❧

They pulled back in unison and her eyes flew open. His gaze was clouded with dazed pleasure and astonishment.

It seemed he'd also been shocked by the heat of their kiss and the speed of its intensity. He, a known rake and libertine, looked *aroused* by what surely had to be one of the chastest kisses he'd experienced in a long while.

Except it hadn't been chaste. It had been brief, but their tongues lightly touching had been profoundly erotic, hinting at greater pleasure to come.

He cleared his throat. "That was . . . a welcome revelation."

Her thoughts whirled while her body clamored for more. Hellfire—if this quick kiss had affected her so much, what would happen when they went to bed together? What if she liked it? What if she *loved* it, and her heart followed her body's devotion?

Tamsyn was about to join with this man for the rest of her life. Aside from a few facts, she knew almost nothing about him. He was basically a stranger. Yet in three days, they would share a bed. They would share everything. According to the law, she would belong to him, and her own identity would dissolve.

Was this the right choice? She'd gotten what she wanted, but she couldn't help the fear that poked its sharp fangs into her heart.

I have no idea what I'm getting myself into.

By Eva Leigh

The Wicked Quills of London
FOREVER YOUR EARL
SCANDAL TAKES THE STAGE
TEMPTATIONS OF A WALLFLOWER

The London Underground
FROM DUKE TILL DAWN
COUNTING ON A COUNTESS

Coming Soon
DARE TO LOVE A DUKE

Eva Leigh

Counting on a Countess

❖ The London Underground ❖

AVONBOOKS

An Imprint of HarperCollins*Publishers*

COUNTING ON A COUNTESS. Copyright © 2018 by Ami Silber. All rights reserved. Printed in the United States of America. No part of this book may be used or reproduced in any manner whatsoever without written permission except in the case of brief quotations embodied in critical articles and reviews. For information, address HarperCollins Publishers, 195 Broadway, New York, NY 10007.

First Avon Books mass market printing: April 2018

Print Edition ISBN: 978-0-06-249943-1
Digital Edition ISBN: 978-0-06-249944-8

Cover illustration by Jon Paul Ferrara
Cover photograph by Shirley Green Photography

Avon, Avon & logo, and Avon Books & logo are registered trademarks of HarperCollins Publishers in the United States of America and other countries.

HarperCollins is a registered trademark of HarperCollins Publishers in the United States of America and other countries.

FIRST EDITION

18 19 20 21 22 QGM 10 9 8 7 6 5 4 3 2 1

To Zack

Acknowledgments

This book has been a group effort born through the generous assistance of many hands. Firstly, I'd like to thank my editor, Nicole Fischer, who saw Tamsyn through her evolutions. Many thanks to my agent, Kevan Lyon, who has always championed my work.

And a huge debt of gratitude to those that provided assistance with the numerous important details: Natasha Boyd, Sarah MacLean, Kate Pearce, Caroline Linden, Cat Sebastian, Tessa Dare, Sophie Barnes, Laura Lee Guhrke, Lizbeth S. Tucker, Brooklyn Ann, Kerri Flowers, Maribeth Louise, Susan Helene Gottfried, Samantha Møller, Allie Filippova, Angela Panozzo, Carey McKinnon, KB Alan, Fran Strober Cassano, Lisa Hendrix, Misa Buckley, Lucy Woodhull, Bryn Donovan, Dee Carney, and Gwen Hayes. This book truly could not have happened without your valuable input.

Chapter 1

London, England
1817

Though he had been the Earl of Blakemere for nearly six months, Christopher Ellingsworth rarely entertained sober or virtuous guests in his bachelor lodgings. Today was no exception.

Kit lounged on a sofa in his parlor, a glass of wine in his hand. Warm, indolent pleasure made his limbs and eyelids heavy. His other hand beat time on the back of the sofa as Jeanette plinked out a merry tune on the pianoforte and the unlikely named Bijou pirouetted around the chamber and twirled brightly colored scarves.

"Bravo, my dears," he murmured as the melody and performance came to a stop.

"Another, my lord?" Bijou asked breathlessly. Her French accent wavered, revealing she was more likely born in Leeds, not Lyon, but it hardly mattered. She wasn't in Kit's rooms to provide lengthy discussion about the philosophy of Voltaire. He'd brought them home from the Royal Opera last night—or rather, very early this morning—and they had been such good company, he hadn't sent them away. It was nearly dusk, and he contemplated with anticipation what the night had in store for him.

"Come and join me," he said, patting his thigh.

"Which of us shall join you?" Jeanette asked.

"Both of you," Kit replied magnanimously.

The two women giggled before fluttering over to where he sprawled. Bijou perched on his outstretched leg while Jeanette snuggled beneath his arm. They were silky and fragrant and lively—precisely what Kit wanted.

Bijou's fingers trailed up his torso and dipped beneath the neckline of his open shirt. Agreeable curls of pleasure blossomed on his skin wherever she touched. "I thought earls weren't supposed to have muscles," she said with a playful pout.

"His lordship was a soldier," Jeanette noted, her fingers toying with his hair. "He's had to become very hard, you know."

"I'm much harder in peacetime." Kit grinned lazily as the two women twittered.

"Shall we put that to the test?" Jeanette nipped at his earlobe.

Before he could answer, a smart rap sounded at the parlor door. He frowned. His staff knew not to bother him when he entertained.

"Go away," he called.

Yet the door opened anyway and his butler's apologetic face appeared. The servant didn't so much as glance at the two opera dancers draped over Kit. "Apologies, my lord. I told the gentleman you weren't to be disturbed, but he insisted you had an appointment." He held up a calling card.

Kit disentangled himself from Jeanette and motioned for the butler to approach. Taking the card from the servant, he glanced at the name.

HERBERT K. FLOWERS, ESQ.
THE LAW OFFICES OF CORRAN AND FLOWERS
LINCOLN'S INN FIELDS

"Damn," Kit swore softly. He had a vague recollection of a letter from Flowers, requesting to meet at Kit's earliest convenience, as the solicitor had a matter of some urgency to discuss. "Send him in."

"Yes, my lord." The butler bowed before hurrying away.

Bijou plucked the card from Kit's hand and squinted at the writing. "What's this mean?"

"It means that this Mr. Flowers deals with tedious and exhausting matters all day," he answered.

She made a face. "How horrid."

"Exactly." Surely whatever this Flowers wanted, it would be dull and require the kind of serious, thoughtful consideration Kit avoided as much as possible.

Another knock sounded at the door, and after receiving Kit's permission to enter, the butler stepped inside.

"Mr. Herbert Flowers, Esquire," the butler intoned.

A hale, middle-aged man in well-tailored clothing entered the room carrying a leather portfolio. "My lord, thank you for . . ." Flowers's steps slowed and his polite smile flickered as his gaze fell on Jeanette and Bijou. Face reddening, he coughed into his fist. "Forgive me, my lord, but it would perhaps be best if we conducted our meeting in private. The concerns are of a . . . delicate and confidential manner."

Kit sighed. He did not, however, sit up. "Ladies, if you would be so kind as to await me upstairs."

The women swayed to their feet and ambled past the solicitor, trailing perfume and laughter as they exited the chamber.

Kit waved Flowers toward a nearby chair. "Care for a drink? I might be able to cajole the cook into preparing something edible."

"Your consideration is appreciated, my lord," the solicitor said quickly. "But once we conclude our business, I am bound for home, where my wife and supper await me."

"I suppose you could eat both," Kit offered after taking a sip of wine. "Or take all of them to bed."

Flowers's cheeks blazed. "Ah . . . well . . . yes." He cleared his throat. "Perhaps we might address the matter at hand." Smoothing a hand down his waistcoat, he said with gravity, "I understand you were an intimate of the late Lord Somerby."

A throb of grief squeezed Kit's heart just hearing the old man's name. "I first met him in Roliça in '08."

Flowers's businesslike expression shifted into restrained melancholy. "The marquess had been an esteemed client of my firm for four decades. The news of his death was met with considerable sorrow." The solicitor gazed at Kit with sympathy. "I imagine that you must also feel distress at the passing of your friend."

Kit gave a wry half smile. "I keep expecting him to show up at my door and demand that I join him at his favorite chophouse. He never allowed me to beg off. Said my wenching and carousing could wait two hours."

Flowers echoed Kit's smile. "A forceful gentleman, Lord Somerby. It stands to reason that he served his country so admirably during the War."

"No one said no to him," Kit agreed. "Well," he added with a self-deprecating shrug, "I tried. He had his ideas about troop movements and I had mine."

"And that is precisely what he admired about you," Flowers noted. "The marquess told me so, himself. Always had good things to say about 'young Captain Ellingsworth.' Courageous, he called you. A born tactician."

Kit glanced away. "He was fulsome in his praise. I merely did my duty—nothing more."

"With all due respect, my lord," the solicitor ventured, "he was not the only man of influence with this opinion of you. His Majesty the Prince was much moved by Lord Somerby's accounts of your heroism. You would not have been given an earldom if you had merely performed your responsibilities."

Nothing in the parlor could hold Kit's attention. He kept shifting his gaze from the paintings on the walls to the windows to the plaster friezes on the ceiling. "I suppose so."

Sadly, the title was almost entirely decorative. It came with a middling estate at the very uppermost border of Northumberland—and hardly any income. Much as Kit appreciated the elevation of his status from marquess's third son to earl, it had done little to alter the course of his life.

But he was grateful to Lord Somerby, just the same. Kit's parents loved him dutifully, yet only Somerby had truly *believed* in him, even when Kit himself did not.

"So you and Lord Somerby were close," Flowers noted.

Kit nodded. "He was a lieutenant general on the Peninsula for most of the War, so our paths crossed many times. He had a fondness for *pastel de nata*, and we'd have them in his tent, chasing them with strong whisky and talking about our favorite public houses back in London." Kit smiled wryly. "We talked strategy, too, and the welfare of our men."

Some of the senior officers Kit had met during his time in the army had been cruel or heartless, concerned only with upholstering themselves with glory. Not Lord Somerby. He remained steadfastly focused on the human cost of war.

"Did his lordship ever discuss marriage?" Flowers asked. "Specifically, yours?"

Kit frowned, the question catching him by surprise. "Occasionally." In truth, Lord Somerby had often harangued Kit about taking a wife, particularly when discussion turned toward life after wartime.

"You need a woman," Lord Somerby had often de-

clared. *"And not one of those actresses or demimon-daines you insist on keeping company with. A proper wife. Someone who's got the backbone and sense to keep you in line. A man's got to have a woman of strength by his side."*

Once, Kit had dared to retort, "I don't see you writing letters to an adored helpmeet."

A look of such profound sorrow had crossed Lord Somerby's face that Kit had immediately regretted his rash words. "I am married, my lad," the older man had replied quietly. "She and the babe she carried were brought to the Lord. I'll not replace Lizzie."

Kit swallowed hard. Lord Somerby and his wife were together now.

"Why do you ask about marriage, Mr. Flowers?"

Instead of answering, the solicitor set his portfolio on the edge of a low table. "I do not want to take up too much of your time, my lord." He opened the folder and removed several documents covered in tiny, precise handwriting. "It is regarding Lord Somerby's demise that I requested a meeting with you today."

Kit set his glass aside and sat up, unease plucking along the back of his neck. "You're his executor."

"Precisely so." Flowers glanced at the papers in his hand. "This is a copy of his will, and it concerns you."

"I cannot see how. We were not related by blood or marriage." His mind churning, Kit rubbed at the stubble along his jaw.

"Perhaps not," the solicitor allowed, "but Lord Somerby named you as one of his beneficiaries."

"He *what*?" Kit demanded.

Flowers pulled a pair of spectacles from his coat's inside pocket and set them on his nose. His eyes moved back and forth as he perused the will. "While it is true that the majority of his considerable fortune has gone to relatives, the marquess earmarked a portion for you upon his death. You are to receive an initial sum of ten thousand pounds and an annual allowance of one thousand pounds for fifty years."

Kit's heart seized before taking up a fast rhythm. "Surely not."

The solicitor drew himself up. "I, myself, transcribed Lord Somerby's words as he lay on his deathbed. There is no mistake, my lord. The money is yours, and should you decease before the fifty years has elapsed, then your issue shall be the recipient or recipients."

"I . . ." Words had always been Kit's ally. They were reliable and came to him easily. Yet now, they were nowhere to be found.

His pulse hammered as though he had just liberated a town from enemy forces. Was it true . . . ? Could he believe it?

His allowance as a third son was, at best, modest, and seldom lasted long. The selling of his commission had provided a small increase—but it was short-lived. Like many men of his class, he lived on credit. His rooms, his clothes, his wine. God only knew what he owed at the gaming hells. But he returned to them again and again, staking too much money on steep odds, praying for the win that would secure his dream. A dream he'd held close throughout the War and that kept him sane when the world had turned to mud and madness.

He'd never truly believed he could make it happen. Until now.

"The news is welcome, I wager," Flowers said, glancing up over the rims of his spectacles.

"Quite welcome," Kit answered softly. "I have . . . plans."

He hoped those plans would chase away the darkness that haunted him ever since his return from Waterloo.

Shadows lurked in silent corners and whispered to him in the quiet moments, joyless thoughts that brought him back to the hell of war and the omnipresence of death. He ran from pleasure to pleasure, trying to outpace the wraiths. If he could accomplish his one goal, he might not have to face those ghosts again.

As the War had ground on, his life consisting of boredom and battles, blood and loss, Kit had turned again and again to thoughts of a world where nothing existed but pleasure. Where every day was filled with happiness and beauty.

He'd always loved going to Vauxhall, with its pavilions, gardens, lights, and music—an unending parade of joy. What if he could create a place like that, a pleasure garden entirely of his own design? He'd oversee it, immersing himself not in the business of death but life.

It would be his. Finally.

"Show me what to sign." He stood and paced around the chamber. "There's got to be a pen around here. I'll ring for one."

"Hold a moment, my lord." Flowers got to his feet.

The grave expression on the solicitor's face froze Kit in place. His instincts had kept him alive on the battlefield for more years than he cared to remember. Those same instincts rang like a bell, resonating through him.

"There is a condition," Flowers explained. "It's rather unusual, but Lord Somerby was most insistent."

"Tell me."

The solicitor cleared his throat once more. "Lord Somerby was, as you are aware, a widower, and spoke most effusively about the holy state of matrimony." He paused. "Might I suggest you have a drink of wine, my lord?"

Kit strode instead to a decanter of brandy perched on a small table. He poured a generous amount into a glass and drank it all down in one swallow. He felt the warm burn in his throat and the softening of reality's sharp edges.

"What must I do to claim my bequest?" he demanded.

"As of today," Flowers announced, "you have thirty days."

Kit narrowed his eyes. "Thirty days to do what?"

"Wed," the solicitor answered. "Then, and only then, will you receive your portion of Lord Somerby's fortune. If you do not, then the money goes to the late marquess's distant relative in Bermuda." Flowers tried to smile, but it resembled a grimace.

Blood rushed from Kit's head like deserters fleeing combat. The room tilted, but it had nothing to do with the brandy he'd consumed. "Good God damn." He clutched the neck of the decanter as though it could support the weight of his shock.

The chamber righted itself, but Kit's world had been completely upended. "It appears that I'm getting married."

Staring into the narrow, dark alley, Tamsyn Pearce calculated her odds of surviving the next ten minutes and determined they weren't good.

"Did you bring a firearm?" Nessa asked as she peered over Tamsyn's shoulder.

"I have a knife in my garter," Tamsyn answered.

Nessa clicked her tongue. "A blade won't do much against a pistol."

Straightening her spine, Tamsyn said in what she hoped was a confident tone, "I've learned a few things after eight years of smuggling—including how to avoid the dangerous end of a pistol." She aimed a smile at her friend. "Haven't been shot yet."

"There's a first time for everything," Nessa replied grimly.

Tamsyn shook her head. "A fine way to show your encouragement."

Nessa attempted to look more cheerful, but the worry never left her eyes. She gently smoothed a hand down Tamsyn's cheek. "Ah, my bird, forgive my worry. You've done so much for Newcombe, ever since you were but a child, and your poor *mabmik* and *tas* at God's table."

An old, familiar ache resounded in Tamsyn's chest, even though it had been ten years. Her parents, Adam and Jane Pearce, had taken their pleasure boat out to sail along the rocky Cornish coast of their home, leaving fourteen-year-old Tamsyn behind to finish her schoolwork. They had not returned alive.

The barony had passed to Tamsyn's uncle, Jory. But if the villagers of Newcombe had hoped to find in the new baron the same measure of concern for their welfare as his brother had demonstrated, they were bitterly disappointed. A poor fishing yield and strangling taxes decimated Newcombe's livelihood. To Tamsyn, orphaned and adrift, there had been one audacious solution to the village's plight.

But all that could come to an end if she couldn't move this sodding shipment of brandy and lace. She'd journeyed all the way to London to help the village and if she failed, she imperiled over four hundred souls depending on her.

She glanced back into the alleyway. It smelled of copper and standing water, and shadows gathered thickly. Somewhere in that gloom, a tanner named Fuller kept a storefront, but that business was merely a pretense for a much more profitable enterprise.

"Can we be sure of this bloke?" Nessa pressed, giving words to Tamsyn's own worries.

"He's the best lead we've had in a fortnight." Everyone else had fallen through. "Come on." She stepped into the alley.

More than once, Tamsyn had evaded customs officers, running down the beach and hiding in caverns to lose her pursuers. She had learned how to fire a pistol and where to stick a man with her blade so that she dealt a punishing but not fatal wound. Every time a new shipment needed to be offloaded, she faced danger.

The fear that made her palms sweat had little to do with physical peril. So many relied on her. She couldn't fail them.

Nessa's nervous steps tapped behind her as she strode deeper into the alley, echoing her own rapid heartbeats. But Tamsyn vowed that she would brazen this out just as she'd done with everything else in her life.

She passed a man sleeping on the ground. He opened one eye as she went by and gave a grunt of surprise. Women of quality didn't haunt shabby London alleys. Not for the first time, Tamsyn wondered if she ought to have changed her clothes before leaving Lady Daleford's this morning. Too late to do anything about it now. She had to move forward.

Fuller's shop front was little more than an awning-covered table strewn with hides in different stages of tanning. The reek of lime brought tears to Tamsyn's eyes, and she heard Nessa gag quietly behind her. A jowly man in a heavy apron stood behind the table, warily watching Tamsyn's approach.

He said with barely concealed disdain, "Looking for fine leathers, miss?"

Tamsyn fingered one hide, pretending to contemplate it. "Bill Conyer said you could help us." In desperation, she'd gone to the docks to look for leads. Conyer, an out-of-work stevedore, had given her Fuller's name and direction—though he'd had to be financially compensated for the information.

Fuller scowled. "Conyer don't send no one to me for leather. Only . . ." His eyes widened. "But you're a lady. Ladies don't—"

"This one does," Tamsyn interrupted. "Are you interested?"

"How do I know you ain't playing?" Fuller demanded. "No ladies in this business."

Tamsyn fingered the diaphanous fabric around her neck. "Chantilly lace. Fifty yards of it." She calmly pulled a flask from her reticule and held it out. "This is a sample of my brandy. Five hundred gallons are sitting in Cornwall this very moment. I'm looking for the right buyer for both."

Fuller glared at the flask but didn't take it.

"Go on," Tamsyn urged. She fought to keep her tone calm. It would scare Fuller off if she showed her desperation. "You'll never taste anything finer."

He snatched the container from her hand and took a drink. After wiping his mouth with the back of his hand, he said with reluctant admiration, "That's prime fuddle."

Her heart rose, all the while she kept her expression calm.

"But I ain't going to be your fence," he added.

An icicle pierced her chest. "Why not?"

"On account of I don't do dealings with gentry morts. Can't trust 'em."

"I assure you, I am most trustworthy. I have been in this line of work for nearly a decade and—"

"Then why don't you got a fence?" Fuller demanded. "Why come crawling to me?"

She opened her mouth, but no words came out. How could she possibly explain? The smuggling operation ran through the family's ancestral home, Chei Owr. Caverns beneath the house led directly to a cove, which was the perfect location to receive smuggled goods from a ship at anchor. Those same caverns served as the holding place for the brandy and lace, and they sat there until they were purchased by their fence, Ames Edmonds, who distributed the goods both in Cornwall and all over England.

It was a perfect system. Jory and his wife, Gwen, knew nothing about the smuggling operation, which was precisely how Tamsyn wanted it to stay.

Everything would have proceeded apace—if Jory hadn't announced a month ago that he intended to sell the crumbling, neglected Chei Owr. He had every right to: he was Lord Shawe, and the manor house wasn't entailed. He already had letters to agents in London, though no buyer had yet stepped forward.

Tamsyn's horror at losing her home and last connection with her parents was doubled when she had received a hastily scrawled note from Ames stating that, with the possible sale of their base of operations, their partnership was over.

The latest shipment of brandy and lace had nowhere to go—and the village was in dire need of cash. Tamsyn had hurriedly concocted a plan wherein she and Nessa, acting as her maid, would travel to London under the guise of her finally having a Season. Her parents' old friend Lady Daleford had offered her a place to stay and entrée into the city's most elite gatherings. All the while, Tamsyn would undergo a frantic search for a new fence. Balls and soirees in the evening, haunting London's seediest corners during the day.

There was one other component to her reason for being in London. But she hadn't been pursuing it with the same dedication as the hunt for a buyer.

None of this could be relayed to Fuller, of course. The less he knew about her personally, the safer both of them would be. Hanging was always an option for smugglers. Or, given that she was of gentle birth, she'd likely be transported. Neither option was appealing.

"I fail to see what difference my motivations make," Tamsyn answered coolly. "I have top-tier merchandise to move, and I'm giving you the option to buy it. We'll both make out nicely."

Fuller squinted at her as if she were tiny, illegible writing. He spat upon the ground. "If you was a bloke, I'd be singing a different tune. But you're a mort."

"I oversee an operation that successfully collects thousands of pounds' worth of merchandise, from making connections with the ship's captain to unloading the goods to its storage and sale," Tamsyn noted, her words dry. "But I am not in control of my sex."

"Ain't my problem, Miss Lacy Drawers. Unless you want to show me what you got under them skirts."

"Don't you talk to her that way!" Nessa interjected hotly.

Tamsyn held up a placating hand. Fishermen and sailors had notoriously foul language, so she was well acquainted with salty words aimed at her person.

"If I did," she said calmly, "would you buy my lace and brandy?"

Fuller grinned. "Naw. I just wanted to see how low a gentry mort would go."

"Then we have nothing further to discuss." Tamsyn turned away, feeling heaviness weighting down her limbs. With Nessa following, she moved toward the entrance to the alley, though she walked with deliberate slowness in case Fuller was merely trying to drive a hard bargain. She waited for him to call her back. He didn't.

When she and Nessa emerged back onto the street, Tamsyn finally exhaled. She leaned against a brick wall and stared up at the greasy, gray London sky—so different from the bright blue that stretched over Cornwall.

"What do we do now?" Nessa practically wailed.

Tamsyn uncapped her flask and, after using her fichu to wipe off its mouth, swallowed a healthy mouthful of brandy. It burned a path through her body, strengthening her resolve.

"I have to find myself a husband," she said.

Chapter 2

"How is it," Kit said, "that I can happily find an eager lover with ease, yet the moment my thoughts turn to matrimony, none of the women I encounter are at all suitable as a bride?"

Kit surveyed the Eblewhites' ballroom with a disheartened gaze. To be sure, the mansion in the heart of Mayfair boasted one of the most beautiful ballrooms in the whole of the city, and it was currently filled with pretty, marriageable women looking for a husband. They wore gowns in a kaleidoscope of colors, adorned with ribbons and flowers and expensive jewels, and to a one, they were lovely, with bright eyes, easy smiles, and soft skin.

Despite the elegance and gaiety around him, his gaze alighted on the corners of the room, searching out areas where an enemy could hide, and locating the best routes for an escape. The war had been over for two years, yet he couldn't shake the skills that had kept him alive.

Someday, perhaps, that ever-alert part of him would realize that the threats had passed. For now, he endured his wariness and caution, and reminded himself to unclench his fists and loosen his jaw.

"It's a deuced mystery." Thomas Powell, the Earl of Langdon and heir to the Duke of Northfield, shook his head with wry dismay. He spoke with a faint Irish accent, evidence of his early years having been spent in County Kerry. "I've told you again and again that you ought to just pick one, marry and bed her, and then acquire a mistress. It's what I would do in a similar situation."

"You're a duke's sodding eldest son," Kit noted tartly. He and Langdon stood near the punch bowl in a desperate bid to locate one young lady who would make a fine countess. "You'll never find yourself in a similar situation."

"I suppose someday I'll have to find myself a wife," Langdon mused, "but that day is thankfully a good distance away." He and Kit bowed as a handsome, statuesque woman walked by with her debutante daughter in tow. The mother nudged her daughter and both sent enormous smiles in Kit's direction. "Lady Briscoe is eager to offer up her daughter for your consideration."

Kit nodded politely in the women's direction, but he only gave the debutante a cursory look before his gaze moved on.

"What was wrong with that one?" Langdon demanded impatiently.

"Too pretty. I'd exhaust myself fighting duels." It didn't really matter to him, though. Remaining faithful to his future wife wasn't in his plans, and so long as she kept her fidelity until she birthed an heir, he didn't much care what his spouse did—or whom she took as a lover.

Yet impatience gnawed on Kit. His body was primed and tense, the way it was in the moments before battle. He felt the clock ticking, more precious minutes and hours lost in his desperate search.

His friend sighed heavily. "You're a bloody piece of work." Langdon sipped at his punch and made a face. "Is there any decent wine in this place?"

"None that I've seen." Kit wouldn't have imbibed

anyway, much as he wanted to. He had to present an appearance of faultless respectability in order to attract a prospective bride.

"We're clearly not going to find anything worthwhile to drink here." Langdon set his punch glass on a passing servant's tray. His expression brightened. "There's new dancers at the opera tonight. It's early enough for us to catch a performance. And meet the ladies afterward." He raised a dark brow with an appreciative leer.

Much as he wanted to go . . . "I can't leave." Kit fought to avoid exhaling in frustration. "Time's running out. I have only a week to find myself a bride."

The punch bowl gambit was a loss. Anyway, he was too restless to stand idle, so he began to walk the perimeter of the ballroom. Langdon kept pace with him, and together they skirted the edge of the guests making their way through the complex patterns of a country dance.

The women dancing all looked at him as he walked, but the moment he caught their gazes, he found something else to attract his interest—the twinkling chandeliers or the vases of hothouse roses positioned at the perimeter of the chamber.

"You're doing it again," Langdon observed. "Dismissing girls left and right as though you're deciding what waistcoat to wear." He grinned at a willowy blonde widow, who sent him an inviting smile. Yet he continued to walk beside Kit as they made a circuit around the ballroom.

"It cannot be helped," Kit answered. He nodded his head toward different young ladies in the chamber. "Her laugh is too abrasive. That one's as shy as a fawn. She'll spend all my blunt and leave me foundering in even greater debt."

That last shortcoming was one he couldn't permit. He *needed* Lord Somerby's money to make his plans for the future come to fruition.

After learning about the matrimonial condition of Somerby's will, Kit had immediately gone to Lady Walford, the *ton*'s most accomplished gossip. He'd informed her—in strictest confidence—of his intention to marry within a month. She had agreed to hold his confidence, and by the following morning, everyone in Society knew that Lord Blakemere had given up his dissolute ways in order to secure himself a wife and fortune.

"Here I am," he grumbled lowly. "A titled man about to possess a considerable fortune, healthy, young, reasonably attractive—"

"*Reasonably,*" Langdon noted drily.

Kit shot him a quelling look. There had been a time not so long ago when he'd been full of good humor and jests, never wasting an opportunity for droll banter. But his sense of humor had disappeared the longer he was in the marriage market.

"And I cannot locate one woman who'd make for a suitable wife," he continued. He didn't understand himself or his mystifying impulse to find fault with each female to cross his path. None of them seemed quite right.

"I blame Somerby," Langdon said. "God rest his soul. If he hadn't gone on about what a sterling marriage he'd had and how he was utterly devoted to his late wife, you wouldn't have such lofty ideals about what constitutes matrimony."

"Don't be an ass," Kit answered at once. "I know what marriage is supposed to be." His own parents esteemed each other, just as any aristocratic couple should, and behaved accordingly in public and in private. The love Lord Somerby had felt for his dear Elizabeth was highly unusual, almost gauche in its effusiveness. Love was not part of genteel alliances.

Neither was fidelity. Kit knew the concept existed in theory, but he'd never practiced it—nor did he want to.

Sharing a bed with just a single person for the duration of one's life seemed both impossible and terrifically dull.

And searching for someone he could love . . . That was nigh impossible. For a number of reasons. You didn't just bump into a young woman at a ball and realize that she was your soul mate. It was ridiculous to think that he might entertain such a thought.

Duty was for wives. Passion for mistresses. And love . . . Love was a dream as elusive as peace.

As he said this, a comely blonde nearby smiled at him. He felt a rise of hope as he returned the smile. But then he observed the whitening of her knuckles as she clutched her fan.

Too desperate.

Kit bit back a growl of frustration as he glanced away. At this rate, he'd be lucky to marry a drunk donkey.

"You're not precisely the ideal potential husband." Langdon smirked.

"I'll have money, won't I?" Kit demanded hotly. "They gave me an earldom. What more could a girl ask for?" His could feel his pleasure garden slipping from his grasp, and the obstacle in his path was himself.

Langdon sent him a wry glance. "Oh, not much. Only temperance, fidelity, and fiscal responsibility."

"Bah," Kit scoffed. "Who needs such a dullard?"

"Most women of marriageable age," Langdon replied.

It would have been better if Kit had never been given the opportunity to inherit any amount of money. He could exist in the same pleasure-filled haze he always did, dreaming his dreams but without the expectation of fulfilling them.

"I've been haunting every ball, tea, and soiree," Kit muttered, fighting frustration and despair. "To no avail."

"A sticky conundrum," Langdon agreed. He yawned into his hand. "There's a reason why I avoid these dull assemblies. A decided lack of nudity." He glanced around the ballroom and made a scoffing sound. "I'm off to the theater. Come with me?"

Kit longed to leave, finding society balls as interesting as a sermon about dirt. But . . . "Got to stay here. No future brides wait for me in the demimondaines' theater boxes."

His friend nodded in acknowledgment. "When you tire of your hunt, you know where to find me."

Kit gave him a distracted wave as he strode away, too busy brooding over his predicament to pay much attention to Langdon's departure. They'd see each other on the morrow, anyway, at White's. Ever since Kit returned from the War, he and Langdon had met at the club and then gone out every night—with a few exceptions—wringing excitement and diversion from London's most disreputable attractions.

He'd done his best to avoid those attractions these past three weeks. He'd been so respectable, it fair turned his stomach. But his sacrifice was in vain. He was as brideless as he'd been at the beginning of those three weeks.

Frustrated, impatient, Kit muttered a curse and started for the card room at the other end of the chamber. He wouldn't find a wife there, amidst the games of *vingt-et-un* and loo, since the amusements were set up primarily for men and married women. But at least it would help relieve a fraction of the tension that knotted his muscles and made him grit his teeth.

Distracted as he was, his head tucked low, his gaze fixed on the parquet floor, he didn't see the young woman in his path until it was almost too late. They nearly collided, but he pulled himself up just before smacking into her.

"Excuse me, miss," he exclaimed.

The girl spoke with a distinct Cornish accent. "No harm done, sir." She smiled at him.

Her smile set off fires throughout his body. She fairly glowed with vibrancy.

Kit didn't recognize her, and he wouldn't have forgotten meeting a girl with such vividly red hair—coppery and bright beneath the light of the chandelier—and he had a fierce need to see it loose about her shoulders. He was drawn in by her wide-set, light brown eyes, slightly tilted at the corners. Her full, rose-hued lips stirred a need in him, baffling in its swiftness.

She had an elfin look, with a long, sleek form. The neckline of her pale green gown highlighted her modest but well-formed bosom, and his hands twitched with the desire to know the feel of her. Though the pink in her cheeks alluded to a life spent frequently out of doors, he easily imagined the same flush in her skin when roused to passion.

The hell? Kit wondered dazedly. He'd seen women and desired them within minutes of meeting, but never had he looked upon a woman and been suddenly dragged under the tide of sensual need.

It had to be because he'd been celibate these last three weeks, a drastic measure undertaken because he'd had to be on his best behavior whilst searching for a bride.

He waited for his reflexive dismissal of her. Yet it never came.

Her eyes were bright with intelligence as she looked at him, and her smile lingered, as though she liked what she saw. That baser part of himself puffed up and preened.

He gave her his best, most winning smile. "I—"

But that was as far as he got before a swain stepped between them. "I believe this dance is mine, Miss Pearce."

"Of course, Mr. Carroll," the girl answered. She sent Kit an apologetic look as she was led to the dance floor. He fought the urge to take her hand in his and run off into the night like some underworld king claiming his companion.

It's finally happened. I've lost my goddamned mind.

He could wait for her. Bide his time, and then swoop down on her the moment she was free from this Carroll's clutches.

Yet his response to her was too powerful. Frightening.

He had to regain control over himself. He needed balance. The only time he'd been this close to losing control of himself was on the eve of his first battle.

Kit turned away from the sight of Miss Pearce swaying on the dance floor like a living flame and made his way toward the room set aside for gambling. At least there, he knew the rules of the game.

THOUGH Tamsyn did her best to keep her attention on her dancing partner, her gaze strayed to the blond man with the wary gaze and wide shoulders as he swiftly exited the ballroom. She ought to stay focused on Mr. Carroll—dancing often led to conversation, which could in turn become a morning call, and a few social calls might give way to an amicable connection, and then, hopefully, an offer of matrimony—but she was unable to help herself. Not only had the blond man been exceptionally handsome, but he carried himself with a singular determination, and sharp intelligence gleamed in his eyes.

Three weeks in London searching for a man she might consider marrying had revealed that, while there were a good deal of attractive men, very few of them possessed lean, athletic bodies, and almost none had a sense of purpose or keen intellects.

However, she didn't need or want a husband to be observant. Or attentive. The more distracted and heedless the better.

It didn't matter what she wanted for herself, that she had once dreamed of a marriage as devoted as her parents'. Such hopes were merely fancies, never to come to pass.

Yet as she moved through the figures of the dance, she found herself asking Mr. Carroll, "Who was that gentleman?"

Mr. Carroll seemed to know exactly to whom she referred. "Lord Blakemere." He gave a puzzled frown when she only looked at him blankly. "You really *are* a country gel if you don't know him either by face or name."

She couldn't feel embarrassed about her Cornish origins. Some London girls had a pale, pinched look and probably couldn't walk over the moors without calling for a carriage.

But she couldn't snap a tart reply to Mr. Carroll—not without seriously damaging her marital prospects—so she merely smiled. "We hear so little about the sophisticated city in Cornwall."

"Can't be faulted for being born in a backwater, I suppose." Mr. Carroll sniffed.

She had considered Mr. Carroll moderately handsome, in a rather watery, overbred way, but her opinion of him took a sharp plummet. It would be bad form to simply walk away and leave him alone on the dance floor, so she kept moving through the figures of La Gaillarde.

"Tell me more about Lord Blakemere," she said with as much sweetness as she could muster.

"Third son of the Marquess of Brownlowe," Mr. Carroll said dismissively.

"But he's *Lord* Blakemere," she pointed out. She fell silent as she walked through the steps, pulling her away from her dance partner.

"He bought a commission, the way third sons do," Mr. Carroll explained when they came back together. "Went off to war. Must've shown off over there like a trained lion because he came back and they gave him an earldom. But it didn't come with any money," he added quickly, clearly seeing her interest. "He's strapped. Barely has a groat."

Tamsyn's heart sank. So much for Lord Blakemere. The second part of her objective in coming to London was finding herself a rich husband. If she was going to buy Chei Owr from her uncle and keep the smuggling operation alive, she needed a spouse with considerable wealth.

"You didn't tell her the best part," the man dancing next to Mr. Carroll added. Before Mr. Carroll could object to the interruption, the other man continued, "Blakemere's got *one week* to find himself a bride."

"What happens in a week?" she asked, trying to listen and concentrate on the steps at the same time.

"He loses his chance to inherit a fortune," Mr. Carroll snapped. "No wife, no money. That's the end of it."

Inherit a fortune. The words reverberated in Tamsyn's head as she fell into distracted silence.

It was certainly something to contemplate.

At the end of the dance, she curtsied to Mr. Carroll. "Thank you, sir."

"Might I get you some refreshment?" he offered.

"That's kind of you, but I believe I see my sponsor, Lady Daleford, standing alone. I must keep her company. Do excuse me."

He looked annoyed by her dismissal as Tamsyn backed away from him, but his expression of irritation lifted when the same talkative gentleman from the dance whispered in his ear. Mr. Carroll glanced at Tamsyn with the look of a man who had narrowly escaped a ravenous ghoul.

She suppressed a sigh and turned away. Doubtless her lack of dowry was the topic under discussion. In the weeks she had been searching for a potential groom, all the men who had shown promise eventually disappeared when they learned of her impecunious circumstances.

Lady Daleford looked at her with sympathy as she approached. "My dear, you mustn't let the chatterers deter you," the older woman declared. She fanned herself slowly. "Your dear papa, God rest him, did you no favors by leaving this world intestate."

The heaviness in Tamsyn's chest pressed down. "I suppose he believed he could attend to that matter later." His brother, Jory, hadn't seen fit to make any provisions for her, and it was only through Lady Daleford's largesse that Tamsyn had any fashionable clothes to wear during her brief, disastrous Season.

"We, all of us, think we have more time than we do," Lady Daleford agreed.

Seeking a change in topic, Tamsyn said, "It cannot be factual that Lord Blakemere has only one week to find himself a wife."

The older woman's brows rose. "Heard the gossip, have you?"

So it was true, incredible as it might seem. "Why isn't he swarming with debutantes?"

Lady Daleford's expression grew sober. "He is. But no matter what gel seeks his favor, he continues on his hunt. But you would do wise to avoid him. Lord Blakemere wants a bride and will indeed come into a fortune, but he will make the most appalling husband."

"Strong words, Lady Daleford," Tamsyn said with surprise. She looked toward the card room.

"Though he fought bravely against our enemies abroad," the older woman acknowledged, "on English soil Blakemere is the veriest rogue. He's in a class by himself—well, Lord Langdon belongs in that class, as well." Her expression became pinched. "Before he learned of his possible inheritance, he never attended a single respectable gathering. He consorts with dancers and actresses, and is a habitué of gaming hells."

"Most men of his rank do the same," Tamsyn pointed out. "As for gambling, ladies do that, too. Even in Cornwall the gentry play cards for coin and wager on horses."

Lady Daleford shook her head. "Here in London, a city full of spendthrifts, he is the *ne plus ultra* of profligates. The considerable number of his vowels is said to be unprecedented." She held up one gloved finger. "Mark my word, if he does manage to inherit that money, he will surely tear through it within a year." She patted Tamsyn's cheek. "My dear, when I agreed to let you stay with me for the Season, I swore a solemn oath to myself that I would steer you clear of any unsuitable candidates. You are here to make a good match, and by heaven, I will make certain that happens."

"It's impossible for me to fully express my gratitude," Tamsyn replied sincerely.

"The very least I could do to honor your parents' memory was to see that their daughter had her Season. Dearest Adam and darling Jane would want this for you." She eyed Tamsyn critically. "Though you are a little on the mature side for a debutante."

Tamsyn smiled wryly. At twenty-four, she was definitely older than most of the girls vying for husbands, and she'd wager had a good deal more worldly experience than her rivals.

Lady Daleford continued, "Despite your age, and the paucity of your dowry, you come from an ancient lineage and can make a relatively advantageous match. Mr. Simon Hoult has been staring at you all night, and he's a baron's second son. You could do far worse."

Tamsyn risked a glance at Mr. Hoult. He was a tall gentleman with dark brown hair and a cheerful face. His smile widened when he caught Tamsyn looking at him.

"Would he make an attentive husband?" she asked Lady Daleford.

The older woman beamed. "Oh, he'll assuredly be dutiful. His parents are devoted to each other, and I am certain he will follow their model."

Much as she desired that for her own selfish reasons, Tamsyn's mood pitched lower. So much for Mr. Hoult. However, likely encouraged by her brief look in his direction, the gentleman began making his way toward her from across the ballroom. He'd unquestionably ask her to dance, or request the honor of getting her a glass of punch, and Tamsyn didn't have the heart to encourage him when his chances were futile.

"I need to find the retiring room," she murmured. "Excuse me."

As Lady Daleford protested, Tamsyn slipped away before Mr. Hoult could get any closer. She hurried down the corridor leading to the retiring room, but she didn't go inside. Instead, she sat down on a settee. Running her fingers over the tufted upholstery, she mentally reviewed all of the Earl of Blakemere's attributes.

1. He was a careless libertine.
2. He was terrible with money.
3. He only wanted a wife in order to claim a fortune, which likely meant he'd be a negligent husband.

In short, he was *perfect*.

Her pulse leapt at the thought of him, and a flame of attraction burned to life. Usually, she didn't find herself drawn to blond men, but he had caught her eye from the moment she'd set foot inside the ballroom. He had wide shoulders and carried himself with supreme confidence, as if capable of conquering any obstacle that presented itself. No surprise that he was a former soldier.

He had a somewhat-long face, with a distinguished, largish nose and curved lips. Up close, she'd seen that his eyes were lake blue, and sharply discerning. He'd looked at her with sensual awareness—and judging by the ease with which he moved, his promise of carnality would be readily, enthusiastically fulfilled.

She shook off her thoughts. Lord Blakemere as a lover was not her purpose. She was here to land a husband, the more desperate and inattentive the better.

A flare of unusual nerves tightened through her body. Lord Blakemere fit the bill exactly, but the question was, could she make him want her?

Chapter 3

❦

$\mathcal{W}$arily, Tamsyn approached the card room. Masculine conversation rolled out, borne aloft on fumes of a considerable amount of imbibed brandy. A handful of ladies' voices joined in, sopranos to the basses, but overall, the room sounded occupied mostly by men.

Her heart made a hard, unsteady beat as she contemplated what she was about to do. She'd never deliberately set her cap for a man, laying out all the pretty little traps women were supposed to cunningly employ to ensnare suitors.

She wasn't afraid of men by any means. At home in Newcombe, she often worked long hours side by side with the roughest of farmers and fishermen. She believed they tempered their words in consideration of her gender and status. Yet sometimes a barrel would crash down, spilling its contents everywhere, and colorful, profane curses were employed. She came from the countryside, too, where talk was likely more honest, more coarse than the way people spoke in London.

Tamsyn hadn't had the luxury of being sheltered. But that also meant that she never truly learned the art of simpering or coquetry.

Yet somehow, she was supposed to attract Lord Blakemere's notice, enough to let him know that *she* was interested.

She exhaled ruefully. She'd spent many a moonless night standing in freezing seawater, hauling crates of fabric and half ankers of brandy, knowing that the custom officers might discover her at any moment—and yet the task of flirting with a handsome, eligible man made her palms damp.

"Are you going to enter?" a young woman asked, fanning herself as she stood beside Tamsyn. "I'm not certain I want to go in. It's so dull everywhere I turn."

"I don't know what you plan on doing," Tamsyn said to the woman beside her, straightening her shoulders, "but *I* feel the need to gamble."

Taking a deep breath, she stepped into the card room.

The setting was far more elegant than any of the taverns where she'd seen card and dice games played. Instead of seamen and farmers crouching around games played upon a coarse stone floor, fashionable men and women sat encircling polished mahogany tables. Rather than rough hands clutching battered cards, the guests wore gloves and played using cards so clean they had to be new, or rolled dice made of shining ivory. Everything here spoke of privileged leisure, so different from what she'd known.

Tamsyn's gaze skipped quickly from table to table. Her heart jumped when she finally spotted Lord Blakemere in a corner, playing cassino.

God help her, he seemed to have grown more handsome in the half an hour since she'd seen him last. No wonder women—both respectable and otherwise—were drawn to him. She felt pulled in his direction, lured by carnal potential.

Look at me.

But the earl was too absorbed in the game to notice any newcomers, and she tried not to feel disappointment that he didn't look up when she entered the room.

Trying to appear as nonchalant as possible, Tamsyn slowly made her way around the room, pausing at different tables, pretending to watch the play. She applauded when one of the guests won their hand, but all the while, she was acutely aware of Lord Blakemere's nearby presence.

What was she going to do once she reached his table? She couldn't very well throw herself across his lap and cry, "Marry me, my lord!"

She needed to be crafty and calculating, perhaps even more so than she was when storing smuggled French spirits in the caverns beneath her family's ancestral home.

Finally, she reached Lord Blakemere's table and found herself struck by the clean angle of his jaw and the hedonistic curves of his mouth. She barely noticed that one gentleman acted as dealer while the other players— another man, the earl, and a dowager in ropes of pearls— studied their cards.

Tamsyn positioned herself behind an empty chair opposite Lord Blakemere, but her target didn't look up from his hand. It wasn't until the round was over that he glanced in her direction.

His gaze met hers, and she felt a hot jolt travel the length of her body. Her breath left her in a sudden rush.

Forcing herself to inhale and exhale slowly, she smiled at him. Gradually, he smiled back. It wasn't a gentleman's polite smile, but one that seemed to promise wicked things leisurely done under cover of darkness.

Another bolt of electricity moved through her. She'd had men look at her with sexual interest before, but none of those looks held the seductive power of Lord Blakemere's sultry smile.

He asked, "Would you care to play, Miss . . . I'm sorry, please remind me of your name."

"Pearce," she said breathlessly. "Tamsyn Pearce."

"Odd name," muttered the dowager. "Tamsyn."

Tamsyn's cheeks heated with a flare of temper. Back home, hers was a commonplace name. But she wasn't one of the thousands of Annes or Catherines or Marys that seemed all the rage in London.

"A charming name," the earl corrected the dowager. "Cornish, yes?"

"That's right." A point for the earl for not dismissing her as a country mouse.

"Never been to Cornwall," Lord Blakemere said, "though I hear it's lovely."

"And a smuggler's paradise," the other gentleman at the table added.

Tamsyn forced herself to laugh, and it came out a little shrilly. "The tales of Cornwall's criminal side are exaggerated by ballads and print sellers."

"I should hope so," Lord Blakemere said darkly.

She didn't like the grim tone of his voice, so she said in a cheerful voice, "Fishing and mining, that's how we earn our bread." She smiled brightly, hoping it might cover up the sheer drivel pouring from her mouth.

Lord Blakemere continued to smile, as well. Their gazes held—with that curious heat unfolding deep within her as she stared into his deep blue eyes—and who knows how long they would have simply stared at each other if the dowager didn't snap, "Are we playing or napping?"

"Miss Pearce, will you join us?" Lord Blakemere asked. "We can be a partnership."

Oh blast. She hadn't thought about this possibility. "I would very much like to," she said, then added ruefully, "only I haven't any cash with me."

"I'll stake you," he offered at once. "Say, three pounds?

No, four." He reached into his coat, pulled out a sizable wad of cash, and peeled off four one-pound notes, which he set on the table.

She felt her eyes widen. Goodness, he really was profligate with money if he offered her—a stranger—the loan of four pounds. That amount of money could feed a dozen families in Newcombe.

The other gentleman at the table and the dowager merely shook their heads, as if familiar with Lord Blakemere's extravagance.

"That's kind of you, my lord," she murmured.

"Sit down, gel," the dowager snarled, "or I may perish of acute boredom."

With a Herculean effort not to snarl back, Tamsyn took her seat opposite Lord Blakemere. He winked at her and her stomach fluttered.

Concentrate, Tam. You're here to snare his *interest, not fall all over yourself like a newborn calf.*

Everyone anted one pound note. Her pulse hammered at the thought of risking so much money on a game, but people played deeper in London than they did in Cornwall.

"You know how to play cassino?" the other gentleman asked as he dealt each of the players four cards.

"She had better," the dowager said tartly. "I'm too old to explain the rules."

Once the hands had been dealt, the dealer laid out four more cards in the center of the table—the queen of clubs, the four of diamonds, the seven of spades, and the ace of hearts. Tamsyn studied her cards.

She'd negotiated more than one shipment of smuggled goods over card games in smoky taprooms. Surely playing against these stiff necks was easier.

The gentleman opened by setting the three of diamonds atop the four. "Sevens," he announced. Tamsyn remembered that this was known as *building*.

Next was Lord Blakemere. He laid the two of hearts on the seven. "Nines."

Clearly, then, he held a nine, and hoped no one would capture it before he had a chance to.

The dowager grumbled as she set down the jack of clubs, unable to build or capture anything with the card.

Now it was Tamsyn's turn. She set the nine of diamonds atop the earl's pile of cards. "Nines," she announced.

He gazed at her with curiosity that gave way to admiration. She could have captured the build, but instead, she left it for him to take. It wasn't unheard of for partners to assist each other in game play, but it seemed evident he was surprised she wanted to bolster him. They would both benefit when it came time to tally points, yet by helping him capture the build, she employed strategy.

And he liked her for it.

The other gentleman captured his sevens, and then Lord Blakemere captured the nines. As he did, he sent Tamsyn a slow-burning look. *If we're this good together at the card table,* his gaze seemed to promise, *imagine what we'd be like in bed.*

The cards became slippery in her damp palms. She'd met her share of country scoundrels, braggarts who were crude in their attempts to woo her. It was easy to dismiss their thinly veiled efforts to get her to lift her skirts because they wanted only their own gratification—she was just a means to an end.

With Lord Blakemere's knowing looks, however, her blood felt hot, gathering warmth in secret places. She forgot the other people at their table, and in the room.

He offered so much more with just his gaze. He guaranteed not just his pleasure, but *hers,* as well. Hours of it.

God above, but he was a rake of the first water. The men she'd known in Cornwall were mere awkward, fumbling boys compared to him, and it didn't appear that he was even trying that hard to impress her. He simply *was*. How intoxicating.

The card game continued, with play following a similar pattern. Sometimes the earl helped her capture a build, and sometimes she came to his aid. They worked together seamlessly, give and take, and every time he gazed at her with greater and greater appreciation. With each look, Tamsyn felt flushed and powerfully aware of herself as a woman. She saw how his eyes lingered on her mouth or the curve of her neck, sometimes dipping even lower to follow the neckline of her gown—as though he was entranced by what he saw.

This is what a siren feels like.

He was clearly too fond of women to believe in fidelity. Perhaps he would be so distracted bringing willing females into his bed that he'd pay his wife no mind. And when the vast fortune was his, he'd hardly notice the cost of buying a run-down manor in Cornwall.

He'd make for a truly terrible husband.

I have to marry him.

At last, the game ended, and the points totaled.

"Blast it," the dowager muttered.

"We win," Tamsyn said, blinking with surprise. She'd been too caught up in the moment, and him, to notice the actual play of the game. But she collected herself enough to say, as Lord Blakemere handed Tamsyn her share of the winnings, "Oh no, you keep it."

His brows rose. "The prize belongs to both of us," he said with surprise.

"I only wanted to play for amusement," she demurred, though she couldn't manage to sound coy. It wasn't the truth, but saying, "I played to flirt with you," wasn't very strategic.

"Are you certain?" he pressed, his voice low and seductive. He leaned closer to her, and she felt her cheeks flush in response to his nearness.

"I am a woman who knows my own mind, my lord," she answered pertly.

His grin was sudden, white, and dazzling. She—a woman who'd never fainted once in her life—grew dizzy from his smile, and wanted to lean into him.

No wonder he possessed such a reputation. What woman could resist his charm? "And I'm too much of a rogue to persuade you to change your mind." He tucked his winnings into his coat. "We make a good partnership," he murmured in a deep voice. "Shall we play again?"

Oh, yes.

"Tamsyn!" a disapproving feminine voice said behind her.

Turning in her chair, Tamsyn fixed Lady Daleford with a cheerful smile, which was difficult to maintain in the face of censure. "You've found me," Tamsyn said brightly.

"So I did." Lady Daleford eyed the earl guardedly. "I find myself fatigued. It's time we head home."

Tamsyn's chest constricted. She wasn't ready to leave yet. Not when things with the earl seemed so promising. On many levels.

But first and foremost, she had to think logically. Though she had attracted Lord Blakemere's interest, she feared it wasn't enough to warrant him calling on her. He'd found other women wanting as potential brides. Why should she be different?

I can only be myself. That had to be enough.

Rising from her chair, Tamsyn looked at him with frankness. "I enjoyed our game."

"The feeling is reciprocated," he answered, standing. His movements were economical but smooth. He had command over his body.

They stood close. Far closer than was respectable. She had an aching awareness of the breadth of his shoulders and the way his evening clothes skimmed over his muscles. The earl was a soldier still, after two years of peace.

A small frown appeared between his brows, as though he was attempting to puzzle through an enigma. "Might I—"

"*Now*, Tamsyn," Lady Daleford said in a clipped tone, already heading for the door.

Damn and hell, Tamsyn thought. Throwing Lord Blakemere a regretful look, she followed her companion out, though she could practically hear her body cry out, *Wait! Go back!*

Had she been successful? Was he intrigued enough to call on her? But she hadn't given him leave to, nor had she told him where she was staying.

It seemed all she could do now was hope.

$\mathcal{K}$IT's eyes followed the intriguing Miss Tamsyn Pearce as she hurried out of the card room. He liked the way she moved with long, purposeful strides rather than using tiny, dainty steps. It wasn't difficult to picture her tramping over wild, rolling countryside with her cheeks reddened by the wind, unconcerned by the mud edging the hem of her plain gown. He could well imagine that she was the sort of woman who needed to *do something* rather than restrict herself to being decorative.

He couldn't deny his visceral reaction to her, either. Even now he felt the hot grip of desire, which had been heightened all the more by the seamless way in which they had played together. It had been a rhythmic give-and-take that had primed his body and excited his mind.

If nothing else, they would be a good match in bed. He knew this with a bodily certitude, an innate recognition of her sensual potential.

Was it enough on which to build a marriage? As he

gazed at the door to the room—long after she'd vacated it—he searched for the instinctual aversion that had kept him from pursuing other ladies. But it wasn't there. If anything, he yearned for more of Tamsyn Pearce.

She'd made her own interest clear. Yet she gazed at him not as a potential to keep her in luxury, but in the dark, elemental way women and men looked at each other.

He wasn't a stranger to women making known their interest in him. Usually, such ladies were older, more familiar with the worldly ways of the *ton*. Tamsyn Pearce wasn't a debutante fresh from the schoolroom, but she had only just come down from the country. She ought to be shy and diffident, yet she didn't glance away when he looked at her.

She had refused to take the money they had won at cassino. So she wasn't entirely mercenary.

Perhaps Miss Pearce was just as drawn to him as he was intrigued by her.

But she'd been dragged away by her sharp-eyed companion before he'd been able to ask about calling on her. Damn.

"The gel's gone, Blakemere," Lady Haighe said, rapping her knuckles on the card table. "So you can stop mooning after her like a sailor on shore leave."

He always did like Lady Haighe. But now wasn't the time to enjoy the baroness's company.

"Please excuse me." Kit bowed and hastened out of the card room, ignoring Lady Haighe's muttered curses.

It took the work of a few moments to locate the night's host, Lord Eblewhite. The viscount stood amidst a group of men and women gathered at one end of the ballroom. Someone had just said something mildly amusing, because the assembled company was all chuckling.

Kit set his hand on the viscount's shoulder. "May I have a word in private, Eblewhite?"

"Of course, my lord." The older man disengaged from his guests and together he and Kit walked to a quiet corner of the chamber. "How goes the search for a bride?" he asked heartily.

Kit fought to keep his impatience in check. Whatever drew him to Miss Pearce, he felt the snap of attraction. He couldn't ignore the fact that time slipped by.

"You may be of assistance in that matter," he replied. "What can you tell me about Miss Tamsyn Pearce?"

Lord Eblewhite frowned in thought. "There are so many girls here. I've trouble recalling 'em all, like picking out one sugared cake from a banquet full of 'em."

"This particular cake comes from Cornwall and has red hair," Kit noted.

The viscount's brows rose. "Ah. Lady Daleford's guest. She's hosting the girl here in London."

So that was the woman who snapped at him like a terrier. "What do you know of Miss Pearce?"

"A spinster, if I recall correctly." Lord Eblewhite cast his gaze toward the ceiling as he scoured his memory. "Old Cornish gentry. Not much of a dowry—she's from impecunious circumstances."

Would that make her quick to spend his money, or would she watch every ha'penny? "Describe these circumstances," Kit urged.

Eblewhite looked impatient to return to his guests, but said, "Lady Daleford spoke to Mrs. Osterland, who told Lady Eblewhite that the family manor house is falling down around them. There may be mines on the property. Perhaps not. The nearby village is barely getting by on farming or fishing, but I can't recall."

"Her family," Kit pressed as Eblewhite started to edge away. "Tell me more about them."

His host sighed. "A fount of information, Lady Daleford. Said her father was Baron Shawe, but he and the baroness died in a boating accident when the girl was in her teens. Went on a pleasure sail one morning and didn't come back. Their wrecked boat was found a week later, but the bodies were never recovered. But there wasn't a will, a damned shame. The girl barely brings a groat to her future husband." Lord Eblewhite shook his head. "Frankly, I'm surprised she'd try for a Season in London, given her age and lack of dowry." He shrugged his shoulders. "She's pretty enough, I suppose. Make someone a good mistress." The viscount rocked on his feet. "Already got one, myself, and can't afford another. But you ought to give her a go." He knocked the side of his fist against Kit's shoulder in a show of manly bonhomie.

"Right now, I'm not looking for a mistress," Kit answered. "Many thanks, Eblewhite."

"Good luck on the hunt, Blakemere," the viscount replied.

Kit bowed as he and Lord Eblewhite parted. Though the dancing and revelry would continue for several more hours, Kit was ready to leave. He avoided Society balls as much as possible, finding them dull and tedious, with an unfortunate lack of indecent behavior—a far cry from the revelry of a pleasure garden. But he'd gotten what he needed from the Eblewhite assembly, and it was time to go home and ponder his options.

Making his way out of the ballroom, he considered all he knew of Miss Pearce.

Item the First: she was poor with few prospects, so
   she wouldn't mind a short courtship.
Item the Second: she didn't appear to be a fortune
   hunter.
Item the Third: he could easily envision them
   spending pleasurable hours in bed together.

Conclusion: she was *perfect*.

Chapter 4

$\mathcal{K}$it stood at the foot of the front steps leading to Lady Daleford's town house on Boswell Street, readying himself for the world's shortest courtship. He had five full days remaining to meet the conditions of Somerby's will.

He didn't know if Miss Pearce would accept his brief attempts at wooing, let alone agree to marry. Ladies wanted long walks through sun-dappled fields and soul-stirring looks. They wanted romance. Or so Kit assumed, not having much experience with pursuing ladies' hearts. He had considerable practice pursuing their *bodies*, however. That part could come after the wedding. Kit practically salivated as he imagined Miss Pearce's taste. As a woman of gentle birth, she likely didn't have much experience—and he couldn't wait to show her the many ways he could give her pleasure.

Yet if romance was what Miss Pearce wanted, the lack of time meant that Kit would have to disappoint her. He wasn't entirely certain how to go about offering a genteel young woman marriage two days after meeting her. He would have to try, however. He'd faced Napoleon's cannons—he could speed a lady through the wooing process and proceed directly to marriage.

Now that he was poised outside Lady Daleford's home, he wasn't as certain about the bouquet of red gerbera daisies he carried. Perhaps he should have gone with the more traditional roses. Yet the cheerful, unaffected daisies recalled Miss Pearce's open, guileless countenance, and the red indicated the passion that lurked just beneath her surface. He'd purchased the flowers without questioning his preference.

Would his title be nothing but a courtesy with no fortune to support it, or would the money slip away and be granted to that distant relative in Bermuda?

The only way to land the blunt is to climb the sodding stairs, he told himself sternly. Miss Pearce was also at the top of the steps, and that quickened his pace and brought him to the front door.

He knocked smartly before a footman opened it with a polite, professional expression, the one he surely used for visiting hours.

Kit handed the servant his card.

"Is her ladyship expecting you, my lord?" the footman inquired politely after reading it.

"Well, no," Kit admitted. He hadn't gotten permission to call. Lady Daleford hadn't told him where she lived, either. That information had been gleaned from Anderson, his valet, who was a trove of information about matters both high and low, and knew the addresses of everyone in the *ton*. "Just present them with my card."

The servant murmured, "You may wait in the foyer, my lord." He stepped back to admit Kit into the house.

With a bow, the footman strode down a hallway, leaving Kit alone. The servant didn't ask to take Kit's hat, since it was known that callers never stayed for more than fifteen minutes—which suited him very well, since he hadn't the luxury of long, protracted conversations.

As he waited, a throb of edginess moved through him. Idleness often gave space for wariness to move in—a habit from so many years in combat.

There are no enemies here. You're in the heart of London, and safety is all around you.

As he pushed the wariness back, unexpected anticipation rose up and strummed silver fingers along his arms and the back of his neck. Miss Pearce had vitality and spirit, with a hint of daring, as evidenced by her willingness to accept his staking her cards, and the directness of her gaze. Their mutual attraction couldn't be ignored, either.

Come find me, her eyes had said as she'd left the card room.

Kit didn't hunt, but he knew a lure when he saw one.

He couldn't question his rationale as to why Miss Pearce had been the lone woman to snag his interest. His instincts had kept him alive for nearly a decade of warfare, and he wouldn't ignore them now.

A clock somewhere chimed the quarter hour, and he checked his pocket watch to see that a full ten minutes had passed since the footman had departed with Kit's card. Which meant that he was currently being debated by Lady Daleford and Miss Pearce.

Straining to hear, he caught faint tones of women's voices speaking in hushed, urgent whispers. A corner of his mouth curved up ruefully.

The voices reached a peak, and then stopped abruptly. Kit's heart thudded in the silence. His fate had been decided. Had Lady Daleford won? Or did Miss Pearce emerge victorious?

The footman appeared, but the expression on his face gave nothing away.

Kit's breath halted.

"Follow me, my lord," the servant said.

Kit exhaled, thinking to himself, *Well done, Miss Pearce!*

He trailed after the footman down a short corridor before stepping through the doorway to a drawing room.

"Lord Blakemere," announced the footman before disappearing.

A wall of windows permitted sunlight to stream into the chamber, forming halos around the furnishings. Miss Pearce, standing with her back to a window, became a fiery saint as her vivid hair caught the light. She wore an equally brilliant smile, full of surprised pleasure as she turned to face him.

For a moment, Kit forgot the mechanics of breathing before they came back to him in a rush. Both he and Miss Pearce took a step toward each other.

He held out the flowers. "Forgive my presumption, but I was compelled to bring these."

She crossed the room, her eyes bright as she accepted the bouquet. "Daisies! My favorite!"

Perhaps she was telling the truth, or perhaps she prevaricated for the sake of politeness. Yet he had the feeling she wasn't given to dishonesty, and his smile grew to see the picture she made, cradling the cheerful flowers. The flowers' vivid hue matched the lushness of her mouth—a mouth that was perfectly made for kissing.

A maid appeared and took the flowers from Miss Pearce. It was only then that Kit remembered that they were not alone in the drawing room. He turned to the older woman seated with an embroidery hoop near the fire.

"Lady Daleford," Kit said, bowing. "I am glad to find you at home."

The woman could not have looked more displeased to see him. Her lips were thin and her cheeks nearly red with indignation. "Lord Blakemere."

How had Miss Pearce convinced the old dame to admit

him? Though he was curious, he would gladly accept the results.

He glanced to Miss Pearce, who watched him with lively, curious eyes. Their looks caught. The distance between them seemed to dissolve to nothing, and the presence of Lady Daleford became a vague, remote annoyance.

Kit felt her gaze like a hot caress down his back. A lick of lust uncoiled, centering in his groin and curling outward with a probing, curious touch.

Her eyes widened, as though she, too, had felt that sudden flare. A candid, carnal flush bloomed in her cheeks. With her redhead's complexion, she wasn't able to hide her responses.

Intriguing, their reactions. As though they were both surprised, and neither had anticipated anything other than dutiful acceptance of an unwanted situation.

She cleared her throat. "Tea, my lord?"

Lady Daleford coughed with displeasure.

"A kind offer," Kit answered. "The company is refreshment enough." He inwardly grimaced. What a bloody trite thing to say.

A corner of Miss Pearce's mouth turned up as if recognizing the ridiculousness of the situation. She waved toward a chair. "Please."

He took his seat as she sank down on a nearby sofa.

A small clock on the mantel ticked. They sat in silence for a full minute.

What could he say to Miss Pearce now, anyway? *We don't know each other at all but let's join our lives together forever* seemed like an odd way to begin a conversation. *I want to touch you everywhere and feel your hands on my naked skin* also seemed inappropriate. And with Lady Daleford hovering like a vulture, he found it even more difficult to speak.

He had to think of something. "Are you enjoying London, Miss Pearce?"

"I get so blessedly confused here," she said honestly. "The minute I set foot outside the door I don't know west from east or north from south." She spread her hands. "The curse of the first-time visitor."

"You've never been here before?" He oughtn't be astonished by this. Many people lived away from London, but other than his years fighting, he'd always returned to the metropolis. Anything a man wanted could be found here.

"All my life has been spent in Cornwall." Her smile turned self-deprecating. "I must sound like the country mouse."

"There's very little about you I'd ascribe to being a mouse, Miss Pearce."

Her lips pursed into an amused bow. "There's another thing I'm not acclimated to—a city gentleman's suavity."

"I'll endeavor to speak more coarsely so I can put you at ease," he teased.

Her laugh was low and rich, sending another flicker of sensual curiosity careening through him. "If you could curse like a disgruntled fisherman, I'd be ever so much more comfortable."

Kit's laugh caught them both by surprise. He hadn't felt much like laughing these past few weeks—but she brought lightness out in him.

Lady Daleford audibly grumbled.

"May I interest you in a walk to Russell Square?" he asked Miss Pearce. "For once, the smoke in the air is tolerable enough. We might even be able to see a glimpse of blue sky." He glanced at Lady Daleford. "Of course, we'll bring along your maid. It will be entirely appropriate."

Lady Daleford opened her mouth, but Miss Pearce spoke first. "Yes, please."

"I'll await you in the hallway," Kit said, standing as she also got to her feet. He bowed at the older woman, who looked as though she gnawed on salt cod.

He took a few steps past the door before stopping in the hallway. It was absolutely unforgivable that he eavesdrop, but Kit never claimed to have unimpeachable morals. In fact, his amorality had long been one of his greatest strengths.

"My dear," Lady Daleford said lowly and urgently. "Please reconsider. Feign illness or a turned ankle. Anything rather than giving *that man* a moment's privacy. He is a poor investment."

What's wrong with me? Kit's pride gave an indignant throb.

"I've already agreed to go," Miss Pearce answered. "And I *want* to go. I like him." She sounded astonished by this fact.

A quick burst of brightness popped in his chest.

"Besides," she continued, "I don't think he's a poor investment."

"He'll make a terrible husband," Lady Daleford warned. "Men like him take *mistresses*. They stick their wives in the country and never see them. He'll be exactly the same."

Damn—the older woman seemed to have read his mind. He'd never desired marriage, but to hear her discredit his husbandly attributes irritated him.

"He's precisely what I need," Miss Pearce countered.

And what might that be? he wondered silently.

But whatever her motivations, the end result matched his own desire for a woman he could see himself marrying, and a woman who would be amenable to the world's shortest courtship. She also seemed unconcerned by the fact that he'd have lovers or deposit her at a far-flung country estate.

"I *will* go," Miss Pearce concluded in a tone that would brook no argument.

He couldn't decide whether or not it was a good thing that she possessed a strong spine. If they were to marry, she would have to accept the fact that he had no intention of changing the way he lived his life. So long as he kept her comfortable, he reasoned, she'd have no cause to complain. He'd give her a comfortable allowance while he used the lion's share of his income to fund the pleasure garden. Everyone would have what they wanted.

But all that was irrelevant unless she agreed to marry him. Though she might not if she found him lurking in corridors and eavesdropping, so he hurried to the foyer to wait.

Miss Pearce smiled at him as she entered the vestibule, then she passed Kit to go upstairs and change. She made a pretty shape as she ascended the staircase, moving with confidence mixed with instinctive sensuality.

Kit could hardly wait for the wedding night. *If* she agreed to marry.

"Ahem."

He turned in mid-ogle to see Lady Daleford glowering at him.

She advanced on him, her eyes sharp and piercing. "I know why you're calling on Tamsyn," she said darkly. "You're panting to get your hands on Lord Somerby's blunt, and she's the key."

"It doesn't seem like my being an earl, and making her my countess, is an abominable fate," he answered blandly.

"The title doesn't trouble me," she retorted. "It's your reputation. Gaming hells, demimondaines, opera dancers . . . hardly the pursuits of an honorable gentleman."

"Perhaps I can reform," Kit replied. *I won't.*

"You won't." Lady Daleford sounded confident. "Tamsyn deserves better."

Kit wasn't precisely the ideal upper-class man, however her words were little barbs digging into his flesh.

He might not be admitted to Almack's, but, damn it, he'd fought Napoleon. One didn't return from the blood and mud and boredom and terror without needing some relief—and it wasn't found at the bottom of a cup of watery lemonade.

"Let's allow Miss Pearce to decide what she wants," he countered.

It looked as though Lady Daleford wanted to say more, but her mouth clamped shut as footsteps sounded on the stairs.

Kit turned to see Miss Pearce descending the steps, a shy but eager smile playing about her lips. His chest constricted with pleasure at the sight of her, and he felt his blood quickening.

He barely noticed a ruddy-cheeked woman in plain clothing trailing behind her—instead, he couldn't tear his gaze from the young woman. She'd donned a lavender redingote and wore a straw bonnet with a matching pale purple ribbon, making her look like a flower from a tropical climate. The color highlighted her complexion and made the light brown of her eyes shine. Everything about her spoke of freshness and vigor, and she seemed ready to meet any experience with unconcealed energy.

Even though she knew he watched her, she didn't make a show of descending the stairs, prolonging his admiration. Coming to stand in front of him, he caught her fragrance—something warm and spicy—and he flared his nostrils, trying to inhale her all at once. She tilted up her chin. This close, he could see the many tiny freckles that danced over her skin.

Each one a place to kiss, he thought unexpectedly, and wondered if they covered just her face or if there were more on her body.

"Shall we?" He offered her his arm.

Wordlessly, she moved to stand beside him and placed

her fingers on his forearm. She wore gloves, and he a coat and shirt, so there was no flesh-to-flesh contact. Just the same, his heartbeat jolted at the pressure of her hand on him.

Normally, he associated with women of a far faster character. Their touches were more bold, but from this simple contact, his whole body came alive.

Miss Pearce's fingers pressed down with more firmness, meeting the solidity of his arm. She glanced at him quickly, as if surprised by the feel of him. He wasn't a brawny country lad, but he had been a soldier, and he continued to visit the fencing and pugilism academies to keep his body healthy and strong. Kit allowed himself a moment's vanity by flexing the muscles of his arm, and was gratified by her interested look.

"Don't forget that we're expected at the Newtons' tonight," Lady Daleford reminded her.

"I'll have her home in time for supper," Kit promised.

Lady Daleford looked unappeased, but Miss Pearce didn't seem fazed by the older woman's disapproval.

Realizing that his future depended on this innocuous walk, Kit led Miss Pearce out the door and into the sunlight and uncertainty.

Chapter 5

$\mathcal{T}$amsyn tried to will her heart to beat at a steadier pace, but it staunchly refused to listen, thudding away with abandon as they ambled down the street. She couldn't help her mingled nervousness and excitement. He clearly needed to wed quickly, but she didn't know how long he'd spend courting her—provided she allowed him to.

"Russell Square isn't far," Lord Blakemere said as they walked.

She chanced a look at him through lowered lashes. The sunlight was his ally, tracing the planes of his long, handsome face with a loving hand. She felt flushed all over from being this close to him and sensing the potency of his body.

Tamsyn had often heard that a life of sin left its mark upon a person, yet that hardly seemed the case with him. Potency and virility radiated from him, as if nourished by his dissolution.

Perhaps if any of her acquaintances ever fell ill, she would recommend a thorough course of gambling and debauchery to set them back on the path to health.

She looked back at Nessa. Her old friend mouthed something at Tamsyn that she couldn't understand, but judging by Nessa's ogling of the earl, she approved of Tamsyn's choice for a potential husband.

"A little green park isn't far from here," she noted. "There's a good deal more privacy there than Russell Square."

"By all means," he said readily, "lead us there."

It was a strange dance they did, she and Lord Blakemere. She imagined that he'd made inquiries about her, and knew some—but not all—of the reasons for her eagerness to wed. Further, he likely understood that she knew the nature of his own predicament. Yet neither of them could address this directly. Not yet, at any rate.

"London's rife with entertainments," he said as they headed toward the tiny park. His voice was deep with a faint, delicious huskiness. "I hope you've had a chance to visit some of them."

"Lady Daleford has no fondness for frivolity. She sees assemblies and balls as a necessary evil, but won't countenance other amusements."

"That's a shame. A pretty young woman needs her share of pleasures."

Her stomach leapt at his suggestive words. She had the feeling he wasn't referring to Astley's Amphitheatre or strolls in the park.

"You sound like one well familiar with the city's . . . pleasures."

His gaze turned wicked and knowing. "There's no better guide. Although," he murmured half to himself, "the places I'm most familiar with aren't quite appropriate for a gentlewoman."

She didn't doubt it. He could probably put to shame a sailor on leave.

"Before I return to Cornwall," she mused, "I'll convince Lady Daleford to let me see something of the city. Vauxhall, at the least."

He grinned. "Pleasure gardens are amongst my favorite places."

"From what I've heard, they're rather wild."

His grin widened and his eyes gleamed with excitement. "Precisely—the mix of all walks of life, the ecstatic chaos, the unpredictability and dedication to wringing joy out of every minute." He looked as though he was about to say something further, but then seemed to reconsider it and was silent.

"I'm not much familiar with gentlemen of fashion and their interests," she confessed. Farmers, fishermen, and smuggling sea captains—those were the men she knew best, but she couldn't tell him that.

He lifted his brows. "I'm a gentleman of fashion?"

She eyed him, from the crown of his beaver hat to the toes of his gleaming tall boots. Today he wore buff breeches, a wine-colored waistcoat, and a bottle-green coat, all of the finest materials and assembled with an expert hand. No one in the whole of Cornwall had a fraction of his sartorial gloss, and that included Penzance. But he didn't quite resemble a dandy, given the fact that the body wearing the garments seemed more suited for the battlefield. Or the bedroom.

"You're no elderly farmer," she replied.

He shook his head and exhaled. "I suppose that's better than most of the names I've been called."

That comment would have to be explored in greater depth—another time.

He guided her around a puddle on the sidewalk. "For one with scant practice talking to a polished gem such as myself, you're doing admirably. London's not known for plain dealing, but you speak your mind."

"I try to be truthful." Which was only partially true. "I'm not always successful."

"No one can be completely honest all the time," he said

with the air of a man who had a few secrets of his own. What were they? Did she dare find out?

"I agree." There was only one secret that she kept, but it was a big one.

They reached the tiny square, tucked between homes. It was a little treasure enclosed by iron railings, with a handful of trees and green grass currently occupied by a pair of pigeons. A wooden bench stood in the middle, as if waiting for two people on an assignation.

"I discovered this place on a walk," Tamsyn explained as she and the earl approached the bench. Nessa stood a small distance away, feeding the birds with bread crumbs she pulled from the pockets of her coat.

"Given Lady Daleford's chary eye," Lord Blakemere said wryly, "I'm surprised she let you amble out of her clutches."

"She was taking a nap," Tamsyn admitted, "and I bolted."

His crooked smile was a roguish thing with the power to weaken her knees. He didn't admonish her for being disobedient, or seem particularly alarmed that she'd gone out on her own.

"If you grasp freedom again," he advised her, "be sure to go to Catton's. The best iced cakes in the hemisphere. It's run by a woman, Isabel Catton." He leaned closer and her mouth went dry. "She's a scandalous woman, Mrs. Catton. A marquess's daughter who shocked Society by marrying a commoner."

Tamsyn barely paid attention to the words he spoke. All she could focus on was his nearness, and the warm, masculine scent of his skin.

"I hadn't heard of the place," she said, struggling for calm. She sat down on the bench and he sat beside her, leaving an unfortunately respectable distance between them. "Now I'll be certain to go before I leave London. I do love a scandalous woman."

"Me, too," he said in a low, confiding voice. A frown suddenly creased his brow. "You plan to stay for the entirety of the Season, I hope."

"I haven't decided the length of my stay," she answered, which was a better response than, *I need to find a husband with heaps of money so I can keep smuggling.*

He drew in a breath, then slowly exhaled. His profile was turned to her, so she could see the clean lines of his face, his slightly large nose, the angles of his jaw. His brows were drawn down, as if in thought.

"Let's agree to honesty between us." He turned to her, his expression serious, which seemed an odd contrast to his usual levity.

She made a noncommittal sound. Fortunately, he took that as a sound of agreement.

"In the spirit of that honesty," he went on, carefully selecting his words like a man picking out precious stones, "I'll state it plainly—I need to wed within five days."

Hearing him say it out loud made her heart speed up. "I know," she replied as evenly as she could.

He waited for a moment, as though expecting her to demand to be taken home. When she didn't, he continued. "Your circumstances are known to me, as well."

Her heart knocked into her ribs. "What do you know?"

"You're from an old family," he recited. "You were orphaned, but there wasn't a will, so you have no dowry." He cocked an eyebrow. "Did I miss anything?"

She forced a thin smile. "From stem to stern, that's everything."

Planting his hands on his knees, he went on. "Knowing what you know about me, would you be amenable . . . to becoming my wife?"

Her breath deserted her. She couldn't speak.

"The short of it is," he continued in her silence, "I need

a wife and you need a husband. We'll suit each other's needs."

"What a romantic proposal," she said wryly. "'You'll do.'"

He grimaced. "I've never proposed before, so my skill is negligible. My apologies."

She shook her head as she accepted the death of her final hope for affection. "Romance never figured into the picture for me, anyway."

"Again, I'm sorry I have to be so businesslike," he said with regret. "Time is slipping away, faster and faster. I can vow that, if you say yes, I will make your life very comfortable."

She didn't care about that—all that mattered was buying Chei Owr and keeping Newcombe from the deadly grip of poverty.

But she would also be married. She'd become Lord Blakemere's property after years of almost-complete liberty.

Yet for all that the country considered her to be his possession, the same could not be said about him. He would not belong to her. She would give up her independence, and he'd keep his freedom, which hardly seemed fair. A husband could sue for divorce on the grounds of infidelity, but she wouldn't have the same recourse unless he was physically cruel to her or a bigamist.

"Will you be faithful?" she asked.

He was silent for a long while. "I cannot guarantee my fidelity," he finally said. Grimly, as though delivering a verdict.

Her sinking regret was expected, but that didn't make it less painful. "I see."

"Once you have given me an heir," he added quickly, "you can take a lover. I won't be jealous of you, and you won't be jealous of me."

She knew how city marriages worked. Even so, she confessed, "I didn't think it mattered that we might be monogamous, but hearing it spelled out so plainly is"—she searched for the right word—"strange."

He looked rueful, but not repentant. "Understandable. But I must say again that Lord Somerby was a very wealthy man. His wealth will be mine. You will have any material comfort you desire, so long as your spending is within reason."

With no dowry and all her attention given to smuggling, she'd never expected to marry. She'd resigned herself to living as her uncle's dependent at Chei Owr while she continued to run the smuggling operation.

She'd also reconciled herself to spinsterhood—and all its attendant loneliness. Yet to know that her future husband wouldn't be faithful felt like a disappointment.

Never knew I'd given two figs about romance. And yet she did, seeing now that it would truly be denied to her.

You'll have Chei Owr. That's something.

"Consider us as business partners," he explained, "rather than a romantic couple."

Could she sign her name to an agreement with the man who would be her husband, the man who would have control over her person and her future children?

Did she have a choice in saying no?

"If we wed," he continued persuasively, "we'll get along well. No illusions, no disenchantment."

She could get up. Walk away.

Since her parents' deaths, she'd had no love in her life. She and Nessa were friends, but that was all. None of the village men had ever vied for her hand. Oh, there had been kisses here and there, but nothing further. They couldn't—she was a baron's daughter and they were farmers and fishermen.

Lord Blakemere's candid proposal was the best she

was going to get. She doubted he would be around enough for her to grow attached—and his absence was necessary if she was to continue smuggling.

A fierce part of her didn't want to share her man with anyone. Perhaps if the earl had been less fascinating, less alluring, she could say with confidence that it wouldn't hurt if he went to other women's beds.

What if it does hurt? What if I come to feel something for him?

Don't *care for him. Protect yourself.* That was the best she could do. Perhaps, once she'd given him that heir, she could find love with someone who wasn't her husband. *How very sophisticated.*

"Your silence alarms me," he said, breaking her thoughts.

"No cause for alarm," she replied. She drew in a breath. "My answer is yes."

His smile was sudden and bright. The worry left his eyes, and pleasure with her and the world radiated from him. "This is . . . this is excellent." His brow furrowed. "Are you content with a special license? We can be married in three days."

"So soon," she murmured, but she had understood it would be fast.

"I cannot wait longer," he said with contrition.

"Understandable." She clasped her hands in her lap. "We can wed in three days, if that's what will help you."

"It will," he said eagerly. "Thank you." His gaze narrowed on her face. There was a sudden determination in his eyes. "I'd like to kiss you."

Ah, there went her pulse again. It sped up at his words, making breath hard to find and her palms damp.

"You don't have to," she answered quickly. "I'll consider our agreement binding. Here." She offered him her hand to shake.

He slid his palm over hers, and the thin leather of his

gloves through her own kidskin was as hot as his bare skin touching hers. Tamsyn's heart jumped into her throat at the contact. But he didn't shake her hand. Instead, he cradled it, enfolding her with his broad palm and long fingers.

The corners of his eyes crinkled as he smiled, but there was no mistaking the desire in his gaze. "We may be entering into this union with practical intentions, but I'm a man before I'm a businessman. And I'd very much enjoy kissing my future wife."

"I . . . oh." She glanced at his lips. They were curved and well formed, and she feared what they would feel like against her mouth. She suspected that he knew the art of kissing and could make a woman surrender everything with just his mouth.

"Don't be afraid," he murmured. "I'll make it good for you."

That's what I'm afraid of.

But I want to know. I want to taste him.

She drew in a breath. "You may kiss me."

He leaned closer to her, slowly, as if afraid of frightening her. Engulfed by his masculinity, she grew light-headed. There was faint stubble on his jaw and cheeks where his beard would come in. Would it be gold or brown or even reddish? It was a shame that beards weren't fashionable, because there was something so definitively masculine about them. If she had her way—

Her thoughts stuttered and died as he pressed his lips to hers, and her eyes fluttered shut. She sank into the sensation of his mouth gently stroking back and forth, as if learning her, testing the feel of him and her together. He lingered that way for a while, as if in no hurry to speed the process along. If kissing was music, then he was a maestro, building gradually, allowing the melody to take shape before plunging ahead.

The press of his lips grew firmer, and she found herself meeting him, leaning into the kiss and letting it delve deeper. At her response, a low sound of approval rose up from his chest. He slowly urged her lips apart and took the kiss further. The very tip of his tongue dipped to taste her. Without thought, she nipped at his tongue and met it with her own.

Hot electricity shot through her. It coursed along her body, forking into bright strands that wove through her breasts and between her legs. She inhaled sharply, stunned by the sudden, powerful sensations.

I'm going to be married to this man? Mercy.

They pulled back in unison and her eyes flew open. His gaze was clouded with dazed pleasure and astonishment.

It seemed he'd also been shocked by the heat of their kiss and the speed of its intensity. He, a known rake and libertine, looked *aroused* by what surely had to be one of the chastest kisses he'd experienced in a long while.

Except it hadn't been chaste. It had been brief, but their tongues lightly touching had been profoundly erotic, hinting at greater pleasure to come.

He cleared his throat. "That was . . . a welcome revelation."

Her thoughts whirled while her body clamored for more. Hellfire—if this quick kiss had affected her so much, what would happen when they went to bed together? What if she liked it? What if she *loved* it, and her heart followed her body's devotion? Then she'd have to reconcile herself to him leaving her bed for another.

"I should be getting back," she said.

"Yes."

She stood, and he did the same, but it was then that she realized their hands were still clasped. She let him go at once, dropping him as though he burned.

"Let's get you home." He held out his arm.

Still shaken by the kiss, her legs wobbled slightly as they headed toward Lady Daleford's town home, with Nessa trailing after them. Tamsyn looked back at her friend, who responded with a grin and a raised thumb.

"I'll go for the special license tomorrow," the earl said. "I can pick the venue, too, unless you'd like to make the selection."

"I trust you." Did she? Tamsyn was about to join with this man for the rest of her life. Aside from a few facts, she knew almost nothing about him. He was basically a stranger. Yet in three days, they would share a bed. They would share everything. According to the law, she would belong to him, and her own identity would dissolve.

Was this the right choice? She'd gotten what she wanted, but she couldn't help the fear that poked its sharp fangs into her heart.

I have no idea what I'm getting myself into.

Chapter 6

The campfire on the night before the Battle of Nivelle seemed festive by comparison to this evening. Only an hour had passed since he'd pledged his troth to Miss Tamsyn Pearce of Cornwall, and the atmosphere still snapped with tension.

The setting couldn't be faulted. Kit's friend, the Duke of Greyland, had offered his expansive, elegant home for the ceremony and reception. The wedding itself had been held in the dining room, which had been cleared out and specially decorated for the occasion with garlands of boxwood leaves and roses. Once the vows had been exchanged, the rites concluded, and the parish register signed, servants had brought in tables laden with delicacies and cakes, bowls of punch, and decanters of wine.

A string trio played softly but cheerfully in one corner. Candlelight glittered on cut crystal chandeliers, making the polished silver plates and goblets shine. Everything *looked* splendid. But the mood remained stubbornly dour.

Kit stood with a glass of wine by a large arrangement of gerbera daisies, watching the guests attempt to socialize. He fought a melancholy sigh. Men didn't give melancholy sighs on their wedding days.

"Naturally, an original such as yourself had to buck tradition and have a wedding at eleven o'clock in the evening." Langdon approached and gave Kit's shoulder a good-natured shake. He stood beside Kit, and together they observed the reception.

"My parents came all the way from Yorkshire to be here," Kit noted, "and their carriage became stuck in the mud *four times* today. I couldn't have the ceremony until they arrived."

The majority of wedding ceremonies had to be before noon in a parish church, but Kit's expensive purchase of a special license—using a loan from Langdon—from the Archbishop of Canterbury ensured that he could be wed at the place and time of his choosing. Unfortunately, it had taken two days longer than Kit had anticipated. Added to that was the excessive amount of time it had taken his parents to travel from Yorkshire, and he'd barely an hour left by the time the vows had been exchanged.

"And on the very last day you had left," Langdon added. He whistled. "I knew you were fond of gambling, but I didn't think you'd risk your fortune."

"It wasn't by choice," Kit grumbled. "I swore to my parents that I wouldn't marry without their presence."

He glanced over at his family. All of them appeared as though they had been drinking unsweetened lemonade.

"None of them are especially forthcoming with their felicitations," Langdon observed drily. "You'd think they would be happier with their youngest son no longer being their financial responsibility." He eyed Kit. "And I would think *you* would be happier, too."

Kit took a drink of wine, but it didn't round the sharp edges of his humor. "Nothing is settled until tomorrow. I'm to go to Lord Somerby's solicitor's office and finalize the paperwork. Until then, I'm the very impecunious Lord Blakemere, and my wife is the impoverished Lady

Blakemere. Speaking of her . . ." His gaze skimmed over the small gathering. "Where is she?"

"Being watched over by a disapproving sentry." Langdon nodded toward a corner of the room.

Tamsyn stood off to one side, her only company being the censorious Lady Daleford. Tamsyn's expression was one of barely suppressed frustration.

"Excuse me," Kit said to Langdon.

He crossed the room to reach her, aware of many gazes upon him. Nearing her, he observed how bewitching she looked in her pale silver gown adorned with tiny pearls and silver lace. It had been purchased ready-made, due to the time-sensitive nature of the wedding, yet she was a ravishing bride, the color and cut flattering her complexion. She wore a crown of white flowers, which gleamed against the fiery hue of her hair.

She'll be mine tonight. That hair would spread upon a pillow, and he'd feel her arms around him. He'd learn the delicious secrets of her body and show her how much pleasure two lovers could create together.

He could barely restrain his eagerness.

"May I have a word with my wife, Lady Daleford?" he asked, feeling the strange shape and sound of the words *my wife* on his lips.

The older woman fixed him with a sharp glare. "You both have walked into a horrendous mistake," she snapped before storming off toward the punch bowl.

Tamsyn rolled her eyes. "Lady Daleford's candor was one of the qualities my parents admired." She looked rueful. "I wouldn't mind a little dissembling right now."

"I would have liked to have met your parents," he said.

"I would have liked the same," she answered.

They both seemed to realize at the same moment that, had her parents been alive, there would have been no need for this wedding.

"Please excuse me for a moment," Tamsyn said, and slipped out into the corridor.

Langdon, Greyland, and Greyland's wife approached him. Kit couldn't help but notice the way the duke and duchess kept close to each other, with Greyland's hand possessively on her lower back as if he needed to touch her at all times.

"Best wishes on your marriage," the Duchess of Greyland said cheerfully, raising her glass of wine. "She's a lovely woman."

"Felicitations," Greyland added heartily.

Langdon also lifted his glass. "Blessings on you both. Though," he added with a furrowed brow, "I fear for my own unattached state, given that my two closest friends have fallen prey to matrimony."

"A duke's heir *must* marry," Greyland pointed out, ever practical.

"But at the time of *my* choosing," Langdon replied. "With my father as hale as ever, I pray that time is long in coming."

"Besides," Lady Greyland noted pertly, "whoever she may be, your choice of bride is entirely at your own discretion. Even someone as entirely unsuitable as me."

"Love, there's nothing unsuitable about you." Warmth shone from Greyland's eyes as he gazed at his duchess, and she gave him a private smile that radiated devotion.

Though Kit and Langdon glanced at each other with exasperation, Kit admitted to himself that it was a rare luxury to have someone with whom you shared that kind of connection. Would he and Tamsyn ever grow as close? Unlikely. They'd sealed their bond on the basis of practicality. So long as they tolerated each other, they ought to do well enough. He knew with certainty that they would enjoy their physical connection, and when that paled—for desire always cooled—they could seek pleasure elsewhere.

Something odd and hot jabbed Kit in his belly. He frowned at the unfamiliar sensation. Perhaps the wine had spoiled. Or was it—no. He couldn't be *jealous* at the thought of Tamsyn taking someone else to her bed. He never felt jealousy when his past paramours found new lovers, and besides, he barely knew Tamsyn. How could he possibly feel that strange emotion for her?

Yet it was there, just the same. Smoldering like the edges of paper moments before bursting into flame.

Out of the corner of his eye, Kit saw Tamsyn slip back into the chamber.

Before anyone could speak, he announced cheerfully to his family, "Your carriages are waiting."

His father scowled. "I didn't order my carriage to be made ready."

"But I did." Kit smiled, relying on the charm that had gotten him out of many a childhood scrape, including the time he painted a very detailed illustration of a dairymaid on the wall of the drawing room.

"How gracious of you," Tamsyn said enthusiastically. She gave Kit a discreet wink, and when he winked back, she coughed into her hand, barely concealing a laugh.

"Lady Daleford," Kit said, turning to her with as much charisma as he could muster, "your vehicle also awaits."

Tamsyn managed to suppress her laughter enough to press a fast kiss on the elderly lady's cheek. "Thank you so much for being here. And my sincere gratitude for your hospitality. I'll have the remainder of my things brought to me tomorrow."

"Where *are* you staying?" Lady Daleford demanded. "You cannot mean to make a home in his *bachelor* lodgings."

"I've rented a house on Bruton Street," Kit said. "Until we are settled in more permanent accommodations, it should suit us well. The house comes complete with a full staff," he added for Tamsyn's benefit. For the gathered crowd, he continued, "Lady Blakemere and I will spend tonight in a hotel, and then tomorrow we shall move into our new home."

Nothing truly has to change, he told himself. *I'm not going to alter all of my life simply because I'm* married.

"But that's all on the morrow," he said cheerfully. "For now, I bid you all a very heartfelt good night." He held out his hand, ushering his family and Lady Daleford toward the door.

As everyone began to file out, grumbling, Tamsyn stepped close to whisper in his ear, "They think your behavior to be scandalous."

He sent her a lopsided grin. "What's one more scandal?"

"Indeed," she said with a mischievous smile.

Ah, damn, I think I truly like this woman.

Finally, after receiving one last affronted glare from his father, they were gone.

"There's always the possibility that we've disappointed them," Tamsyn said wryly.

His smile didn't waver. "A third son is *always* a disappointment, even if he becomes an earl." He ran a placating finger down her cheek, and the softness of her skin roused him.

Soon.

Coming back to himself, he continued brightly, "Now that we've liberated ourselves from our oppressive guests, the celebration can happen in earnest."

"Truly, though," she said, laying a hand on his arm, "you didn't have to send your family away on my account."

The spontaneous touch of her hand upon his sleeve sent a jolt through him. Their kiss formalizing their union had been quick, chaste—a far cry from the heat that had risen up between them so quickly days earlier—yet the feel of her now stoked the furnace of his growing desire.

"They'll recover from the indignity," Kit said optimistically. "In time, when I'm generating more wealth than my father, everyone will come to an accord."

"Nonetheless," she said, smiling, "your gallantry on my behalf is appreciated."

He pressed a hand to his chest and executed an extravagantly old-fashioned bow. "Your servant."

His reward was the trill of her low, husky laughter. The sound trailed heat into his chest and traveled lower.

Since when did virgins laugh like sophisticated, earthy women of pleasure? There was more to Tamsyn than he'd first realized.

"We need to improve the atmosphere in here," he declared, then strode to the musicians. "Enough of elegance," he said to them. "Play something more festive and lively."

At once, the musicians struck up a sprightly country tune.

"A fine improvement," Kit proclaimed. He made his way back to Tamsyn, who watched with amused interest. "Come." He offered her his arm. "Let us attend to the other guests." He guided them toward Langdon, Greyland, and Lady Greyland.

Tamsyn whispered with a hint of awe, "You're truly friends with a *duke*? And a *duke's heir*?"

"Lord Langdon and I were at university together," Kit explained. "After, he and I had a few years subsequently of knocking around London until I joined the army. When I came back, Langdon introduced me to the duke, and the three of us have been wreaking havoc over the city. Well, Greyland has always been a bit, shall we say, *sober*. And since his marriage to Lady G., he's become as sanctimonious as a parson. Wouldn't you agree, Greyland?" Kit added once they'd joined the others.

"I pray for Blakemere's soul," Greyland confirmed with a wry tilt of his lips, "but it comes to nothing. He'll surely burn in the afterlife."

"But I'll be there, too," Langdon added, "so at least we'll enjoy our time in Hades."

"I'd add my prayers with yours, my darling," Lady Greyland said sardonically, "but I'm afraid my avowals of righteousness hold no weight."

"Love," her husband answered, "where you go, I follow. Paradise would be a dark place indeed without your light."

Langdon rolled his eyes. "My God, the two of you."

Greyland's hand curved over his wife's waist. "You're jealous because, unlike you, when my woman professes her devotion to me, no money changes hands."

Kit couldn't hold back his laugh. "A hit, a very palpable hit." He glanced at Tamsyn, who watched the interplay with amused fascination. "Forgive us. The habits of long familiarity must seem appalling to you."

"Oh, no." A smile lifted the corners of her mouth. "It's rather like going to the zoo, only better, because the animals are not caged."

For a moment, everyone was silent. An expression of horror crossed Tamsyn's face as she clearly regretted her humor. But then everyone began to laugh, and not only did her face brighten, but the little knot of anxiety wrapped around Kit's chest loosened. He didn't need to worry how well Tamsyn would fit in with his friends.

That would presume, however, that there would be interaction between them beyond tonight.

As Langdon chatted with Greyland and Lady Greyland, Tamsyn turned to Kit. "How did you know?"

"Know what?"

"That once Lady Daleford and your family left, things would get better?"

He said lightly, "I learned in the army that you can't build a decent campfire with too much kindling. The fire won't breathe if there's too much fuel. Take a little out and"—he waved his hands—"you have a cheerful blaze."

"A ship can't float with too much ballast," she agreed.

He motioned for a servant and flourished his arm. "We have our music, and now some liquid cheer."

The footman stepped forward with a decanter full of dark amber liquid.

"Ah, perfect," Kit exclaimed. "A glass for everyone in the company."

"Is this . . . brandy?" Tamsyn asked, peering into the goblet that was placed in her hand.

"So it is," he said with good humor. "All the way from Cognac. You needn't drink it if you don't care for spirits."

As the words left his mouth, she tilted the glass back and downed the contents in one swallow. Then she held out her goblet for more. The footman refilled it immediately.

Well. Every day with Kit's new bride would be a surprise.

A peculiar expression crossed her face, as if, in the most unlikely place, she recognized someone after they had been absent for a number of years.

"Where did this come from?" she asked the duke.

"It's perfectly legal," Greyland assured her. "I'd never serve Blakemere anything that wasn't strictly aboveboard."

"Why is that?" Tamsyn wondered.

"For all his wild reputation," Langdon drawled, "Blakemere doesn't look kindly on criminals."

"I didn't see good men die to protect their country," Kit said grimly, "only to have the rule of law in England sneered at. Felons and offenders deserve whatever punishment is meted out." His jaw hardened as he felt anger rise.

Color drained from Tamsyn's face.

"You seem distressed."

"Not a bit," she said at once, but the merriment in her eyes had faded.

"I'm about to stun myself by cautioning that we shouldn't overindulge tonight. Tomorrow afternoon, we go to the solicitor's office and finalize the transfer of Lord Somerby's fortune. You're the Countess of Blakemere now, but in less than twenty-four hours, neither of us will be poor as church mice." And he'd be so much closer to building the pleasure garden. So close to fulfilling his dream and finding peace.

Tamsyn's expression turned thoughtful. Kit tried to decipher her countenance—was she forming plans for his money, or did the thought of possessing *any* fortune bewilder her?

"To the bride and groom," Langdon said, lifting his glass. His look was practically devilish. "May the marriage be as fruitful as it is prosperous."

Greyland and his wife lifted their own glasses and said, "To the bride and groom."

Everyone merrily drank. Then Greyland pulled the duchess into his arms and waltzed her around the room, as Langdon tapped his foot and Tamsyn clapped her hands in time with the music.

Kit couldn't tear his gaze from her. Despite the stressors of the day, she glowed with a radiance he'd seldom seen before, and it drew him like a wolf edging closer and closer to a welcome fire.

She was his wife now, and whatever the future held, tonight belonged to them.

The clock chimed midnight.

Chapter 7

"Good night! Good night! Try not to make the morning newspapers!"

With these questionable words, Lord Langdon, Lord Greyland, and Lady Greyland waved Tamsyn and Lord Blakemere—*Kit*, she reminded herself—off as their carriage pulled away.

She'd married a man who hated lawbreakers. *Good God.*

Not only that, soon, she and Kit would spend their first night together. By morning, she'd no longer be a virgin.

Tamsyn tried to grasp the fact that she was now a married woman, with a wife's duty to her husband in the home, and in bed. Everything in her life had changed. She was no longer Tamsyn Pearce, but Tamsyn Ellingsworth, the Countess of Blakemere, and inside half a day, she would be wealthy—well, her *husband* would be wealthy, but she'd likely be given a substantial allowance.

She had plans for that money and knew precisely what to do with it. But when it came to the mysteries of the nuptial bed, she had little experience. Men wanted to marry virgins but they preferred a courtesan in the bedchamber—or so she'd been told. Almost everything she knew about sex was relayed to her by the women of Newcombe. Fortunately, the village women were outspoken and opinionated.

Through her lowered lashes, she studied Kit. They had never been truly alone until this moment. He wasn't an especially big man, but he was strapping and hale and irrefutably masculine. Nothing buffered the small space between them, and each breath felt shallow due to his nearness.

He filled the silence and darkness of the carriage with easy conversation.

"Greyland's cook turned out a repast that would put Prinny's banquets to shame," he said idly. "I think my brother Franklin ate a dozen seed cakes. He never had to be coaxed into cleaning his plate. I wouldn't have been surprised if his wife filled her reticule with sugared fruit. Pamela is parsimonious to the point of agony. You wouldn't believe she stood to become a viscountess upon the passing of my father. Given the long lives enjoyed by Ellingsworth men, I can see the point of her concern."

"They must have been proud of you today," she replied.

He wryly quirked his lips. "Relieved of their responsibility, more like. I'm not certain if *pride* is quite the feeling they've ever had where I was concerned." He sounded fatalistic about being dismissed by his kin, as though he never expected otherwise.

There was no affection between Tamsyn and her aunt and uncle, yet when her parents had been alive, she had been treasured and loved. She clung to memories of their care, using it to sustain herself in darker moments.

But to never have had that—as Kit seemed to—seemed lonely and cold.

"Surely they felt pride when you were given an earldom for your service," she objected.

"They thought my role in the army was merely decorative," he answered. "No one in my family has any idea what war is like." The brightness around him dimmed as memories seemed to swarm behind his eyes.

"Did you fight in many battles?" There had been men in Newcombe who'd gone off to fight. Either they hadn't returned, or many of them bore terrible injuries. Few had been willing to talk about what they'd seen. Katie Davis told Tamsyn that her husband came back without any visible scars, but he couldn't sleep in a dark room, and often woke Katie with his nightmare-induced screams.

He shrugged. "A few."

"You were decorated," she recalled.

He waved that aside like an invisible insect. "They dole out medals with a liberal hand."

His modesty intrigued her. Most men would savor the opportunity to extol their own virtues.

"You cannot say the same about your earldom," she noted. "Not many received the same honor. Clearly, your heroics deserved approbation."

He glanced away. "Lord Somerby was a good man. It was only because of his efforts that I was given the title."

His unwillingness to discuss his commendations tugged at her. Was he being modest? Were his recollections too horrific to speak of? Would he ever entrust her with his memories?

She reminded herself that she couldn't afford to have her and Kit reach that point of trust and intimacy. The more they were apart, physically and emotionally, the easier it would be for her to keep her secrets safe.

However, she wondered, perhaps Kit slept with a light burning, too. Maybe *his* dreams pulled him back to bloodstained battlefields. Yet she would never know, because she would never let them grow that close.

"It's our wedding night," he said, clapping his hands together, "and I won't bore you with tales of the War. Let's talk of something more pleasant. You wanted to see more of London's amusements, and now you shall, loosened from the yoke of Lady Daleford's aversion to frivolity. Let's start right away with Vauxhall. Sadly, Ranelagh closed years ago, but it was said to rival Vauxhall for spectacle."

"We had traveling fairs come through Newcombe," she said with a smile. "There were games where we could win ribbons or toys, jugglers and acrobats, and pig races."

"Ah, you see! You know the joy that can only be felt at such places. Though," he added drily, "I've not yet experienced the bliss that is pig racing." He reached across the narrow space of the carriage and took her ungloved hand in his. Eyes bright with humor, he added, "Perhaps someday we can share in that delight together."

She tried to share in his droll humor, but the feel of his touch made her breath scarce and head light. With just a brush of skin against skin, her senses flew into disarray.

Having heard the blunt and earthy talk of the village women, Tamsyn understood that the first time would likely be uncomfortable or even painful. But then it got better—provided a husband was attentive enough.

The way some women back home talked, having sex was the greatest pleasure they'd ever experienced.

It would soon be hers. *He* would be hers.

But what if she liked sex with Kit so much she wanted him all the time? Even more alarming, how would she stand it when he left her bed to find satisfaction with another woman?

"Perhaps," she said, trying to keep her voice sounding as light and easy as his.

He let go of her hand, yet his heat continued to linger in her flesh. "Tomorrow morning," he said, "we'll tour our new home. It's temporary until we can find a permanent residence in London. The Blakemere estate in Northumberland is rather in need of attention, but you'll have free rein to renovate and improve it."

She wasn't certain how to broach this important topic. Best to just say what she thought and get it over with. "Cornwall is where I'd like to spend most of my time," she ventured. "At my family home."

The interior of the carriage was dim, so she couldn't quite make out the look on his face, but his words showed his surprise. "You won't stay in London?"

"I'm a country girl," she said, spreading her hands. "For all its pleasures, I don't know if I will ever be comfortable in this city."

He fell into a stunned silence.

Oh, blast. They hadn't worked out the details of where each of them would live, and now they had to tackle the logistics of how to make their marriage work. She could evade customs men while timing the tide on a moonless night, but the particulars of being married eluded her.

Finally, he said, "How about this—once you're pregnant, you can live in Cornwall as long as you like."

That would mean being away from Newcombe for what could be a long while. Could they manage without her? When she bought the house, she'd place Nessa in charge. At least until Tamsyn got with child.

"Ah, here we are," Kit said eagerly, peering out the window as the carriage rolled to a stop.

The streets were utterly silent at this late hour. A chill mist obscured the sky and clung to the pavement.

A liveried footman opened the vehicle's door and helped Tamsyn alight. Kit followed, and together they crossed the threshold of a large and elegant building.

She had a brief impression of rich fabrics and stylish furnishings in the empty lobby before a neatly dressed balding man rushed forward to meet them.

"Ah, Lord Blakemere and his new bride!" The man bowed. "I am Chapman, the night manager of our fine establishment. Welcome, my lord and lady, and felicitations. We have everything on hand to ensure you have a most pleasant night."

"Much appreciated," Kit answered politely, yet she could sense waves of impatience emanating from him as his gaze moved restively around the hotel entrance.

"You have a lovely establishment," Tamsyn added.

The night manager beamed. "If you'll follow me, I will show you to your rooms." He waved them toward the stairs adorned with gilded railings and covered with plush deep red carpeting.

She tried to take in the details of the hotel. She'd never stayed in anything finer than an ordinary coaching inn, so to spend the night at one of London's best hotels was a privilege she didn't want to waste. The crystal lamps sparkled and the thick floor covering dampened the sound of her footsteps.

Kit didn't appear to notice or care. He kept looking at her as though she was a sweetmeat he wanted to devour.

Her stomach fluttered in response.

After climbing two more sets of stairs, they at last arrived. Mr. Chapman unlocked the door and said, "We have smaller chambers nearby for your valet and maidservant. And, of course, our staff is available at all hours to accommodate your every need."

Kit nodded distractedly, his mind clearly on something else.

Mr. Chapman opened the door and waved them inside. Kit waited as Tamsyn slowly entered, then he and the night manager followed her into the room.

It was a spacious chamber, the walls covered in floral wallpaper that surely came from France, and a row of curtained windows. A fire burned merrily in the grate, and candles had been lit in anticipation of Tamsyn and Kit's arrival. Other furniture occupied the room, but all she saw was the substantial four-poster bed. It towered as large and looming as the Colossus of Rhodes.

Once you climb in me, it promised, *there's no going back.*

"Is there anything you require?" Mr. Chapman was all solicitousness. "I can have refreshments brought up."

"We have everything we need." Kit hastily handed him a guinea.

"My gratitude, sir," the night manager said with a bow. "I'll just see myself out."

Tamsyn's heartbeat was thick in her throat when the door closed, leaving her alone with her new husband. She tore her gaze away from the bed to find him watching her with a careful, curious expression, as though she were a doe who had wandered into a ballroom.

"My valet and your maid should be here by now," he said neutrally. "Shall I send her to you?"

To help her undress.

"Yes, please." She tried to discreetly wipe her damp palms on her skirts. *Damn these nerves!* She had no reason to be afraid. Pain was merely pain—it came and it went. She could manage that kind of hurt.

A wound to her heart, however, was more difficult to heal.

After giving her a warm, encouraging smile, Kit left quietly.

She walked to the fire and watched the dancing flames, as if their shifting light could somehow ease her mind and calm her body.

A soft tap sounded on the door, and Nessa let herself into the room. Seeing her cheerful, familiar face in this decidedly unfamiliar place was a balm, and Tamsyn walked quickly over to lay her head on Nessa's shoulder.

"Ah, child," Nessa said, patting her back. "Here I am. Naught to worry about."

"I'm not worried," Tamsyn replied automatically.

"'Course you aren't," Nessa said in a soothing voice. "You're a brave lass. Come on, then," Nessa said, stepping back. "Can't have you climbing into bed wearing all your clothes."

Tamsyn nodded. With brisk, businesslike movements, Nessa began divesting her of her gown.

"He's a handsome one, so it won't be a chore," Nessa noted in a matter-of-fact tone.

"He pleases my eye," Tamsyn agreed. "That much is certain."

Nessa's fingers stilled on the fastenings running down the back of Tamsyn's dress. "How much do you know?" she asked. "About what goes on between a man and a woman?"

"I understand the process." Tamsyn couldn't stop the heat that washed through her. "What goes into what and so forth."

"That's good." Nessa's fingers, well trained in the fixing of fishing nets, made short work of the gown's fastenings. Once the silver dress had been removed, Nessa put it in the clothespress. "I was afraid I'd have to draw you pictures, and I've no skill with a pencil."

"It's one thing to understand how bodies fit together," Tamsyn admitted. Blast, but she hated this nervousness. It wasn't like her at all. "Another thing entirely to know what sex is truly *like*. What if I do something wrong? It's supposed to hurt the first time." It seemed like it had to, given what she'd seen of male parts. Like other girls of Newcombe, she'd spied on boys bathing in the sea—but Cornish waters were chilly, and, one girl said with confidence, *that part* shrank in the cold. It got bigger and harder when properly motivated.

"There's some pain," Nessa said plainly. She worked at Tamsyn's stays. "Can't be helped. But it's not a forever pain. Remember when you fell off John Pricher's wall and twisted your ankle?" When Tamsyn nodded, Nessa said, "That was far worse."

"Ah," Tamsyn said, struggling to quiet her anxiety.

Nessa patted Tamsyn's cheek. "Oh, child, it's not all pain. Tell me a time when something felt good."

"There used to be a swing set my father put up in the big apple tree in the West Meadow," Tamsyn recalled. "When I was small, I'd swing and swing, trying to get as high as I could. As though I could float away right up into the sky. I liked that an awful lot."

"It's better than that," Nessa said decisively. She sighed wistfully. "I miss it, I do."

Nessa had been married for a decade before her husband had drowned a few years back. But given the way village men circled around her after mass on Sundays, she didn't have to be unmarried for long.

Perhaps it did feel good. Babes were born to unwed women all the time.

With her stays removed, she stood in her underthings and shoes. She kicked off her dainty slippers and helped Nessa pull off her shift.

"Ah, but you're in an enviable place tonight, my girl. No need for fear." Nessa clicked her tongue. "That husband of yours, he's no stranger to bedsport."

More heat suffused Tamsyn's body. Men had the luxury of indulging their sexual appetites whenever they liked, without consequence. It wasn't the same for women. Kit was relatively young, exceedingly handsome, and privileged. It stood to reason that he'd had his share of sexual experience. Even so, thinking about him bedding legions of women made her stomach feel strange and tight.

He'd said plainly that he had no intention of being faithful—and that he didn't expect fidelity from her. Would she come to regret this agreement?

"Yes," she said, fighting to sound sophisticated. "I know."

"He'll be an artist under the covers," Nessa assured her. "Think he'd be so popular with ladies if he just stuck it in and spent without a by-your-leave? Not hardly."

"I suppose not," Tamsyn said. That wasn't the most encouraging description of sex she had heard. She glanced at the bed, but it only seemed to have grown larger and more intimidating in the intervening minutes since she'd last looked at it. "A woman can lie with a man and keep her heart safe, I imagine."

Nessa planted her hands on her hips and asked sternly, "What's this talk, girl?"

Tamsyn considered prevaricating, but she could never withhold the truth from her friend. She said flatly, "He told me he won't be faithful."

"The devil he did!" Nessa looked outraged.

"In the park that day he offered marriage," Tamsyn confirmed. "He said he wasn't going to keep his vows of fidelity. But I was free to take a lover if I wanted—after I gave him an heir."

Nessa's cheeks darkened with fury and she balled her hands into fists. "I'll give him a pummeling, I will. Earl or no, he can't say things like that."

"It's not uncommon, though." Tamsyn felt strangely obliged to defend him. "People of rank and fashion often have lovers."

"They don't say so when they're courting!" Nessa fired back.

Tamsyn sat down on the edge of the bed. "Better this way," she reasoned, trying to convince herself as much as Nessa. "If he paid me too much mind, he'd get suspicious about what we do in Newcombe." She affected a shrug. "It doesn't trouble me. I may grow fond of him, but I'll never *love* him."

Nessa walked to her and placed her hands on her

shoulders. Her expression mingled sadness and resignation. "I know you, my girl. You can't do anything by half measures."

"What would you have me do?" Baffled, Tamsyn lifted her hands in supplication. "I can't refuse him his husbandly privileges."

"Just have a care with your heart," Nessa answered, and pressed a kiss to her forehead. "Now, stand up so we can make you ready."

Tamsyn rose and remained still while Nessa took down her hair, removing pins and ornaments. At last, her hair came down to hang in loose waves around her shoulders. Fear and excitement warred within her. She couldn't tell if she craved being intimate with Kit, or if it filled her with dread.

Nessa cupped Tamsyn's chin in her hand. "Remember this, my dove. If he wants to kiss you *down there*, by God, you let him."

"Oh," Tamsyn said faintly. She didn't know people kissed each other's parts.

A soft rap sounded at the door. "It's Kit," his muffled voice announced.

Instead of answering, Nessa handed Tamsyn an embroidered robe—presumably purchased with Kit's money—before giving Tamsyn's cheek a pat. Then she hurried out the door. Tamsyn quickly pulled on the robe, then sat on the edge of the bed, her hands tapping against the tops of her thighs.

"Come in," she called, her voice oddly loud.

Kit entered, looking just as delicious as he had all evening. With his neckcloth gone, she could see a glimpse of his throat. He carried a decanter of wine and two glasses. "I thought we could—" He stopped, a puzzled frown on his face. "Wouldn't you be more comfortable *in* bed?"

"There's no hurry, is there?" she answered brightly.

Kit raised a brow but didn't speak. Instead, he poured two glasses of wine, then sat beside her. The mattress dipped with his weight, and warmth radiated from his body. "Go slow with this." He handed her a glass. "To make you comfortable, nothing more. No one enjoys making love with a drunken partner."

Trying to follow his advice, she took a few sips of wine, rather than downing the whole thing in one gulp. "Damn these nerves," she muttered ruefully.

He watched her before drinking from his wine. "You've been so brave about everything."

She pushed out a laugh. "Not so courageous tonight." After taking another sip, she spoke, her words edged in frustration. "I *want* to be a wife to you. Please understand that." His frame radiated warmth, and she wanted to sink into it, and the strength he offered. While her body craved his touch, her mind and heart held back warily. "It's all been so fast. We don't know each other at all, and now we're supposed to be . . . intimate."

"People do this knowing each other far less," Kit noted. At least he didn't sound angry or impatient. "Do you understand how sex works?"

After a moment, she nodded.

He let out a small exhalation, sounding relieved. "I'll tell you something and you must promise me you won't jeer or call me silly."

She wasn't certain he was serious, but at his prompting gaze, she answered, "I promise."

He leaned close, his lips hovering by her ear. His warmth and scent enveloped her, and she fought for breath.

"I'm nervous, too," he whispered.

Her eyes went wide. "You?"

He edged back, giving her some much-needed space. A small smile curved his mouth. "Why not me?"

"But you've done this loads of times," she protested.

"With ladies of experience," he answered. "With a virgin? No."

"Surely your first time . . . ?"

A slightly faraway look came into his eyes. "I was fifteen and she was a worldly seventeen. She wanted a conquest. I was happy to provide one."

"So . . . we're both in the dark here," she ventured wryly.

"To an extent," he allowed. He took a sip of wine, and then set it down on a bedside table. He had to reach across her to do so, and his arm brushed against her breasts. She started. Kit held himself still, then chuckled softly. "Unintentional, that, but I don't regret it."

It hadn't felt bad, just different. She'd touched her own breasts before and knew they could give her pleasure. Clearly, men liked them, too, because they were often the sought-after prize the few times she'd kissed lads. But they had pawed at her like trying to catch fish with their bare hands. Not exactly delightful.

"Let's start slowly," he offered, plucking her glass from her hand and putting it beside his own.

She struggled for calm. "How?"

"With a kiss," he answered.

Chapter 8

*K*it slowly moved his hand to cup the back of Tamsyn's head. Her pupils were huge, her breath shallow, and her body tense as an iron beam. He'd never kissed a skittish woman before, and now here he was on his *wedding night,* trying to guide a virgin into bed.

Damn and hell, he wanted her. The ferocity of his desire was shocking. She was both bold and innocent, and the combination inflamed him. He could look for hours at the juncture where her neck met her shoulder, while he ached to learn the feel of her and taste her again.

In every way, this was far beyond his usual experiences with women. Yet none of them mattered at this moment.

There was desire and something more. Though he didn't know Tamsyn very well, what he'd learned of her he genuinely liked. Hurting her, or making her do anything she didn't want to do, never entered his mind. He truly wanted to make this good for her. Perhaps that desire was selfish. Having a wife who was unenthusiastic about lovemaking made everyone's life difficult and disagreeable. But if he could teach her that sex was, in fact, one of the greatest pleasures that existed—everyone benefitted.

"Easy," he murmured, gentling her as her breathing accelerated. "It's nothing but a kiss."

"We've kissed before," she whispered.

"Did you like it?"

She nodded.

"Now shouldn't be any different," he said.

"It shouldn't," she agreed. She glanced at him with trepidation. "But . . ."

"It does feel different," he deduced.

Another nod.

"Don't think about where it leads," he said gently. "All that matters is this moment."

Slowly, he lowered his head and brushed his lips over hers. Ah, she was soft and lush. Her skin smelled of warm flowers.

He softly stroked the curve where her head met her neck. Her abundant silky hair spread over his palm, and at his touch, she drew in a breath. As though gaining strength.

He pressed his lips more firmly to hers. At first, she held herself still, but then she stirred, kissing him back with growing confidence. Taking a chance, he parted his lips slightly and stroked her with the tip of his tongue. She tasted faintly of wine and a hint of sugar. Tentatively, her tongue touched his.

God knew he'd had far more deliberately carnal kisses than this. Yet his blood roared in his ears and his groin tightened in reaction. This was new for her. She was discovering herself, and that made her response all the more potent.

"There," he purred. "That's my girl. Give me a little— just a little."

He took the kiss deeper, his tongue now caressing hers, their mouths opening. She made a soft, low sound of pleasure. The honesty of her response inflamed him far more than any practiced kiss. She was finding her path, learning the ways of her desires. It was a humbling, wonderful sensation to be the man lucky enough to partner her in this exploration.

He brought his hand up to rest at the curve of her waist where her warmth seeped into him. As he caressed her, she exhaled again and made more noises of pleasure.

She angled her body toward his. It was a silent demand for more.

Yes, he thought. *Yes.*

With a leisurely pace, he eased his hand up and up over her rib cage. Then higher, until he cupped the full, velvet weight of her breast.

She pulled away abruptly. Her eyes had gone wide, and she wore the expression of one who'd misjudged the distance to jump from one side of a chasm to the other.

Kit struggled for breath, shocked by his own reaction to hardly any touching at all. The artlessness of the desire she'd shown—its complete candor—shook him. He was hard as a pike, his body primed for more.

"I'm not very good at this," she said, her words tight with frustration.

"You're doing very well." He, however, felt like a boy barely out of the schoolroom, ready to spend in his breeches without even being touched.

"I didn't think I would be this nervous," she confessed.

"Perfectly logical, given the circumstances." He offered her a smile, which she tentatively returned. There had to be another way to reach her and break through her fear. "Tamsyn."

"Yes?"

"Have you ever touched yourself?" When she didn't answer, he said, "Not like taking hold of your own wrist or scratching your nose. I mean *touched yourself.*"

Her redhead's complexion hid nothing as she blushed furiously. But she held his gaze. "No one's ever asked me that before."

He reached out, taking her hand between his two palms, and said with humor, "I can tell you that I most assuredly have given myself pleasure. Many, many times."

Her eyes widened. "Really?"

"Especially when I was fighting," he admitted. "We'd go weeks without meeting any women, and, as I'm not inclined toward the amorous company of men, I needed to do something or else I'd tear off my uniform and throw myself into a freezing river."

"That's understandable." Her lips curved slightly.

"It's a natural thing, to touch yourself. Everyone does it."

She looked dubious. "Everyone?"

"Those who claim they don't are likely either lying or very unhappy people."

A laugh escaped her, then she grew more serious. "It's said to be sinful."

He shook his head. "The only thing that's sinful about it is when we deny ourselves. I like to think that our Creator wanted us to feel good, or else why would he give us such delightful toys to play with?"

"A persuasive argument," she said wryly. After a moment, she said, "I do. In the bath, sometimes. Or when I'm in bed."

And there went his cock again, rising up with interest. He tried not to picture the pretty Tamsyn slipping her hand between her thighs and fingering her sweet pussy until she came with a soft cry. The image alone would keep him hard for days.

He cleared his dry throat. "You know that exquisite feeling you get when everything breaks apart? That rising pleasure that builds and builds until it explodes?"

A pause. And then, "Yes."

"I can make you feel that," he said earnestly, "over and over again. It might even be better than when you're alone."

She lifted a brow. "Is that because you've done . . . *it* a lot?"

How to approach this? "I'm not a stranger to what happens in bed," he allowed. "Think of my experience as leading up to this moment, ensuring you'll feel good."

She was silent for a long while. He made sure to wait, giving her the time she needed. Then she lifted her chin. "I'd like to try again." She closed her eyes and held her head in such a way that indicated, *You may kiss me now.*

Go slow, he reminded himself. *Take your bloody time.*

He stroked his hand up the column of her neck, feeling the hard beat of her pulse, and let his palm rest at the juncture between her throat and her jaw. She was so delicate here, but he reminded himself that, knowing what he did of her, she possessed considerable strength.

He leaned closer, until their lips met. He kissed her lightly, little sips of kisses, until she returned them, and then he went further. His lips made silent promises. *This will be so good for us, I swear it.*

He'd never made such promises before or felt this surge of protectiveness holding him to his vow.

She seemed to understand the unspoken pledge, and when his tongue slipped into her mouth, she sucked on it lightly. Most likely, she didn't know what she mimicked, but it was enough to send his already-hot blood to a boil. He cupped her breast and thumbed the nipple to a firm point.

She moaned. Yet the sound seemed to startle her. Frowning, she edged away from his touch.

"You don't like it?" he asked, genuinely puzzled.

"I do," she answered. "But . . ." Her brow knotted. She shook her head.

Kit wanted to growl in frustration. Yet he felt her uncertainty and something in his chest softened.

"It's all right." His voice sounded an octave deeper, and raspy. "We're virtually strangers." He dragged a hand through his hair, barely believing what he was about to say. "Let's wait. Give things between us time."

She looked so relieved, and he wanted to groan. "I'd like that."

What an enigma she was—her strength and her vulnerability coexisting side by side.

"Time to get some sleep," he announced. Feeling reasonably certain he wouldn't send her into a panic by the state of his cock, he stood. "We've a full day tomorrow." He strode toward the small dressing room that adjoined the bedchamber.

He stripped off his clothing, and, for the first time in years, slipped on a sleep shirt. Normally, he slept in the nude, but that was *absolutely* not happening tonight. Or any night for the near future. Ah, God help him.

As he readied for bed, he heard her slip between the covers and struggled not to picture her satiny limbs or the soft outline of her breasts or the shadowy vale between her legs. Was her hair down there red, too? His cock enjoyed his speculation and sprang back to attention.

For half a moment, he considered doing precisely what he'd advocated for earlier. It would help dull the edge of his desire.

No, he'd just have to think of battle formations and frigid water, which he did until his erection subsided. After pulling on a robe, he exited the dressing room.

She waited for him in bed, the covers pulled up to her chin. Her gaze was a palpable thing, skimming over his body as he doused the candles around the bedchamber. When the room was submerged in near darkness, he dropped his robe, and then climbed into bed.

She lay on her back, staring up at the canopy. A narrow span of bed stretched between them. It was a sizable bed, but as he shifted slightly, his arm and leg brushed hers. She didn't pull away, yet she didn't draw closer, either.

It was novel to share a bed with a woman without making love to her. This was a night of firsts.

Kit struggled to tamp down his need that simmered and pushed beneath his skin. Nearly a month of celibacy had been difficult—now it would be prolonged indefinitely.

He recited what he could remember of Vegetius's *De Re Militari*, but that part of his education had been a long time ago, and he kept returning to the touches of her body against his.

"I thought two in a bed would feel crowded," she said into the darkness, "but I like it."

"How fortunate humans aren't covered in quills like porcupines."

"Or scales like armadillos," she added. She yawned. "Thank you, Kit."

"Of course," he answered.

Within moments, her body went lax as she slept. But then she murmured quietly and rolled toward him, her breasts snug against his arm while she rested a hand on his chest—covering his thudding heart. Her touch went straight through his body.

He gritted his teeth as though having a limb amputated. Rather than gather her close, as he longed to do, he kept his arms at his sides.

I'm not a praying man, but for the love of all that's holy, grant me patience.

She trusted him, and he had earned that trust. Of all the awards and commendations he'd received, this one felt the most important, and the most fragile.

I⊤ wasn't unusual for Kit to wake up alone. He seldom brought women home, preferring to have his trysts in their rooms. This enabled him to leave when he pleased and not have to face any awkwardness in the morning, when both he and his lover made strained conversation over breakfast, their use for each other gone.

This morning, he stretched in bed and encountered nothing. A moment later he realized that he wasn't supposed to be alone.

Tamsyn wasn't there.

He sat up quickly, the covers pooling at his waist. There was no sign of her in the room. It was as if he'd invented a bride and dreamed the whole of last night—their kisses, her uncertainty, and his offer for them to postpone the consummation until she felt more at ease.

"Tamsyn?" he called. She could be in the dressing chamber or perhaps seeing to her personal needs. But a moment went by, and there was no answer.

Hurriedly, he climbed out of bed and checked the dressing room. She wasn't there. Her bridal gown was folded in the clothespress, but she likely brought a change of clothes. Where *was* she?

An irrational thought leapt into his mind. What if she had decided she wanted no part of this marriage, didn't want anything to do with him, and had fled in the night?

Kit summoned his valet, then, when Anderson appeared, he hastily washed and dressed. As he shrugged into his jacket, Kit told himself that his thoughts were ridiculous, his fears unfounded. Or so he hoped.

On his way out the door, he caught a glimpse of himself in the pier glass. Nothing out of the ordinary stared back at him, but he certainly didn't wear the contented look of a man who'd made love to a willing woman all night.

He nodded politely as he passed other guests in the hallway, quashing the impulse to grab them and demand if they had seen a pretty redhead in flight.

As he strode through the lobby on the ground floor, a man in tidy dark clothes approached him. "My lord, I am Ives, the day manager. I hope you had a pleasant night."

Kit resisted telling Mr. Ives that his night had been confusing and oddly humbling. Instead, he attempted a smile. "I did, thank you."

"Lady Blakemere is in the dining room," Mr. Ives said, gesturing to a room off the library.

"Ah, she said she'd have an early breakfast," Kit answered. There was no benefit in telling the day manager that Kit had no earthly idea where his new wife had hared off to.

"If you care to join her, I'll have some tea brought out to you straightaway."

Kit nodded his thanks, then headed for the dining room. Tables were arranged throughout, while the occupants of the sunny chamber consisted primarily of couples and families with a handful of lone men dotted here and there. Few paid him any mind as he came in—including the redhead at a table for two, staring out a bow window at the far end of the room.

The pressure in his chest released as he approached. She was here. She hadn't run away to a distant corner of England.

Sunlight outlined her clean profile, highlighting her strong features and making her glow. Her throat was a long, elegant line. An urge to run his lips along her neck and taste her flesh gripped him.

It was a positive that he was attracted to his wife. Better that than the alternative. Yet it only compounded his sexual frustration. But he'd have to endure more abstinence, at least until Tamsyn was ready. He'd be damned if he forced her to do something she didn't want to do.

The floor was thickly carpeted, his boots making no sound as he approached. But she caught his reflection in the window and turned with a smile at his approach.

He bowed. A kiss on the cheek wasn't seemly in public, and he didn't want to risk her pulling away from him.

"I woke and you were gone," he said without rebuke as he sat opposite her.

"I've been in London a fortnight and I cannot get used to town hours," she admitted. "It's an early day for us in the country. And early to bed." At the word *bed*, color crept into her face, and she covered her cheeks with a look of consternation.

He shook out his napkin and thanked the server who brought him a pot of tea. "The fashionable rise from bed before ten only if the house is on fire. Even then, if the fire isn't in their bedchamber, it can be ignored."

"I'll attempt to remember that," she said with a nod, "should a conflagration engulf our home."

Another server brought Kit a plate of eggs, streaky bacon, and toasted bread. After taking a few bites, he said, "Which reminds me, you recall that I've taken a temporary home for us." When she nodded, he continued, "I've leased it for six months, but the lease can be extended if we don't find anything that suits us on a more permanent basis."

"I do love my home in Cornwall." She smoothed her hand over the tablecloth. "Yet after staying at Lady Daleford's home, I've grown used to roofs that aren't full of rot and floors that don't buckle under each step."

Kit frowned. He hadn't realized that she lived in such terrible conditions. No wonder she'd been ready to marry him with barely any courtship.

Yet her confession seemed to catch her off guard, and she pressed her lips together in consternation. As if she didn't want him to know of her dismal circumstances.

"That's a pity," he said lightly. "The house I rented is built of soggy pasteboard. It'll blow over with the next stiff breeze."

His teasing had the desired effect as her concern faded. "You were thinking of my needs, and for that I thank you."

The corners of her eyes crinkled, and he was relieved she shared some of his rather whimsical humor.

He continued, "At five this afternoon, we're expected at the chambers of Lord Somerby's solicitor to finalize the transfer of the fortune. Mr. Flowers specifically mentioned that I was to bring my new wife with me. Most likely, that's to ensure I'm actually married."

Without the marriage being consummated, it might still be annulled, but Kit didn't want to mention that.

Yet it seemed that Tamsyn's thoughts strayed in that direction, as well. She looked away for a moment, then met his gaze.

"Thank you," she said softly. "For what you did last night."

It took courage for her to confront something so potentially embarrassing, and he nodded in acknowledgment.

"Most men would demand their due," she noted candidly.

"I'm not most men," he pointed out.

A corner of her mouth tilted up. "So I am learning."

As he looked into her eyes, a pang of confused longing reverberated through him. They'd entered into this marriage with their eyes open, knowing it was merely a means to an end. Yet he'd been drawn to her from the first when every other woman had been mysteriously lacking. There was desire for her, but there was a stronger pull beyond the needs of his body.

He wanted her to come to him willingly. For that, he'd wait as long as necessary.

Even if it killed him.

Chapter 9

$\mathcal{A}$ rare anxiety gnawed on Kit as he and Tamsyn looked at the facade of their new home. The town house on Bruton Street had pleased him the first time he'd seen it. Standing three stories tall—plus an attic where the servants slept—it had an elegant, modern appearance with a columned portico and rows of windows to let in plenty of sunlight. He'd toured it briefly two days earlier, but now found himself a little nervous as he awaited Tamsyn's opinion.

"We can't make too many changes," he explained, "but I thought it would suit us. For a few months, anyway." When she gave no reply, he held out his arm. "Shall we go inside?"

In response, she placed her hand on his sleeve. One of the staff that came with the house already had the door open, so Kit and Tamsyn strode inside.

They walked through the town home together, drifting from one room to the next, with Kit leading the tour. As he described the features of each chamber, he kept a close eye on her expression, trying to discern her thoughts.

"The drawing room has a good view of the street," he pointed out, walking to the windows. "Lots of afternoon sun for callers."

She said nothing as she turned in a small circle in the middle of the chamber. Her gaze touched here and there—on the aforementioned windows, at the plaster detailing on the ceiling, on the blue moiré sofa. Yet she kept quiet.

What was she thinking?

"I rented the furniture, too," Kit went on. He walked to the sofa and ran his hand over the back upholstery. "It came with the place, but if you want something else, anything can be arranged."

She nodded.

"Over here," he said brightly, striding toward another chamber, "is the dining room. The table can seat sixteen comfortably." He sounded like a sodding estate agent showing off properties to a client.

Tamsyn peered inside the dining room. The furnishings were more masculine here, with a long mahogany table in the middle and sixteen matching chairs arranged around it. Metal candle sconces on the walls would cast a pleasant light during dinner parties, especially gleaming off silver serving dishes and crystal goblets.

Again, she nodded, but didn't speak.

She was silent, too, as they viewed the parlor on the ground floor and the large music room up a flight of stairs.

With each new, stylish room, he waited for her response. A smile, a frown. But her expression remained carefully neutral.

As they both looked at the sizable chandelier in the music room, he finally burst out, "For God's sake, say *something*." At her puzzled expression, he continued, "Do you love it? Hate it? I can't sodding tell."

"Does my opinion matter?" she asked with a puzzled frown.

"You're going to live here," he said, "and I want you to be happy, so of course it matters."

A warm smile wreathed her face. "It's wonderful, Kit. All of it. I couldn't be more pleased."

Relief and exasperation warred within him. "Why didn't you say so?"

"I thought if I looked too eager, you'd think I married you for your money." She wrinkled her nose.

His laugh was unexpected. "Oh, my dear," he said between chuckles, "*of course* you married me for my money. Or at least," he added, "for the money I *will* have."

She looked as though she wanted to say something, but then she pressed her lips together and shook her head. Yet the dispassionate expression she'd worn had given way to something more open, almost happy.

He *did* want to make her happy. Why wouldn't he? She was his wife, and though they'd entered into a marriage of convenience, he wasn't a brute. Her contentment was his responsibility.

She hadn't said much about what her life had been like since the death of her parents. Thinking back to the way she'd described the condition of her home, her uncle had most likely neglected her as much as he did the ancestral house.

God only knew what else she'd endured. She deserved pleasure and ease in her existence. If he could give that to her, maybe he wasn't such a selfish bastard after all.

"Shall we see the rest of the house?" he offered.

She gave him a wide smile that shot through him like a bullet. "Yes, please."

They moved on to a bedchamber, furnished in hues of cream and peach. It faced the garden in the back of the house. "The lady of the house's rooms," he announced, then nodded toward a door set into the wall panels. "That leads to the master's bedchamber. Convenient, no? Saves on chilly feet during treks in the night."

She frowned. "We're to have separate bedrooms?"

"Naturally." Her bafflement was a puzzle.

"It's only . . . my parents shared a room."

"What of your aunt and uncle?" he asked.

"There's only a handful of usable rooms at Chei Owr," she said, spreading her hands. "They have one bedchamber, as well."

Kit cleared his throat. "I can't speak for everyone in London, but it's common practice amongst the *ton* that husbands and wives sleep apart. Too much affection is seen as rather gauche."

"Of course," she said at once. "City manners, and all that."

"However," he continued, "what is fashion but a set of arbitrary rules made by people we shouldn't care about? If you want to share a room, that can certainly be arranged."

"But," she said persuasively, "I don't want anyone to think less of you because you married some country vulgarian. If it's the custom for a husband and wife to have separate beds, let's follow that tradition."

"As you like." He'd planned on them not sharing a bedchamber, so why was he disappointed? "Would you like to see the rooms on the next floor?" The nursery was located there, but given the tenuous state of their current sexual situation, he opted not to point that out.

Before she could answer, her maid appeared. The woman bobbed a curtsy. "Forgive me, my lord, but I need to speak with the missus."

"It's likely some household business," Tamsyn said hastily.

"No need for explanations," Kit said with a wave of his hand. "The law may declare you my property, but as far as I'm concerned, the only person who owns you is you."

Tamsyn smiled, then slipped out into the corridor with

her maid. Their mingled whispers faded as they walked away down the corridor.

Kit gave the lady's bedchamber one last look—hopefully, he'd be journeying here regularly—before moving on to the room that he'd occupy. He'd seen it before, though that had been more of a cursory examination. Now he walked to the windows that also looked out onto the garden and stared at the view that would be his for the foreseeable future. It was a dapper little garden, with neatly trimmed hedges and an oyster shell path, a fine place to take a cheroot on warm evenings.

How positively domestic.

Kit tapped his fingers on the glass, mulling over the way his life was unfolding. A bachelor one day, a married man the next.

He usually dined at a chophouse before seeking out the enjoyments of the night. Theaters, gaming hells, private rooms abundant with women.

He'd return to that soon enough.

In the meantime, they'd find a way to live comfortably together as husband and wife, learning each other, discovering how to make a marriage work.

There would come a time when Tamsyn would welcome him in her bed. The getting of an heir would be an agreeable thing—for all of her trepidation, he felt her desire for him. At the proper moment, he would show her the many pleasures of the flesh. And then it would be good. Extremely good.

A fizzy feeling bubbled up in his chest, as though he'd had too much sparkling wine. It took him several moments to realize it was a sense of expectation. It had been too long since he'd felt that.

This was a new beginning.

Today, at five o'clock, he would go see Mr. Flowers

and then—and then he could begin working on the dream he'd held close to his heart for many years. The pleasure garden was a hope he shared with no one but his own thoughts. It would be his, at last.

Finally, he could be free of the War's lingering darkness.

"WHAT's going on?" Tamsyn whispered.

Concerned, she followed Nessa down the hallway and into a small alcove.

After checking to make certain no one was within listening distance, Nessa spoke quietly but quickly. "I didn't want to tell you yesterday because it was your wedding day and such."

Tamsyn put her hands on her friend's shoulders. "Tell me what is happening."

"Got a letter." Nessa pulled a piece of paper from her pocket. "There's a problem." She handed the missive to Tamsyn, who read it with a sinking heart.

There was, indeed, a problem. Due to her uncle's decision to sell Chei Owr at some point in the near future, the villagers had gotten panicky. They had elected Fred Wren, one of the village men, to bring the latest shipment of smuggled goods closer to London in advance of Tamsyn finding a buyer. Fred had found shelter for the merchandise at a cousin's barn halfway between Newcombe and London. But the cousin had grown nervous and declared that Fred had to take the contraband and leave within the next few days. Yet Fred didn't know where to go. While he dithered, several hundred pounds' worth of brandy and lace languished in a barn because there was nowhere to store it in London. So he'd written to Nessa in a terror.

"We've got no buyer to trek out to the barn to inspect it, and bloody Fred is worried that without anywhere to put the stuff in town," Nessa said apprehensively, "he's stuck."

"I'll have to find a place to warehouse everything," Tamsyn replied, feeling an odd comfort stealing through her. She had been ripped from one world to be forced into another—from touring her sumptuous new home with Kit into a colder reality, where starvation and danger lurked. But this was a world she knew, and knew well. It was far more familiar to her than navigating marriage. "It's been damned difficult trying to find a buyer here, let alone somewhere to store the goods."

Nessa wrung her hands and made small fretting noises while Tamsyn tried to work out a solution.

"There must be *someplace* that will suit our needs," she muttered to herself. "Somewhere large enough, but close at hand so that we can ensure the goods' safety."

Her whole body snapped to attention.

"How much of this house have you seen, Nessa?" she demanded.

The other woman shrugged. "Not much. The butler, Mr. Stockton, he showed me where I'll sleep and also the room where the servants take their meals."

"Take me to Mr. Stockton."

With a puzzled frown, Nessa led Tamsyn down the stairs to the ground floor, before they descended a narrower set of stairs leading to the kitchen. Curious servants watched, likely surprised that the mistress would deign to visit the working part of the house. The kitchen was already bustling with preparations for tonight's dinner, but Tamsyn didn't have time to introduce herself to the cook.

"This here is Mr. Stockton's office," Nessa said, pointing to a door standing ajar.

Tamsyn approached and knocked. She entered when the butler called for her to do so.

"If you're wanting tomorrow night off, John," Mr. Stockton said, bent over a ledger on his desk, "the answer's still no."

Tamsyn cleared her throat, and the moment the butler glanced up, he shot to his feet.

"My lady," he exclaimed. "Your presence here is an unexpected pleasure. I am Stockton, the butler." He bowed.

Damn. He seemed terribly principled. That wouldn't work in her favor.

"My apologies for disturbing you," Tamsyn said with as much warmth as she could muster. "It's not my habit to stalk my employees to their dens."

"No need to apologize, my lady. I am at your disposal, as is the rest of the staff. Shall I fetch Mrs. Hoskins, the housekeeper? You will have much to discuss with her, I imagine."

"Perhaps later," Tamsyn said hastily. "I have a request of you."

"Anything at all, my lady," the butler answered.

"Could you tell me if there's a storage room here in the house?"

If her request was an unusual one, Mr. Stockton was too well trained to show it. "We have a sizable space here belowstairs where we keep spare furniture and other items not in current use."

"I would like to see it."

"Please, follow me." Mr. Stockton led Tamsyn and Nessa from his office and into the hallway. With a key, he unlocked a door, pushed it open, then stepped inside.

Tamsyn and Nessa followed. It was, as the butler stated, a goodly sized room that contained several tall-backed chairs, a demilune table, and a few pictures covered with protective fabric. Most of the low-ceilinged chamber stood empty.

"This room looks to be about twenty by forty feet," Tamsyn speculated.

"I imagine that you are right, my lady," Mr. Stockton said, "though I can have it measured, if you like."

"That won't be necessary." Tamsyn exchanged a glance with Nessa, who nodded her approval. Now came the more difficult part of this process. "Mr. Stockton," Tamsyn began, "I do not mean to be vulgar, but I must approach this directly."

The butler gazed at her with a puzzled frown. "My lady?"

"I hope," she went on, "that you are paid an amount commensurate with your estimable skill."

"I am . . . comfortable," he allowed.

"What would you say if I told you that I can generously increase your wages?" she asked.

"I would say that I am most interested," Mr. Stockton replied. "While I enjoy my employment, I am getting older, and I need to think of my future."

"I've need of two footmen," Tamsyn continued. "Men of physical strength who would also like to supplement their income. It is extremely important that they be trustworthy and not given to gossip."

The butler nodded. "I know just the fellows."

Better and better. "A shipment of goods will arrive within the next few days," she explained. "It must be brought into the house and stored here. This is the most crucial part: *my husband cannot know about it.* Not a word can be whispered to anyone—most especially the master of the house." Despite Kit's reputation as a libertine, the very fact that he had been honored for his military service meant he had considerable loyalty to the law of the land. He'd said as much shortly after their wedding. He'd be furious if he knew about her illegal activity, and repudiate her without a second thought.

She might be his wife now, but she had it from his own lips how much he valued king and country. He might even report her to the authorities.

"I see," Mr. Stockton murmured.

"If you agree to this," Tamsyn went on, "you and the footmen you select will get a percentage of the sales of these goods."

He was silent a moment, and Tamsyn could only wait. She understood from experience that people could not be hurried, or else they would get nervous and all negotiations would be spoiled.

"These . . . goods, as you describe them," he said speculatively, "what are they?"

"It doesn't matter," she answered. "All that matters is the money lining your pocket if it's stored here securely."

"This isn't legal, is it?" Mr. Stockton asked with a raised brow.

"It isn't condoned by the Crown, no," she allowed.

The butler's eyes widened slightly. But he did not sputter in outrage, nor give notice. Slowly, very slowly, he nodded his head.

Silently, she exhaled. "When the shipment arrives, you must notify me immediately. I will direct the operation from there. I cannot stress enough that all of this must take place with as much discretion as possible. Should the master or anyone on the staff—or indeed anybody at all—have the slightest inkling about what we are doing, it will be disastrous for everyone. Further, the percentage I promised you will never materialize."

"Yes, my lady." The butler bowed again. He said with a gleam in his eye, "I thought I detected a hint of Cornwall in your accent."

"Not all of us Cornishmen and women participate in

this trade," she felt obliged to point out. As of eight years ago, her own hands were entirely clean. "Now, bring the two footmen to me."

"I'll fetch Dennis and Liam," he said with another bow before briskly leaving the storage room.

Nessa let out a gusty breath. "Thank the heavens. I thought we'd be sunk for sure."

"I won't disappoint Newcombe," Tamsyn vowed. "We'll have to get word to Fred. Let him know that we've finally got a place to house everything. He'll have to move quickly, in case any customs men are prowling around."

Two young men in livery cautiously entered the storage room. Tamsyn noted with approval that they were both tall and sturdily built.

One of them said warily, "Begging your pardon, my lady. Mr. Stockton said you wanted a word?"

"Who are you?" Tamsyn asked.

"Liam," he answered, coming into the room. He wore the livery of a footman. "Liam McBride."

"And I'm Dennis Bell," the other piped in.

"What I'm about to tell you cannot leave this room," Tamsyn said firmly. "If you feel that you might have trouble keeping secrets—even from your families—you must leave immediately."

Both footmen exchanged glances. Finally, Dennis spoke. "What's in it for us?"

"Money," she answered without prevarication. "Enough to substantially supplement what you make now."

"I don't know about Dennis," Liam said quickly, "but I'm game."

"Me, too," Dennis threw in.

As briefly as possible, Tamsyn explained the situation to them. While she spoke, their eyes went wide, but neither of them looked outraged.

"Will it prove to be a difficulty?" she asked pointedly.

Both footmen shook their heads. "My family back home has no love for the law," Liam added.

"And do you care for legalities?" Nessa demanded.

"I like having a steady job and a full belly," Dennis said, "but it don't hurt to have a little extra in my coffers."

Though she was pleased with the arrangements as they fell into place, she pressed, "And which of you two grew up poorest?"

Dennis shrugged, but Liam raised his hand. "Left Ireland as a tyke and lived in a Whitechapel rookery until I was old enough to go into service."

"What do you know about buyers here in London?" Tamsyn asked. "Buyers of things that aren't precisely sanctioned by the Crown." When Liam hesitated, she added encouragingly, "Trust me, Liam. I won't turn on you."

"There's a bloke," the footman finally said. "A jeweler in Clerkenwell. Mr. Jayne. He's known for doing some selling on the side. Might be able to help you, too."

"Thank you," Tamsyn said, feeling a slide of relief. "You can go now."

"Thank *you*, my lady," Liam answered fervently.

The footmen bowed before hastily exiting through the door.

"At least that's settled," Tamsyn said, and exhaled. "We might have ourselves a buyer. In the meantime, I'd better get back to Lord Blakemere."

She started for the door.

"You think we can do this without him knowing?" Nessa wondered.

"We're going to have to," Tamsyn said over her shoulder. "The alternative is too calamitous to contemplate." The best she could hope for was transportation. As for the villagers, she would never incriminate them, but they would starve without the smuggling profits.

She hurried out and made her way back up the stairs, hoping Kit wouldn't be too concerned about her prolonged absence. She found him in a small parlor at the back of the house. He stood in front of the fire, hands braced on the mantel as he nudged the decorative andirons with the toe of his boot as if to test their weight.

He glanced behind him at her entrance, and his smile was warm. It shot straight into her chest, and she felt momentarily giddy. Ah, he was a fine thing to look upon. How bloody lucky for her that her best candidate for husband also happened to be the handsomest.

She had to remember to stay alert and not be distracted by his good looks or charm.

He hadn't been angry when she'd been beset by nerves last night, nor had he demanded his husbandly rights. Instead, he'd been patient and kind. That kindness presented its own dangers, because at that moment she'd felt that she could trust him with anything. Yet for her own safety, and the security of the people of Newcombe, that couldn't happen.

"Everything sorted out?" he asked.

"She had a few questions about unpacking my things," Tamsyn answered. "But I have so few possessions, it shouldn't take long to tend to them."

"After today," he said brightly, striding toward her, "that won't be a concern. You'll have a substantial allowance to spend however you like."

Hopefully it would be enough to put a down payment on Chei Owr. "That's generous of you," she murmured.

He waved off this compliment. "By agreeing to marry me, you've ensured my future happiness. In thanks, there's nothing I won't give you. Within reason," he added belatedly. His grin was sheepish. "I'm not particularly adept at curtailing my spending. The curse of the third son—to have his munificence constrained by circumstance."

"It's the curse of the poor country gentry that we can never scale the pecuniary heights of our city cousins," Tamsyn replied. "I can assure you that my financial demands will be minimal." Perhaps now was not an ideal moment to mention buying Chei Owr. "I've had to learn frugality the hard way. I hold on to my pennies, like this." She lifted her clenched hand.

He covered her hand with his, and the gesture felt both comfortable and thrilling. "You *should* give yourself every luxury," he advised.

"Is that your express command?" she teased.

He affected a stern look. "Do not gainsay me in this, Lady Blakemere." Then he ruined the effect of his severe expression by grinning, looking very much like a boy who'd been given a barrow full of sweets. "Come, let's find ourselves some luncheon. I find the prospect of inheriting a fortune increases my appetite."

Kit released her hands and strode from the parlor. She followed at a more sedate pace, and her gaze alighted on Dennis, standing at his post in the hallway. He gave her a wink, and she sternly put her finger to her lips. Chastened, he snapped his gaze to attention, staring into the middle distance the way a footman was supposed to.

Storing smuggled goods right under the nose of her new husband? She must be certifiably mad. But what choice did she have?

A knot formed in her belly. Kit might be a reckless libertine, but she couldn't deny how very gentle he was with her. She hadn't missed the sag in his shoulders when he agreed to let them have separate bedchambers, either.

Her own disappointment had been something of a revelation. No matter what she'd told herself, it hurt to let go of her hope for romance and affection. It wouldn't be very challenging to grow attached to Kit, to care for him.

But it was better this way. Keeping herself guarded meant that her deception would be easier.

"I could absolutely *obliterate* a pork pie right now," Kit said cheerfully from the foyer. "Oh, and a tankard of ale. Doesn't that sound blissful? Let's buy the whole chophouse a round."

Damn and damn. How would she keep from growing closer to him? Every moment in his company proved more dangerous to her heart.

Chapter 10

Kit was largely unfamiliar with the industrious side of London, including those men and women who kept society functioning. It was something of a shock to see anyone doing anything at five besides riding on Rotten Row. Yet the offices of Flowers and Corran were still bustling by the time Kit and Tamsyn arrived that afternoon.

He opted not to voice this to Tamsyn as they followed a clerk through the maze of rooms stuffed with papers tended by ink-stained young men. Though he'd secured her hand and needn't fear her changing her mind, it was probably better that she didn't think him *entirely* indolent and shiftless.

Anxiety prickled along the back of his neck and down his spine, though he kept himself strolling with an easy gait. Why should he be anxious? He'd fulfilled the terms of Lord Somerby's will, and now there was nothing left to do but transfer the money to him.

He had already earmarked a portion of it for the pleasure garden. Once the fortune was in his possession, he'd get to work on making it a reality.

"It's like a rabbit's warren in here," Tamsyn murmured to him. "I'd get lost if I ran for the door."

"Thinking about bolting?" he asked quietly. "There's no cause for it." He gave her a reassuring smile.

She returned it, though the corners of her mouth seemed tight with apprehension. He supposed she was just as concerned as he was.

"When everything is settled," he said, "I'll buy you a fine little curricle and a pair of matched white horses so you can jaunt about London as much as you please. It's not a far ride to Hampstead Heath. Plenty of green and open space there. You'll like it."

The tension eased from her smile. "Never driven a curricle, just a wobbly dog cart."

"A countess has no need for a wobbly dog cart," he proclaimed.

Mr. Flowers came forward to meet them, all attentiveness as he held out his hands in greeting. "Is this Lady Blakemere?"

"It is," Kit said, noting how much less reticent the solicitor was today as opposed to the last time they had met. "Tamsyn Ellingsworth, née Pearce, of Cornwall."

"A pleasure, Mr. Flowers," Tamsyn said, and the solicitor bowed over her hand.

"I see that Lord Blakemere is indeed a fortunate man," Mr. Flowers said cordially. "And might I add that Mrs. Flowers and I once spent a fortnight in and around Penzance, and found Cornwall most enchanting."

"You must return someday and visit my village of Newcombe," Tamsyn replied. "The country's a bit wild in my part of Cornwall."

"The most rugged cliffs yield the most beautiful blossoms," the solicitor answered, and a delighted smile wreathed Tamsyn's face.

Kit's already-quick pulse accelerated at the sight.

"I say, that's very good, Flowers," he exclaimed. "Charming my bride of less than twenty-four hours."

The other man chuckled. "Mrs. Flowers would be cross indeed if I started angling for pretty Cornish lasses." He snapped his fingers, and one of countless clerks appeared. "Bring some refreshment for the earl and countess. Have Keane fetch the Somerby file."

The lad scurried off, presumably to find Keane, as well as scare up a tea set and something to nibble on besides paper.

"This way, if you please." Mr. Flowers waved for them to enter his office.

Inside, legal tomes were neatly shelved and stacks of documents were piled in some kind of order over a large rosewood desk. Two chairs were positioned in front of the desk, and Kit held one out for Tamsyn. When she took her seat, Kit sat in the other. Mr. Flowers lowered himself into a wingback leather chair behind the desk.

"My felicitations on your marriage," the solicitor said as they waited for refreshment and paperwork. As Tamsyn searched for something in her reticule, Mr. Flowers took the opportunity to send Kit a look rich with meaning. *Well done, my lad*, he seemed to say.

Kit raised his brows. *Of course*, he answered silently. *This* is *me, we're talking about*.

But he hadn't been nearly as confident a week ago, when he could not find an eligible, willing miss who seemed suitable. He'd seen too much suffering on the battlefield to believe in anything like providence, but clearly, if there was any goodwill in the universe, he'd received some of it when Tamsyn had crossed his path.

There was still the matter of consummation, however. He couldn't be comfortable as a husband and a man until he'd taken her to bed and shown her a good time. His honor as a libertine demanded it. He wanted it, too. Wanted her.

Focus, damn it.

A thin lad in his late teens hurried in carrying a substantial leather portfolio. "The Somerby papers, sir." He deposited the portfolio carefully on Mr. Flowers's desk before bowing and scampering off.

Kit leaned forward as Mr. Flowers opened the portfolio and removed several sheets of a document.

"These are the papers that will require your signature," the solicitor explained, "which will make binding the transference of your portion of Lord Somerby's fortune to your name." He took a large stack of sheets from the document and turned them to face Kit. "I've indicated the places where you are to sign." He offered Kit a sharpened quill.

Kit got to his feet and took the quill. It surprised him, how unsteady his hand was. After everything he'd faced, the countless brushes with death, including when his shako had been shot off during a march in Belgium, that he should feel any trepidation *now* struck him as ridiculous. Yet an unmistakable tremor made his hand shake as he bent over the documents.

Much as Kit wanted the money, it saddened him that it had to come into his possession for the price of Somerby's life. He'd been a good friend—exacting in his demands, but generous with his praise when those demands had been met. Would Somerby approve of Kit's plan to build a pleasure garden? Or would he frown and grow silent in that way he did whenever someone made a foolish choice?

Kit glanced back at Tamsyn, who sent him a small, encouraging smile. The steadiness of her presence acted as a balm, and within moments, he felt himself grow more stable.

The novelty of signing his name to the transfer papers soon dimmed as he had to provide his signature again and again. He wrote his name so many times, his fingers cramped.

"As you may surmise," Mr. Flowers said, dusting sand onto the papers while Kit shook out his hand, "it is a complicated business to transfer this great an amount of money. Be grateful you did not have to draft these papers. They made more than one clerk cry."

"You rewarded them for their efforts, surely," Tamsyn said pointedly.

"The law is a difficult and sometimes tedious industry," the solicitor answered. "In law, as in life, there are no rewards for doing your job as it's supposed to be done."

"True," she said with the air of someone speaking from experience.

Kit glanced at her and saw a tiny birthmark behind her left ear he'd never noticed before. Damn—he knew barely anything about his wife. He had certain particulars, but there was so much more to her than what he'd grasped. It was like noticing one leaf rather than seeing the entire tree. Would he ever come to truly understand her? If everything went according to the plans they had set out before their marriage, they never would fully know each other.

She'd been so adamant that she wanted to return to Cornwall, and he had been content to let her go, so long as an heir had been produced. This was the scenario Kit had wanted, and yet now he wasn't certain whether he liked it or not.

But this wasn't the time to contemplate these intricacies. He bent himself back to the task of signing countless papers.

Finally, the last page was reached. Kit scrawled his name, his handwriting far worse than it had been at the beginning.

Mr. Flowers sanded and blotted the last sheets, then tucked them back into the portfolio. "It's done. Congratulations, Lord Blakemere."

Kit took his offered hand and shook it. Then he turned to Tamsyn. "Lady Blakemere," he said with a little bow.

"Is it real?" she asked, wonderingly.

"Indeed it is, my lady," the solicitor answered with a chuckle. "Your husband has inherited a substantial fortune." He also offered a small bow.

"Well." She exhaled. "That doesn't happen every Monday."

Kit held out his hand to help Tamsyn to her feet. "Shall we return home for a celebratory supper?"

Mr. Flowers cleared his throat. "There's one more item to attend to, my lord."

Turning back to the solicitor, Kit saw something that looked suspiciously like a sealed letter in Mr. Flowers's hand. "More?"

"Please sit." When Kit did so, the solicitor explained, "The late Lord Somerby provided instructions to my firm. After you were married and the documents securing the fortune's transfer had been signed, I was to read you this." He held up the missive.

"What's in it?" Tamsyn asked.

"The contents are unknown to me," Mr. Flowers said.

Kit frowned, but dismissed his trepidation. It had to be some words of warning from Somerby, or perhaps a stern admonition to be a good steward to the fortune. "Go ahead."

Mr. Flowers broke the wax seal, then donned a pair of spectacles. He cleared his throat again, and read aloud.

"My dearest Ellingsworth—or should I say, Lord Blakemere,

I offer my blessings on your marriage. You made myself, your family, and country proud with your service abroad. All I ever desired for you was to find a measure of stability and happiness—thus my requirement that you marry in order to inherit a measure of my wealth. The greatest joy I ever experienced was with my beloved Elizabeth. If you might experience a fraction of the contentment I felt with Lizzie, I go to my grave at peace. I die serene, knowing that I am to be reunited with my precious wife once more."

Tamsyn made a soft noise, and Kit glanced over to see her dash a knuckle across her eyes. Lord Somerby's sentiment clearly moved her, the words of a man who had once loved deeply.

Kit had been blunt with Tamsyn about his own fidelity and expectations for the marriage. He doubted this was what Somerby had in mind. Would his old friend be disappointed?

The solicitor continued to read.

"There is one aspect of your life that concerns me, and that is your appalling habits with money. I fear that you will recklessly decimate my fortune in your relentless pursuit of pleasure.

To that end, the transfer of the money is not complete unless you agree—in writing—to let your new bride control the finances."

Mr. Flowers dropped the letter, stunned. But the solicitor was no more aghast than Kit.

"That cannot be what Somerby said," Kit choked out.

"I assure you, Lord Blakemere, I did not fabricate the contents." Mr. Flowers held out the letter, and Kit snatched it up.

He scanned the letter. And found that Lord Somerby did, in fact, stipulate that all of the financial control would belong to Kit's bride. Tamsyn.

Absently, Kit handed the letter back to the solicitor, but his focus was on Tamsyn. All the color had left her face, leaving her freckles to stand out starkly, like drops of blood. Her chest rose and fell quickly, as if she was running away from something.

A strained laugh broke from Kit's lips. "Dearest Lord Somerby is trying to control me from the afterlife." He forced out another hollow chuckle. "Never knew the old fellow could be so ruthless."

"Is there more?" Tamsyn asked, her voice strained. "In the letter?"

Mr. Flowers picked the sheet of paper up and read aloud.

> "My directives for how the capital will be controlled are as follows:
>
> The new Lady Blakemere cannot simply settle an amount of money on you. She must approve all financial requests. Further, if you think to bully your wife or in any way forcefully take money from her, you are sorely mistaken. All applications for cash must go through the bank and be reviewed personally by my banker, Mr. George Bradley. Such requests for money must include documentation of what you intend to do with it, as well as Lady Blakemere's explicit approval of this use.
>
> Lest you think I am a tyrant, let me assure you that Lady Blakemere will settle a modest quarterly allowance on you. Everything else beyond this nominal figure will be in her control.
>
> I imagine that you are baffled by me now, Kit. Rest assured that I derive no pleasure

*from these conditions; but I want nothing
more than your happiness, and see your own
impulses as the greatest impediment to that. If
you curse me, do so because I loved you too
well to permit your self-destruction.*
   Your friend,
   Prescott Lamb, Lord Somerby"

Mr. Flowers lowered the letter and tapped his finger-tips against the paper, as if trying to nudge away its significance. Silence reigned in the office for several moments.

Kit sat back in his chair, stunned. "Congratulations, Lady Blakemere," he said, his voice tight. "You are a wealthy woman."

"Is this true?" Tamsyn asked Mr. Flowers. Her voice was raspy. "Kit signed the papers. The fortune rightfully belongs to him."

"There is a postscript to the late Lord Somerby's letter, intended for my eyes." The solicitor pointed to a few lines at the bottom of the missive. "It declares all other documents relating to the financial holdings to be null and void without Lord Blakemere's signature here."

Kit looked at his wife, the woman he barely knew, and yet who was the key to giving him what he most desired. Either he signed and had her managing his fortune, or he didn't sign and the money went to someone else.

"We didn't quite take this situation into account, did we?" Kit said wryly to Tamsyn.

Her face was still chalky as she gazed at him. "I didn't know such a thing was possible."

"I imagine there will be some . . . negotiations," he answered carefully.

"Will you sign?" she wondered.

"Better to have my money in your hands than in someone else's possession."

He rose and grabbed the quill from its stand. He scrawled his name along the lower edge of the letter, then returned the quill to the stand, his hand feeling a thousand miles away.

"There," he said and exhaled. "It's done."

The solicitor said, "I'm certain the two of you will come to an amicable arrangement."

Kit sank down in the chair, rubbing at his temple. "You can buy yourself that curricle now," he said to Tamsyn. "You don't need me to approve your purchases. *I*, however, appear to need you."

"I suppose you do," she said, looking appalled.

A leaden weight settled in his chest. This marriage was supposed to be convenient for both of them, but now everything had been thrown into chaos.

Would his dreams of the future come to nothing, now that he had to ask his wife for every penny? The cost of the pleasure garden was considerable and would eat up most of their newfound annual income. Very likely, she'd balk at the expense. Most reasonable people would, or at the very least question why he would want to sink such an amount into a folly.

She'd come from poverty and she had said only today that she held on to money tightly. Tamsyn would never agree to throwing money into a pleasure garden.

But she had to agree. She *had* to.

Whether she wanted it or not, his happiness was in her hands.

Chapter 11

❦

Tamsyn felt as though her stays had been laced too tight. She couldn't catch her breath, and everything squeezed her, harder and harder.

The carriage seemed impossibly small as they rode back to their new home. Kit brooded across from her, staring moodily out the window while a steady rain fell, turning the streets muddy and slick, and darkening the buildings.

"You have to know that I had no foreknowledge of this," she said to Kit.

"Of course," he answered distractedly.

Before they had left Mr. Flowers's chambers, the solicitor had informed her that on the morrow, a Mr. George Bradley would visit her at home to review documents relating to the fortune and all its holdings. She'd learn precisely how rich she was, which, given Mr. Flowers's solemnity and Kit's distance, meant she must be mistress of a great deal of money.

After nearly a decade in genteel poverty, economizing and watching every cent, making do without, her circumstances had been completely, radically reversed. She didn't know how to feel. Happy? Appalled? Managing a fortune was entirely new. She was in charge of the money earned through smuggling, but that was likely a pittance compared to the earnings of the title and its holdings.

But to review and approve Kit's purchases? Could she do it?

She had no choice. They would need to figure out some way to traverse this unknown territory.

She watched London scroll past, dirty and cold. Clearly, Lord Somerby thought that his actions would yield a positive result. A husband had all the power in a marriage—but that had been inverted. Kit had to be as baffled as she was.

Somehow, they would need to manage this new paradigm.

The carriage came to a stop outside the town house on Bruton Street. A footman opened the door to the vehicle, and with his help, Tamsyn alighted. Kit followed, but he seemed deeply distracted. Instead of offering her his arm, he drifted up the front steps and into the house.

Their lives were inexorably intertwined now. Precisely the opposite of what she had wanted going into this marriage. She had hoped for polite disinterest; instead, it could shift into a bitter attachment.

She hurried from the carriage to the foyer, dodging the rain. Inside, she gave her hat and bonnet to a waiting footman. She briefly considered going in search of Kit before rejecting that notion. He likely wanted to be alone right now, and pursuing him could create tension between them.

"Send my maid to me," she said to the footman. "I'll be in my room."

Slowly, she made her way up the stairs. Candles had been lit to combat the cloudy gloom outside, but they barely penetrated the dimness. A surprising wave of homesickness struck her and her heart felt leaden. If only she could roam the seaside cliffs as she longed to do, taking consolation in the ceaseless rhythm of the ocean as it pounded the shore. When the pressures of shouldering the village's burdens became too much, she often went on daylong rambles, losing herself in the eternal Cornish countryside. She didn't know her way around London, and the endless, dangerous city would give her no comfort tonight.

She reached her room, where a low fire burned, and drifted inside to stand at the window to watch the raindrops course down the glass and obscure her view of the garden.

"I heard the master came wandering in as distracted as a cloud," Nessa said as she entered, shutting the door behind her. "Didn't talk to nobody, just went to his chamber and shut the door."

Tamsyn turned to face her friend. She planted her hands on her hips. Briefly, she explained what happened at the solicitor's office.

Nessa walked to one of the chairs by the fire, then sank down into it. Her expression was opaque, until it cleared.

She beamed at Tamsyn.

"But this news is first-rate," she exclaimed.

"I cannot see how," Tamsyn answered grimly. "Kit and I will have to be in each other's pockets."

Nessa shooed this away with a wave. "You'll find a way through this. The important thing is that you're rich—and *you* control the purse strings."

"I don't want to," Tamsyn objected.

"Listen, my girl." Nessa rose and walked to her. "Ever since taxes were raised and the catch dried up, the folk of Newcombe have been scraping by. We took to smuggling because we had no choice. But we don't have to worry anymore. You've got more than enough to keep the roofs over our heads and fresh bread on the table."

Tamsyn stared at her. "Just hand over the Blakemere fortune to the village?"

"Why not?" Nessa challenged.

Pacing away, Tamsyn said, "That's not a solution to our difficulties. Subsisting on charity is no way to live."

"How would you know?" Nessa demanded.

Tamsyn threw up her hands. "I live in a house that's less than a mile from the center of Newcombe. I might not live in the village, but it's my home, and yours. And . . . we're proud people. Too proud and hardworking to depend entirely on alms. When Will Fox's house burned down and everyone came to fix it—he patched up all the boats and sails in the harbor to pay everybody back."

"Aye, I remember," Nessa said with a nod.

"The villagers smuggle because it doesn't hurt anyone. None of us are criminals. We're not going to steal all of the earl's money."

For a moment, the other woman was still. Then her shoulders drooped. "You're right, blast it. I can't see Alan Hammett or Susan Bligh going a-begging. They'd never countenance it."

"No," Tamsyn said with a shake of her head, thinking too of the independent, dignified fisherman and the washerwoman, "they wouldn't."

"Shame we can't touch that money, though," Nessa murmured.

"But . . ." A thought occurred to her. "I'd been planning on using my allowance from Lord Blakemere on a down payment for Chei Owr."

Excitement filled Nessa's face as she realized where Tamsyn was heading. "And now—"

"I can buy it outright."

The house would be hers. The smuggling could continue, and nothing had to change.

Thank you, Lord Somerby. I never knew you, but you've helped me in ways you'll never know.

TAMSYN went down to supper a short while later. As she suspected, Kit wasn't in attendance.

"Where's Lord Blakemere?" she asked a footman.

"He went out, my lady," was the answer. "Didn't say where or when he'd be back."

Her feelings of celebration dimmed as she sat alone in the large dining room. The chamber seemed even more cavernous, occupied as it was by only her and a retinue of servants. Liam and Dennis were there, but neither of them winked or sent her a knowing look.

On her plate, she made neat piles of peas and potatoes, and aligned the fish so that it was perfectly horizontal.

I've gotten what I needed. The village is going to be safe. So why am I not happier? Beyond the money to buy the house, what she wanted, what she needed, was an inattentive husband. The more her spouse was away, the easier it would be to continue smuggling. It was a simple equation.

Yet her stomach was knotted as she barely ate her elegant supper.

She could solve one problem, but there were so many others to consider. Everything at home was in suspension, waiting for her return. There was a secret door leading to the caverns beneath Chei Owr, the same caverns where the smuggled merchandise was stored before buyers were secured. Tamsyn was the only one who had the key to that door, and it would remain locked until she came home.

She needed to get back to purchase the house from Jory. He was a suspicious man and wouldn't agree to anything in a letter, so the transaction had to be done in person.

How long would it be before she was able to return? Kit had stated he wanted her to stay until she was with child. But at this rate, with him too stunned by their new arrangement, that would happen precisely never.

Further, if her nerves kept her out of his bed, that made the possibility of pregnancy nil. She was going to have to overcome her trepidation.

Kit might make sex feel good, but if she thought of it as merely a transaction she wouldn't have to fear him damaging her heart. He would move on to his actresses and opera dancers while she kept Newcombe alive. Everyone got what they wanted.

Abruptly, she stood from the table. Solitary meals had a way of curtailing her appetite.

She wandered into the library and ran her fingers over the spines of the books on the shelves. It was such a luxury to have books, especially ones without mildewed pages. These volumes had come with the house, so they did not reflect Kit's reading tastes. She didn't know if he enjoyed books, or indeed, what gave him any pleasure. He liked to play cards and gamble and Lady Daleford had said he went to the theater often, as well.

Tamsyn wasn't a child. She knew men met courtesans at theaters, or else chose a lover from the dancers and actresses.

Was Kit there now? Was he selecting a woman for the night—or was he already in her bed?

Despite her resolution, a cold burning lodged in her stomach. He'd said plainly that he wasn't going to be faithful, and it seemed especially likely in the absence of consummating their marriage. But did it have to be so *soon*?

To distract herself, she chose a book at random and sat down in one of the chairs by the fire. But a history of Roman London couldn't hold her interest, not when pictures of Kit kissing an eager opera dancer kept flitting through her mind.

Exasperated, she left the library without returning the book to its shelf and went up to her bedchamber.

Nessa gossiped amiably about the other servants as she helped Tamsyn undress, but Tamsyn could only offer monosyllabic answers.

"Why aren't you smiling?" Nessa asked. "Our troubles are over."

Tamsyn shook her head ruefully.

"Ah, child," her friend murmured. "You're worried about that man of yours. I wouldn't fuss overmuch about it. He'll get used to the way of things."

"If he does," Tamsyn answered, "he'll be in my pockets every moment. Men of fashion spend extravagantly. He's supposedly one of the worst of them. Everyone said he goes through money as if it fell from the skies. And I'll be the one bankrolling it—if there's anything left over after purchasing Chei Owr."

A thought struck her. If Kit wanted to keep a mistress, Tamsyn would have to approve the costs of that woman's keeping. The house, the carriage, the clothes and jewels. All of it. In essence, she'd be paying another woman to sleep with her husband.

"God above," she muttered. "What was Lord Somerby thinking?"

"He probably thought he was doing you both a favor." Nessa *tsked*. "If he loved his wife as he claimed, he didn't think his lordship would go chasing after lightskirts. That Lord Somerby wanted the same kind of love for you both. With each other," she added.

"That's an impossibility," Tamsyn answered. It could never come to pass, for so many reasons.

Nessa gasped. "I forgot to ask you—did his lordship treat you right in bed? I'm certain he made your first time agreeable."

"He didn't. That is to say," she added quickly when her friend scowled, "we didn't. Consummate the marriage."

"The devil you didn't!"

After glancing away, Tamsyn said, "I got to thinking about how he'd make me care about him, and I can't do that."

Nessa crossed her arms over her chest. "Men of his station want heirs, and you don't find babes floating down the Thames, like Moses in the bulrushes."

Tamsyn threw up her hands in exasperation. "I know!"

"You'd best harden your heart and open your legs, or he'll file for an annulment, and then where will we be?"

Rubbing her forehead, Tamsyn groaned in frustration. "You aren't helping."

Nessa sighed. "It's not precisely an enviable place you've found yourself, 'tis true."

Tamsyn shot Nessa a dry look. "Can you at least *pretend* to cheer me up?"

"Ah." Nessa forced a smile on her face. "Everything will work out fine and you've nothing to fret over." She looked at Tamsyn expectantly. "How was that?"

"I feel much better," Tamsyn drawled.

When she'd finished changing into her nightclothes, and Nessa had gone for the night, Tamsyn climbed into bed. It was the finest bed she'd ever lain in, and yet with her thoughts in a furious jumble, the mattress felt stuffed full of tacks and glass. Sleep didn't come, not for many hours, but she told herself that she wasn't waiting up for Kit.

Yet she was still awake at four in the morning, when she heard footsteps in the corridor. Someone paused outside her door. Her breath caught and held as she waited.

But then the steps moved on, and she remained alone.

Chapter 12

His billiard cue balanced in his hands, Kit tried to line up his shot. It ought be a straight trajectory to the corner pocket—but then, very little in his life seemed to follow a direct course lately.

The turmoil ought to have passed by now. Twenty-four hours had elapsed since he'd learned of Lord Somerby's stipulations, which should have been enough time for Kit to settle into this new mode of being. *Should have been* but *wasn't*.

Fighting to steady his hands, he took the shot. The ball rolled toward the pocket. Kit held his breath in anticipation.

The ball clipped the corner and went spinning off into the expanse of green baize covering the table.

"For fuck's sake," he muttered as he straightened.

A man at the next billiard table coughed at Kit's language. Kit fought from rolling his eyes. It wasn't as though profanity had never before crossed the threshold of White's. But the club could also be stodgy and straitlaced. He should find another club—except all of his friends belonged to White's and he wasn't certain if foul language should be the hill upon which he should die.

"Marriage has certainly sanitized your vocabulary," drawled Langdon as he chalked up his cue.

Kit shot him a warning look. "You're so amusing you should join a company of strolling players—and stroll away."

His friend feigned a look of horror. "I'm not amusing? But . . . Mother always said I was witty!"

"Go find her, then," Kit growled. "She'll be at her favorite gin house across from the soldiers' barracks."

"You wound me, sirrah," Langdon said pleasantly.

Kit exhaled roughly. "I came here seeking solace."

"A pity that you found me, instead." He peered at Kit. "But why should you need solace? I assume Somerby's money has been transferred."

"It has. Signed a mountain of papers yesterday."

Langdon thumped him on the shoulder. "Felicitations, old man. Welcome to the world of wealthy, titled wastrels."

"Here I believed I already lived in that world," Kit said drily.

Langdon waved his hand. "Third sons dwell in another circle. The nonessential laggards. Of course, there were some alterations to your status when you were made an earl. But now you've ascended to the heights of the rich aristos." He titled his head in contemplation. "Yet there's an air about you . . ."

"Are we playing or not?" Kit demanded, gesturing toward the billiard table.

But Langdon ignored his demand and studied Kit closely. Finally, he said, "You've the obstructed look of a man who hasn't rogered anyone lately. But that can't be. You're newly wed. Unless . . ." His eyebrows shot up. "Good Christ, you haven't swived her yet."

Kit scowled at Langdon. "She was too nervous on our wedding night."

"And the last night?" Langdon pressed.

"I was too busy drinking myself into a stupor to make an attempt—on her or anyone else." Alcohol was an old crutch, there to help him sort through confusion. But instead of aiding him in sorting through the tangled web of his life, he'd only fallen into more uncertainty.

His head still felt a little tender from the effects of too much wine. Or brandy. Or was it both? Damn, but he couldn't remember. He had vague recollections of taking a solitary supper at a chophouse, and then . . . Did he go to a gaming hell? He might have. He'd gambled deep, and now he owed an obscene amount of money to the proprietors. Money he'd have to pay back by asking *his wife* for the funds.

Langdon shook his head before walking around the table, assessing his position to set up his next shot. "Married barely two days and already you're drowning yourself in drink. I thought the gel fit all the necessary requirements to be your bride. She looks beddable enough."

Kit's jaw hardened. "We may have married for the sake of convenience," he rumbled, "but you don't speak of my wife that way. Have some sodding respect."

He started at his unexpected defense of Tamsyn. It seemed that, despite yesterday's tangle and the earthquake that followed, his attraction to her persisted.

His friend held up his hands in surrender. "As you please." Langdon sized up the layout of the table, then positioned himself to shoot. "Your temper is remarkably terrible, considering you're a wealthy earl." He took his shot, and, to Kit's disgust, the ball sank neatly into its pocket.

"An earl in a quandary," Kit said moodily. As concisely as he could manage, he told Langdon about what had transpired with the reading of Somerby's letter. "Today, the bankers came to our home and told my wife about the vast fortune she now controls. I made certain I wasn't home for that appointment."

For several moments, Langdon seemed immobilized,

save for the opening and closing of his mouth. Finally, he said in a stunned voice, "Your friend Lord Somerby was a son of a bitch. No offense," he added hastily.

"You aren't expressing thoughts I haven't already entertained." Kit sighed and stared at the oil lamps illuminating the table. "I believe that the legal term for my situation is: *fucked*."

"Surely she'll agree to give you whatever money you ask for," Langdon objected.

"Perhaps. We haven't discussed it. And there's a project I've got my eye on that's ruddy expensive." Kit thought of that dream, how thoughts of the pleasure garden had sheltered him through years of war, offering him solace in the middle of misery. Now it seemed to grow dimmer and dimmer with each moment.

She would never agree to committing so much of their income to something that was, admittedly, a risky investment. A pleasure garden wasn't a mine or canal or shipping operation. It could fail.

He refused to consider that possibility.

But something couldn't fail if it never came to pass in the first place. *I hold on to every penny*, she'd said.

Langdon frowned. "What project is that?"

"No point in discussing it if it's not going to happen." Kit tossed his cue onto the billiard table. "I can't play tonight. My hand's as unsteady as your morals."

"If I recall correctly," Langdon mused, "we *both* agreed to climb onto the roof of the girls' academy. So your accusations hold no weight." He placed his cue in the rack on the wall. "How much does this plan cost?"

"Ten thousand pounds—minimum," Kit said flatly.

"Good God."

"Precisely," Kit agreed. "It's not exactly a sum that one parts with readily. Somehow, I doubt Tamsyn will simply hand me the cash and send me merrily away."

"I don't see why she wouldn't," Langdon said with a puzzled frown. "If you tell her what it's for . . ."

Kit tapped his fingers on the baize covering the table. "I can't. She'll think it frivolous and a waste of money. She doesn't come from the most affluent circumstances."

"So you think she'll hold on to her new wealth," Langdon surmised.

"From what I've learned of her"—which admittedly wasn't much—"she doesn't like to spend money. Told me so herself. More than likely," he speculated grimly, "she will refuse to sink such a vast amount into my scheme, and I'll be back to where I am now, which is precisely nowhere."

"Ever the officer, planning a battle," Langdon noted.

"I fought for eight years," Kit answered wryly. "Hard to break the strategic habit."

"You know the best way to win a battle," Langdon prompted.

"To have the enemy surrender before a single shot is fired."

Langdon slapped his hand on the wooden side of the table. "Exactly. Lady Blakemere won't have cause to obstruct your fiscal desires, no matter how extravagant."

"And how is this supposed to come to pass?" Kit demanded.

A grin spread across Langdon's face. "You're going to seduce your wife."

Kit and Langdon left the billiards table and ensconced themselves in two wingback chairs by the fire. A servant brought them brandies, but Kit waved off his glass. Spirits didn't help his thought process.

"Out with it," Kit demanded. "Tell me what you meant."

Langdon swirled the brandy around in his glass, then took a sip. "All the money must pass through the countess's hands, correct?"

Kit grunted in response.

"If you were to go to her today, this very evening, and tell her you need . . . How much did you lose last night?"

"Eight hundred pounds," Kit muttered. "All on credit. I was trying to raise the blunt I need."

His friend grimaced. "Christ in heaven, no wonder Somerby wanted to protect you from yourself."

Leveling a look of sincere displeasure at Langdon, Kit said darkly, "This from the man who bought a fleet of phaetons."

"I had to see which was fastest," Langdon said defensively.

"Did you ever consider simply *asking*?"

Now it was Langdon's turn to look irate. "We're deviating from my point."

"Which is growing cloudier by the moment." Kit drummed his fingers on the arm of his chair.

His friend exhaled loudly before continuing. "So you go to Lady Blakemere and ask her for eight hundred pounds to cover your gaming debts. What would she say?"

"I have no sodding idea," Kit said, fighting exasperation. "I barely know her."

And wasn't that the problem? He'd discovered pieces of her here and there, but there was still so much left to learn.

Langdon held up a finger. "Ah. Here's the crux of the matter. You and your wife began your marriage already estranged. How can she approve anything about your spending if she doesn't have a farthing's worth of knowledge about you?"

"I'd think to preserve marital harmony," Kit mused, "she'd simply agree to whatever I demanded."

"There's another of your problems." Langdon leaned forward. "Your impulse is to *demand*, not *ask*."

"In my experience," Kit noted, "there are certain demands to which women are perfectly happy to cede."

"The bedroom is a separate arena," was Langdon's rejoinder. "I'm speaking specifically of money, which has its own set of rules."

"How would you know?" Kit demanded. "You're the bloody heir. You've always gotten whatever you want. A fleet of phaetons?" He snapped his fingers. "Done. A fortune to spend on grisettes and gambling?" Once more, he snapped his fingers. "Done."

"This ad hominem attack helps no one," Langdon said with an equanimity that made Kit want to punch him. "We're moving away from my argument. Certainly you've heard the old chestnut about flies and vinegar and honey and so forth."

Kit lapsed into a contemplative silence. Finally, he said, "Once or twice."

"Let that be your guide," Langdon answered. "If you set out to win Lady Blakemere's favor, she won't deny you anything. Including," he added, "this secret project that you refuse to disclose to me." He drained his brandy. "You won't get anywhere if you continue on this path of befuddled stasis."

A servant reappeared immediately to refill Langdon's glass.

As Kit watched his friend drink, he pondered what Langdon advocated. There was logic in his counsel. If he courted Tamsyn—properly—she'd soften toward him. Once favorably inclined, surely she would grant him the funds for whatever he desired. She might even do so with a smile.

Kit let out a breath. "Here's an upside-down strategy. Usually a man seduces a woman *before* marriage."

"Yes, well," Langdon said with a self-deprecating twist of his mouth, "when it comes to the nuances of actual courtship, I might not be the best mentor."

Kit smirked. "What a marvelous gift of understatement you have."

"Silence, you ass." But there was no rancor in Langdon's words. They had known each other too long to take offense at anything the other said. "You're the military man. Use those gifts of strategy that kept you alive to do something much more difficult—namely, endearing yourself to your wife."

Slowly, Kit nodded. It would take some work on his part, but then, nothing truly worth having came easily. In Portugal and Spain, he would lie awake at night listening to his men asleep, men he might have to send to their deaths. A reliable way he could get himself to sleep was to think of his plans for the pleasure garden. He'd go over every detail, every nuance, until he surrendered to unconsciousness. Now that he was home, whenever memories of death loomed close, he returned to that dream. It soothed him now as it did then.

Langdon frowned at him. "What are you doing sitting here?" He made a shooing motion with his hand. "Get thee home, miscreant, and charm your wife."

"I will." Kit rose quickly and smoothed a hand down his waistcoat. After giving Langdon a nod of thanks, he headed for the door. He had, in fact, survived a considerable amount of combat. Scars marked his body, though they were hidden by his clothing. He'd weathered so much, yet the prospect of making a woman care about him was far more intimidating.

KIT cautiously crossed the threshold of the town house. He'd made himself quite scarce since yesterday, and if Tamsyn waited for him with a fire iron clutched in her hand, ready to brain him, he couldn't quite blame her.

Aside from a footman, who assisted him with his coat

and hat, the foyer stood empty. No waiting, angry wife. Yet her absence spoke just as loudly as an aggressive assault.

"Where is Lady Blakemere?" he asked the footman. He didn't want to have to search all over the house, seeking his wife in some kind of treasure hunt.

"In the study, my lord," the servant answered.

Kit took two steps before stopping. "And where is the study?"

"Follow me, my lord."

He trailed after the footman as they moved down a corridor, deeper into the house. They passed several chambers of different sizes, including two separate drawing rooms, before the servant stopped outside a closed door.

"That will do," Kit said in dismissal. He didn't relish the idea of the staff watching him when there was a distinct possibility he might have to grovel.

The footman bowed and disappeared. When Kit was certain he was alone, he knocked. Tamsyn's muffled voice called, "Come in."

It would be better to enter with confidence rather than timidly poking his head in and pleading for an audience. He opened the door and stepped inside.

The study was typically a masculine sanctuary, and this one had indeed been decorated for a man. Dark wooden bookshelves were set into paneled alcoves, and important morocco-clad tomes stood upright in neat rows. Leather chairs were arranged around the room in small groups, as if encouraging sober tête-à-têtes where men decided the fate of nations, if not discussing the turn of an actress's ankle. Hunting scenes hung on the walls. The centerpiece of the room was a massive mahogany desk situated in the middle of the chamber, as though whomever sat at it was the sun and everyone else merely satellites.

As the lord of the house and holder of the title, by right

Kit should find himself behind that desk—reviewing letters, petitions, or whatever pieces of paper that titled men read assiduously, wearing a pair of spectacles and being Important. Other than his years in the army, and the few months he'd been an earl, Kit had never been Important.

But he was the Earl of Blakemere now—it was about time he took on that mantle.

Except seated behind the desk was Tamsyn.

She cradled her head in her hands, a stack of those significant papers in front of her.

He hadn't seen her in twenty-four hours. Hardly enough time for anyone to long for the sight of somebody. And yet his gaze moved over her with a restless demand, taking in the details of her.

Something quieted and stilled within him, and he realized that she was responsible. Being near Tamsyn seemed to calm the restlessness within him.

Her slim fingers threaded through the flames of her hair. He itched to touch that delicious curve where her neck met her shoulder and ease the knots that bunched there.

Why had he stayed away so long?

"Are our finances as bad as that?" he asked, breaking the silence.

She looked up abruptly. The arch of her brows lifted. "I thought you were Mrs. Hoskins."

"As you see," he said, raising his arms, "I wear no apron and have no keys dangling from my belt."

To his surprise, she gave him a thorough looking-over, from the toes of his boots to the crown of his head. His blood heated as her eyes lingered on his thighs and torso, then skimmed over the width of his shoulders.

The bold examination heightened his awareness of her—and it seemed to affect her, as well. Her redhead's complexion couldn't hide the flush in her cheeks.

She visibly collected herself before exhaling. "No need for concern. Lord Somerby left us an ample yearly income. Neither of us will want for luxury." She frowned.

"That troubles you?" Kit eased closer.

"The gowns I've been wearing for my abbreviated Season were all generously gifted to me by Lady Daleford." She touched the sleeve of her peach-hued dress, delicately stroking the fabric. The movement hypnotized him. "They were the first new articles of clothing I've had in five years."

Coming back to himself, Kit recalled that after her parents' deaths, her uncle had inherited the title, the house, and, apparently, the keeping of her. It appeared that the baron neglected his responsibilities—especially to Tamsyn.

Anger swept through Kit, stunning him with its speed and force. "You should buy yourself a whole trousseau. *Three* trousseaus. Velvets and satins and hundreds of yards of silk." The image of her beautifully adorned filled him with a strange sensation, one of purity and light.

It was pleasure. Not the voluptuous sort that usually filled his nights, but a simpler, richer kind. "You deserve that much," he said, his voice low.

Her eyes went faraway and glassy, as though she imagined herself in gown after gown, but then she shook her head. "What I have is sufficient." At his sound of exasperation, she said with a wry smile, "It's going to take more than a day of wealth to undo years of living frugally."

Cold shards pierced his gratification. She would never agree to financing the pleasure garden, not with such an entrenched attitude about money.

"We can work to unlearn that." He tried to smile.

She shuffled through the papers. "My mind is dancing like a paper boat in a tempest." She shook her head. "It seems impossible that I'm responsible for so much money. But I am."

Sympathy tightened his chest. "This wasn't precisely what you thought would happen when you married."

"Quite the opposite," she agreed wearily.

"Lord Somerby put a weighty burden on you." He raked a hand through his hair. "And I haven't exactly helped you, either."

She was silent for a moment. "No," she finally allowed. "You haven't."

Guilt stabbed at him. He would never abandon the troops under his command, but that's what he had done with her.

He came closer, as though approaching a tiger, unsure whether she would bite his head off or let herself be petted. Finally, he stood just on the other side of the desk. This close, he could see shadows beneath her eyes. She hadn't slept well last night, and he was the cause. He really was a bastard.

"When I was about seven," he began, "I had a collection of tin soldiers. Far too many for one child to own. My mother's sister visited us, and she brought her huge brood of children with her. It feels like there were a dozen of them, but that's probably an inaccurate assessment. In any event," he continued, "her youngest son accidentally left his favorite wooden toy at home. He was disconsolate. My mother suggested I lend him some of my soldiers, merely for the duration of their visit."

Kit shook his head. "I threw the whole lot of them into the pond just so I wouldn't have to give up any."

Tamsyn watched him carefully through his little monologue, her expression opaque.

"What I'm trying to say," he went on, "is that I'm a selfish son of a bitch who needs to learn how to share. I needed time to work my way through this puzzle."

She let out a breath. "It's a shocking thing, and a strange

thing, this arrangement your friend constructed. If you're confused and angry about it, I cannot blame you. But," she said, leveling her gaze at him, "the only way we can truly move forward is to do this together."

"Agreed," he said. "And so, I'm sorry for running away when you needed me."

A long moment passed and his stomach clenched in worry. Apologizing wasn't something he had much practice in.

"Apology accepted," she said, and he exhaled.

"We'll find a way to make this work," Kit vowed.

"I made arrangements with the banker," she added. "Your quarterly allowance has been set aside and is already in your account. And your debts have been settled."

Humbled, he bowed his thanks. It wasn't all that different from financially relying on his father. On the morrow, he'd withdraw a sum of cash to help him further his plans.

"Have you dined?" Kit asked. It was nearing six o'clock.

She blinked at the abrupt change of subject but answered, "Not yet. Despite the lateness of the hour." Her mouth curved winsomely, and he recalled the kiss they'd shared in the hotel room on their wedding night. Its sudden heat and the strength of their responses to each other. "At home, we dine by five and sleep by eight."

"A respectable city gentleman doesn't *think* of going to bed before three in the morning," he announced with faux grandeur. "Anything else is bourgeois."

"No one would ever mistake you for a sleepy burgher," she affirmed.

Kit planted his hands on the desk and leaned closer. "Would it be entirely conventional of me to ask if you'll join me for dinner tonight?"

Her lips parted. "Just us?"

He picked up her hand and stroked his thumb over her knuckles, back and forth in a slow, spellbinding rhythm. But who was being ensorcelled—her, or him?

"You and me," he murmured. "Here."

"I . . ." Her pupils were dark and large as she gazed up at him. "Yes."

He could do it now. Lean down and take her mouth with his—God knew he wanted to. His gaze strayed to her mouth.

She blinked and cleared her throat. "Let me finish up a few items here, and then I'll be up to change for dinner." Carefully, she removed her hand from his, but she curled it into a fist and rested it against her chest as though holding on to the feel of him.

I can win her—if I don't lose myself in the process.

"Of course. Is there anything I can help you with?" He gestured to the paperwork.

She smiled slightly. "Thank you for the offer, but I think I have the matter in hand. It's fortunate that my childhood governess was very insistent that I learn mathematics."

"I'll leave you to your work." He bowed before retreating. His last glimpse of her was the brilliant crown of her head bent over a sheaf of documents.

Turning away from the study, he went in search of an available servant. Finding a maid in the parlor, he said, "Please send Lady Blakemere's abigail to me in my bedchamber."

"Yes, my lord," the girl answered with a curtsy.

Kit pensively climbed the stairs to his room. What he had planned verged on calculating, yet there wasn't another option. The pleasure garden had to be made real, for the sake of his own peace. Seducing Tamsyn would not be a chore, either. The air between them already sparked with attraction. He had but to urge that spark into a flame.

His heart thudded in anticipation of them burning together.

Kit entered his chamber and a minute later the ruddy-cheeked Cornishwoman appeared in the doorway, her expression cautious.

"You wanted to see me, my lord?"

"Come in," he said, "and close the door."

"Am I in trouble?" she asked, brow furrowed.

"Not at all," he assured her. "But close the door so that we may speak in confidence."

She did as he asked, but didn't move farther into the room.

Sitting down at his dressing table, he fiddled with the silver grooming set that his valet had neatly arranged. "You have known my wife for a long time, is that correct?"

"Aye, my lord. Ever since she was no bigger than an idea."

He smiled at that. "I think, then, that you're the right person to advise me."

"On what, my lord?"

He spread his hands. "On my wife." At the maid's puzzled expression, he continued, "We knew each other so briefly before our wedding, and now I find her mostly a stranger to me. And what I need from you is information. Her likes. Her dislikes. Things that make her happy."

She was silent for a moment. Likely tallying up the different ways he could please Tamsyn.

"Excuse me, my lord," the maid finally said, "if I just tell you those things, that's cheating."

"Cheating?" He stood. "This is marriage. There is no *fair* or *unfair*."

"Begging your pardon, my lord, but seeing as I've been married before and you haven't, let me tell you that there's most certainly *fair* and *unfair* in marriage. And the fact that you don't know that means you really *do* have to learn the rules."

Tamping down frustration, Kit took a step toward her. "I can make it worth your while."

Her brows climbed up. "Firstly, my lord, I don't accept bribes. Secondly, even if I did, you'd have to get the money from my mistress."

He ground his teeth together. He had no cash on him since he hadn't made it to the bank to receive his allowance. Grabbing his silver comb, he growled, "Pawn this or keep it for yourself."

But the stubborn woman shook her head. "I'm not taking anything from you, my lord. If you want to know something about my mistress, you're going to have to ask her yourself."

"But . . . but . . ." He rubbed at his jaw. "I don't even know where to start."

She gave him an enigmatic smile. "You fought Bonaparte himself. I'm sure finding out your wife's favorite color will be simple by comparison. Now, if you'll excuse me, my lord, I need to prepare her for dinner. I only just heard from a footman that you're dining at home tonight," she said pointedly.

Lowering himself into a chair by the fire, Kit managed a grunt to let her know they were done. He stared at the flames, watching them shift and dance with alchemical grace.

Why should this vex him as much as it did? He couldn't understand himself. He'd never had a shortage of female company and knew precisely what to say to a woman when he desired her. But this was different. Even knowing her on such short acquaintance, he could see that Tamsyn was singular.

He sifted through what he knew of her and the labyrinth of their current circumstances. There was so much to take into consideration. He was her husband, yet theirs was no ordinary marriage. Nothing about them was ordinary.

In the middle of this thicket, Kit was going to have to learn who she was. What she loved. What she despised. Her girlish fancies and the deepest dreams of her woman's heart.

He'd never had a bigger challenge.

Chapter 13

❧

$\mathcal{T}$he enormous dining room felt far more intimate to Tamsyn when taking a meal with Kit. He insisted that, rather than sitting at opposite ends of the long table, they actually sit *beside* each other.

"This way I don't have to shout at you like a sergeant barking orders," he said with a cheerful air as waited for her to take her seat.

"I don't obey orders very well," she answered pertly.

He raised a brow as he sat. "Disobedient, eh? You know what we do with willful countesses."

"Actually," she replied, propping her chin on her hand, "I don't know."

Shaking out his napkin, he said, "Neither do I. But," he added, smiling wickedly, "I'm certain I can devise a suitable punishment."

Her stomach fluttered as she held his gaze. "Have to catch me first."

"Daring words, my lady." His eyes heated. "I look forward to the chase."

Oh, dear.

She sipped her wine as she struggled for a level head. A flirtatious Kit ought to be considered a weapon.

In his evening clothes, he was all things masculine and

dangerous. The dark indigo of his coat brought out the blue in his eyes, and the immaculate tailoring fit snugly to his lean, muscular body. She could stare for hours at the clean lines of his jaw highlighted against the white of his neckcloth.

He watched her with a hooded look as she helped herself to the artichokes in cream sauce and then the roast lemon capons.

"Difficult to concentrate on this excellent food with you observing me like a patrolman," she murmured.

"Forgive me." He didn't take his eyes off her, however. "I am congratulating myself."

She took a bite and had to focus very hard on enjoying her meal, but he was so blasted distracting. "For what?"

"For finding myself in the enviable position of being your husband." He served himself and began to eat.

A drink of wine didn't cool her heated cheeks. "You're awfully adept at flattery."

"I was in the army, ma'am," he answered. "Flattery is hardly worth a ha'penny when you're struggling to keep your men fed and your brains firmly ensconced inside your skull."

Talk of his service piqued her interest. In the time they'd been together, he seldom mentioned that period. "Then you don't miss it," she wondered.

"What's to miss? Maggots in the bread or some Frenchman wanting to shove a bayonet in my chest?" At her appalled silence, he muttered, "Apologies. I shouldn't have spoken so bluntly."

"There are men in my village who went off to war," she answered gently. "Only some of them came back. I imagine it takes a great deal of strength to live with those memories."

His jaw tightened as he determinedly cut his capon into bite-sized pieces. "We all have our ways of enduring."

Perhaps that was why he'd devoted himself so whole-heartedly to being a libertine. It was a means to keep thoughts of the War at bay. She'd seen veterans at taverns drinking with single-minded determination, washing away the faces of the fallen and the sounds of battle.

"Come, let's not spoil this evening with dull topics," he said with determined lightness. "Tell me about your life in Cornwall."

Panic chilled the back of her neck, but she tried to soothe herself with the rationalization that he knew nothing about her illicit activities. "You'd find it very dull compared to London life," she demurred.

"Whenever you speak of Cornwall you go bright as a star."

Heat pervaded her cheeks. Compliments were rare—the men and lads in Newcombe respected her too much to say anything potentially untoward, and she had been such a poor matrimonial prospect in London that few gentlemen had taken the time to dole out honeyed words.

"What do you want to know?" she finally answered.

He waved his fork. "Anything. Everything."

A laugh burst from her. "Sizable topics."

"I'll be more specific. Who do you dine with? Besides your aunt and uncle."

"There aren't many genteel families within easy distance of my house," she explained after taking a bite. "Though when my parents were alive, we had guests nearly every night. The vicar, of course."

"Of course." Kit nodded gravely. "Can't leave out the man of God."

"Yeoman farmers," she continued, "some merchants from Newquay or Truro—they'd stay the night." A smile touched her lips at the memory. "No shortage of company. My mother played the pianoforte and we'd dance."

She recalled the feel of the smooth leather of Father's

shoes beneath her feet as she stood on them in her stockings, and they would sway back and forth as Mother plinked out "Sweet Nightingale."

She started at the touch of Kit's fingertip on her cheek.

He turned his finger to show her the sheen of moisture that gleamed on his skin. Her hands flew to her cheeks, and to her horror she found them wet with tears. Quickly, she brushed them away.

"Lord," she said in a muffled voice, turning her head away, "I haven't done that in ages."

"There's no harm in it." His voice was unexpectedly gentle. "You loved them."

Gratitude surged within her at his kindness. Surreptitiously, she dabbed at her nose with her napkin. "I lost them so long ago."

"And life with your uncle and aunt?" She must have made a face, because he said with wry sympathy, "As bad as that?"

"They're . . ." She searched for the right way to phrase it. "Related by blood, but it's not much of a bond." After nudging around the food on her plate, she went on. "Where I'm concerned, it's benign neglect. They leave me to my own devices."

"But . . . ?" he prompted, his expression one of intense listening.

Anger welled up and she balled her free hand into a fist. "The house is nearly a ruin because Jory refuses to maintain it. 'Why keep up a moldering heap of bricks?'" She gritted her teeth in frustration. "He'd rather spend money on trips to Penzance and Falmouth, or even Cheltenham. Gwen doesn't care what the house looks like so long as she's kept in Chinese silk and Indian shawls. And the way they care for the village—" She stopped herself a moment before blurting anything incriminating. Yet it was too easy to talk with Kit.

"What of the village?" he urged.

"It's a fishing village like any other," she said, her words deliberately airy. "Hardly worth a gentleman's interest."

"Your aunt and uncle sound like a right pair of bastards," Kit said bluntly.

This startled another laugh out of her. "I've thought the same," she confessed lowly. "But never said it aloud."

"I'll give voice to whatever you want to say but can't," he declared. "Just write it down on a piece of paper and I'll bellow it from the rooftops."

"Our neighbors might take issue with that," she cautioned. "I think an awful lot of things that shouldn't be spoken. Don't forget, I grew up around fishermen."

His grin was sudden and wrapped her in warmth. "I knew there was a reason why we were well suited for each other."

His praise felt far too good, yet she wanted to bask in it. And the way he looked at her—as though she was the most enthralling creature alive—made her hot and shaky and excited all at the same time.

For the remainder of the meal, she tried her best to keep from falling under his spell, but she struggled. His irreverent humor made her laugh, while his direct, unwavering gaze sent her pulse fluttering. He told her the story about the near disaster that had been his presentation at court—"Watch how many drinks for courage you have beforehand"—and described the exhibit of Lord Elgin's Grecian marbles in such a thorough manner she felt as though she had seen them with her own eyes.

Yet he never talked again of the War or his time in the army.

In fact, all he spoke of was strictly related to amusing and diverting issues. No unpleasant topics. Nothing grave or serious. As though he avoided such things. As though he pretended they didn't exist.

But she saw how his head turned slightly when a footman entered the room carrying a tray of cake and fruit. Kit seemed aware of his surroundings at all times, marking where the servants stood, or the distance between his seat and the window, in case a threat suddenly appeared.

As the meal came to its close, she rose. He looked up at her with a quizzical expression. "Where are you going?"

"To the drawing room," she explained. "So you can enjoy the company of your port and tobacco. Isn't that the way of fashionable folk?"

He waved this aside. "It's a bloody foolish concept. Never happier than when I'm in women's company."

"A glutton for adoration." She raised a brow. What woman wouldn't fall all over herself to earn one of his smiles or be on the receiving end of his attentive gaze?

"Nothing of the sort." He scowled with aversion to the idea. "Everyone knows that women are more logical than men. They can also have conversations that don't center on their . . ." He glanced down at his lap.

Her cheeks bloomed with heat as she realized his meaning. Oh, she'd heard more candid talk in taverns, but context changed everything. A handsome, elegant man in a handsome, elegant room didn't speak so openly around ladies.

She liked that he could feel so comfortable around her, however. That he didn't think her in need of coddling or pretty obfuscations. Unlike most of the aristocratic men she'd met in London, Kit talked to her like an equal. And that was something she appreciated.

But she realized suddenly that she stared at Kit's groin. He followed her look, and then gazed back at her, interest hot in his eyes.

A wave of need pulsed through her. Yet she wasn't certain what to do with it. She didn't know how to feel about him. He was her husband, but she had to protect herself and her secrets.

"Are you very tired?" he asked her suddenly.

"I'm not seeing double yet," she answered.

"Then join me in the parlor." He stood and offered her his arm. When she took it, he nodded with approval. She tried to keep herself from squeezing his forearm just to feel its solidity, but he looked so blasted attractive and trim in his evening clothes it was all she could do to touch him lightly.

They left the dining room and they strolled to the parlor, with her profoundly aware of his large male presence beside her.

Once in the parlor, he moved away from her to the sideboard. "A drink to celebrate our first evening at home." His hands moved from bottle to bottle. "There must be cordial water around here. That's what ladies drink, correct? Cordial waters and ratafia?"

"Brandy," she said at once.

He lifted his brows, but poured them two glasses. As he did, she drifted to stand by the fireplace.

Holding the drinks aloft, he went to her. "To domestic suppers." He raised his glass.

She took her drink from him. "To unexpected pleasures," she answered.

The corners of his eyes crinkled. Together, they drank.

Tamsyn made a sound of appreciation. This was fine brandy, even better than the kind she smuggled.

But Kit's brandy wasn't contraband. A vine of ice wove down her spine as she considered this.

"I'm glad you like it," he said admiringly.

"In the absence of ratafia," she answered, "I'll do my best to choke it down."

He smiled before taking another sip. "We'll make our debut as a married couple soon." She tried to keep her expression neutral, but must have shown her dislike because he said in a teasing voice, "Surely I'm not as disgraceful as that."

"*You* are perfectly delightful," she answered with a shake of her head. "Only . . ." How to phrase this politely? "What I've seen of London Society hasn't been precisely enchanting."

He lifted a brow. "Balls, regattas, teas? None of them charmed you?"

"You sound shocked."

"I thought respectable ladies of quality *adored* the Season's whirlwind," he admitted.

She held up one finger. "Firstly, I would take issue with describing myself as a 'respectable lady of quality.'"

He looked intrigued. "What are you, then?"

Tamsyn pondered this. "I'm . . . more wild than tame. If I had to choose between a ballroom and the prow of a fishing boat, I'd take the fishing boat every time." She waited to see a disgusted or appalled look cross his face, but instead he appeared thoughtful.

"Those are in short supply in London," he finally said.

"I know." She sighed wistfully.

For a moment, he studied her, and she felt his scrutiny in the way one wolf assessed the other. It was fed by curiosity rather than wariness.

"And secondly?" he asked.

She held up another finger. "From what I have heard, you aren't much enamored of virtuous Society, either."

He tipped his head in acknowledgment. "Touché. Though I'm a man."

"I am well aware of that," she murmured, taking in the width of his shoulders and the length of his legs. Her heart sped in response to his masculinity. Though they kept a few feet apart, he seemed profoundly close, almost oversize in comparison to her.

There was no mistaking the carnal shift in his gaze. His eyes were fiery blue as he contemplated her face, her mouth, and the skin just above the low neckline of her gown.

Her breasts grew sensitive, and warmth coursed low in her belly. She felt dazed by his proximity.

"As a man," he continued, his voice husky, "there are certain privileges I enjoy. Certain desires I am free to pursue."

Images of him entwined with lithe, worldly women jabbed her. His reputation as a voluptuary was based on fact. She tried to shove the mental pictures away but they lurked in the back of her mind.

At some point, he would return to that world of pleasure, leaving her to spend her days and nights like any sophisticated woman, taking lovers—or not—as she wanted.

It seemed a very lonely way to live. She'd gone over a decade without the love of her parents. Could she endure without the love of her husband, too?

Yet she couldn't hold him off forever. She had agreed to this marriage and its conditions—including giving him an heir.

No one ever got with child through long, lingering glances. All she had to do was keep her heart protected, and she wouldn't be hurt.

Just go slowly. Step by step.

She drained her glass and set it carefully on the mantel before facing him.

"Are there desires I might pursue, as well?" she asked, her voice going husky.

His brows went up in surprise for half a moment before that look of need burned brighter in his eyes. He moved closer to her.

She held up a hand, holding him at bay. "Tonight, I want only kissing," she asserted. "It cannot lead to anything else."

He swallowed. "As you wish." His voice was low and gravelly.

"Good." She tried to will her heart to stop pounding

frantically, but it wouldn't listen. Instead, blood roared in her ears as she stepped nearer, turning the distance between them to mere inches.

She slid her hands up the front of his waistcoat, feeling his strapping body beneath the brocade, and his own energetically beating heart. He seemed to hold his breath as her hands went up farther to rest on his shoulders. The flesh beneath her palms was tight and solid, and it shifted under her touch. He watched all this with heavy-lidded eyes.

"I'm going to touch you now," he rumbled.

She couldn't find her voice to agree, but nodded.

Unhurriedly, his hands moved around her waist, fitting to her curves. His heat soaked into her flesh. He gently pulled her even closer, until their bodies met. She bit back an exclamation of shock and pleasure at the feel of him, so very potent, so different from her. She wanted to run and she wanted to lean into him and absorb this moment, this intimacy. The cold from years of isolation thawed slowly, leaving her exposed and open.

He lowered his head as she tipped hers upward, and their mouths met. Desire flamed brightly at his touch. They moved quickly past tentative caresses to fuller, deeper kisses, stroking against each other. His tongue moved in a hypnotic rhythm in her mouth. She yielded and she took, growing bolder, feeling her own power. When she sucked lightly on his tongue, he growled and pressed her tightly against him. Her fingers wove into his hair.

Everything in her body went warm and liquid. She felt intoxicated yet also powerfully aware. A new ache started to throb, demanding more.

He will devastate you, her mind whispered.

I don't care, her body answered.

Abruptly, she pulled back.

His eyes slowly opened as his hold on her waist loosened slightly. He looked as though someone had taken away the very air he needed to breathe. And yet he didn't try to grab her or force his kisses on her.

"I think . . . that's enough for tonight." She couldn't quite catch her breath.

He said nothing, his jaw tight. But he nodded.

"It's been a long day," she continued, her voice sounding overloud, "and I really do need to go to sleep. Have a good night."

"Good night," he answered hoarsely.

She spun on her heel and hurried out of the parlor, putting much-needed distance between them.

$\mathcal{K}$IT watched her go, his heart pounding and his cock hard. Goddamn it—his need for her grew like wildfire whenever he touched her, nearly burning him to ash.

He stalked to the sideboard and poured himself another drink, which he quickly threw back, bracing himself and fighting to return to sanity.

Everything he had learned of her tonight revealed her courage, her strength—and her solitude. She was a rare elemental creature, one that demanded respect, even as her innate sensuality inflamed him. He could lose himself in her.

He'd made plans for tomorrow evening, hoping that what he had arranged would please her.

I want to please her.

The thought struck him like a sniper's bullet. But when he conjured images of her smiling and laughing, warmth seeped through him and he felt both calm and purposeful.

He strode to the window and parted the curtains to look out at the darkness that mirrored his own shadowed thoughts. Too much silence unnerved him, reminding him of the calm before an ambush.

Remember your objective. Woo her, get the money,

build the pleasure garden. It was the light to his darkness, illuminating his way back to life in peacetime.

There was no reason why he couldn't enjoy courting his wife. But Tamsyn wasn't the cure for his somber illness. She wouldn't lead him out of the perpetual war being waged in his mind, his heart. He knew of only one thing that could finally give him tranquility.

Tonight he'd go to his solitary bed, planning the next step in his campaign of seduction.

Chapter 14

$\mathcal{A}$ny rake of value knew that the theater was the prime place to find mischief. Like other young men of breeding, Kit had stalked many of London's playhouses. He'd gather with other bucks in the lobby, trading barbs and posturing, all the while on the lookout for pretty, available women. Then it would be on to the pit and even more roguery.

Despite his long history of pleasure seeking at the theater, a new excitement pulsed just beneath the surface of his skin as he escorted Tamsyn through the doors of the Imperial Theatre.

He paid little attention to the elegant lobby, or the smartly dressed crowd milling around before the first performance. All his attention was focused on his wife.

She held on to his arm as she looked with wide-eyed fascination at the exhilarating milieu. Her gaze was never at rest—staring at a puffery of dandies posturing near a column, following the progress of some daringly clothed courtesans as they tried to catch the attention of the dandies, or lingering on a well-to-do matron's elaborately dressed hair. Voices clashed together and reverberated off the lobby's low ceiling, and all around was the press of many bodies as everyone fought to see and be seen.

A thread of apprehension wove up his back, but he tried to ignore it even as the sound crushed him and the walls loomed close.

Push it back. Don't give it room to breathe.

Damned war. Since its end, large, noisy crowds could inspire notes of uneasiness in him. Only when he tracked an escape path did the concern fade.

It was an irritating habit, yet he managed to live with it. He made himself focus on the delights of the evening rather than give any more attention to his darker thoughts. He donned the mask of a man fully at ease with himself and the world.

"Are you all right?" Tamsyn asked with concern.

How had she seen through his disguise? No one else ever had, not even Langdon.

"Never better," he answered.

Despite his disquiet, his gaze lingered on Tamsyn's lips while his body revisited the kiss they'd shared last night. He'd gone to bed hard and aching, wanting more of her. But he would go as slowly as necessary, moving forward incrementally, until she came to him willingly.

Tonight was for her enjoyment. He'd mulled over ideas about what she'd like, what would bring her pleasure—and then he'd come up with this plan. A novel kind of nervousness danced along his limbs as he escorted her through the theater. Would she like what he'd arranged for her? Would it bring them closer together?

"Don't mind the crush," he said into her ear, trying to be heard above the din. He caught her floral fragrance and it acted as a balm to the edginess he felt in crowds. "Some prefer Theatre Royal or the Haymarket," he replied, guiding her around another clutch of young bucks. "But they can get tiresomely overcrowded."

"This isn't?" she asked. "Any more people packed in here and I think the roof will pop right off."

He grinned. "The Imperial's grown more popular since Mrs. Delamere, the playwright, married the Viscount Marwood and became a viscountess. Helps, too, that she writes a damned fine burletta."

"Is one of her burlettas on the bill tonight?"

"Oh, yes."

He was about to elaborate on the talent of the viscountess when a male voice cried out, "Beggar me, is that Blakemere?"

"So it is," Kit said smoothly as he turned to a ruddy-faced gentleman moving toward him. Several other finely attired men followed, their faces also flushed from heat and—more likely—imbibing a healthy amount of wine before the performance. "Hatfield, how the deuces are you?" He stuck out his hand.

Edwin Hatfield shook his hand with the same eagerness with which he did everything. His gaze moved appreciatively over Tamsyn, lingering on her face and the low neckline of her peach gown.

Kit's chest tightened and his jaw went rigid. "My dear, may I introduce Mr. Edwin Hatfield. This is my wife, scoundrel, so keep your ogling to a minimum else we'll have an appointment at dawn." He realized a moment later that he'd said this only half in jest.

Tamsyn offered her hand and Hatfield bowed over it. He said gallantly, "The luck that kept Blakemere alive on the Continent must have surely followed him here, to marry such a gem as yourself."

"Perhaps, on both counts, it was more strategy than luck," she answered.

Hatfield laughed heartily, his laughter followed a moment later by his hangers-on.

Kit quickly ran through introductions to the set of young men he'd recently been a part of.

"Will you be joining us in the pit?" Hatfield pressed.

Men of leisure almost always paraded their way through the theater's pit, boasting, flirting with ladies of fast reputation, and generally making nuisances of themselves.

At Hatfield's query, Tamsyn looked at him, her brows lifted in a question.

"My days of shouldering through that mob have passed," Kit said without much regret.

"I see how it is," Hatfield answered glumly. "Get yourself a wife and full coffers, and suddenly you're a stranger."

"It's a sad, old story, my friend," Kit replied. "Who am I to change the narrative? Now, if you'll excuse us, we're heading toward our seats."

Before Hatfield or any of the others could speak, Kit guided Tamsyn away.

"We didn't linger," she noted. "But they're your friends."

"*Were* my friends," he corrected. "Heirs and younger sons, the lot of them. They've little to do with themselves all day but run from one amusement to the next." He led her toward a curved staircase, and together, they ascended.

"Sounds rather aimless," she mused.

"It is. Dedicated to filling time with meaningless diversions."

She eyed him as they continued to climb the stairs. "You miss it."

He waited for a pang of longing for that life. Oddly, none came. If anything, he felt more wearily tolerant than envious of his former set. It felt far better to be at her side and watch the play of excited emotions across her face. "Lately, there are other matters vying for my attention. Far worthier matters."

"You could continue to join them," she offered, which puzzled him. He had little experience with marriage, but he would have thought a wife demanded the presence of her husband at home.

"Let's not discuss those purposeless reprobates," he said. They reached the top of the stairs and he took them down a corridor lined on one side with curtains. "Tonight, we have eyes only for the stage. Ah, here we are."

He swept aside one of the curtains, revealing a theater box. Several seats were arranged near the railing, and there was also a bench. The box itself stood empty.

As he moved into the enclosure, Tamsyn stopped at the entrance. "Kit, this is a private box."

He turned to face her. "What of it?"

"This is where the wealthy and important people sit."

"We *are* the wealthy and important people," he reminded her.

"Did your allowance cover it?" She had accompanied him to the bank that afternoon when he went to withdraw a goodly portion of his quarterly allotment of money.

"This is mostly on credit. It's how everyone of fashion pays for everything." He tried to smother the worry that churned in his gut. "I wanted to please you with a surprise. I hope I wasn't wrong to do so." He gave her a smile that had softened many women's hearts.

After a long moment, she shook her head, murmuring, "Not wrong," and he let out his breath.

He held out his hand.

Slowly, she took it. His body tightened at the slide of her gloved fingers as they glided over his palm. But other sensations threaded through him—elation and tranquility.

He brought her forward, leading her to the chair set up in front of the railing. Instead of sitting, she looked around, from the empty stage to the crowded pit, to the tiers of seats where the more well-to-do audience members sat. Finally, she gazed at the other boxes as they filled with London's elite.

A few people called up to Kit, some from the pit and others from the boxes. He nodded a greeting but didn't invite anyone to join them. He wanted this time alone with Tamsyn.

Glancing at his wife, he noticed her scowling.

"Would you like to change boxes?" he asked. "I know the management. We can have it done in a trice."

"Do any have screens?" At his perplexed look, she explained with an irritated expression, "People keep staring at me."

He scanned the crowd. Many pairs of eyes turned in Tamsyn's direction, some bold, others more discreet in their attempt to study her.

"They want a look at the scandalous woman who consented to a one-week courtship," she said grimly.

"Possibly," Kit replied, gazing at her. "More likely, it's because you're one of the loveliest women here."

Though her cheeks were already flushed from the heat of the theater, her blush deepened. "You're lavish with compliments."

"I am truthful," he returned. With her russet hair piled artfully atop her head, showing off her slim neck, her peach gown bringing out her complexion, and her hazel eyes bright as she gazed back at him, he spoke the truth.

Kit nodded and waved at a few more audience members vying for his attention.

"Feels like I'm standing beside the sun," Tamsyn noted wryly. "Everyone wants to bask in your glow."

"Some are friends," he answered offhandedly. "Others only see me since I received the earldom. I'd rather be appreciated for who I've always been than what I've become."

Yet—he hadn't always felt this way. He'd been married all of a few days, and in that time, he sensed something shifting within him with an internal realignment. Last night had been so much quieter than how he normally spent his evenings. However, the hours he'd spent in her company had been pleasurable and gratifying. He hadn't longed to be with his wild compatriots or carousing with people of easy morals.

He'd wanted to be with Tamsyn.

As he did tonight. If given the choice between joining the bucks in the pit or staying in the theater box with his wife, he'd rather be with her. To see her smile, listen to her stories, flirt with her just to see more of her magnificent, redheaded blushes.

Movement on the stage caught Kit's eye. The curtains lifted as the orchestra struck up a dramatic tune.

"The performance is beginning," he murmured in Tamsyn's ear. "We're lucky—tonight is the debut of the viscountess's newest burletta."

Tamsyn took the seat he proffered, and he sat himself beside her. Only when they were both ensconced in their chairs did he realize that they continued to hold hands. Rosy-colored happiness stole up his arm and wove through him as he contemplated their intertwined fingers. He realized at that moment that there was more to physicality than the satisfying of bodily needs. There was closeness, and the warmth that came from being near someone extraordinary.

Tamsyn didn't appear to notice their hands were still joined. Instead, her gaze was riveted on the stage as a trio of actresses appeared. Because the Imperial didn't have a royal patent, unlike Covent Garden or Drury Lane, the works presented here had to include music. The performers half sang, half spoke their lines, like a recitative in an opera. As the actresses onstage sang, the audience quickly fell under their spell. Some cried out encouragement to the characters or hissed at the villains, but on the whole, comments from the crowd remained at a minimum.

Both he and Tamsyn leaned forward in their seats, gazes fixed firmly on the performance as it unfolded before them. There were disguises, secrets, kidnappings, love lost and found. More than a few times Kit glanced over at Tamsyn and saw a shining tear roll down her cheek. His own eyes felt a trifle hot and itchy, especially when the two lovers were reunited after much tribulation.

As the curtain fell, the audience roared its approval. Those who were seated surged to their feet as they clapped—including Kit and Tamsyn. The actors came out to take their bows, and finally, one of the performers pulled a diminutive dark-haired woman from the wings. The applause grew louder.

"Is that the Viscountess Marwood?" Tamsyn asked above the din.

"The very same," he answered. "Usually, the author of the works isn't brought out at the end."

"She deserves her own accolades," Tamsyn said, then cried out, "Brava!"

The cry was repeated around the theater, and the viscountess gave a grateful, humble curtsy before hurrying back into the wings. Finally, the actors retreated backstage and the applause quieted.

"There's a comic farce and some dancing after the intermission," Kit noted.

"I doubt anything could top what we've just seen," Tamsyn answered with a laugh. She eased back into her seat. "But I'd like to stay."

"I'll get us some refreshments. A lemonade for my lady?"

Her eyes gleamed as she looked up at him, her smile wide. "Yes, please, my lord."

Kit hurried out into the massing throng in the corridors. He maneuvered quickly through the crowd, hardly stopping whenever someone tried to get his attention. Generally, he loved lingering between performances, feeding off the excitement and energy of the other theater-goers. Yet impatience nipped at him whenever some buck blocked his path and congratulated him on his newly acquired fortune. He barely glanced at the courtesans batting their eyes at him.

Bellying up to the refreshment stand, he purchased a lemonade and some sugared nuts, then wove through the crowd to return to the box.

As he neared, Tamsyn's laughter spilled out, followed by the deeper tones of a man's voice. Frowning, Kit threw back the curtain and stepped inside.

Tamsyn was still seated, but she had turned to face a gentleman who stood close by. The gent in question stood a little shorter than Kit, but his darkly handsome and roguish looks would make any female entertain improper thoughts. Clearly, he'd been using his considerable skills at flirtation on Tamsyn.

"Hell, Marwood," Kit grumbled, coming forward, "if I had known you'd be here, I would have gotten another lemonade. To throw in your face."

"I've had far worse thrown at me," Lord Marwood answered with a grin. He took Kit's offered hand and shook it heartily.

"You've met Lady Blakemere," Kit noted. He handed Tamsyn her beverage as well as the packet containing the sugared nuts. She murmured her thanks.

"Indeed, I have." Marwood had a keen and discerning eye when it came to women, and it was with genuine appreciation that he gazed at Tamsyn. "I was just telling the delightful lady about my own poor attempts at playwriting when I was a youth."

"Your wife has enough talent for the both of you," Tamsyn said.

"And thank God for her." The look of pure adoration

that came over Marwood's face when he mentioned Lady Marwood quelled any jealous thoughts that threatened to smother Kit. "Did you enjoy the performance?"

"I was enthralled," Tamsyn answered without reservation.

Marwood rubbed his hands together. "Excellent. Excellent. Maggie still gets nervous before any new work is put on. It'll do her good to hear that Lady Blakemere was, what was your word? *Enthralled*." He turned to Kit. "You're still coming over to our home tonight, yes? After the performance?"

"We'll meet you backstage after the final curtain call," Kit replied.

"Brilliant. Until then." Marwood bowed to Tamsyn before retreating out of the box.

Kit took his seat and plucked the packet of sugared nuts from Tamsyn's hand. He popped a few of the sweets into his mouth, enjoying the look of puzzlement on her face.

"Will there be a fete at Lord Marwood's?" she asked.

"Not a fete," he answered.

"Supper?"

"No supper."

"Dancing? Cards?" She gave him a playful swat on the arm. "You're delighting in my torment."

"Perhaps a little." He rather adored being teasing and lighthearted with her, watching the humor and enjoyment in her eyes. "But I will relent and end your suffering. Marwood has the best cellar in London. The finest brandy and Scotch whisky." He chewed a few more nuts.

"Ah." She nodded sagely. "You'll enjoy that."

"*We* will," he corrected her. At least, he hoped she'd find it pleasurable. A tiny spark of concern flared. "After last night, I saw how much you appreciate a fine dram. So we're having a tasting at Marwood's. Just you, me, Marwood, and his wife." At her silence, he pressed, worried, "If you'd rather not go, I can—"

"That sounds wonderful, Kit." A soft smile illuminated her face and his heart squeezed in response. "Thank you. For being so considerate."

Her gratitude warmed him. After he'd sent a note in the morning requesting time in Marwood's cellars, he'd gnawed on his decision. Would she take offense at the idea? Would she be pleased by it?

"Whisky's better than cordial water, I should think." He glanced at the glass in her hand. "And lemonade."

"It depends," she replied, her smile shining in her eyes, "on who's bringing the lemonade."

Unseen electricity crackled between them. She had been pleased with everything he'd done for her tonight. Surely that meant she was warming to him. He couldn't be more gratified with how his plan was unfolding—yet he knew from combat-tested experience that, when it came to the future, every plan could fall apart. Nothing was certain.

TAMSYN planted her feet to avoid being barreled over by a stagehand carrying a painted, flat wooden castle. She ducked just in time to keep the back of her head from getting smacked by a curtain valance. Kit, too, was buffeted by a group of dancers pouring off the stage as they hurried toward the dressing rooms.

The controlled anarchy backstage at the Imperial matched the chaos at the front of the house. A black man stood in the middle of the bedlam, shouting in a Caribbean accent as he directed the traffic. There were no collisions or fights, so the man—Tamsyn assumed he was the theater's manager—seemed to have everything running smoothly, if not quietly.

The manager's role reminded her strongly of her own function when smuggling, with her trying to keep a level head when all around her was madness.

Kit's expression was wry. "Disenchanted?" he asked above the din.

"Why should I be?" She dodged a trio of trained dogs wearing ruffled collars. Their trainer, wearing a similar ruffled collar, ran after them.

"It's not precisely glamorous back here."

"That makes what they do onstage all the more extraordinary," she answered. "To work so hard and have the end result fall smoothly into place. Not unlike planning a battle, I imagine."

His smile grew distracted, a shadow passing over his face.

She wasn't imagining it. He spoke sometimes of his experience in the military, but only lightly and in passing. She thought of Katie Davis, back home, and Katie's husband, Bill. He'd struggled to return to civilian life. Bill would get that same dark, troubled look whenever anyone talked of the War and would quickly change the subject.

What had Kit seen? What had he done? She might never know—and she recognized that she wanted to. She craved discovering more about him despite her vows to keep her husband at arm's length.

He quickly shook off his mood and looked around with his usual good humor. "I thought I'd need to lie down on the floor during the farce that followed Lady Marwood's play. That bit with the hat and the ham. Guffawed so hard I couldn't breathe."

"The actress who made all those puns." She pressed a hand to her ribs. "My sides hurt from laughing." She'd also been spellbound by the sound of Kit's laugh, so deep and rich and full of joy. She'd heard him chuckle before, but never that full surrender to mirth. It suited him.

It was as though two men existed side by side within him. The exuberant, sensual, curious Kit, who simply enjoyed being—and the grim, harrowed Kit with shades behind his eyes. Each shaped the other. She struggled to understand all aspects of him.

"A good evening so far," Kit said with a touch of hesitancy, as though testing her reaction.

"One of the best I've had in London," she answered. An expression of relief eased his features. After their conversation about paying for the theater box, it had occurred to her that he hadn't yet asked her for a penny. Strange. Surely he expected some amount of money from her beyond his allowance.

"But it's not over yet." As he said this, Lord Marwood approached, holding the hand of a petite dark-haired woman. This was the famous Lady Marwood, the author of wondrous words that had made her laugh and cry.

Bashfulness stole over Tamsyn. Kit's friend, the Duke of Greyland, was intimidating in both looks and status, but Lady Marwood was a *celebrity* and a woman of exceptional talent.

Tamsyn felt profoundly ordinary by comparison.

"Lord and Lady Blakemere," Marwood pronounced fondly. "My lovely wife. Maggie, these are the charming folk who will be sampling our cellar tonight."

"A pleasure," Lady Marwood said warmly. Her accent differed from the smooth, rounded tones used by the aristocracy. It was rougher, more streetwise.

Instead of curtsying, she stuck out her hand. She shook first with Kit, then Tamsyn. Holding a quill all day had given the writer an exceptionally strong grip—but then, Tamsyn wasn't a stranger to hauling rope or lifting casks.

Kit smiled widely. "Magnificent performance tonight."

"I heard sniffles from every corner of the house when Angela thought she would never see Eduardo again,"

Tamsyn added, despite her shyness in the viscountess's presence.

Yet Lady Marwood looked skeptical. "You don't think the scene needs more anguish? It felt rather shallow to me."

"Not at all," Tamsyn quickly assured her. "Any more anguish and a legion of doctors would have to come and bleed everyone to balance their humors."

A cautious smile tilted the corner of Lady Marwood's mouth. "You are kindness itself." She glanced up at her husband, who looked at her adoringly, as though Lady Marwood had personally invented the dramatic arts.

Some of Tamsyn's trepidation dissolved. It seemed that, despite all her success, Lady Marwood still entertained thoughts of uncertainty, making her less of an exalted personage and more human.

"You came in your own carriage?" Lord Marwood asked Kit. In response to Kit's nod, Lord Marwood continued, "We'll meet you at our modest cottage in a quarter of an hour. And mind," he added, holding up a finger, "we *won't* race this time. Had to pay the constabulary a ruddy fortune because we nearly ran the poor sod down."

"Thank God he could jump far," Kit answered. "We'll reconnoiter shortly."

His arm slid around Tamsyn's shoulders and he guided her away. Pinwheels spun in her belly at his touch. She simply couldn't get used to his nearness or the feel of him. She'd hoped that, by now, his good looks would have mellowed in her eyes, but precisely the opposite had happened. He had only to look at her or take her hand and her heart rate leapt.

He'd been so attentive tonight, so concerned for her happiness, and an excellent companion. Her husband treated her with respect but not cringing deference.

The longer she knew him, the more handsome he seemed to become.

More than a few actresses and dancers stared at him as he and Tamsyn made their way through the backstage. Tartly, Tamsyn wondered how many of them had been his lovers—and how many wanted that role for themselves. Her reticence might drive him right into their arms.

Last night, aroused by his kiss, she'd lain in bed and all but smoldered between the crisp cotton sheets. When she'd seen the light beneath the door that adjoined their rooms, she had been sorely tempted to go to him and end their celibacy.

But she hadn't.

Once she and Kit emerged from backstage, the audience had thinned out in the rest of the theater. A group of young men lingered near the stage entrance, presumably waiting for the female performers to come out.

Kit had been one of those men, not so long ago, but he barely considered them as he escorted her toward the exit.

Their carriage stood outside the theater and he guided her to it. When the footman moved to help her into the vehicle, Kit stepped forward and offered her his hand, instead. "My lady," he murmured. She blushed at the wicked promise in his tone.

"You make an excellent footman," she said after they were both ensconced in the carriage.

"Good to know I have a career to fall back on, should this whole earl business come a cropper." He stretched out his long legs as he sat opposite her then rapped on the roof to signal they were ready to depart.

"You've been an earl for several months," she objected as the carriage pulled away. "They won't take the title away from you."

"I've learned that, in this life, it's best not to take anything for granted." He looked sardonic. "Expectation leads to disappointment."

She said nothing, but could not stop herself from wondering what his expectations of her might be—and what she wanted from him. At first, she'd wanted only a husband with money who paid her little mind. But now, with Kit, she sensed she wanted much more from him. She wanted his wit, his intelligence, his joy in simply experiencing the world.

Tamsyn wanted *him*, and that frightened her far more than any raid by the customs officers.

Chapter 15

✦

*T*amsyn tried to maintain a calm outward appearance, though she was all but vibrating with nervousness and excitement. From a private theater box to a viscount's residence in one night was a far cry from her usual sedate evenings at home curled up with a book.

Other than the nights she smuggled, of course. Those were a touch more eventful than reading.

The carriage came to a stop on Mount Street, outside an impressively large residence. Tamsyn fairly gawked at the size of the place as she stepped onto the curb.

"You neglected to mention that your friend has a sprawling mansion," she said drily to Kit when he stood beside her.

Kit smirked as he gazed at Lord Marwood's home. "Likely overcompensating for his masculine deficiencies."

She coughed at his outrageous comment, then rallied enough to note, "The viscountess seemed rather satisfied with her husband—deficiencies or no."

Kit chuckled and led her toward the front entrance. She felt his hand warm at the small of her back and his solicitous concern, causing warmth to travel all the way through her.

A butler stood waiting by the open door.

"It wasn't so long ago that Marwood hosted London's most notorious parties in this very house," Kit noted. "All that changed when he proposed to Lady Marwood right onstage in front of half the city."

"He didn't!"

"I assure you, he did. I saw it myself. One of the most romantic things anyone's ever witnessed," he muttered, so low Tamsyn barely heard him, "I should ask him for advice."

Just as they crossed the threshold, the viscount and his wife came forward.

"So brigands didn't kidnap you, thank the heavens," Lord Marwood said with a grin.

"They wouldn't dare attempt it," Kit answered. "Not with my rapier-like wit to slice them into ribbons."

"A fearsome weapon, indeed," Lady Marwood agreed with mock solemnity.

"Welcome to my home, Lady Blakemere," her husband said, and bowed.

Tamsyn curtsied. "This is no modest cottage. I could dock a boat in here." She eyed the foyer ceiling that soared above them. "You were having me on, my lord. I didn't know London gentry played so loosely with the truth."

"My lady, you wound me." Lord Marwood pressed a hand to his chest. He glanced at Kit. "Did you know you married such a cruel woman?"

Kit's gaze was warm as he looked at her, and she felt a blossom of pleasure in response. "Lady Blakemere is insightful but never cruel. At least," he added, "I hope to never give her reason to unleash her cruelty, which I'm certain is more devastating than any twelve-pounder."

"Perhaps a tour of our cellars will round any sharp edges." Lord Marwood waved toward a corridor branching off the foyer. "Unto the breach."

He grabbed a lit candelabra, and then he and Lady Marwood led the way. They strode past vast rooms and an abundance of beautiful things—silver, porcelain, paintings—that spoke of an ancient lineage. Watching the viscountess walk beside the viscount, their hands clasped, Tamsyn had to wonder what it must be like to come from a commoner's background into this eminent opulence.

They were somewhat alike, Lady Marwood and herself. Though her family's baronial title was an old and distinguished one, Tamsyn had little experience with the dazzling life of a titled Londoner. Now that she was Lady Blakemere, a countess, she'd have to get used to it. It seemed as though Lady Marwood had become comfortable with her surroundings—though it helped that she was her husband's beloved.

She stole a glance at Kit's profile. Would he ever look at Tamsyn the way Lord Marwood looked at Lady Marwood? And, more importantly, did Tamsyn *want* him to?

"Down into the depths we go," Lord Marwood said when they reached the top of a staircase leading toward the basement. "If I was in one of Maggie's burlettas, I'd be leading you toward my hidden abattoir where I take all my hapless victims."

"But then my heroine would cosh you over the head with a statue," Lady Marwood said decisively as they proceeded downward. "Thus liberating the ghosts of your victims."

"I like the way your mind works, my lady," Tamsyn declared. "Let the heroine save herself."

"But what shall us poor males do if we're not needed to wave our swords around and feel important?" Kit asked.

"We'll just have to find other uses for our swords," Lord Marwood said with a roguish smile.

At last, they reached the basement, and Lord Marwood made his way past the kitchen and pantries. He took them to a heavy door. After removing a key from his pocket, he unlocked the door and pushed it open. Cool, slightly damp air rushed out, reminding her of the caverns beneath Chei Owr.

"Enter, my friends," he said magnanimously, directing them forward. "The spirits you will find inside are of the benevolent variety." He strode in, then set the candelabra on a low counter, illuminating the space.

It was a square, windowless room, roughly ten feet by ten feet. Shelves lined two of the walls, on which stood a proliferation of bottles filled with various shades of amber liquid. Tamsyn estimated the value of the cellar's contents at hundreds of pounds, if not thousands. No wonder Lord Marwood kept the key on his person.

"Ah, I almost forgot!" Their host darted out of the cellar and returned moments later with four glasses, which he arrayed on the counter beside the candelabra. "We won't pretend to be pirates and drink straight from the bottles."

He walked to one of the walls covered in bottles and studied them like a man in a circulating library. "Where to begin . . ." he mused aloud. "Ah!" He pulled a bottle from its spot on a shelf.

Lord Marwood poured two fingers of amber liquid into each waiting glass, then handed them around with the genial air of a taproom host.

Kit lifted his glass. "To the ladies," he announced. "Whether they need us or not, we need them." His gaze held hers, and she basked in the tenderness in his look.

"To the ladies," everyone repeated. The glasses clinked together with a chime.

After studying her whisky for a moment, enjoying the color of the drink, she brought it to her nose and inhaled. "Smells of . . . green apples and . . . honey," she said between sniffs.

"So it does," Kit agreed.

Everyone took a sip. The rich, creamy whisky lingered long on the tongue and warmed gently on the way down.

"This is from a distillery on the Dornoch Firth," Lord Marwood explained. "North of Inverness."

"I taste a bit of chocolate," Lady Marwood noted, and her husband nodded in agreement.

"If given a choice between drinking cordial water every day or having just one sip of this for the rest of my life," Kit declared, "then give me this."

The others also drank the last of their whiskies, and in short order, Lord Marwood returned to the shelves to make their next selection.

"This one's from Islay, an island in the Hebrides." He brought a bottle forward.

"How have you amassed such a collection, Lord Marwood?" Tamsyn asked.

"Got a man on retainer who searches for spirits far and wide and brings 'em back to me every few months. Malcolm Ross—a genuine Scottish laird with an ancient but poor lineage. Met him one wild night in Edinburgh. Of course, I was a bachelor at the time. But he had such a skill with finding the best bottles, I hired him on the spot." He poured out four deep golden glasses. "I take my hedonism seriously."

"Surely you could find sellers of quality liquor here in London," she objected, stunned by the extravagance.

"He could," Lady Marwood answered. "But there's no fun in something so ordinary. Right, my love?" She winked at her husband.

"What astonishes you, Lady Blakemere?" Lord Marwood asked. "The cost or my eccentricity?"

Tamsyn glanced at Kit, who watched her carefully. She chose her words with deliberation, perceiving that her answer meant a great deal to him. "One has to weigh something's price against one's happiness."

"Which wins?" Kit asked, his look penetrating.

"It has to be assessed case by case," she answered after a moment.

His jaw firmed and he glanced away.

She sensed her response didn't quite satisfy him, and it made her wonder if he was thinking of something in particular when he'd asked his question. But what could it be? She longed to peel away the many layers of her husband to find the man behind the playfulness.

"This one smells sweet," Lady Marwood said, interrupting the silence. She delicately sniffed her glass. "Like molasses."

After taking a sip, Tamsyn noted, "Yet it tastes smoky."

"Almost savory," the viscountess added.

Lord Marwood chuckled. "It starts as dessert and finishes as dinner."

Kit's frown smoothed as he rejoined the conversation. "Which is what I preferred when I was a child. Pudding first, then roast."

"And now?" Tamsyn pressed, eager for any bit of information about him. "Which do you favor—sweets or savories?"

"No preference," he replied. "So long as something tastes good, my appetite isn't easily sated." His seductive smile heated her far more than the whisky. She knew the alluring power of his lips, and could still feel his kiss from last night.

I want that kiss again. I want so much more.

Tamsyn hid her reaction by taking another drink. The whisky was easy to swallow, and by the time she saw the bottom of her glass, she felt a pleasant looseness through her body, as if all her burdens had been taken away.

She looked at her husband and a surge of feeling moved through her. He was so kind, so giving. Would he mind if she wrapped her arms around him and simply held him tight? But she kept her arms at her sides, uncertain how he'd react to a semipublic embrace.

"One more whisky!" Lord Marwood declared. He hummed to himself while he picked out another bottle. "The malt in this one's triple distilled. Comes from the Scottish Lowlands, near Glasgow."

As before, Lord Marwood served up the drink, but he was getting far more generous with his pours as the evening progressed. Tamsyn didn't want to be rude, yet as she eyed the amount of honey-hued whisky she had to drink, she feared she'd be well in her cups before too long.

"Reminds me of Christmas oranges," Kit said after he took a sip.

"And almonds," Tamsyn noted, then gave a small hiccup. The others laughed quietly at her approaching inebriation. But she didn't feel embarrassed and drank her liquor.

When she finished her glass, the room seemed to have unmoored itself from gravity, drifting gently about the world. Or maybe that was her head. She wasn't entirely certain.

"What did you think of the dancers tonight at the Imperial?" Lady Marwood asked Tamsyn. "Did you like the music?"

"Only the fiddlers at the Tipsy Flea play better," Tamsyn declared. "That's our public house, you know, in Newcombe. The Tipsy Flea. Everyone gathers there after a night of—"

She slammed her mouth shut. God, she'd been so close to simply blurting out her secret. Tamsyn glared at her empty glass. Damn that tongue-loosening whisky.

Lady Marwood continued, her own words slurring slightly, "Bloody good tune, methinks. I won't sing it, on account of me sounding like an ill cat, but I can hum with the best of them." She hummed a melody and thumped her hand upon the counter in a rhythmic beat. It was a reel that made Tamsyn's toes tap.

"Shall we dance, Blakemere?" Lord Marwood set down his glass, then bowed at Kit.

"I would be charmed, Marwood," Kit answered loftily, performing his own bow.

The two men hooked elbows and spun around the small room in time with Lady Marwood's humming. Tamsyn clapped along as they danced, her smile making it impossible to add her voice to the impromptu music.

Kit twirled away from Marwood and toward her. Before she knew what was happening, she was in his arms, whirling around the cellar. Lord and Lady Marwood also embraced as they took up the dance.

But Tamsyn only saw and felt Kit. His grip was sure and steady, and the solidness of his body surrounded her. He beamed at her, his smile turning his handsome face into something wondrous. She couldn't stop the laugh that broke from her lips. Free—she felt free.

Was it the drink or Kit that made her head spin? She didn't know and it didn't matter. All that mattered was this moment, her charming, thoughtful husband holding her, dancing with her.

"We partner well," he said as they moved. "Should dance together more often."

She had no answer for him, turning with him, feeling the strength of his body and the brightness of his essence.

"One more drink!" Lord Marwood cried. He strode on not quite steady legs to the array of bottles. He pulled one out that was a little rounder and squatter than the others, its contents a dark, gleaming gold. "Armagnac from Gascony." Four more glasses were poured. "A little more bold and fiery than Charente cognac."

Tamsyn and Kit pulled apart slowly, but his heat lingered as it resonated through her. The room continued to move as she went to pick up her glass.

The first sip and its flavors of caramel and ripe pears brought her immediately back to Newcombe. This was a taste she knew well—French brandy. Many times had she felt its warmth on her tongue, taking a celebratory drink after a successful run. The faces of so many friends and allies would grow rosy with each toast, until they all staggered into the night, seeking home.

Her eyes felt hot as she blinked back tears. She missed everyone so much. She missed home. But she was fighting for them, for all of them.

They'd like this Armagnac, though. It was exceptional. At Newcombe, they mostly moved cognac brandy of decent but not exceptional quality. She could drink rather a lot of this Armagnac.

"Oh, this is—" She shut her lips, once more preventing herself from giving away too much. They would all be suspect if she pointed out that the drink had to be from Bas-Armagnac, rather than Haut-Armagnac or La Ténarèze. "This is good," she finished awkwardly, then moved to tip back the rest of her drink.

Kit's hand stayed her. "Supper was a long time ago," he said gently as she swayed on her feet.

She tried to focus her gaze on him, but the cursed man insisted on being hazy. "Was it?"

"Yes—hours, and you haven't had much to eat since then." He carefully plucked the glass from her hand and set it on the counter. "Let's be charming guests and leave before Lord and Lady Marwood find us tiresome."

"We'd never do that," Lady Marwood pronounced. Her cheeks were flushed and she leaned against her husband. "Would we, Cam?"

"Never." Lord Marwood pressed a kiss to the crown

of her head. "But I think we're all a trifle tired from the night's adventures. We'll see you out."

It was quite complicated to walk down the hall, and climbing up the stairs required all of Tamsyn's skill. Kit's hand was warm and solid on her lower back as he helped her ascend. He offered encouragement with every step.

"Just lift your foot a little," he coaxed, "there's a lass. One more. And again. There! The heights have been conquered." He put an arm around her shoulders when they reached the top of the steps.

Victorious, she lifted her arms into the air while Lady Marwood clapped. "I am the vanquisher of stairwells! Look ye, and tremble at my might!" Goodness, but her Cornish accent sounded stronger even to her own ears.

"Our carriage waits, mighty one." Kit kept pace beside her as helped her to the front door. He was like a knight of old, her husband. Pure chivalry.

A sleepy footman was there with hats and coats, while Lord Marwood mused, "I don't know why they say married life is dull. We always have a rollicking good time, don't we, Maggie?"

"The very *best* of times, my love." She stood on tiptoe to give her husband an extremely enthusiastic kiss, which Lord Marwood returned. For a moment, it seemed as though they had forgotten about Tamsyn and Kit entirely, particularly when Lady Marwood's fingers began undoing the buttons of Lord Marwood's waistcoat.

Tamsyn watched with longing.

"Let's leave them to it," Kit murmured, then guided her out the open door.

"Good night!" Tamsyn called over her shoulder. "Thank you for the"—she hiccuped again—"refreshments." She giggled at her own wit.

It took a small amount of intricate choreography to get into the carriage. She toppled in before clambering onto the seat. Kit did the same difficult maneuver with enviable effortlessness.

"How do you do that?" she accused as Kit settled into the seat opposite her. "Make everything look so easy?"

He rapped on the carriage ceiling and they were off. "It takes a good deal of work to appear graceful."

"Always so ruddy handsome and strong," she muttered.

"You think me handsome?" He asked this lightly, as if her answer didn't matter. But his look was keen and curious.

"You know I do, scoundrel. And I know that makes you happy." Yet she swam in affection for the good-looking rogue. She patted the cushions beside her. "Come here."

He looked as though he considered refusing, but then the carriage tilted as he moved next to her. Their thighs pressed securely against each other, and she was aware of every fiber and sinew in his body. Wanting to feel more of Kit, she wrapped her arms around his bicep, her breasts snugly fitting to him.

"That's another thing," she announced. "You feel brawny like a laborer, but you're not. No man can have muscles like these just from being a rakehell." She squeezed the unyielding mass of his arm.

"Perhaps wenching and wine keep a man fit," he offered. She made a rude noise, so he went on. "On Mondays and Thursdays I go to a fencing academy. Tuesdays and Fridays are for pugilism."

"And Wednesday, Saturday, and Sunday?" she demanded.

His grin flashed. "There are other kinds of exercise."

"You mean the *horizontal* sort," she deduced. She poked a finger into his solid chest. "How much of that exercise have you gotten lately?"

"That sounds suspiciously like jealousy, Lady Blakemere," he said wryly.

"No jealousy, right? That's the rule." She blew a strand

of loose hair from her face. She added sullenly, "I always break the rules."

"My lady," he said softly, putting a fingertip beneath her chin, "if you've want of my amorous services, you have only to demand them, and they're yours."

In response, she released his arm and grabbed the back of his head. "Kiss me."

He carefully pulled her hands away and set them on his chest. "No need for an attack, my love. I'm not running away. Here. Like this." He lowered his head and softly, gently, took her lips with his. Then he pulled back just enough to ask, "Better, yes?"

"More," she murmured.

He brought his mouth down on hers. This time, there was greater heat and intent. She responded at once, all of the pent-up yearning and emotion within her rising to the surface. He tasted delicious and masculine, kissing her skillfully. But then his restraint seemed to slip, and he nipped at her, as though unable to control his desire. She loved his loss of control, that she could inspire him to forget what he knew and simply respond naturally. When his tongue slipped between her lips and stroked hers, she moaned, opening for him.

Her concern about this, about what his touch would do to her, was forgotten. Who cared about sheltering her heart? All she knew was her body's needs and her soul's yearning for Kit.

His hand skimmed up along her ribs. She held her breath, waiting for his touch. At last, he cupped her breast, and no sensation had ever been better. His finger circled her taut nipple. She gasped with pleasure.

Then he was gone.

She opened her eyes to find him staring at her ravenously, his breath coming fast.

"Don't stop," she said.

"Three whiskies and one brandy equal an inability to control one's faculties." His voice was low and rough. "If you want me like this when you're sober, we'll take up where we left off."

Before she could complain, he moved to the rear-facing seat. He winced a little as he sat, and Tamsyn risked a glance at his crotch. The front of his breeches tented. Shock and arousal battled within her to see how he was affected.

She pressed a hand to her vertiginous head. The rocking of the carriage made her dizziness worse.

"Close your eyes, love," he said. "If there's anything to be said, it should wait for a more sober moment."

"Wise," she murmured, her lids drifting shut as she leaned against the side of the carriage. "You're a wise man, Kit."

"Only sometimes," he answered, his voice sounding quite dry.

The next time Tamsyn opened her eyes, she was in his arms. The ceiling above looked vaguely familiar before she realized that they'd arrived home at some point. He now carried her upstairs.

She kept her lashes lowered, so he wouldn't know that she was awake.

How easily he supported her! She felt his strength as he took the stairs without struggle, even though she was sprawled in his arms.

In a few moments, they had reached her room. Kit walked to the bed, then gently laid her down atop the covers. She held still as his steady hands undid the ribbons of her slippers. He pulled the shoes from her feet and, presumably, set them on the ground.

She thought that with his duty discharged, he would leave. Instead, he came back around the side of the bed and gazed down at her with an unreadable expression. He brushed a few strands of hair off her forehead, yet made no other move to touch her.

Kit exhaled. "Right," he said softly. Then he turned and left, shutting the door quietly behind him.

She lay in bed, unmoving. The only sound in the room was the crackle of the fire and the tick of the clock.

The sound reminded her of important obligations. Despite Jory's dislike of letters, she'd written him early in the day asking that he wait before selling Chei Owr to any prospective buyers because she had a lead on one here in London. That would have to do until she could find some way to return to Cornwall and offer for the house herself.

Then, using coded language, she'd sent another note this morning to the fence recommended by footman Liam. Mr. Jayne had responded also using veiled words, agreeing to meet her tomorrow. Getting out of the house without attracting too much of Kit's attention would be a challenge.

He'd been so attentive tonight, so focused on her enjoyment and her needs. And he'd been honorable, too, in refusing to take advantage of her inebriated state. Her heart and body craved him powerfully as though he'd taken up space beside her very bones. And her lonely, tender soul wanted everything he could give her—companionship, affection, respect.

Against her better judgment, she was developing feelings for him. Dangerous feelings.

Chapter 16

"*I* have an errand to run," Tamsyn announced off-handedly.

Sitting at the breakfast table, Kit looked up from sorting through a stack of invitations. After their appearance at the theater, word had apparently gotten out that he and his new wife were out in public. Now he and Tamsyn received invitations by the heap, including social functions with some of the *ton*'s most respected figures. When he'd been a bachelor, the requests for his presence had come with a little less frequency, likely because everyone knew he wouldn't go anywhere that was part of the Season's sanctioned events.

Tamsyn gazed at him with an easy smile, the morning light painting her in soft hues as she sat beside him at the table. She showed no signs of her worry that, after last night's heated kiss, he'd lunge across the table and ravish her in the breakfast room.

He was still reeling from it, how fast and hot the desire between them could rise up. He'd known from the beginning that they shared a powerful chemistry, and to his surprise, he saw that the more he knew of her, the more he desired her.

Kit felt himself set at a constant simmer. He'd been

chaste for too long, having had to resort to hard, fast wanks before being able to fall asleep. Yet more than that, he wanted to know what would happen once he and Tamsyn finally let go—and how brightly they would burn.

She had to feel the attraction between them, too—last night had shown him that. Unguarded, she'd given voice to and acted on the pull of desire that had them circling each other like hawks in a mating dance. Now she gazed at him with warm familiarity, either pretending that last night hadn't happened or that it didn't affect her.

He wanted her, yes, and he craved having her close. He yearned to wake up beside her and hold her closely as she stirred from sleep. Kit had always believed it the height of banality to discuss dreams, and yet he wanted to hear his wife's. Did she journey to places of happiness or fear? And if she did dream of fearful things, he wanted to be there beside her to offer comfort.

Despite her relaxed manner today, she was a little pale, most likely from the aftereffects of drink. He was slightly tender in the head this morning, but he'd developed a strong constitution when it came to alcohol. Still, despite recovering from intoxication, she'd risen at a decent time—which was notably different from ninety-five percent of the *ton*, sober or crapulous.

"I can accompany you," he answered. It might provide more insight into who she was—though after the last few nights, he recognized her courage and determination.

"You'd find it dull," she replied lightly. "And a carriage is a very uncomfortable place to take a nap."

"Anything dull I can make amusing." He'd gotten through the worst of the War's tedium by finding ways to entertain his men. They'd have knife-throwing contests, and dirty rhyme competitions, or else Kit would challenge them to see who found the most weevils in their bread. No prizes were given out—what with all things of value being in short supply—but winning bragging rights could often spur someone to great heights.

Tamsyn rose from her chair and strolled toward the door. "This would strain even your ability to be diverted. I'll take Nessa. I should be home sometime this afternoon."

"Are you interested in any of these?" He gestured to the stack of invitations. "There are no fewer than five different balls, fetes, and dinners requesting our presence." At her profoundly disinterested expression, he said, "Quite right. It's all a lot of tedium. Let's dine alone together tonight."

A flush of pleasure stole into her cheeks. "I'd like that."

"We'll see each other later, then?" He couldn't keep the eagerness out of his voice.

"Look for me," she answered. "I'll be the one in lavender."

"Thank God you told me, or else I'd have trouble picking you out from all the other redheaded countesses milling about the dining room."

Their shared smile warmed him everywhere, from the tips of his fingers to his smallest toes.

Before he could say another word, she had gone.

He sat alone with the invitations, trying to make sense of his excitement over tonight. The moments with her seemed all too brief, and he found himself wanting more and more.

Yet he sensed that part of her remained hidden from him. She seemed as private as a fairy guarding enchanted treasure beneath the earth. He could ask her questions and hope she'd reveal herself to him, or he could learn more about her.

Intelligence gathering had been part of the war effort. More than once, Kit and some of his most skilled men had gone in search of information, tailing the enemy while keeping hidden so that he might gain important knowledge about troop placements or the strength of the enemy's defenses.

This was peacetime. One simply didn't *spy* on other people—especially one's wife.

On the other hand, if he didn't find out more about Tamsyn, wooing her became that much more difficult and the pleasure garden would remain out of reach.

He exhaled heavily at the dilemma. Ethics versus the attainment of his dream.

After a moment, he got to his feet and hurried upstairs. In the hallway, he heard Tamsyn speaking with her maid as the two of them got ready to leave. He darted into his room, grabbed a hat and coat, and sped downstairs, his conscience pricking him all the while.

To the footman by the door he said, "If Lady Blakemere asks, I went to White's." It was far too early for anyone of interest to be at the club, but it was unlikely that she would know that. "I'm leaving the carriage for her use."

"Yes, my lord."

With that, Kit threw on his coat and hat and left. He hurried down the block before hailing a cab.

"Where to, my lord?" the driver asked as Kit neared.

"In a few minutes, a carriage is going to pull in front of that house," he answered, pointing at his own front door. "After a woman gets in the carriage and drives off, I want you to follow it."

"Here now," the driver said fretfully, "I don't cotton to following ladies, especially them of quality."

"She's my damned *wife*." Kit spoke between his teeth. He didn't need anyone reminding him that what he was about to do wasn't precisely ethical. Clamping down on his principles, he handed the driver a shiny guinea. "There's more in it for you, so long as you stay on top of the carriage, avoid being seen, and keep your opinions to yourself."

The cabman's brows rose, but he nodded in agreement. "Get in, my lord."

Kit clambered into the cab and prepared himself for a short wait. He drummed his fingers on the seat, tamping down his unease. Following Tamsyn was an impulse. He wasn't entirely certain what it might yield, but he had to believe it was better trying to discover who she was than simply retreating into habitual self-indulgence. He could argue with his morals later, after he'd purchased the land for the pleasure garden.

His thoughts snapped to the present when Tamsyn emerged from the house with her maid. She glanced up and down the street before a footman helped her into the carriage. With a flick of the reins, the vehicle pulled away from the curb.

"This is your cue," Kit called up to the driver.

"Right, my lord." The cabman clicked to the horse and flicked the ribbons. In a moment, they were in pursuit.

Kit watched the passing scenery with an alert eye. Would she be heading to Bond Street? The shops on Oxford Street, or maybe Covent Garden? She had a fortune at her disposal and despite her concern over money, she could buy anything she wanted.

The cab followed the carriage into the City, until they reached Clerkenwell. Jeweler's shops were abundant here—which made sense now that he thought about it. Tamsyn seemed to own almost no jewelry or adornments. Most likely, if there were any family treasures, her uncle and aunt had control over them.

The carriage came to a stop on a side street. Kit called up to his driver, "Pull over here."

When the cab halted, Kit jumped out and threw money

at the driver. Then he hurried back toward the narrow lane.

He peered around the corner, watching the carriage. A footman got down from the back of the vehicle and opened the door for Tamsyn, who stepped out cautiously. Again, she glanced up and down the street, which seemed a curious thing to do, until he recalled that she was unfamiliar with the City and was most likely acquainting herself with her surroundings.

Her maid descended the carriage and, together, they walked down the street.

Keeping a safe distance back, Kit followed.

TAMSYN paused in front of a jewelry shop, drawn by the display of earbobs arranged in the window. Baubles seldom caught her eye, but these were so brilliant she had to admire them.

"Fine bit of stone to have hanging on one's ears," Nessa murmured beside her. "You could get yourself a pair."

"They're so frivolous," Tamsyn answered.

"Can afford to be frivolous now," her friend pointed out.

"I—" Tamsyn's words died as she spied a familiar figure in the glass. She didn't dare turn around to investigate, but then she peered closer at the man's reflected image and cursed.

"What is it, dove?" Nessa asked.

"My husband," Tamsyn replied through her teeth. "He's on the other side of the street. Half-hidden behind a cart. Don't look," she warned. Damn—she thought he'd gone to his club.

Nessa's eyes were round. "What's he doing here?"

"I don't know." Perhaps it was only a coincidence. He had no known reason to follow her. Unless he suspected her of something. Had he talked to Mr. Stockton, or Liam and Dennis?

"He can't know where we're going," Nessa said urgently.

"He won't." Tamsyn wasn't quite as certain as her words implied. "Stick close to me."

Feigning casualness, she turned from the window and ambled down the street. The trick was losing Kit without him knowing that she'd done so on purpose. She stopped periodically in front of shops, all the while keeping track of him surreptitiously. He maintained a degree of distance, but was always nearby.

Hellfire, he *was* following her.

She walked into one of the jeweler's shops and contrived interest in the wares before leaving. She did this twice more. At the fourth establishment, a clerk came over to her.

"How may I be of assistance, my lady?" he asked.

"Does this shop have a back door?"

The clerk seemed puzzled by her request, but said, "It does. Straight through the curtains, down the hall, and then there's a door that opens onto an alley."

"Thank you." She held up a twopence. "If anyone asks after me, I was never here."

"Yes, my lady," he said, quickly pocketing the coin. He held the curtain back for her, and she swept into the corridor, with Nessa following.

Within moments, they were in a narrow, brick-lined alley, the cobblestones slick at their feet. Tamsyn hastened down the narrow passageway until she reached its end, which opened onto a street. After giving the street a thorough inspection and finding no sign of Kit, she consulted a map that she had tucked in her reticule.

Once oriented, she walked with quick, decisive steps toward her destination.

KIT waited across the street, using a newspaper to shield his face. Minutes passed. Tamsyn and her maid didn't emerge. Perhaps something had caught her eye, and she was arranging for its purchase.

Yet time stretched on until a full half an hour passed.

Curious, Kit made his way to the shop and glanced through the glass. Inside, a gentleman in a long coat examined a case of watch chains, attended by a clerk, yet there were no women inside.

The hell with caution. Kit entered the shop, and the clerk greeted him.

"Excuse me," Kit asked, stepping beside the other customer. "Did a redheaded woman and her maid come in here?"

"No, my lord," the young clerk answered.

Strange. Kit could have sworn that *this* was the shop she'd entered. He drifted out of the jeweler's and stood on the curb, looking up and down Turnmill Street. But there was no sign of Tamsyn or her maid. It was as if both women had vanished.

Where had his wife gone?

You've gone and spied on her—for nothing.

Not for nothing. I've learned something very important about her: despite her frugality, she craves something pretty and frivolous. That's a significant discovery.

He had to believe it was worth it.

"THIS is it," Tamsyn said quietly to Nessa.

The sign outside read, A. JAYNE, PURVEYOR OF FINE JEWELRY, WATCHES, &C.

A bell rang as they stepped inside the jewelry shop. The sound matched her jangling pulse as she fought to keep her expression calm.

It had been close, very close with Kit. Thank God she'd lost him in the maze of London streets. She would have to think about his reasons for following her, but not now. Not here.

She didn't know much about the world inhabited by the upper echelons. But she'd been a part of the criminal sphere for years. Stepping inside a fence's front felt natural and comfortable. Yet she didn't feel too at ease—so much was at stake.

Tamsyn glanced about curiously. She hadn't truly paid attention to the interiors of the other jewelry shops, too focused on shaking Kit. After her experience with the tanner and his stinking booth weeks ago, the elegant luxury of A. Jayne's showroom came as a surprise.

"*Areah,*" Nessa exclaimed softly. "Don't see much like this back home. Not even in Penzance."

"Or Newquay," Tamsyn agreed in a low voice.

A plush Oriental carpet covered the floor, and polished brass fittings gleamed in the sunlight. Locked glass cases were arranged atop wooden counters. The contents of the displays dazzled with their brilliant array of gold and silver, pearls and diamonds, all arrayed on black velvet-covered cushions. Though she was here on a different kind of business, she found herself drifting to one case with an array of necklaces. They ranged in design from large and showy to delicate and understated.

One in particular caught her eye. It was a fine gold chain with a single teardrop pearl pendant. Next to the other pieces, it seemed almost plain. But the simplicity of the design highlighted the iridescent allure of the pearl. It reminded her of the white foam atop the waves as they rushed toward the shore.

"A good eye you've got."

Tamsyn looked up at the man standing behind the counter, gazing at her expectantly. He had dark brown skin and black hair that was going silver at the temples. Dressed finely but soberly, he sported a very stylish watch chain draped over his waistcoat, and a ruby ring glinted on his right hand.

"Most people go for the diamonds and emeralds," the man continued. "It takes discernment to appreciate pearls."

"Are you Mr. Jayne?" Tamsyn asked.

"I am," he answered with a nod. "Alfonse Jayne, and this is my establishment. That lass over there," he continued, pointing at a girl of about twelve years who was wiping down one of the cases, "is my daughter, Lydia."

Tamsyn nodded at the girl, who shyly curtsied in response.

"Your shop is lovely," Tamsyn said, turning back to Mr. Jayne.

He smiled broadly. "Make everything in the back, myself and my wife. The finest diamonds from Brazil and gold from the Balkans." He looked at her attentively as he rested his hands on the back of the case. "Is there something special you're shopping for today, madam?"

"Today is not for shopping." She drew in a breath. "Today is for selling."

A faint frown appeared between Mr. Jayne's eyebrows. "Are you a dealer of gems?"

She leaned forward and said very quietly, "Not gems, but items that you might find of interest. Continental items— from France, specifically."

His expression shifted slightly, smoothing out and becoming unreadable. He walked quickly to the door and locked it, then returned to her.

"You wrote me yesterday. You're the one from Cornwall," he said briskly. "With the lace and brandy."

She nodded. "A shipment is on its way now, and looking for buyers. It will be in London before week's end."

"Go in the back, Lydia," Mr. Jayne said to his daughter. At once, the girl obeyed, disappearing behind a heavy door. Turning back to Tamsyn, he continued, his expression slightly distant. "Your letter didn't indicate your sex.

I wasn't expecting a Cornish *woman*. When it comes to moving contraband, I don't usually work with females."

Tamsyn straightened. "If you don't want to do business with me on the basis of my gender, you'll be losing out on substantial profits—profits I'm happy to take elsewhere."

She didn't have a lead on another dealer, but Mr. Jayne didn't need to know that. Thankfully, Nessa held her tongue.

He appeared unconvinced. "What sort of inventory will I be expecting?"

"Nearly five hundred gallons of brandy. And fifty yards of Chantilly lace. All of it would fetch fine coin here in London." She pulled the flask from her reticule. "A sample of the brandy."

Mr. Jayne took a sip, then nodded thoughtfully as he handed the flask back to her. "And when would all this arrive?"

"By the end of the week, no later," Tamsyn answered. "You'd have time to line up buyers."

He stroked his chin and was silent. Tamsyn gazed at him with what she hoped was perfect indifference. She'd played this game before and knew the rules.

"People are tired of the War's deprivations," she said casually. "They want to indulge and spoil themselves. You'll have no trouble moving my goods, with a generous profit for you and your family."

After another pause, he said, "I know half a dozen members of Parliament who'll want that brandy. Their wives will want the lace."

Silently, Tamsyn exhaled.

Mr. Jayne looked past her to Nessa. "You. Come to me when the shipment arrives. We'll make a plan on moving the goods out for sale."

"Aye, sir," Nessa answered.

"In the interim," Tamsyn added, "you'll find buyers." She stuck out her hand. "Seal the bargain?"

He glanced down at her outstretched hand, then shook it. "For a woman, you have a good head for this trade."

Tamsyn bit back a tart reply. Now wasn't the time for upbraiding him about his bias. Instead, after shaking his hand, she headed toward the door. "Communication from me will turn up shortly."

"Pleasure doing business with you," he replied. He stepped forward and unlocked the door.

She gave him a nod, then moved out onto the curb with Nessa following. After giving the street one last look and finding only the usual tradespeople and shoppers and no sign of Kit, Tamsyn walked toward the waiting carriage.

They reached the vehicle without incident, and she allowed the footman to open the carriage door and help her inside. Nessa took the seat opposite her.

"Drive on," Tamsyn called up to the coachman.

Only when the carriage was in motion did she allow herself to fully relax, sinking back against the padded seat with a loud exhale.

"Nicely accomplished, my dove," Nessa said brightly. She patted Tamsyn's knee. "No need to fret. His lordship knows nothing. We've got our fence, and there's naught to do but bide your time. Then . . ." She rubbed her fingers together.

"First, the goods have to get here," Tamsyn reminded her. "There's the matter of storing it all, keeping the servants and Lord Blakemere from finding out, and getting people to buy everything."

Nessa clicked her tongue. "A worrier, you are."

"If I don't do it, who will?" Tamsyn glanced out the window. At least the first task was taken care of. And she'd done it without Kit's knowledge. Or so she hoped.

She pressed a hand to her chest, pushing back against

the thudding of her heart. All night, her thoughts had ricocheted back and forth between worry about securing a fence and reliving the kiss with Kit. It had been so potent, so seductive. Yet she couldn't attribute her distraction to the alcohol clouding her brain. In truth, all of her intoxication had been because of him.

It reverberated throughout her body. She could still taste him.

Once she had gotten with child, she could return to Cornwall. He would have his heir, and she'd go home to run the smuggling. With her situated far away, he'd take lovers.

Everyone would get what they wanted.

Wouldn't they?

Chapter 17

"Tamsyn."

Her eyes closed, she muttered and stirred. It had taken her so long to fall asleep last night. Now a man kept saying her name, forcing her out of fitful dreams.

"Tamsyn, wake up."

A hand rested on her shoulder, giving her a slight shake. Her eyelids dragged open, and Kit's face swam into focus.

Several moments passed before she registered what this meant. Kit was in her room. He sat on the edge of her bed, pale morning sunlight filtering through the windows behind him.

Consciousness hit her like a slap. She pushed herself upright, then rubbed her face, forcing back the heavy smoke of lethargy. Something had to be wrong, or else why would Kit be in her bedchamber, fully dressed, and up at—she squinted at the clock on the mantel—six in the morning?

"What is it?" She scanned his face for some sign, something to indicate what was happening or a hint at his mood, yet his expression was opaque.

"Get dressed," he said. "Quickly." He stood and loomed over the bed.

"Tell me what's going on," she urged.

"A surprise," he answered. "However, you must hurry. I'll wait for you downstairs in the foyer."

"I—"

But he was already striding out of the room, leaving her alone with her confusion.

She clambered out of bed and tugged the bellpull for Nessa. While she waited, she speedily took care of her morning needs, then began to wash.

As she worked a brush through her tangled hair, her thoughts tumbled over each other in hazy confusion. She'd returned home from her meeting with Mr. Jayne— and shaking Kit as he'd followed her—worried that she would find her husband distant and suspicious. But their dinner at home together had been altogether delightful. He'd entertained her late into the evening with tales of his youthful misadventures at school. When he'd pressed her for more about her life in Cornwall, she'd recounted her favorite legends about alluring mermaids and mischievous piskies.

After their meal, they'd gone to the drawing room and played piquet. It had turned into a game of who could cheat more outrageously, culminating in her finding a stash of aces tucked into the top of Kit's boot.

She'd thought he would try to kiss her again, but he hadn't. Instead, they'd gone to their separate beds, where she'd spent the night wondering if she'd merely imagined him following her earlier in the day. Everything was as snared as her hair, and she set the brush down in frustration, still mystified by Kit's strange appearance in her bedroom.

Nessa hastened in, clothed but her hair wasn't yet up. "A trifle early," she said with a hint of remonstrance, "even for you."

"Lord Blakemere woke me minutes ago," Tamsyn explained. She scrubbed a washcloth over her face. "Didn't tell me anything but I was to get dressed as soon as possible." A thousand probabilities ran through her mind, none of them good.

"Do you think he knows?" Nessa asked, going pale.

"He didn't say, and I can't read his bloody mind," Tamsyn snapped. Anxiety made her patience thin—but she regretted her tone the moment she spoke.

"All right, all right." Nessa delved into the wardrobe and removed a teal walking gown as well as the necessary underpinnings.

Tamsyn tried to calm her racing pulse as Nessa helped her into her clothes, including a russet-colored pelisse. Finally, when she was dressed, she grabbed a bonnet, jammed it on her head, and rushed out. Whatever was happening, it was best not to keep Kit waiting for long.

He stood at the foot of the stairs, already wearing his hat and coat. Drawing a deep breath, she tried to descend the steps with some grace, but her equanimity was difficult to hold on to when she could make out nothing in the lake-blue of Kit's eyes.

"The carriage is outside," he said when she stood before him.

"We're going somewhere?"

In response, he offered her his arm.

She planted her feet. "I'm not going anywhere unless you tell me what the deuce is happening."

"We're taking a short trip," he finally answered, "and that's all I can tell you."

She might control the purse strings, but he was her husband. Realizing that she had little choice, Tamsyn took his arm. A footman held the front door open, and they emerged onto a street that was just barely coming awake for the day. One laborer pulled a cart loaded with rags and buckets, and a milkmaid carried her pails hanging from a yoke. Certainly no one from fashionable London was about.

Kit waved her toward the carriage. There wasn't much to do besides climb in and take a seat, her limbs stiff. Once he had gotten in and knocked on the roof, the vehicle jolted into motion.

"Mrs. Hoskins had the cook pack a hamper," Kit said. He nodded at a covered basket on the floor. "Rolls and such, to break your fast."

"Thank you," Tamsyn answered, but her appetite had deserted her.

Neither spoke as the carriage rolled westward, passing through unfamiliar neighborhoods. Eventually, the buildings came with less and less frequency, with more stretches of green. Kit offered no commentary or guidance. He was unusually silent, save for drumming his fingertips on the edge of the window. Occasionally, he'd glance in her direction, yet she couldn't tell if his gaze was accusatory. Other than the time before they had gone to finalize the transfer of the fortune, she'd never seen him this preoccupied or distant.

Perhaps she hadn't lost him in the jewelry district, as she'd hoped. Perhaps he knew everything.

Was he taking her somewhere to confront her about her smuggling? Running her out of town? Or maybe he'd use his knowledge to wrest control of the fortune back to him.

The urge to confess hovered on her tongue. She hated having to keep lying to him, and if she told him everything, maybe he'd be lenient. Perhaps he could forgive her. At the least, maybe he wouldn't turn her in to the magistrate. He'd shown that he did care for her to some degree. Possibly that would be enough to keep her from prosecution.

Yet the confession remained merely an impulse, and she said nothing.

Finally, the carriage came to a stop. A medium-size town perched on either side of the river. Glancing out the window, she observed another river intersecting the Thames, with barges and other small craft moving up and down the water.

"Where are we?" she asked.

"Brentford," Kit answered. "The other body of water is the River Brent."

The footman opened the carriage door and waited, his hand extended. She had no alternative other than get out.

As she set foot on the ground, she scanned the area, looking for law enforcement. Perhaps Kit planned on having her arrested, but he didn't want to do it in the city where everyone could see her brought to justice.

When Kit stepped down from the carriage, she whirled on him.

"I need to know what's happening," she demanded. *"Now."*

"Turn around," he replied.

Slowly, she did so, expecting to see someone waiting to clap her in irons.

Instead, she looked at several small boats moored thirty feet away on a dock. They bobbed and swayed on diminutive waves, and their sails were furled. On one of the dinghies, an East Indian man was in the process of preparing the mainsail, making it ready to venture out on the water. As he did this, a fair-haired woman stood on the dock, watching as she held a basket. The man on the boat, dressed in a cap and the traditionally loose clothes of a sailor, caught sight of Kit and Tamsyn and waved.

Her husband nodded in an answering signal.

"Kit," Tamsyn said, trying to keep her voice level.

"That gentleman over there is Mr. Sanjay Singh," Kit

said. "One of the finest lascars to sail for the East India Company. The lady on the dock is his wife, Alice. I've hired Mr. Singh's services for the day, as well as the use of his ship."

"Boat," Tamsyn corrected automatically. "A ship has three or more square-rigged masts."

He blinked at her. "Ah. Yes. Well, I've engaged Mr. Singh's *boat* to sail us on the Thames today."

"But . . . why?"

"You're a Cornishwoman," Kit explained. "From a sea-side village. But you haven't been home for some time. I imagine you must be eager to escape crowded, noisy London and get out on the water. So," he finished, "here we are."

He fell abruptly silent, his expectant gaze fixed intently on her face.

It suddenly made sense. Kit's reserve and silence on the ride here. His refusal to tell her anything about their destination. Even his tenseness now.

He was anxious. He feared her response.

Because he wasn't planning to have her arrested or run her out of town. He'd arranged a special outing for her, to make her happy.

Her heart expanded, filling her chest. Inundated with emotion, she felt like laughing and weeping at the same time. Not since she'd lost her parents had anyone done something so thoughtful for her. No one had believed she was worth the effort. Yet Kit did.

The hard armor she'd carefully used to shield her from tender, vulnerable feelings fell away. He understood her. He cared.

It was the most precious gift she could have ever received.

"I can't think of a better way to spend the day," she said, and smiled. She squeezed his hand. "Thank you so much."

His tight, high shoulders visibly relaxed, and he grinned. "It pleases you?"

"Very much." Everything about him pleased her, most of all his innate kindness. He had been a soldier and seen untold horrors, and yet he hadn't lost his humanity or ability to give of himself.

He exhaled. "Thank God." Weaving their fingers together, he led her toward the waiting boat. "It's going to be a splendid excursion. Nothing has been left to chance."

Her throat tightened and her eyes became hot. The stiffness in her limbs ebbed away as her fear receded. He'd gone to so much trouble on her behalf. Each day, he'd worked so hard to make her happy. Today was no exception. He'd been generous and thoughtful and truly seemed to care about her. Her heart had responded, warming and opening to him.

At that moment, holding his hand, she felt herself falling, falling headlong into feelings that would not be held back.

$\mathcal{K}$IT fought to master his pleasure at seeing the happiness on his wife's face, but it was a losing battle. The last time he'd experienced this euphoria had been . . . Damn. He couldn't remember. It was as though his life had been divided into two distinct parts: before Tamsyn and after. The time before had been shrouded in fog and shadow, and the time after was luminosity and contentment.

He wanted to gift her the world—mansions and gowns and the stars themselves, if only to see the happiness in her eyes.

You haven't given her everything yet.

That would come later. All he had to concern himself with now was sailing and Tamsyn's enjoyment of it.

They approached the dock, and Mr. Singh climbed nimbly out of the boat.

"Everything is nearly ready, my lord," the lascar said after bowing. His wife bobbed a curtsy and glanced at the basket in her arms. "Mrs. Singh has prepared a fine luncheon to enjoy while you are on the water."

Tamsyn accepted the basket with a smile. "Can I help make ready the boat?"

"There is nothing for you to do, Lady Blakemere, except enjoy yourself," Mr. Singh answered. "This way, if you please." He waved them toward the waiting vessel.

Stepping into a rocking boat was not an easy task, but Mr. Singh helped both Kit and Tamsyn in. Cushions lay on the benches that skimmed along the interior edges. Tamsyn sat on one side, setting the basket down on the floor, and Kit carefully lowered himself down beside her.

"Don't get too comfortable," she murmured to him as Mr. Singh performed a number of mysterious tasks to get the boat ready. "A dinghy this size . . . we'll be switching sides to keep from heeling."

"What's that?"

"Tipping over." She glanced at a flag flying from the top of a boathouse roof. "There's some wind today but it oughtn't require too much tacking. That means turning the boat through the wind so it changes from one side of the vessel to the other," she explained. "The boom will move from side to side, so we should be prepared to duck."

"Here I'd brought you for a pleasure cruise, but I'd no idea you were so conversant with the technical aspects of seafaring." He felt a throb of pride at the depth of her knowledge.

"My father kept a boat."

Kit felt the blood drain from his face. "Oh God, I didn't think . . ."

She shook her head. "It's all right. Being on the water doesn't upset me anymore."

"We can do something else," he offered, feeling like an ass. "Hire horses for a ride."

"No," she answered with a smile. "It's good to be under sail again. And I miss being on the water. I'd go with sundry folk from Newcombe. Fishermen, sailors, and such."

Had any of those fishermen or sailors or such been her sweetheart? If he'd been one of their weathered number, he surely would have tried to steal a kiss from her as they'd glided over the waves. He could picture it now—the wind loosening locks of her fiery hair, her skin turning golden from the sun, and all around the gray blue of the water. She'd be irresistible.

Tamsyn had never mentioned a beau. Perhaps she'd had to bid him a tearful farewell in order to secure the hand of a wealthy gentleman in London.

His chest constricted and he realized with shock that what he felt was jealousy. It was an unknown emotion to him where people were concerned, and he wasn't certain he liked it. In fact, he knew he didn't.

"That's rare," he finally said with effort, "to have that kind of closeness with your neighbors."

"We look out for each other," she agreed.

"I grew up in London," he explained, "and spent childhood summers at the family estate, but relations between the lord of the manor's family and the villagers were never very congenial."

"Hopefully you weren't too lonely during those summers." Her eyes shone with concern, and his chest ached in response to her sentiment.

"I found ways to get into mischief."

She smiled. "That I don't doubt."

"I imagine there isn't a lot of mischief afoot in a small Cornish village," he mused.

Her smile faded and she seemed suddenly fascinated

by the various ropes attached to the sails. "I suppose not," she murmured quietly.

It distressed him to see her mood shift, but before he could speculate on what caused it, Mr. Singh was untying the vessel from the dock. He used an oar to row them out, and then they were underway. Once the captain raised the sails, the boat skimmed away and Mrs. Singh grew smaller and smaller as she waved her goodbyes.

Wind filled the fluttering sails and it was as though they flew over the surface of the water. It wasn't long before they'd put Brentford behind them. Houses of different sizes perched close to the riverbank, peaceably coexisting beside the water. A child and her dog ran to keep up with the boat but soon were outpaced. Washing on lines snapped like medieval pennants. A fresh scent rose up from the river, far different here than the thick mire it was in the city.

Mr. Singh hailed the other vessels they passed as he deftly steered. He was in constant motion, either adjusting the lines or else working the tiller. True to Tamsyn's word, periodically they had to move from one side of the boat to the other.

Kit's gaze seldom left Tamsyn's face. Her smile returned while she chatted with their skipper about his seafaring experience. It seemed that Mr. Singh had seen much of the world in service to the East India Company, and he had many thrilling and harrowing tales of life as a sailor.

Kit tried to keep up with the conversation, but it was a morass of mystifying nautical terms and he contented himself with her endless enthusiasm, her interest in other people's lives. She had been hurt by life, but it hadn't beaten her down. Her resilience awed him.

"Hard not to miss this," she said to him, her eyes roving the passing scenery. "Being on the water, it gives one such freedom."

"There's possibility in it," he agreed. "You could go anywhere."

She nodded. "You master nature, but you give yourself over to it, as well."

"Would you care to take the tiller, my lady?" Mr. Singh asked.

Her expression was one of pure elation. "Might I?"

"I welcome it."

Balancing carefully, she made her way over and, at Mr. Singh's signal, she took over steering the boat. Her expression became focused and serious while she piloted their vessel, her hand holding firm to the tiller. With Tamsyn and Mr. Singh at the back of the boat, it wasn't necessary for Kit to change sides when they occasionally zigzagged. Despite the traffic on the water, she kept them moving in a steady course.

She'd called herself a wild creature unsuited to life in a ballroom. He saw now that she was so much more than that. She fearlessly tackled life's challenges, yet she wasn't jaded or cold. The warmth of her smile could thaw the deepest freeze, and he realized at that moment how his thoughts of the War seemed to retreat when he was near her. He hadn't scanned the horizon for enemy threats once today.

What a lucky sod he was, to have become her husband.

"Very good, my lady!" Mr. Singh exclaimed.

"Indeed," Kit added with enthusiasm. "Excellent seamanship. Or is it seawomanship? We should invent a new word for women on the water."

"Oh, we've always been sailors," she said brightly. She added with a wink, "Don't tell the British Navy."

They sailed on for several minutes before Tamsyn announced, "It's bad form to take command of another man's vessel. I return the tiller to you, Mr. Singh." She ceded the wooden bar.

"All this nautical hubbub has given me a considerable appetite," Kit declared.

"I'm also famished," she admitted. "Didn't have much breakfast."

A pang of remorse hit him. He didn't want to cause her any distress. "I didn't mean to alarm you with my skulduggery." Yet he wondered, what precisely had she been afraid of?

Tamsyn opened the lid on the basket. "Let's see what Mrs. Singh has packed for us." She pulled out a loaf of bread, slices of cold meat and cheese, apples, and a flagon. "Will you join us, Mr. Singh?"

The captain politely waved off her offer. "It is custom for my wife and I to sup together. I shall wait."

Kit pressed a hand to his rumbling stomach. "Well, I, for one, cannot."

They ate their luncheon with gusto. The brush of their fingers as they passed the flagon of ale back and forth sent heat and awareness pulsing through him. As he drank, he realized he had his mouth where hers had been moments earlier.

He hadn't kissed her last night, even though he'd desired it. But their companionship had been so easy during and after dinner he had wanted to preserve their harmony. Now, seeing her come alive on the water, full of vivid energy, the need to touch her and feel her close rose up like a tide—powerful and immutable.

He tried to concentrate on their unassuming meal, to enjoy simply being out with her on the river, but all the while, a box in his coat pocket kept demanding attention. He'd been so confident when he'd acquired it, but now that the moment approached, uncertainty took hold.

Once the food had been consumed and the remainders

packed away, he decided that the time had finally arrived. His hand slipped into his pocket.

"I, ah, have something for you." The nervousness in his voice was strange and unwelcome, but he couldn't stop it. Not when he wanted so much to please her. "Put out your hand."

With a faintly puzzled frown, she did so. He placed the hinged box on her palm.

"It's not a pony," he said with forced brightness.

"Or a steam engine," she added.

He held his breath. Carefully, she lifted the lid to reveal its contents. She made a soft sound, pressing the fingers of her free hand to her lips.

"Oh, Kit." From the box, she pulled out a length of gold chain. A pearl and diamond pendant swayed as she held up the necklace. Her gaze didn't move from the bauble, yet she didn't speak.

Disappointment came hard and cutting.

"It's too plain," he said, his words flat. "There were other necklaces. I should have gotten one of those. A cameo or a whole strand of pearls, or—"

"I love it."

He went quiet. Then, "Truly?"

Her wide hazel eyes met his. "Truly. Thank you."

Kit felt as though he could melt with relief. *Praise God*. He couldn't tell her that he'd followed her to Clerkenwell yesterday, or that he'd noticed she had not returned with any purchases. Not even a simple strand of coral beads.

Between the necklace and this boat ride, most of his allowance was gone. But, damn, it had been worth it just to see her face light with happiness. That was all he wanted.

She turned, presenting him with her back. "Help me put it on?"

He took the necklace from her and looped it around her neck. The tender sweep of her nape was so sweet, he felt his throat grow tight. He wanted to lean close and inhale her scent, drawing her deeply into himself. His fingers grew clumsy as he fussed with the clasp.

"Almost have it," he said through clenched teeth. "There."

She spun around to face him. "How does it look?" She tilted her head from side to side, modeling the jewelry. Sunlight caught on the diamonds encircling the pearl, but nothing shone quite as brightly as she did.

It took Kit a moment to find his voice, and when he spoke, he sounded hoarse. "It suits you."

"What do you think, Mr. Singh?" she asked the other man.

"A lovely gift for a charming young woman," the captain answered, and beamed at her.

She kept touching the pendant as if to assure herself that it was there.

She has so little for herself.

"If I could," Kit vowed, "I'd buy you ropes of pearls and diamonds for your ears, and emerald rings."

"Kit." She shook her head. "This is what I want."

A deluge of pure, unalloyed pleasure inundated him. "I'm glad."

After a moment, she glanced back at Mr. Singh, who suddenly became fascinated by the horizon. With his attention diverted, Tamsyn turned back to Kit. She gently stroked the line of his jaw, then angled her head, her lips hovering close to his.

He breached the distance between them. It didn't matter that they were in public or that they weren't alone. He needed to kiss her.

It was a soft, honeyed kiss, the sweetest of his life, as cool river air swirled around them. She was silken and welcoming, and each press of her lips to his made his heart pound with exultation.

But he could not take the kiss very far. Not here, not now. So, aching with reluctance, he drew back.

Her eyes fluttered open and she smiled up at him. He'd made her happy, and that gratified him beyond measure.

Kit saw then that he was in terrible danger. He'd gone into this marriage for purely mercenary reasons, but, day by day, he lost himself in her. There had been a reason to woo her, but he could barely remember it anymore. All that signified was her pleasure, her joy.

Tomorrow, when he told her of his plans for the pleasure garden, they could each have a part in making that dream a reality. It wouldn't be his dream anymore, it would be theirs, and the sharing of it would make it all the sweeter.

God help them both, but he cared for his wife.

Chapter 18

❧

That night, Tamsyn stared up at the canopy over her bed. It wasn't a particularly exciting canopy, though the white chintz fabric covered with twining, multicolored flowers was a better view than the sagging beams over her bed at Chei Owr. At home, she would fall asleep with the fear that maybe tonight the beams would finally collapse and bury her beneath the roof.

She had no apprehension that anything in her bed-chamber on Bruton Street would tumble down onto her. Everything in the house was solidly built.

So *that* wasn't keeping her awake.

It had been a long, full day. An early morning followed by a lengthy carriage journey, then hours sailing on the Thames, two more hours in the carriage back to London, then supper. Tumultuous feelings had been her constant companion, veering from fear to wonderment to joy.

She *should* be exhausted. In fact, she had been so weary she'd even declined Kit's offer of going to the opera tonight after they'd dined. Instead, she'd gone straight to bed.

Yet now that she had bathed, changed into her night-gown, and climbed into bed with a rather dull novel, her eyes steadfastly refused to stay closed.

Tamsyn drummed her fingers on the mattress, impatient with her unaccountable restlessness. Her thoughts circled back to being with her husband on Mr. Singh's boat—how the sunlight had gleamed on Kit's fair hair, or how his vivid blue eyes seemed to shine from within when he'd seen how much she appreciated his gift of the necklace. The raw emotion in his expression when she'd kissed him.

That emotion had continued on the journey back to London, and was joined by growing desire. At dinner, he all but simmered with it. The conversation had been perfectly polite as they discussed the best places in London to eat, including a few less than respectable chophouses. Yet all the while as they talked, his ravenous gaze had been fixed on her. Excitement and anxiety made her stomach light and fluttery while she toyed with her meal.

He'd kissed her hand when they had parted company for the night. Even now, the feel of his lips on her skin lingered. She rubbed at her knuckles with her thumb as if she could push the sensation deeper into her flesh, making it a part of her.

He wants me.

I desire him.

Her need for him had been building and building, each day, each moment in his presence. It settled within her heartbeat, coursing through her. The more she knew of him, the greater her need became. Not just the demands of her body, but her heart. She craved every part of him, wanting to be as close to him as possible.

At the beginning of their marriage, she had wanted to keep him at a distance, but there was no going back to being two civil strangers entering into an agreement. In a short time, he'd become so much to her. She had to join with him, creating something that united them both in a way more deeply profound than any spoken vows.

She sat upright and pressed her hand to the center of her chest. A furious thudding echoed beneath her palm—from anticipation and trepidation.

The time was now. She didn't want to wait any longer.

She eased from bed. Momentum carried her on toward a destination she feared and longed for. Before she could talk herself out of her decision, she walked to the hidden door that separated her bedroom from Kit's and pressed her ear to the wood. There was no sound, but a thin line of light shone from beneath the door.

Tamsyn knocked. A moment passed, and then another. Had he gone out? Fallen asleep? Should she knock again?

As she wrestled with these questions, the door opened. Kit stood before her, wearing only an open shirt and a pair of breeches. He held a book in one hand. Her gaze took in many details at once—the strong column of his neck; the parted fabric of his shirt, which revealed the upper part of his chest; all the way down to his long, bare feet, which struck her as powerfully masculine.

Only when Kit cleared his throat did she realize she stared at the golden hair that curled on his pectorals. Her gaze flew up to meet his.

His eyes were both wry and curious. "This is an unexpected pleasure."

"May I come in?"

He stepped back, giving her access to his room. Quickly, before she lost her courage, she crossed the threshold. He shut the door behind her.

Dark hues dominated in his bedchamber, with burgundy walls and heavy mahogany furnishing and paintings of dead animals. A waistcoat and jacket were draped over a wingback chair near the fire, and a pair of tall boots stood nearby. Several books had been stacked atop a writing desk in the corner.

"The decor is a trifle aggressive," Kit said conversationally, glancing at one of the paintings. "I call this style *Early Brute*." When Tamsyn turned to face him, he set his book aside and crossed his arms loosely over his chest. She tried, and failed, not to watch how the lightweight fabric of his shirt pulled across his torso and arms. "I expected you to be unconscious in your bed. At dinner, you were half-asleep in the consommé."

"I had difficulty sleeping." She paced to stand in front of the fire, but the dancing flames couldn't hold her attention, and she turned back to face him.

Kit's expression sharpened and he straightened to his full height. "This isn't a complaint, but I feel honor-bound to tell you that when you stand in front of the fire, your nightgown goes transparent."

Tamsyn glanced down at herself in alarm. In her haste, she'd forgotten a dressing gown. Her first impulse was to dart away from the illuminating flames. Instead, she stayed where she was.

Her chin tipped up. "So it does."

He dragged his gaze up to her face. "Tamsyn," he said, his voice low and dark, "if this is some kind of test, you should go back to your room."

"Will you lose control of yourself?"

He exhaled roughly. "No. Any man who says that he can't control himself is a liar. Men *always* have a choice." Glancing down, he dragged a hand through his hair. "However, if you insist on parading your delicious body in front of me, I may need to take my leave of you and go swimming in the nice, cold Serpentine."

"You think my body is delicious?" The idea was wonderful, if a little alarming.

Kit aimed a long-suffering look at her. "Starving men have looked at ten-course banquets with less hunger than I feel for you. And I think you know it." He paced to the door and opened it. "I don't like asking for anyone's pity, but if you have any, please go."

She drew upon her reserves of courage and stalked to him. Gripping his shoulders, she rose up on her toes to give him a firm, demanding kiss. Yet he didn't move or return the kiss.

Pulling back, she frowned. "You don't want me."

"Goddamn it, Tamsyn," he growled. "You're killing me with your kisses."

"I'm ready," she announced.

His brow furrowed. "For what?"

She glanced toward the bed, then back at him. "We've waited long enough."

For a moment, he did nothing. Then, without taking his gaze from her, he closed the door.

He reached for her, but she'd already hurried to the bed and sat upon it. He approached and lowered down beside her on the edge of the bed, placing his hand just above her knee. Fabric from her nightgown covered her legs, but his touch sent crackles of lightning along her body.

His hand lightly curved around the side of her neck as he lowered his mouth to hers. The kiss started gently as he took light sips from her mouth, then it intensified as she opened to him. He stroked his tongue against hers. A flame of arousal flared higher within her and built with each caress.

She gasped when he stroked his fingers over her breast, causing her nipple to firm to a sensitive point. As he fondled her breast, more desire swirled in her, and she leaned into his touch.

A distant corner of her mind registered as his hand moved from her breast to her calf. He gathered up the hem of her nightgown, baring her legs, her thighs, and higher. She gulped air as she felt warm air touch her flesh.

When he cupped her mound, she instinctively jumped. He pulled back and gazed at her with concern. "You're still nervous."

"A little," she admitted.

A minute went by, then he stood and held his hand out to her. Slowly, she slid her hand into his and let him help her off the bed.

"You need to see." He stroked the underside of her chin with his fingertip. "To witness for yourself that sex is natural and pleasurable, not something to be feared. And I know the place where you can learn this."

She frowned. "A brothel?"

"Brothels are places of commercial exchange," he answered. "Where I'm thinking of, all participation is voluntary."

"Places like that aren't precisely pointed out to virgins."

He chuckled softly. "You certainly wouldn't find it in any guidebook. It's strictly word of mouth. You see," he continued, "the Orchid Club is a private society. People from all walks of life gather there. They wear masks to keep their identities hidden. Perhaps you can guess why."

"They have sex there?" she ventured. "With prostitutes?"

"With each other," he amended. "In public. Sometimes there are dramatizations where performers enact scenes from erotic books."

She tried to think of a response but none came. What he described sounded shocking—and arousing.

"For a fee," he went on, "one can indulge every sexual fantasy and desire. No one judges. No one forces anyone to do anything."

"Have you—" She cleared her suddenly dry throat. "Have you been there?"

"I'm not a stranger to the place," he said neutrally. He released her and strode to his dressing table, then pulled something from one of the drawers. "Hold out your hand," he said as he walked back to her.

She did so, and lifted her brows in surprise when he dropped a coin into her palm.

On closer inspection, she saw that it wasn't an ordinary coin of the realm. One side was stamped with the image of a half mask. The other side read *Amici secreta tuentur*.

"*Friends keep secrets*," she said, remembering her Latin.

"That's given to people who visit the club more than three times."

A vast ocean of experience lay between them. He knew so much, had done many things she couldn't even conjure. It was difficult not to feel naive and green beside Kit—a wild, worldly sensualist. Even with her experience as a smuggler, she didn't have his sophistication.

She closed her fingers around the coin. "You want to bring me there. For us to have sex in front of other people."

"No, love. All we are going to do is watch."

"Just watch?" she pressed. "Not participate?"

"Perhaps in the future," he allowed. "Your first time shouldn't have an audience. For now, I think we'll just observe. You can see how natural and instinctive sex can be."

Part of her wanted to tell him that going to this Orchid Club wasn't necessary. But another part of her yearned to see it. It was daring and forbidden and wicked—and she thirsted for it. There were things she knew, and many things she didn't. In some ways, she was still a sheltered country lass, but she didn't want to be that girl anymore—she was a grown woman with a husband and a universe to discover.

"We're in luck," he said with a half smile. "The Orchid Club is open tonight. Would you like to go?"

His question reverberated in her mind. Of all the things she'd ever imagined, attending a clandestine sex society with her husband had never occurred to her.

I want to do this. For him. But most of all for myself.
She realized that she'd fallen silent.

"I'll go," she announced.

He smiled with admiration. "Goddamn, but you're brave. Go and dress. I'll meet you in the hallway in a quarter of an hour."

Once inside her bedchamber, she leaned against the door and pressed her trembling fingers to her mouth. This was going to be a very wicked night, and it would be made all the better because she was going to share it with Kit.

To hell with the consequences.

EXPERIENCE had taught Tamsyn that appearances couldn't be trusted. Any smuggler knew this. False fronts were an integral part of the process—a wagon might have a secret compartment to hold casks of brandy, or a woman's "pregnant" stomach might conceal a bolt of lace.

So it was a surprise and yet not a surprise to see that this infamous Orchid Club appeared to be an affluent home on a city block of other affluent homes. Nothing distinguished the club from its neighbors, save for the occasional masked people going in and out of the front door.

"We don't have masks," Tamsyn said to Kit. They sat in the carriage, parked a discreet distance from the entrance to the club.

"That can be remedied." He poked his head out the window and softly called up to the footman. The servant immediately climbed down from his perch on the carriage.

"Yes, my lord?"

"Tell the manager we're in need of masks," Kit instructed the footman.

The servant bowed and went quickly to the club's front door. He returned a few moments later with two half masks, one blue satin and the other black velvet. With a carefully neutral expression, the footman handed them to Kit, then waited to help them both descend from the carriage.

Tamsyn tied the ribbons of her mask, securing it in place. Kit did the same.

"You look like a highwayman," she noted with a mix of humor and pleasure.

He grinned waggishly. "A dashing highwayman who steals kisses, not gold."

"Every lady prays you hold up her coach." She gave him a smile, but excitement mixed with nervousness made it tremulous.

He reached across the small space of the carriage and wrapped his hand around hers. "Anytime you want to leave, if anything makes you uncomfortable, let me know. We'll be gone in a trice."

Tamsyn nodded. She could do this. She *wanted* to do this.

Now properly disguised, they exited the carriage. Tamsyn took Kit's arm and he led her across the street. Her heart pounded with each step closer, but she didn't balk and she didn't turn around to flee. Soon, she would know what mysteries lay beyond the entrance to this club.

They reached the front door, and Kit knocked. *Tap. Tap tap. Tap.*

The door was opened by a masked woman. She had glossy black hair and tawny skin, and her dark eyes were sharp as she assessed Tamsyn and Kit.

"I've come for the plums," Kit said.

"We haven't any," the woman answered.

"Peaches will suffice."

The woman smiled as she opened the door wider. "Welcome, friends."

Smugglers often used exchanges such as the one Kit and the woman had employed to show that they were allies. It made sense that a secret club would make use of a similar code.

Once Tamsyn and Kit had stepped inside a dimly lit foyer, the woman closed the door and locked it. Before she could speak, Kit showed her the coin with the mask and motto.

"Ah, you are not strangers here," the woman noted with satisfaction.

"It is the lady's first time," Kit explained.

When the woman glanced at her, Tamsyn tipped up her chin. "We are happy to receive you," the woman said in a hospitable voice. "I am Amina, the manager, and the only one within these walls permitted a name. We have a very strict code of anonymity here. Do not speak of anything that may indicate your true identity."

"I understand," Tamsyn answered solemnly.

"Once you cross the threshold," Amina continued, "you must agree to abide by our policy that you will force no one to do anything they don't desire. Consent is mandatory. Further," she added, "nothing about this society leaves the building. Do you agree to obey these strictures?"

Tamsyn felt a particular kinship with Amina. Both of them were women managing illicit operations, and both made sure that anyone they worked with adhered to strict rules.

"I agree," Tamsyn said.

Kit handed Amina a pouch jingling with coins. The manager curled her fingers around it and curtsied.

"Please enter," Amina said warmly. "The night is yours." She swept an arm toward a corridor.

"Ready?" Kit whispered to her.

Excitement rising, she inhaled, then nodded. At her signal, he guided her down the hallway. Voices and music grew louder as they neared a set of open double doors. She and Kit stopped on the threshold.

For a moment, Tamsyn forgot the mechanics of breathing.

Masked people were entangled in groups of two or three on low couches scattered throughout the chamber. Glimpses of naked flesh gleamed in the low candlelight. In the corners of the room, men and women touched and caressed each other, heedless of anyone who might be watching. A man pressed his lips to a woman's bared breasts. Two men embraced, kissing as their hips rubbed together.

Sex happened everywhere. Her gaze alighted from one scene of unbridled eroticism to another.

Moans and sighs floated on the music, and a warm, heavy musk scented the air with a human, sensual smell. Meanwhile, masked servants circulated with trays offering wine and cakes, as calm and disinterested as though they attended to the guests of an afternoon luncheon.

Two women reclined on pillows heaped on the floor. They kissed deeply, and one fondled the breasts of the other. Seeing them, Tamsyn thought of Samantha Markham and Lucy Temple. The two women lived together in Newcombe and had done so since before Tamsyn had been born. No one ever questioned why the women hadn't married. Now Tamsyn knew why.

She fought to suppress a gasp when she saw a woman eagerly sucking on a man's upright penis. The man sat in a chair, his breeches open just enough for the lady to take his member in her mouth and hand as she knelt between his legs. Even though they wore masks, their blissful expressions were evident.

"A place for discovery, yes?" Kit murmured.

"Women talk," she answered quietly. "They say things to each other about what goes on in the bedroom. I'd *heard* about . . . that. But I didn't know people actually did it."

She tore her gaze from the couple, only to land on a woman in coarse, worn garments reclining on a sofa with her skirts up around her waist. A man in fine evening clothing eagerly licked and kissed the woman's bared quim.

"What of that?" Kit asked Tamsyn, his gaze following hers. "Does that intrigue or disgust you?"

The woman's head was tipped back and her mouth was open as she moaned her pleasure. Tamsyn had never seen anyone experience such ecstasy before. The man who lapped at her had his eyes shut as he bent to his task.

Tamsyn stroked her fingers along the neckline of her gown. Her flesh felt feverish and tight, and her own quim heated as she observed the lovers.

She licked her dry lips. "I'd attempt that." She glanced at Kit, who watched her with heavy-lidded eyes.

"Good," he answered, his voice deep. "Because it's something I enjoy doing."

She had no answer for him, but her mind spun to images of his head between her legs, lapping eagerly at her most private place. She felt a liquid warmth gathering between her thighs while the tips of her breasts became acutely sensitive as they rubbed against her chemise.

Glancing away, she caught sight of Amina on the other side of the room. The manager surveyed her club, but as she did so, a strapping dark-haired man approached her. Though he wore a mask, Amina seemed to know him. Her smile widened as he neared. The man stood very close to her, their bodies almost touching. Even at a distance, Tamsyn sensed the attraction between the two. Yet neither moved to touch the other.

Did Amina permit herself to take a lover from amongst her guests? The man was dressed expensively. Was he a gentleman?

"There is more to explore," Kit noted.

Tamsyn's curiosity about the mysterious Amina evaporated when Kit led her into another chamber. This one resembled a ballroom, with an empty stage set up at one end and couples dancing languorously in the middle of the room. The fact that the dancers were essentially embracing barely registered in Tamsyn's mind—not when she beheld a partially dressed woman pressed up against a wall, with a man holding her up, vigorously having sex with her. The woman held tightly to her lover's shoulders, and her legs were wrapped around his waist. Their sounds of pleasure mingled with the melody supplied by nearby musicians.

"Oh," Tamsyn said on an exhale. "I didn't know that was possible. To make love standing up."

"One can couple many places," Kit answered. His voice continued to get deeper, and his arm beneath Tamsyn's hand was iron hard. "Especially if you are motivated. Lying down is just the beginning. You can stand, or kneel, or one person lies down while the other stands. Any number of combinations."

He moved in front of her. His pupils were large and dark as he stared at her with undisguised desire.

"You see, love," he murmured, "people have sex because it's what all creatures do. Because there are few pleasures as extraordinary. I want us to share that. Will you take this journey with me?"

His gaze was hot and intent, but his question didn't make her feel pressured into doing something she wasn't ready to do. The next step was hers to take.

$\mathcal{K}$IT's heart beat thickly as he awaited Tamsyn's answer. She glanced around the ballroom, and he watched where her gaze landed—the couple fucking against the wall, a man sinking to his knees in front of another man, two men and one woman swaying together as their hands roamed each other's bodies.

He used to appear at the Orchid Club regularly with Langdon. Tonight, in fact, Kit had spotted his friend flirting with Amina. After several visits, though, Kit's fascination with the club had waned. The idea of fucking in public and watching others fuck lost its forbidden allure. As a precaution, after it had become known that Kit was on the hunt for a wife, he stopped attending evenings here altogether.

He hadn't expected to become so aroused tonight. Yet being here with Tamsyn, watching her genuine response, inflamed him. He pictured himself licking her pussy, or her taking his cock in his mouth, or them standing up and urgently fucking. Everywhere his body was primed and ready, his aching cock most of all.

Kit couldn't remember wanting a woman more. But he would wait and wait, until she was ready.

He'd taken a gamble, bringing her here. He hoped he hadn't scared her further.

Tamsyn's lips parted and her chest rose and fell rapidly. She turned her wide eyes to him.

"I want to leave," she said breathlessly.

Guilt lanced him. He'd wanted this so much for them, and his instincts had been wrong. He'd brought her here to help alleviate her trepidation and show that sex was something to be celebrated. Yet he'd been terribly mistaken.

"The fault is mine," he said grimly. "I'd thought, I'd hoped—but I was wrong." He started toward the door.

She stepped in front of him and placed a surprisingly strong hand on his chest. "You misunderstand me," she said, her voice husky. "It's time for us to become husband and wife in fact as well as in name."

For a moment, he could only stare at her. Perhaps he'd

misheard. Yet the raw arousal in her gaze told him otherwise. She meant what she'd said.

"You've always been a bold woman," he said. "I understood that the first time I saw you."

"This bold woman wants her husband." Her hand slid up to cup his jaw, and her touch aroused him beyond measure.

He threaded his fingers with hers and kissed her wrist, where her pulse throbbed. "That husband is hers to command."

Chapter 19

There was a stretch of coastline back home that consisted of a twenty-foot-high cliff that plunged into the sea, with a small beach and cove beside it. Since time immemorial, village children had been daring each other to jump from the bluff into the water, then swim to the beach in triumph. Only a handful attempted it.

Though Tamsyn was the daughter of a baron, she'd always played with the local children, all of them disinterested in any class system that would keep them separate. Just a few days past her twelfth birthday, she'd been racing along the craggy coast with Julia Rowe and Louise Turner, when Louise had challenged Tamsyn to leap from the cliff into the sea.

Tamsyn had taken a deep breath, and then ran right over the edge of the bluff.

Riding in the carriage with Kit, she felt exactly the same as she had in those seconds running toward the cliff's brink. Giddy, elated, uncertain. Afraid of the unknown but welcoming it. Her whole body was electric with anticipation.

She was a grown woman now and made choices because she wanted to, not because someone goaded her into it. Doubt fell away.

Kit sat opposite Tamsyn, his gaze never leaving her face, except to dip down along the length of her neck to linger at the skin exposed by the low neckline of her gown. Wherever he looked, she felt heat and a surge of awareness, as though he touched her with his fingers—or his mouth. From time to time, he brushed his lips with his knuckles, as if he already anticipated the taste of her. They had both removed their masks, so it was impossible to miss the raw desire that gleamed in his eyes.

He said nothing, and the silence only built her tension higher.

But she wanted this, wanted *him*, badly. She'd been ready to yield to the demands of her body, and seeing all that she had at the club only ignited her further.

At last, the carriage reached their home. Kit got out on his own and helped her down. His hand was hot as it held hers, and he didn't relinquish his hold on her once she stood beside him on the curb.

They climbed the front steps together and entered the foyer. Most of the servants were already abed, so a lone drowsy footman shut the door behind them and handed Kit a lit taper to navigate the darkened house. Side by side, she and Kit ascended the stairs. Her heartbeat thudded with each step. In the flickering light, he was sinfully handsome and she marveled that this dazzling, sensuous man would soon be her lover as well as her husband.

At the top of the stairs, he turned to her. "Whose room would you prefer?"

"Mine."

Within moments, they were in her chamber. As Kit shut the door, Tamsyn released his hand and went to the fire burning low in the grate. She bent and stirred the embers with a poker, urging the flames to life.

Tamsyn stood as Kit approached, moving toward her

with intent. Keeping his gaze on hers, he uncurled her fingers from the poker and set the tool aside.

He narrowed the space between them, until their chests brushed against each other. Slowly, he reached up and removed pins from her hair. The pins fell to the carpet but she paid them no mind as he went about his task with a serious, studious thoroughness. Locks of her hair tumbled free over her shoulders. When all of her hair had been unpinned, he combed his fingers through the strands. His careful attention made her heart contract with pleasure.

"Woman of fire," he murmured, holding one coppery curl between his fingers. "A phoenix."

She'd been called many names on account of her bright red hair and used to wish she'd been born a brunette, but seeing the desire sharpening Kit's features, she wanted only to be herself.

"Will your lips burn me?" he mused softly, his mouth hovering over hers. "Shall you turn me to ash?"

"Perhaps we'll both go up in flames," she answered breathlessly.

"We'll burn together." With one hand, he cupped the back of her head, and sensation bloomed at this simple touch.

Their lips met hotly. The time for tentative exploration was over. His tongue delved into her mouth and she stroked it with her own. She clung to his shoulders as he wrapped his arm around her waist and pressed their bodies close. They devoured each other. The kiss was wild, unchained from propriety or artifice. He felt hard and taut against her—the length of his thighs, his broad torso, the solidity of his arms—and she willingly fell into him as she spun into greater and greater pleasure.

Heat spread across her back, soaking into her skin. Only when silk fabric bunched and sagged did she realize he'd undone the fastenings at the back of her dress, and the warmth she felt came from the fire behind her.

She pulled back enough to send him a wry look.

He lifted a brow but there was no apology in his expression.

All his worldly experience didn't matter to her anymore. A rake and a virgin—they were who they were. Yet they were also so much more than their conscribed roles.

"Help me out of the rest of it," she whispered urgently.

Together, they stripped her out of her gown, her stays, and her petticoat. In a few moments, she wore only her chemise, stockings, and garters. When she bent down to untie them, he stopped her hands.

"Leave them on," he said huskily, causing arousal to flood her body.

He eyed her greedily as she stood in a nearly transparent chemise. His gaze stroked along her breasts before skimming lower. She looked down and saw the red of her woman's curls barely concealed by the fabric. Earlier, she'd been in a very similar situation when she'd stood before the fireplace in Kit's room. She hadn't covered herself then, and she wouldn't now.

She tilted up her chin. "It's time for me to see you, as well." She toyed with the buttons of his waistcoat, dipping her fingertips between them to feel the fine lawn of his shirt and his body beneath.

A smile curved one corner of his mouth. "At your pleasure." He quickly shucked his coat and let it fall to the floor, then went to work undoing his waistcoat. That, too, was tossed to the ground, which was also the fate of his neckcloth. Before she could admire him in his shirtsleeves, he pulled the garment off over his head, completely baring his torso.

"Oh," she exhaled.

She'd seen shirtless men before. One didn't live in the country without witnessing bare-chested men in the fields or working on their ships. And while some of those men's bodies had been pleasing to her eye, none of them made her lose her breath the way Kit's did.

He was lean and hewn, with each muscle sharply defined, from the breadth of his shoulders to his pectorals and lower to his flat abdomen. Blond hair curled over his chest and wound down to a thin line that vanished beneath the waistband of his breeches.

His was a body that had been forged by combat, and though he had left his service behind, he hadn't lost his warrior's physique or potency. The war had touched him in other ways. Puckered flesh denoted old injuries—a slash across his right bicep, a round mark on the back of his left shoulder from a bullet—proof that he wasn't merely a reckless libertine but rather a man who had fought and survived.

Unable to stop herself, she stepped close and ran her hands over him. His skin was iron hot, and he seared her as she touched him. He went tight beneath her palms. When she stroked along his stomach, the muscles there contracted and quivered. He sucked in a breath.

"You're putting me under a spell," he said hoarsely as she fingered the dip above his hip bones.

"I'm exploring," she answered. Her hand stopped just before she reached the column of his erection pressing against the front of his breeches.

"Let me be your guide." He covered her hand with his. But he waited for her nod before he moved them both down lower, until she cupped his length. He rasped, "That's my cock, love. And it wants inside you."

Fire coursed from her hand up her arm and all throughout her body and between her legs. Urged on by a primal need, she stroked him, learning his size and shape. As she caressed him, he muttered curses and prayers. The look on his face was one of tormented bliss.

"I need to feel you," she breathed, "with nothing between us."

"Not yet," he said with a rueful chuckle, "or this production will be over before the curtain rises." His smile turned wry. "It's been a very long time since I've felt anyone's touch besides my own."

The image of him stroking himself made her dizzy. Her breasts felt acutely sensitive and her nipples tightened.

"I saw so much at the club." She licked her dry lips. "But I don't know what to do next."

His eyelids lowered. "Do you know what I'd like to do right now?"

She shook her head.

"I'd like to make you come," he rumbled.

Her breath left her in a rush, but she managed to say expectantly, "Yes."

With a knowing, carnal smile, he led her toward the bed. He released her to pull off his boots, then he climbed onto the bed and leaned against the headboard with his legs stretched out. "Recline against me."

There was something so potent in his direct, forthright words. No prevarication, only a man and a woman together seeking pleasure. She got onto the bed and positioned herself between his legs, with his chest snug against her back. His arms encircled her, and she was acutely aware of his cock rising between them.

"Kiss me," he urged.

She turned her head to meet his lips. It was a long, deep, drugging kiss that robbed her of thought. When his hands cupped her breasts, she gasped into his mouth, and when he took her nipple between his fingers and gently pinched, her gasp turned into a moan. Her legs fell open.

He stroked and caressed her breasts, toying with her

nipples, all the while intoxicating her with his kiss. She arched up into his touch. When his hand slipped down from her breast to curve over her mound, she realized that he had gathered up the hem of her chemise.

The feel of his bare skin on her most private place jolted her. But it felt so very good. Her body released its tension.

"Ah, that's it," he said on a sigh as she relaxed against him. "I've been waiting so long to do this, to feel you here." As he spoke, his fingers stroked lower, between her lips.

She sucked in a breath. *Oh, God.*

"You're so wet," he growled.

She reveled in her blatant display of arousal, claiming it as part of herself. Thought itself vanished as he caressed her folds, and when he massaged her bud, the boundaries of her body dissolved, lost in a golden haze of pleasure. She heard her long, wild moan as he circled her opening.

His finger slid into her.

"Yes," she gasped. She felt no sense of invasion, only rightness.

He stroked in and out of her while his thumb flicked over her bud. With his other hand, he continued to stroke her nipple. Sensation consumed her. He pressed inside her, into a bright, swollen spot. She bowed up as pleasure cascaded over her in shining waves.

Hoarse sounds climbed up from her throat as he played her body. She abandoned herself to his touch, needing only him and the way he drew forth ecstasy. Her hips moved without thought.

"That's it, love," he urged. "Take what you want."

Her climax hit her with the strength of a tempest. It was an unstoppable force that leveled everything in its path. She cried out as it crested and ebbed and crested again.

Her release slowly receded, leaving her limp and spent in Kit's arms. He took her chin in his hand and kissed her, his tongue lapping against hers.

He slid out from behind her to stand beside the bed. She had just enough strength left to prop herself against the headboard, but her attention sharpened when he unfastened his breeches and pushed them down his legs. Then he was naked.

It was impossible not to stare at his cock, curved and hard, with a shining bead of moisture emerging from the slit at the top. Ravenous desire rose up in her like a high tide, submerging her in need.

"The way you're looking at me," he rumbled. "Like a lioness eyeing her prey."

She pulled off her chemise, but kept her stockings and lay down as she widened her legs. "We're the hunters and the hunted."

Kit inhaled deeply, then climbed onto the bed, arranging his long body atop hers. He lay between her legs, his weight balanced on his forearms. Their bodies fit together, flesh to flesh, his cock snug against her belly, and she looked up into his face to see a pleat of worry between his brows.

"I thought the untried maiden was the one who was supposed to be afraid," she murmured with a smile.

"But this is my first time with a virgin." He stroked a few strands of hair off her face. "It needs to be good for you."

She kissed him tenderly. "You already have made it better than I could've ever imagined."

He lowered his head and kissed her with such thoroughness she lost awareness of where she ended and he began.

Shifting slightly, he reached down and positioned his cock so that it lay between her folds. She gasped as he slid his length up and down, teasing her bud, coating himself with her wetness. Then he fit the head of his cock at her entrance.

She held her breath. He cupped her head with both of his hands, their gazes holding tightly.

Slowly, he sank into her, inch by inch. Despite the discomfort, she breathed into the unfamiliar sensation, urging her body to relax to this new presence. He stretched and filled her.

Sweat glossed his brow and his jaw clenched. He didn't exhale until he'd seated himself completely. Then he held himself still, as though waiting for her to grow accustomed to the feel of him within her.

"Yes?" he said through gritted teeth.

"Yes," she answered breathlessly.

He drew his hips back, then slid forward. Gradually, her body eased, and the feeling verged between pain and pleasure. When he set up a slow rhythm, in and out, discomfort receded. She found herself rising up to meet his careful thrusts, gleams of sensation growing brighter with each stroke. Her fingernails dug into his shoulders as his pace increased.

"Ah, God," he growled.

She wrapped her legs around his waist, opening herself fully to him. He lifted up on straightened arms, gaining leverage to plunge harder, deeper. Sounds came out of her mouth, rising from a profound place. His low rumbles and exhalations joined her own wordless noises of pleasure.

The world tilted as he rolled them over so he was on his back and she straddled him.

"Ride me, love," he rumbled, gripping her hips.

This was wondrous. This was power. Bracing her hands on his chest, she experimented with angles and motions until she discovered the precise point where she could grind her bud against him with each stroke. A hot ecstasy gripped her. She felt wild and fierce, creating pleasure with him and taking what she wanted.

"Ah, sweet." His words were low and gravelly. "I could come just from seeing that look on your face."

"Then do it." She didn't recognize her voice—surely an untamed siren had taken her place.

"You first." He bared his teeth. "Fuck me, Tamsyn. Fuck me until you come."

His raw words untethered her. She let go and pumped her hips hard against him, and he bucked beneath her. Release beckoned. She raced toward it, riding Kit hard.

She cried out as her climax struck. It filled her and shattered the boundaries of her body, her mind. She only knew the feel of Kit under her, within her, and the rapture they made.

The pleasure withdrew in long, slow pulses, taking her strength with it. She draped over him. But no sooner did the last waves pass before he thrust up powerfully and threw back his head. He groaned as his orgasm seemed to rack his entire body, and she felt him pulse within her.

They collapsed and panted together, slick with sweat. He stroked her hair, her back, her arse. She soaked in the feeling of his touch. Their mouths found each other.

"We burn together," he murmured between kisses.

She couldn't speak, but if she could, she would have agreed. Had they done this on their wedding night, with them practically strangers, they might have felt some physical pleasure but missed the profound connection that bound them together now.

But she'd been right to fear this, because she knew with overwhelming certainty that in giving her body pleasure, he'd won her heart.

$\mathcal{K}$IT lay with Tamsyn in his arms, contentment filling him. Leisurely, he ran his hand back and forth from her shoulder, down her arm, to her hand, then back. He loved the feel of her skin. He could touch it forever and never tire of the sensation.

He was wrung dry, his body sated, yet the need to make love to her again drummed through him.

Perhaps his unquenched desire was a result of having withheld for so long—yet that wasn't what drove his need. He'd wanted her almost from the very beginning, realizing on a deep level how magnificent they would be together. He'd been right.

Tamsyn's honest, frank responsiveness had aroused him beyond measure, and the fit of their bodies together sent him into a frenzied fever. God, she'd been sweet. His cock stirred at the remembrance of being inside her. And there was so much wonderment in making love with someone he cared for. The experience had been transcendent, and he wanted to share it with her again. But she needed time to recover from her first time.

His first time, as well. He'd tried so hard to please her, wanting that above all else. Had he been successful? Given the way she all but purred in his arms now, he had to think that he was. He permitted himself a moment's pride, reveling in the glow that came from pleasuring a woman. Not just any woman. His wife. There were men who talked of mechanically having sex with their spouses, saving passion and creativity for mistresses. They were sodding fools.

What a damn idiot he'd been, thinking that he would sleep with Tamsyn long enough to get an heir, then find himself a mistress and look the other way when she took a lover. The idea of touching any woman besides her was abhorrent. As for Tamsyn's future lover—he couldn't even allow himself to complete that thought.

At the very back of his mind, he remembered his plan to get closer to her, for money's sake. Yet he let that idea scatter like a dandelion on the wind. They had started a journey together, a journey that bound them to each other. Now he wanted to win her heart because he'd given her his.

She trailed her fingers over his chest, her touch lingering over the scar he'd received in Vimeiro from a bayonet. The fever had been worse than the wound, nearly killing him as he'd sweated in a hospital tent with dozens of dying men. He still heard the screams of those undergoing amputations, though the rattle of gaming dice usually chased away the phantom sound.

Yet her brightness burned away lingering shadows.

"Kit?" Tamsyn murmured, snapping him back to the present.

"Mmm." He rubbed his lips over the crown of her head.

"You don't need to tell me anything about the War," she said softly. "I won't ask. But if you do want to speak about it, anything at all, I'm here."

No one had ever said such a thing to him. Not his family, nor his friends. Even Langdon and Greyland had merely clapped him on the shoulder upon his return and maintained what he imagined they thought was a respectful silence on the subject. So he'd been alone with his memories and his scars, shouldering their weight because he had to. It was either that, or collapsing beneath the burden of a thousand ghosts.

He'd never tell Tamsyn about the brutality of war. She shouldn't have the knowledge that warfare killed a man's sense of divine justice. No one needed to live with that poisoning their souls.

Yet her offer struck him to his marrow, humbling him.

"Thank you." He wove their fingers together, and her touch pushed back the specters. "For now, this is all I need."

They fell into an intimate silence. Her breath fanned

across his chest where she rested her head, the soft puffs of warm air soothing him.

"Kit?"

"Yes?" It didn't matter what she asked of him, he'd agree to it.

She sifted the fingers of her free hand through the hair curling on his chest. "I'd like to do this again."

"Of course," he answered. "We are married, after all. We can share a bed whenever we want."

"No," she said, raising herself up enough to turn and look at him. "I mean, right now, I'd like to . . ." Her cheeks flushed.

"Ah." His body was ready in an instant. "You're not too sore?"

"I am, a bit," she admitted. "But I don't want to wait."

He bowed his head. "Your servant, madam." Pulling her closer so that their mouths aligned, he said on a murmur, "I'm glad we took our time with this."

"I am, too," she said, her eyes soft.

They kissed, and he had the vertiginous realization that he could have thousands of nights with her, but it would never be enough.

Chapter 20

❦

*T*amsyn awoke with a deep feeling of peace, the kind of peace she hadn't known in many years. As though all the storms that had been raging within her finally subsided and the sea was mirror calm and the sky was a deep, jeweled blue. It was odd and strange, this sensation, and she searched her memory for a reason why she ought to feel this way.

With closed eyes, she moved to stretch out her arm and her hand encountered something solid and warm moving rhythmically. Pressing her hand to this mass, she discovered it was a male torso.

Her eyes flew open and she turned to behold a very naked Kit sleeping beside her. A faint blond stubble shaded his jaw, and the blanket had crept down his chest, revealing a body she wanted to study for hours. She drank him in as though desperately parched.

Which she had been, in truth. For so long, she'd resigned herself to a life of responsibility and duty, a life of solitude. Then Kit had come along and while she'd found him handsome and alluring, she'd tried her best to hold him at arm's length.

Yet he'd been so gentle, so patient and generous, giving her the affection and care she hadn't realized she craved.

Last night, she'd yielded to the demands of her body and her heart. She couldn't regret her decision.

Tamsyn tamped down the urge to sigh blissfully, but it was a challenge. She'd fallen for her husband.

Her lips curved into a smile as she decided the best way to mark this significant moment was to kiss Kit awake. Then, as he stirred, she'd kiss him even more, rousing him to full awareness, and then . . . Her body heated at the thought as her soul welcomed their profound joining.

Tap tap tap tap.

Tamsyn frowned at the sudden sound. Rising up on her elbow, she looked around the room. Perhaps it was a wood-pecker, or a leaky ceiling.

But no birds perched on the windowsill, and the ceiling seemed free of drips. Sitting up farther, she looked down at Kit, who slept peaceably on, undisturbed by the tapping.

She would have happily gazed at her handsome husband while he slept—but that bloody noise wouldn't let up.

It came from the door.

She slid out of bed and threw on a robe. Clutching the silk around her body, she hurried to the door and cracked it open to reveal Nessa's concerned face.

Instantly, Tamsyn's irritation vanished. Anxiety prickled along her arms. "What is it?"

"The shipment," Nessa whispered. "It's here."

Any lingering feelings of love-struck peace clinging to Tamsyn disappeared. She snapped to attention. "I'll be down in five minutes."

After Nessa nodded, Tamsyn quietly shut the door. She turned back to look at the bed, where Kit continued to slumber. Praying that he was a heavy sleeper, she padded as silently as possible around the chamber, gathering up her clothes and hastily dressing.

This was not how she wanted to spend the morning

after discovering that she'd developed powerful feelings for her husband and finally making love with him.

Tamsyn gave him one last enraptured look, then slipped out of her room. She sped down the stairs and through the house, going down another flight of steps to reach the basement.

Hurrying into Mr. Stockton's pantry, she saw Nessa waiting with Liam and Dennis.

The butler stood as she entered. "My lady. I believe your items have arrived."

"Do any of the other servants know?" Tamsyn demanded.

"I told them the delivery was for his lordship's cellar."

"Very good," she said with a nod. "I'll speak to Fred. Liam and Dennis, follow me."

With the footmen trailing after her, Tamsyn exited the back door. It opened to the mews, where Fred Wren stood with a hay-filled wagon. The tall Cornishman's shoulders sagged with relief to see her.

Even though she missed a familiar face from home, this was no time for reunions. She approached him and asked briskly, "You've brought the harvest?"

In response, he moved aside some of the hay, revealing that the damp mass was only a few inches deep. Beneath it were wooden boards. Fred tugged off a slat to uncover a sizable space full of small casks.

"And the rest?" she pressed.

He pulled a basket down from behind the driver's seat. Apples lay at the very top of the basket, and under the apples were several bolts of Chantilly lace.

Tamsyn nodded in approval. She turned to the waiting footmen. "Take these and put them in the storeroom. Be quick," she added.

As the servants hurried to follow her directions, she handed five pound notes to the driver. "You shouldn't have left Newcombe without being summoned," she said, "but you did, and that's behind us. The five pounds is for your trouble."

He blushed with embarrassment and tugged on the brim of his hat. "Thank'ee, Miss Tamsyn."

She didn't bother telling Fred that she was Lady Blakemere now—she knew him too well to stand on ceremony.

While Liam and Dennis unloaded the wagon, Tamsyn supervised, directing the footmen to minimize stacking the casks too tall so the ankers would be easier to move quickly. The basket of lace was stashed in a corner. Finally, the emptied wagon drove off, presumably heading back to Cornwall.

Tamsyn addressed Liam, Dennis, and Mr. Stockton as Nessa looked on. "We'll be moving the merchandise in the next few days. In the meantime, none of you can breathe a word of this to anybody. Not your friends, your family, or the pie man who sells you your breakfast. The merest whisper to my husband would be disastrous. He's a veteran, and will be furious if he learns of us subverting the Crown. Should anyone get wind of what we're doing here, each and every one of us could be transported. At the very least, you won't see a cent from the profits. Do you understand me?"

"Yes, my lady," the three men chorused.

"Very good." She exhaled. "Excellent work today." She nodded at Nessa before sweeping past them and making her way upstairs.

Later today, she was going to have to ask Kit if she could take a brief sojourn to Cornwall to tie up loose ends—namely, buying Chei Owr. Much as she needed to undertake that journey, the thought of leaving him now, when things were so good between them, caused a throb of pain to press down on her.

After she shut the door to the basement stairs behind

her, she turned and collided with something warm and solid.

"There you are," Kit said. He was partially dressed, several of the buttons on his waistcoat undone and his neckcloth missing. His uncombed hair stood up in unruly patches.

She summoned a smile as her heartbeat struggled to return to a normal pace. "Good morning."

"Imagine my surprise when I awoke to find my bride missing," he noted wryly.

"A small domestic emergency," she explained, leading him back into the main part of the house. "All taken care of."

"Anything I can assist with?"

She waved a hand. "Not a bit. I didn't mean to alarm you," she added apologetically.

"I wasn't alarmed." He stepped nearer and looped his arms around her, drawing her close. "But I wakened hoping to share with my wife the delights of a morning abed."

He bent down and kissed her with an erotic intensity that made her blood heat. She clung to him, her mind spinning from the pressure of maintaining her deception while her body hummed with arousal from his seduction.

"We could return to bed," she suggested when she surfaced.

"We'll save our energies for an afternoon nap," he said with a wicked smile. "But let's begin our day now that we're both up and dressed. Or somewhat dressed," he added on a laugh when she looked at his unfastened waistcoat. "I have plans for us today."

Her heart squeezed with bittersweet happiness. He continually sought to give her pleasure, and she deceived him under his own roof. "More boating?"

"This will be a city outing," he allowed.

She tilted her head. "You won't tell me where we're going? Like you did with the sailing?"

He grinned. "I do like surprising you." Reaching down to take hold of her hand, he said with mock solemnity. "Before we can have our adventure, we must break our fast and fortify ourselves. Though," he added, his look scorching, "you may have changed my mind about returning to bed. You'd make for a delectable breakfast."

"There's no limit to your appetites," she noted, warming from the candid sensuality of his gaze and words.

He walked backward, leading her toward the stairs up to the bedroom. "I can do without food if I have to. But I'm learning that when it comes to my hunger for you, I can't be sated."

Her soul withered even as happiness made her glow. She had entered into this marriage for purely mercenary reasons, and now that she and Kit shared a bond, she was being made to pay the price.

WITH rising excitement—and growing trepidation— Kit watched through the carriage window as they crossed over the Thames to the south bank. When he'd planned on telling her about the pleasure garden, he hadn't anticipated it would follow their first night together. But she'd given him so much happiness, he wanted to share everything with her. That included revealing his long-cherished wish with her.

Yet, he realized, he'd given little thought to the pleasure garden when he was with her. Watching her laugh and cry at the theater, seeing her pleasure in good whisky and better company, her freedom and exhilaration on the water—these things had made him happy because *she* was happy. He wanted to give her that. Again and again until they were old and dozing side by side in front of the fire.

He was close, so very close, to having his heart's every desire. All he had to do was convince Tamsyn that his plan for a pleasure garden was a good one, and worth the exorbitant cost.

She would love his dream as he did. He knew it. And they would spend the rest of their lives bringing each other joy.

My God, I think I've fallen in love with my wife.

She caught him looking at her and gave him a warm smile, as if she could hear this revelation.

Tonight—or perhaps later today—he'd make love to her again. And as they lay together, he would tell her of his feelings. Then he would work very hard to make certain that he deserved her.

Damn, but he'd been a fortunate bastard to find her.

By the time the carriage came to a stop, he was grinning. Once the footman opened the door, Kit sprang out, then reached in to help Tamsyn down.

They would have the pleasure garden, *and* each other. It would be perfect.

He held on to her hand once she'd alighted, and together, they walked to the edge of a large, empty plot of land.

Tamsyn looked confused but interested as she took in the property. It covered roughly an acre, with a few stands of scrubby trees dotting the dusty parcel. The remains of a shack crouched toward one end, its timbers waiting for a determined breeze to knock it over.

"Was this a farm?" She shaded her eyes against the day's brightness.

"Years ago," he answered, walking them farther into the plot. "The tenant couldn't keep up with the rent and moved out about a decade past. It's stood vacant ever since."

"It's very . . . open," she said brightly.

He grinned at her attempt to find something commendable about the property. "Precisely." Letting go of her hand, he walked backward, his arms open wide. "You are looking at the future home of the Greenwood Pleasure Garden. Imagine, if you will, a lantern-covered pergola that stretches from where you are standing to a terrace surrounded by topiary." He waved to the invisible pergola. "At dusk, the Chinese lanterns will be lit, dazzling the eye."

He walked quickly to the area reserved for the terrace. "Tables will be arrayed here for *al fresco* dining on wine-poached fish and fruit grown in the Greenwood's own glasshouse." He turned in a circle, envisioning a multitude of guests seated or strolling as they enjoyed the fine evening.

"And here," he continued, striding farther into the area, "will stand an elegant, open pavilion where musicians from the Continent play the very latest musical compositions. Sopranos from Italy will sing from a gilded balcony. Or acrobats will tumble and walk on tightropes while juggling flaming torches."

Tamsyn walked slowly down the future site of the pergola, her eyes bright as he described the rest of the pleasure garden.

"Beyond the pavilion," Kit went on, "will be the gardens themselves, full of wild roses and mazes for moonlight assignations. An artificial stream will run the length of the property, and guests will be encouraged to purchase little paper boats to float down the stream in daily regattas.

"And every night at midnight," he said excitedly, "fireworks shall brighten the sky as the musicians play in accompaniment." He wouldn't mind the sound of the explosions—their loudness would chase away the booming echoes of cannon fire.

His breath came quickly and his heartbeat throbbed

with exhilaration. He felt the smile stretching his face as he strode quickly to Tamsyn.

"It sounds marvelous," she said appreciatively.

"It will be," he said with conviction. "The culmination of many years' planning and consideration."

"When will construction begin?"

He took hold of both her hands and wondered if she could feel the excited trembling in his. "As soon as you give me the nine thousand pounds the project requires."

Her face went blank. "I beg your pardon?"

"Nine thousand is the initial estimate," he explained. "More costs will likely be incurred, but for now, the amount will be sufficient to begin. A manager will need to be hired, of course, and someone to plan the gardens, plus somebody else to take charge of the entertainment such as the musicians, singers, and acrobats. Lady Marwood might be able to offer some recommendations, as well, since she knows the theatrical world so well. There's also—"

"No."

—*t*HE kitchens where the suppers will be prepared, so a person will be hired to get provisions, and—" He stopped abruptly. "What was that?"

"No," she repeated. Her heart was a cannon in her ears.

He frowned. "I don't understand. 'No' what?"

"I mean," she said, sliding her hands out of his, an agonized expression on her face, "that I can't give you the money. I'm sorry, Kit, but this is a dreadful idea."

"You just said it sounded marvelous," he pointed out.

"For *someone else* to build. Someone who doesn't care if they lose such a vast sum of money." She shook her head. "Now is a *terrible* time to build a new pleasure garden. The country's economic status is in shambles. We haven't recovered from the War. There's famine and crop failures and . . ." She took a breath. "I truly wish I could agree to this, but I just can't, Kit."

Everything she said was true. But most of all, she needed that money. To buy Chei Owr and keep the village alive.

Kit looked as though someone had plowed a fist into his stomach. His lips moved as though trying to find words but no sound came out.

Finally, he spoke in a dazed voice. "All those years I was fighting, trying to survive another day, eating rotten meat and watching the deaths of men who trusted me." He looked down at the tops of his boots, which had collected dust as he'd walked through the vacant parcel of land.

"I didn't have a sweetheart to write me letters of hope," he said, his flat voice a sharp contrast to painful words. "The only thing I had to keep me sane was . . . this."

He looked around at the empty tract, as though trying to conjure up what he'd needed for so long. "This dream of a place where there was no suffering, no death. Only joy and pleasure."

She swallowed hard around the ache in her throat. He wanted this so much—and she had to deny him. She wished she had the resources to see his dream come to fruition *and* to protect the people of Newcombe, but she couldn't do both. Guilt racked her. It was his money, and yet she needed it desperately to keep the village alive.

It felt as though some creature wanted to claw its way out of her chest, leaving her a mass of bloody pulp.

"Is there anything else?" she asked desperately. "Some other dream we can fulfill?"

"There is nothing else," he answered without inflection.

Almost frantic, she glanced around at the land. "A little park, perhaps, for veterans?" That, they could afford.

"Greenwood was to be for them." His voice was wooden.

"Any man who could prove his past military service would be admitted for free." He looked out over the property, which would always be an empty lot.

He glanced around with a stunned, devastated expression. She was the author of that devastation, and it shattered her.

"I'm so sorry," she said, misery heavy in her words.

"Yes, you've said." Dazedly, he moved past her, heading toward the waiting carriage. "Well, that's it. Just an empty plot of land. We can go home."

He reached the carriage and got inside. She followed on legs made weighty by unhappiness. The footman helped her in, and when she settled she saw Kit staring sightlessly. When he didn't move, she knocked on the roof, and in a moment, they were heading back across the river.

"Kit." She reached out and tried to take his hand, but he pulled it away. It felt like a slap.

His silence gnawed at her, but in that quiet, her mind replayed the scene at the parcel of land. His eagerness, and how certain he had been that she would agree to finance the whole scheme. Why would he tell her about the pleasure garden today? Why hadn't he mentioned it sooner? What had changed?

Her thoughts turned toward one conclusion—and every time they did, she wanted to reel away in horror.

Oh, please. No.

Yet it made sense. Horrible, agonizing sense.

"You knew how I felt about extravagant spending," she said, her words cutting her like steel. "You knew I would refuse to fund Greenwood. So you set about ensuring that I wouldn't say no."

Please let me be wrong.

His gaze lifted to hers, and she saw in it the truth.

The heartbreak she had felt at denying him his happiness shifted into a new kind of pain. It leveled everything in its path, leaving her a devastated ruin. She fought the urge to curl in on herself and groan in agony.

"You believed I'd fall into your hand," she said through lips that had gone numb from anger and hurt, "and play the nice, lovesick wife who throws money at you because you deigned to throw crumbs of attention in my direction."

He had the grace to look away. "That's not what happened."

"Isn't it?" She leaned closer to him. "Bring me to the theater, arrange for a tasting at Lord Marwood's house, take me sailing. There's the necklace, too. And," she added, hurt outrage choking her words, "finagling me into your bed. All for your benefit, to make me pliant to your demands."

"You make it sound as though I timed it," he said tautly. "Fuck you, and then get my nine thousand pounds."

"Isn't that what happened?" she retorted.

"No."

"How can I believe you, when you just admitted to wooing me for the sake of money?"

"It wasn't about money," he answered, but he still refused to gaze at her. "I'd dreamed of Greenwood. Hoping but never believing that it could ever be mine." Finally, he looked at her, his eyes showing desperate yearning. "Lord Somerby's fortune was going to change all that. It would chase the darkness away."

"Did it never occur to you to simply ask me rather than go through this pantomime of affection?" she fired at him.

"Would you have said yes?" he shot back.

She had no answer.

His mouth twisted into something bitter and cold, and he spread his hands. "So here we are."

Yes. Here we are. I believed you cared for me, and I have to deceive you. No one wins.

Her mind firmed on a resolution. She would get the

smuggled goods to Mr. Jayne as soon as possible. "I have business to attend to tomorrow," she said into the frigidness between her and Kit. "When that's settled, I'm leaving for Cornwall." Once back home, she'd buy Chei Owr and secure the village's welfare. Lord Somerby had intended that money to be shared between them, but she couldn't give it to Kit. She shoved away her aching conscience.

"We are still married," he pointed out.

"I'm well aware of that," she answered flatly. "Don't worry, your lordship. I'll return to London eventually, and we'll get to the business of impregnating me. But without further sham displays of affection. You see," she said with a hard little smile, "I'm finally learning the ways of you city aristocrats. I can be heartless, too."

Chapter 21

Rolling moors evolved into rugged coastline, and the landscape became more recognizable with each passing mile.

The carriage had already gone through the village of Newcombe, where villagers had come out of their homes to watch the elegant, crested vehicle go by. She'd waved at a few people, though she'd felt shy at returning with her new title of countess. Nessa had gotten out of the carriage to return to her own home, as well as distribute the profits from the sale to Mr. Jayne. As Tamsyn had driven away, she saw Nessa swarmed with villagers all eager to hear stories about London and receive their portion of the earnings.

Newcombe was a collection of neat, whitewashed buildings that clung to a slope descending to the water. The village fronted a beach with a pier where the familiar sight of fishing ships bobbing on the water made Tamsyn smile with fondness. To reach Chei Owr, one had to take a steep road that climbed a line of cliffs. The manor house itself was situated at the top of a bluff, with views of the ocean from the west-facing windows. A cove belonging to the estate lay at the bottom of the cliff.

As the carriage wound its way up the steep cliff, a longing for home rose up like a wave. She'd missed this place so much—the open wildness and the crashing, foaming surf.

She'd journeyed for five days, stopping at inns overnight to rest the horses, and weariness pulsed in her bones despite nearing her destination. It hadn't helped that between lumpy mattresses and her own tormenting thoughts she hadn't been able to cobble together a decent sleep. Memories of Kit tormented her.

Five days ago, he had stood outside their home on Bruton Street, his hands stuffed into his pockets, watching with a carefully blank expression as her trunks had been lashed to the roof of the carriage.

"When will you be back?" he had asked impassively.

"I can't say," she had answered. "But I made sure to leave you extra funds during my absence."

She had hoped that he might press her for more details, or try to argue her out of going, but all he had done was nod wearily. He'd helped her into the carriage, yet he hadn't waved goodbye as she drove away. His lone watching figure had lingered on the curb until the carriage turned a corner, and he'd disappeared.

Was there any part of him that truly cared about her—as she had developed feelings for him? Her chest ached at the thought. Yet everything was a hopeless tangle.

Time and distance were required before she could move forward. She needed to return to Cornwall to purchase Chei Owr, but her own need for breathing space from Kit made the journey that much more necessary.

She didn't know what she would expect upon her return. Chei Owr had once been her home, but for the past ten years, it was her uncle's possession. Still, for all the unhappiness she'd experienced here, as the carriage wound up the lane that led to Chei Owr, some of the layers of her sorrow peeled away. London's soot-stained melancholy couldn't compete with Cornwall's rugged grace. Here, she no longer had to pretend to be anything—all she had to be was herself.

The carriage came to a stop outside the front door. No surprise that neither Gwen nor Jory stood to meet her, even though an approaching carriage could be seen from the house's main south-facing rooms, and the sound of wooden wheels on the rocky drive easily disturbed the silence.

Maybe it was better this way.

But the moment her feet touched on the gravel, Gwen and Jory emerged from the house.

They appeared the same since she had been in London. Jory's snowy hair was still worn in an old-fashioned queue, and white stubble sprouted on his lean cheeks. He shared her father's angled jaw, and his eyes were also deeply set. Jory's resemblance to Tamsyn's father never failed to provoke a sense of loss and disappointment.

Gwen had retained her youthful looks well into middle age, which was a continual source of pride for her. She kept most of her blond hair tucked into a cap, and her fichu ensured that her décolletage never saw the light of day.

"Got your note that you were coming back," Jory said without interest.

"Thought once you'd gotten yourself a husband," Gwen added, "you'd stay in London." Her normally bored expression shifted into one of jealousy. Her aunt always spoke of the city as though it was a paradise she'd been denied.

"I have business to attend to here," Tamsyn answered. She turned to Jory. "You received my letter. Have you sold the house?"

"Some bloke who made a fortune from copper mining is interested." His lip curled, revealing his disgust with the notion of earning money from actual work.

"I want to buy Chei Owr," Tamsyn announced. "Whatever the copper mine gentleman offered, I can meet his price and more."

Jory narrowed his gaze while Gwen gaped at Tamsyn. "With what money?"

"With mine," she replied coolly. She gestured to the carriage behind her. "As you see, I can afford it."

Jory eyed her warily. They had never been close—this conversation was likely the longest they had ever shared.

"I'll think about it," he finally answered.

Frustration prickled her like burrs. "Why not settle the decision now?"

"Because I said I'd think about it," he snapped, and wheeled into the house.

Gwen gave Tamsyn a sour look before following her husband inside.

Once they were gone, Tamsyn shook her head wearily. Jory had always been a man of perverse temperament—he let the house fall apart around him yet spent large sums to finance trips to stylish places such as Cheltenham— which had to account for his refusal to discuss the sale of Chei Owr.

A disdainfully bored footman appeared at the door. None of the servants ever lasted long due to Jory's slowness in paying wages. "What do you want?"

"See that my luggage is taken up to my chamber," she informed him coldly. "And you shall refer to me as *my lady*."

"Yes, my lady." The footman grudgingly approached the carriage.

She said to the coachman, "You'll find the path that leads to the stables off to the left. Hopefully, they'll have what you need to see to the horses. If they don't, go on to the village and ask for Tom Nance. He owns the feed shop and saddlery."

"Of course, my lady," the driver answered.

Squaring her shoulders, Tamsyn walked into the house. The front door opened into a narrow, dark-paneled vestibule with a staircase leading up to the next floor. She peered through a doorway into the Great Hall, where dusty sunlight struggled to break through high diamond-paned windows. Some of the panes gaped where their glass used to be.

She went back into the vestibule, and then climbed the creaking stairs. Once at the top, she walked down the corridor, turned right, right again, and then there it was, the door to the room where she'd lived almost her whole life.

Tamsyn pushed open the door, then stood in shock as she beheld an empty room. Everything had been cleared out—the bed, the clothespress, the washstand and mirror. Only a chair draped in holland covers remained, hovering like a ghost near the cold fireplace.

Steps sounded in the hallway, growing nearer. She turned to face Jory as he stood in the doorway.

"You wrote and said you'd wed," he said without hint of apology. "Didn't think you were coming back, so we sold the lot."

"As you can see, I'm right here."

"Where's your husband?" Jory demanded.

She made sure to keep her face unreadable as she replied, "In London."

"Saw that crest on your carriage," he continued. "You're truly a countess now." His mouth turned down when he seemed to realize that she vastly outranked him.

"I am," she answered. "And your time in this house will come to an end. Soon."

She shouldered past him, then hurried down the stairs and out of the house, moving quickly to the stables. Aside from the coachman seeing to the carriage horses, the stalls were mostly empty, since Jory and Gwen had sold the majority of their cattle. But one old dun gelding greeted her as she passed, nickering in recognition.

"Hello, Jupiter." Tamsyn stroked the velvet between his nostrils. "Be a good lad and take me to the village. I have to buy some furniture." It would have been possible to take furniture from other bedchambers, yet Tamsyn wanted something of her own, something untouched by memories.

Without waiting for the lone groom to appear, Tamsyn prepared Jupiter for riding. Once he was ready, she led him to the steps and mounted.

She nudged Jupiter into an easy walk out of the stables. She passed out of the yard, and then guided her horse to the bridle path that led to Newcombe.

She passed beneath the branches of ancient elm trees that stood sentry on either side of the path. Tall grasses waved in the afternoon breeze, which carried the salty tang of the ocean. It was all so powerfully familiar, so laden with memories—she'd ridden this bridle path with her father on many Saturdays when their destination had been Josiah Williams's all things shop. There, her father would buy her a boiled sweet and they would sit on the pier as they sucked on their candy. Even now, she could still taste the sugary, lemony flavor of the sweets mixing with the briny sea air.

This place brought her so much joy but also devastated her. Happiness and misery lived side by side—Kit had given her joy but also filled her with despair.

The bridle path joined up with the main road leading into Newcombe. She came alongside a mule-drawn cart jouncing down the lane, and the driver glanced in her direction, then looked again. A smile wreathed his weathered face.

"Miss Tamsyn," he said warmly. "Or is it *my lady* now?"

"Miss Tamsyn will do, Ben," she answered, her heart lifting at the sight of the old farmer.

"When did you get back?"

"Only this afternoon. The baron and baroness gave me their usual welcome."

"Which is no welcome at all." Ben shook his head and made a tutting sound. "No mistake, Jory and Gwen Pearce might be your blood, but they're no part of Newcombe."

She exhaled. "I suspect that their hate for the village is reciprocated."

Ben pulled on the reins, and Tamsyn brought Jupiter to a stop. He leaned forward and said in a hushed, confiding tone, "It's good fortune that brought you back today. Captain Landry sent word that he'll have a new shipment for us. Brandy and lace."

All of Tamsyn's nostalgia and hurt faded. She needed all her focus for this. "When's the delivery?"

"In a week and a half," Ben answered. His brow wrinkled. "Since you were in London, I was going to let the captain know we'd have to give this shipment a miss. But if you're here now . . ."

Though she'd sold the goods in London, the village always needed more. The school needed a new roof, and some of the fishermen's cottages required repair. "Tell him that we'll have a landing party ready," she said decisively.

"Aye, I will." Ben peered at her. "Begging your pardon, but when we all heard you'd wed a London nobleman, many of us thought we'd never see you again."

"The villagers were the reason I married. And you should know," she said firmly, "I'll always take care of Newcombe."

He smiled, his face creasing into numerous furrows. "'Miss Tamsyn won't let us starve. She's the backbone of the village.' So I said at the Tipsy Flea." He glanced up at the sun. "Day's moving apace. I'll make certain that the captain knows to go ahead with the next delivery. See you anon."

He urged his mule on, and Tamsyn did the same with Jupiter. The horse soon outpaced the cart, and she was alone again on the road to the village.

Weariness dragged along her body, but she couldn't give in to it. Her responsibilities never ended, and she had to dip back into her reserves to ensure that everything and everyone was taken care of.

Not for the first time, she wished she didn't have to shoulder all her burdens alone. Yet now she found herself longing for someone specific.

Kit could always tease a smile from her. He'd showed her the joy there was to be had in life. But all that he'd given her was just part of a scheme, a means by which he could get what he wanted. She'd surrendered her heart to him and in turn he'd thought of her as someone to be manipulated.

Yet she couldn't stop the ache in her chest when she thought of him. She missed him—even if what they had shared had been based on falsehoods.

Chapter 22

❧

*B*lood sprayed as the heavyweight's fist connected with his opponent's jaw. The crowd shouted its approval, clapping and hooting as the challenger staggered from the force of the blow. The air was thick with the smell of gin and sweat and fetid river water as nearly a hundred men packed themselves around the makeshift boxing ring that had been set up in an old Wapping warehouse.

Kit dispassionately watched the fight, wondering what time it was, and how soon he could reasonably excuse himself from Langdon's company so he might go home.

Yet home was just a large house in Mayfair that contained himself and a cadre of servants. No life existed there. No brightness or joy or energy. It had become simply a place to sleep and eat in between his forays to London's amusements.

He observed the men in the boxing ring, and barely suppressed a yawn as the opponent sank to his knees before sprawling face-first onto the ground. The heavyweight raised his fists in triumph while the crowd's yells of approval poured over him. Two men dragged away the challenger, leaving a smear of blood on the ground.

"The next match should be a rollicking good one,"

Langdon shouted to Kit above the din. "'Murderer' John Grundie versus 'Bulldog' Smythe. Last time they fought, it went thirty-one rounds and ended in a brawl that erupted among the audience." He rubbed his hands together in anticipation.

"Wonderful." Kit couldn't keep the dismay from his voice. Thirty-one rounds would stretch on interminably.

"I can't wait to see your excitement when I suggest a visit to a barber surgeon."

"If he gets me drunk before cutting off a limb, I'll be grateful." Kit checked his pocket watch. It was shortly before one o'clock in the morning, which was smack in the middle of a rakehell's day, yet he felt ineffably tired.

Langdon frowned. "How long has she been gone?"

Kit didn't bother asking who *she* was. "A week. Imagine she's in Cornwall by now. At home and happy." Which he wasn't.

"And you've no idea when she's returning."

"I didn't press her on the subject." The day she had left, he'd gone into her room, drawn by a need he didn't want to examine. Ice had covered his chest when he found the necklace he'd bought her sitting atop her dressing table. His wife had left it behind. "She said she'd return to give me the heir I need."

Langdon shook his head. "Bad business all around."

"I know it," Kit said wearily.

The throng yelled eagerly as two new pugilists entered the ring. Kit didn't know who was Grundie and who was Smythe, but as he had no money on the fight, it didn't matter to him. The preliminaries before the match went quickly, and in a trice, the pugilists were beating the stuffing out of each other. Whoever these men were, they seemed to be made of iron as they took punch after punch without going down.

Kit had once enjoyed attending these boxing matches with Langdon. The gin flowed freely and he'd bet with abandon. Now, it all seemed brutal and pointless.

"There's no possibility she'll give you the nine thousand pounds," Langdon pressed.

"None," Kit replied flatly. "She said it was a terrible idea and a waste of money."

"A pleasure garden," his friend mused. "You never spoke to me about it."

"Some things are too important to talk about." He'd hoarded his dream like a dragon guarding its treasure, afraid to even speak of it—lest it be met with indifference or, worse, ridicule. If his friends had jeered at him for being foolish, for throwing his money and energy into a project that had little chance of succeeding, it would have crushed the nascent hope that had been budding within him.

Now that Tamsyn had flatly rejected his plan, it no longer mattered who knew about it. There wasn't much power in ridiculing something that would never come to pass.

Langdon looked skeptical, but didn't question Kit. "I'd give it to you, old man, but even my allowance wouldn't cover that sum."

"Your would-be generosity is appreciated," Kit answered, yet there was some relief in knowing that his friend wouldn't deride or mock him. Neither he nor Langdon had ever followed the rules of proper—or improper—behavior.

Kit watched as one of the fighters unleashed a furious combination of jabs and hooks. The opponent managed to block or avoid some of the blows, but others landed solidly. Kit imagined the pugilist's body must be hurting like a son of a bitch by now, but the damned fool was too proud to bow out.

"I need to let go of the idea," Kit went on tiredly. "It's

not going to come to pass and the sooner I accept that, the better." Investing himself in something that had no possibility of existing was a sure formula for misery. But, damn, he'd thought that once Greenwood had become real, he could devote all his energy and time in something good and unpolluted. Something that gave back to people rather than took from them.

He glanced around the warehouse, crammed full of vicious men shouting for yet more blood to be spilled, and his heart withered. "I can't stay here anymore."

Thank God Langdon didn't try to argue him into remaining. "There's a tavern around the corner. Might be a bit unsavory, though."

"So long as they have ale, I'll be happy with a midden perched atop a bog."

He and Langdon shouldered their way through the crowd until they emerged from the warehouse. Night in Wapping wasn't particularly pleasant, but something about the place's unrepentant shabbiness felt precisely right. In short order, they reached the dockside tavern. It was every bit as unsavory as Langdon had warned, with a few sailors and stevedores gathered around tables as they nursed drinks served in dented tankards. A handful of patrons looked up at Kit's and Langdon's entrance. Somebody muttered something about *unwelcome toffs*, but no one sought out a confrontation.

Kit and Langdon found an available settle, and took their seats. Without asking them what they wanted, a weary woman brought over two pints and banged them down on the table before trudging off.

After taking a sip and finding the ale to be reasonably potable, Kit said, "She left in fury. Angry at *me* for trying to beguile her into giving me the blunt. Which was *your* idea," he added sourly.

His friend only smirked. "Shift the blame back onto

yourself, you dog. I made a suggestion and it was up to you to decide whether or not to take it up, or what methodology you'd use." He drank from his tankard. "I imagine I'd be steamed as a pudding if I found out someone was playing me nice but only for the sake of themselves."

Kit ran his fingers over the table's scratched surface. "You've got a point, goddamn it." The guilt he'd been trying to hold at bay crept over him, miring him in its heavy fog. For years since her parents' deaths, Tamsyn had been ignored by her aunt and uncle. They had given her no love. Then Kit came along and made her feel cared for and respected—but it had been for his own benefit, not hers.

No wonder she'd been so sad, so angry. It wasn't difficult to see why she felt it necessary to flee all the way to the other side of the country.

He'd spent the past few days returning to his old ways. All the entertainments he'd visited—Vauxhall, Astley's Amphitheatre, the Imperial—had barely moved him. What was the point in going if not to bring her happiness or to see the brightness of her eyes as she made new discoveries? Why do anything if not for her sake?

"I've analyzed the field of battle," he said. "Determined my assets and my liabilities—but I can't figure out the right course of action."

"When it comes to the best way to keep a wife happy," Langdon answered, "I'm no authority. Well," he added with a grin, "I'm rather capable when it comes to some-one *else's* wife."

"You ass," Kit said with a shake of his head. Langdon only dallied with married women whose husbands also took lovers, part of his friend's peculiar ethics. "If you can't give me counsel, what's the point of keeping you around?"

"My roguish good looks," Langdon said sagely.

"Ah, that must be it." Kit swirled the ale around in his tankard. "Damn if I know what to do."

Langdon leaned back. "That soldier's intuition of yours kept you alive for years. What does it tell you now?"

"It tells me . . ." He closed his eyes and waited. For a word, a sign, a voice. A feeling. It began quietly, almost imperceptibly, but it was there. It was a need, an absence of something very important. That need grew and grew until it filled him—to see Tamsyn again, to make her smile, to give her pleasure. He had never felt more fulfilled than when dedicating himself to his wife, and the aimlessness which had characterized his life after the War had been replaced by a sense of purpose and gratification. Her absence formed a sizable chasm within.

The pleasure garden had been a distraction, but not an answer. He'd clung to that dream believing it would take away dark memories of the War—and while nothing could ever completely erase them, they had dimmed considerably when Tamsyn had come into his world.

Together, they might not undo the damage of the past, but they would create enough light to dim the shadows.

He wasn't certain what he could say to repair the rift between them. Better men than him were fashioned for stirring pleas begging forgiveness or knew their way around a proper grand gesture. He could only provide himself and hope that what words he could cobble together might begin to heal the wound.

He opened his eyes and got to his feet. "I need to go."

"You haven't finished your ale," Langdon noted.

Kit threw coins down onto the table. "I'll have more on the road to Cornwall."

NEARLY two years had passed since Kit had actually been on a horseback campaign. In those intervening years, he'd grown used to sleeping on a bed with a genuine mattress, covered by blankets free of fleas. It had taken him months to break the habit of sleeping with his boots on, and even today, he left them right beside his bed. He now could eat hot, cooked meals whenever he wanted and go to sleep beneath a roof, rather than a canopy of branches, and no rats tried to nibble on his fingers or run across his face.

Yet as he woke in a hayloft eight days into his journey to Cornwall, stretching out the kinks that inevitably worked their way into his muscles, he felt strangely free. The artificial constructs of London fell away like so much scaffolding supporting a warship at dock. He didn't concern himself with sleeping in to an indulgent hour, or what witty things he might drawl to the lads at White's, or how he'd fill his long, leisured hours with ephemeral amusements. He was a man on a mission, and that goal kept him moving always forward, paring away anything unnecessary.

Kit's thoughts were filled with Tamsyn. Long hours in the saddle gave him little diversion besides his own mind. He grimaced at his coldness toward her that day, and his anger had been infantile.

His plans for the pleasure garden were merely distractions, a fantasy formed in the darkest depths of war. Yet he should have known better.

Nothing and no one could ever erase what he'd seen and done. Perhaps only time could make those memories fade.

If he built a rich, worthwhile life with Tamsyn—a life she deserved—there might be a chance for him to slow down, an opportunity to stop running from the past. He would learn to be a proper earl, bringing her along for every step.

All he had to do was make her forgive him.

Sitting up, Kit picked straw out of his hair and tossed

the pieces down to the barn floor below. They twirled in lazy circles to lie in the dust and be trampled by animal hooves. Dawn sunlight cautiously slipped through the wooden slats, though full daylight was still an hour away.

A folded kerchief held his spare breakfast provided from the farmhouse, after the farmer had agreed to let him sleep in their hayloft for the princely sum of one penny. The meal the yeoman had provided was simple and devoured quickly.

After gathering up his belongings and attempting to return the hayloft to some semblance of order, he climbed down the ladder that led to the rest of the barn. A half-dozen cows lowed at him from their stalls, and a goat took a liking to the tails of his coat, nibbling at its hem.

Kit snatched the coat away before too much damage could be done. If the roads held, he'd be in Cornwall tonight, and it wouldn't do to have him show up looking like a vagabond whose coat was eaten by goats.

On his way to untie his horse, he passed a large orange tabby sunning himself on a pile of blankets. Kit paused to scratch the cat's chin, which the animal deigned to receive with indulged dignity. Having satisfied the ruler of the barn, he went to his horse and began preparing it for the day.

The barn door opened, and the farmer came ambling in. He was roughly Kit's age, though bronzed from the sun and with a burly build. He had thin, light brown whiskers. Tipping back his hat, the farmer said, "Accommodations suit ye, my lord?"

"I was dead to the world the moment I lay my head down," Kit answered, cinching on the saddle.

"Begging your pardon, my lord," the other man said, resting his arms on the slats that made up the horse's stall. "There's a perfectly good inn not five miles from here. A fine gentleman like yourself shouldn't be sleeping in barns."

"Some princes like to disguise themselves," Kit replied with a wink.

The farmer's eye's widened. "A bloody prince, are ye? If you'd said so, I would've kicked the missus out of bed so she and I slept in the hayloft and you'd have the bed to yourself."

Kit held up his hand. "Forgive my jest. I'm no prince, merely a man who's looking to find his way."

"Ain't you got no money, then?"

"Enough for the necessities," he explained, adjusting the horse's bridle. "But I thought I'd save some coin and secure more economical housing."

"The way you're seeing to that animal," the farmer noted, nodding his head toward Kit's horse, "seems like you've a heap of experience in that department."

"Had my share of getting by with the bare necessities," he answered, rechecking the stirrups.

"Two of my brothers went to fight," the other man said somberly. "Only Joe came back, and he's got but one arm now. Joe does what he can to help on the farm, but . . ." He shrugged. "He's not the same man who left in search of glory."

"Not many of us found it," Kit answered.

"We see 'em coming through, even now," the farmer went on. "Soldiers back from the War. Poor blighters. No work for 'em anywhere, so they wander from place to place like revenants, and some missing parts of 'emselves—like Joe." He shook his head.

Kit dug into his pocket and produced a handful of coins. "Some of this is for you and Joe. And if you see any of those men nearby, give them a cooked meal and a hayloft to sleep in. The expense is on me."

"Thank 'ee, my lord!" The farmer tucked the coins away, and Kit hoped that the money would be used in the spirit in which it had been given.

Kit thought that perhaps their conversation was complete, but the farmer lingered, watching Kit make the last adjustments to his gear. Maybe things in this part of the country were so quiet that the sight of a gentleman saddling his own horse counted as something rare and exciting.

Though he'd mapped his course ahead of time, he asked, "Do you know the way to Newcombe, in Cornwall?"

"Oh, aye," the farmer answered, nodding his head vigorously. "Stay on the main road and turn south, that is, make a left at the church with a collapsed steeple. Go on twenty more miles, and you should reach it. But . . . if you beg my pardon, my lord, what would you want with a place like that?"

"Never been there," Kit answered. The beginnings of alarm tightened the hairs along his arms. "What's wrong with it?"

The farmer shrugged. "It's not a bad sort of village. Everything's clean and kept up, but they hold to themselves in Newcombe, they do, especially since . . ." He glanced away and made a show of dusting off his hat.

"Since . . ." Kit prompted, trying as best as he could not to sound overeager.

The farmer lowered his voice. "There's some dark dealings over there, I hear. Things that ain't quite legal. 'Specially since their fishing catch dried up and taxes came and fair gutted the place."

Kit frowned at that. "What sort of things?"

The farmer waved his hand. "Just the usual country gossip," he said with a grin. "Not much to do around here except watch the barley grow and prattle about the neighbors. Why, last year some girls up in Ivybridge said they saw Old Joe Mann riding a flying cow all the way to Ugborough. Which is ridiculous because Joe Mann makes no secret of how much he hates Ugborough. Sooner see him flying to Ermington!"

"That's perfectly logical," Kit replied gravely. He looked through the open barn door to see the sky turning pale blue with the morning. "Time for me to recommence my journey." He led his horse, Empress, out of the stall and then into the yard before swinging up in the saddle. "Thank you for your hospitality," he added with a nod.

The farmer followed him out. "No trouble at all. And, uh, thanks for this." He patted his jingling pocket, full of coins. "If you do go to Newcombe," he added with a warning hand on Empress's bridle, "keep a chary eye about you. Hate to see that fine head of yours crushed like a pork pie."

Kit automatically fingered his temple. But he had a pistol and ammunition in his saddle, just in case anything happened. He was less alarmed for his own safety than he was concerned about Tamsyn. She'd spoken of her home as a place of unhappiness because of her relatives' neglect, but as to the village itself, she'd talked fondly of it, never mentioning anything suspicious or dangerous about it. Perhaps the farmer was just spinning yarns, or maybe there was more to be learned—and secrets to uncover.

"Good day to you, my lord," the farmer called as Kit urged his horse into motion. "Have a care for yourself. Could be some untrustworthy folk about."

"I'll remain vigilant," Kit answered. He kicked his horse into a brisk trot, then moved into a steady canter.

Today, he'd see Tamsyn again. Today, they would make right the mistakes of their past. When he'd been fighting overseas, he'd awaken every morning not knowing what the day was going to bring. That same ambiguity dug at him now. Though the stakes were different, he still faced a battle. He had very little experience with this kind of conflict. Facing snipers' bullets or cannon fire seemed familiar and almost comfortable by comparison. Would he win the day—and his lady's heart—or would he falter and fail?

The only way to know was to move forward. Into uncertainty.

Chapter 23

❧

The sun set over the golden mirror of the sea, and lightness filled her. How she'd missed this!

Tamsyn rode slowly along the cliffs, returning to Chei Owr from a meeting in the village. Turning her gaze to the west, she watched the sunset gild the waves.

The stillness of the ocean belied its danger. Men died out there, and the sea had claimed the lives of her parents. Death and the water were eternally linked, and she gazed at the ocean with a mixture of love and fear.

There were other dangers, too. Tomorrow night, Captain Landry would sail his cutter close to the shore, its hold full of brandy and lace. Bringing the cargo to land was perilous as she and the others fought the waves. The constant threat of the customs officers conspired to make each landing fraught with danger. There had been a few close calls, but the riding officers hadn't caught anyone—yet.

Tamsyn rode to the cliff above the cove. The inlet formed a neat semicircle of sand and rocks. She'd played there as a child, and now relied on it to keep everyone in Newcombe fed, sheltered, and healthy.

Some of her happiest moments since her parents' passing had been in that very cove, sharing in the communal effort and outwitting the customs men. The villagers had become her family, and they looked to her as their leader. She had a meaningful role. She meant something to someone.

If she couldn't have a family by blood that cared about her, if her husband thought her merely a means to his own ambitions, she'd have to accept what she did have.

Yet she throbbed with loneliness.

"A beautiful maiden silhouetted by the setting sun," a familiar masculine voice said. "A fine sight to greet a weary traveler's eyes."

Tamsyn turned in the saddle to see Kit slowly riding up the path toward her. For a moment, she doubted her vision. Yet he drew nearer, his familiar face and lean body coming into greater focus, and doubt vanished.

"What . . . ?" She struggled to find words. "What are you doing here?"

He drew up so that his horse stood ten feet away. Though he wore his habitual smile, the way his horse tossed its head and shifted revealed that he held the reins tightly. A golden haze of stubble covered his jaw and cheeks.

Her husband looked impossibly handsome and a bit wild. Kit eyed her like a starving man desperate to feast on a banquet. Her body glowed to life, growing aware and sensitive merely by Kit's presence and perusal.

The attraction between them hadn't faded in the intervening time—it had only grown stronger. And her heart ached beneath the cage of her ribs, reminding her how much she had missed him, how she had come to need him in her life.

"Haven't you heard?" he asked drolly. "London is passé and the outer reaches of Cornwall have become *au courante*. Within days, you should expect a monsoon of fashionable people clinging to the cliffs."

She stared at him, still trying to comprehend the fact that her cosmopolitan husband had journeyed all the way to the rural, wild edge of the country. He appeared a little weary, a little tousled—and the sight aroused her on a deep, instinctive level. This was how warriors looked when returning home from battle.

"It's over two hundred and fifty miles from here to London," she noted with amazement.

"So it is," he answered neutrally.

"I don't see a carriage following you," she added. "You rode the whole way?"

Kit gave one slight nod.

He'd been in the saddle for over a week. Yet her amazement was nearly dwarfed by an expanding, stunned joy that he was here with her now. "Is that . . . a piece of hay on the back of your coat?"

Absently, he plucked the hay from behind his shoulder and flicked it away.

"On your journey," she pressed, "you slept where, exactly?"

"Barns, mostly," he replied offhandedly. "Under a hayrick one night."

That explained why it looked as though he hadn't shaved for several days. But why? Why put himself through such a demanding ordeal? "Surely with your allowance you could afford hiring a carriage and staying at inns. I made sure to leave you money before I left."

"True," he answered neutrally. "But I'd rather spend my blunt on something important. Like this." He pulled an object from his saddlebag and held it out to her.

She urged her horse closer and looked at the metallic object in his hand. It was a disk the size of a dinner plate, with markings etched into the brass, and flat plates set into its surface. The patina on it showed its considerable age—and the markings were in a language Tamsyn assumed was Arabic.

Her pulse hammered as she looked between him and

the object, and she felt both humbled and elated that he had done so much for her.

"It's an astrolabe," he explained as she took the object from him. Their fingers brushed, sending pulses of hot awareness to every part of her.

He stared at his hand, and she realized that he'd felt that surge of sensation, too. Then he roused himself and dragged his gaze up to hers. "For navigation on the sea. I picked it up in an antiquaries shop in Exeter. Couldn't arrive empty-handed." He spoke with an airiness contradicted by the intensity in his gaze. Kit tried to smile in an offhand manner, but there was strain in the corners of his mouth.

Tamsyn turned the astrolabe carefully over in her hands. It was exquisitely crafted, a marvel of engineering combined with beauty.

"Kit . . ." She brought her gaze up to his. "Why?"

His smile fell away. He glanced toward the water. "The world's been an awfully gray place since you went away." He turned back to her, naked longing in his gaze. "I'm not certain how to make things right, but I knew it couldn't be done with me stomping about London and you all the way over here. The pleasure garden . . . it was something I'd clung to, thinking it would make everything better. But it wouldn't," he said with somber resolve. "I couldn't tell you all this in a letter. Thus . . ." He exhaled. "Here I am."

Her chest contracted painfully. She'd craved seeing his face, hearing his voice—and here he was.

"What I did was unforgivable," he went on. "I don't expect you to absolve me. Perhaps, in time, you might not hate me."

"I don't hate you, Kit," she said softly. "But you dealt me a hard blow."

He looked down briefly, acknowledging his wrongdoing. "The damned thing is . . . by setting out to win you for my own selfish reasons, I learned how truly extraordinary you are, and how much I—" He swallowed. "How much I care about you. I care *for* you."

His eyes were hot and intense with emotion. "I pray that one day, you will feel for me even a fraction of what I feel for you. That would be enough."

"Kit." She could barely speak around the thick knot in her throat.

"I won't ask you to figure out a way for me to regain your favor," he said hoarsely. "But know that I will spend the rest of my life making you happy in any way I can."

The enormity of the gesture and his words thrilled and humbled her. She wanted to sing, to shout. To throw her arms around him and kiss him until they both forgot how to breathe.

The anger at his actions still lived, yet it faded before the enormity of what he had done to get to her. At the feelings he'd expressed. But—

Heaviness tugged on her heart. She would have to betray those feelings by lying to him—again. Tomorrow night she'd oversee another smuggling run, and he couldn't learn about it. If he did . . . everything could fall apart. He'd been a soldier, serving his king and country. His earldom had been a reward for his heroism. From his own lips she'd learned that he would believe her illegal activities betrayed the very values he'd risked his life to uphold.

If only he'd showed up three days later. If only she wasn't the source of Newcombe's stability. If only . . .

His lips pressed into a line, and she realized she'd fallen silent for a long time.

"I shouldn't have come," he said flatly, "judging by the effusive warmth of your welcome."

She nudged her horse until she and Kit were side-by-side. Cradling the astrolabe with one arm, she curved her free hand over Kit's jaw.

He leaned into her touch, his eyes closing as though he'd found the one place that could give him peace. Curling his fingers around hers, he pressed his lips to her palm.

Heartbreak and desire and affection tore through her, coalescing into a maelstrom that left her breathless and dizzy. She was engulfed in emotions that could not be tamed.

"I am glad to see you, Kit," she said lowly. "Truly. Things at the moment are . . . complicated."

She still hadn't been able to corner Jory to talk to him about the sale of Chei Owr, in addition to planning tomorrow's run. "I have many responsibilities here. Things I bear alone."

He continued to hold her hand to his face, and the brush of his stubble against her skin awakened every nerve in her body.

"A burden is lightened when there's help in lifting it," he murmured.

What could she do? He'd shown her what it felt like to have good things and happiness. Yet she continuously lied to him. He merited better than that, nor was she worthy of everything he'd given her.

Sending him back to London would cauterize any hopes of a reconciliation. If he stayed, however, she risked the safety of the village. The choice clawed her from the inside out.

Gently, she slid her hand out of his grip.

"Chei Owr isn't much to look at," she warned him. "Over a decade of neglect has taken its toll. It's drafty, the fireplaces smoke. And there are bats."

His expression brightened when he realized that she was inviting him to stay. "Much as I appreciate a warm bed and the absence of flying vermin," he said lightly, "good company more than compensates for the lack of luxury. Speaking of which, I haven't done this yet."

He leaned close, and as her heart wheeled in her chest like a kestrel, he lowered his mouth to hers. She opened to him immediately, tumbling recklessly into sensation. Heat exploded between them as the kiss grew ravenous and urgent. His tongue slicked against hers and she moaned at the delicious exploration. All the while, her heart cried out, *Yes. Yes, he is what I want, what I need.*

"Tamsyn," he growled when he finally pulled back. "Wife. I need to have you."

Desire and a need for closeness with him leveled her. "I want nothing more. But they're expecting me at home."

"The hell with them," he rumbled.

She smiled ruefully. "Yes. And I need to get back." She had to confirm that everything was in place for tomorrow's run.

His growl sent a thrill through her. "Very well. But depend on it, my lady, we *will* ravish each other."

"I'll hold you to that," she said, and licked her lips. Every part of her, from her body to her soul, yearned for him.

"Careful," he rumbled, "or I'll drag you out of that saddle and make good on my vow."

Reluctantly, she leaned back, putting necessary distance between them. "We need to go." She cradled the astrolabe to her chest—a precious gift she would treasure all her days—while her other hand tugged on Jupiter's reins to turn him toward home.

"I can't vouch for the company at Chei Owr, either," she said wryly. "Not while the current baron is master of the house." She nudged her horse into a sedate walk.

Kit followed on his mount. "Everyone finds me charming," he said with assurance.

"My uncle barely looks up from his food. His idea of pleasant dinner conversation consists of grunts. And my aunt likes nothing more than to slander the neighbors."

His confident smile flickered, but he rallied. "Facing the baron and baroness can't be worse than Bonaparte."

"If only I could exile them to some distant island," Tamsyn said on an exhale. "Preferably a Patagonian archipelago."

"I have friends in the Navy. Something can be arranged."

For the first time in many days, she found herself genuinely smiling. "Thank you."

"It's just a little kidnapping," he answered. "Hardly any trouble."

She shook her head. "I mean, thank you. For this." She held up the astrolabe. "And for coming after me."

Their gazes held and fiery awareness poured through her. "You're worth fighting for."

In silence, they continued on toward the house, the only sounds coming from the distant beach and the horses' hooves. She shot him furtive glances, watching his expression as he took in the landscape. His gaze was never still, as though he was assessing the geography. The habit of searching out defensible positions and hidden dangers would likely always be a part of him. With his stubble and the slight disorder of his clothing, he looked less polished than he did in London, more like a man on an adventure or expedition.

I'm the quest.

But she wasn't much of a prize, not when she continued to deceive him.

"What's that structure there?" He pointed west, toward a stone shed standing alone in the middle of a field.

Her stomach leapt. He couldn't ever learn of the shed's purpose or what it concealed. "Only an old storage outbuilding. A notoriously favorite place for spiders to build nests."

"Woke up once in Portugal with a tarantula sitting on my chest." He gave a slight shudder. "Not an experience I'm eager to repeat."

She silently exhaled.

Soon, they drew closer to Chei Owr. Sunlight glinted off the west-facing windows, and the brick facade glowed warmly. But there were dark spots in the walls where the window glass was missing, and untended vines clung to the bricks. Familiar dismay filled her at the sight. She chanced a look at Kit, who saw her home for the first time. A small frown creased between his eyebrows. Surely with his soldier's sight, he didn't miss the neglected and care-worn condition of the house. The closer they got to Chei Owr, the more its disrepair showed—holes in the roof, leaning chimneys, and weeds choking the once-pristine grounds.

"How long has it been since your uncle took possession of the house?" Kit asked.

"Ten years," she replied. "He maintained it for the first year."

His jaw clenched. "And let it fall to pieces after that."

"Jory always said it wasn't worth throwing money into a place that should just be razed. Besides, he was always more interested in going to the gaming houses in Falmouth or Truro."

"But it's your *home*," Kit said in a tight voice.

"I didn't warrant much attention."

"I like most everyone," Kit growled. "But, hell, I have no love for your uncle."

"Which warms my heart," she said sincerely. "We'll take the horses to the stables and see to them ourselves. If we wait for a groom, we'll be cooling our heels for hours."

They approached the stables and dismounted in the yard. Even though Kit had been in the saddle for days, he moved with a sleek economy. Leading his horse, he followed her to the stalls. They didn't speak as they tended to the animals—but watching him move with such muscular fluidity made her long for a time and place where they could explore every inch of each other, and speak of all the things lovers did in the aftermath of passion. Their time together in London had been too brief. She wanted to delve deeper to absorb his very essence.

When they had finished, they strode up the rear path toward the house. His saddlebags were slung over his shoulder, and she tried to take comfort in the minimal possessions he carried with him. Perhaps he wouldn't stay long, much as she wanted to have him close.

She walked to the back door and, still holding the astrolabe, put her shoulder to the warped, age-swollen wood. After giving Kit an apologetic grimace, she gave the door several shoves before it finally creaked open. She waved him in. "Welcome to Chei Owr," she said with false cheer.

They emerged in a small room that joined with a long gallery. Dusty tapestries hung on the walls, and a scattering of chairs were shoved to one side. "I used to run here on rainy days," she explained as they walked farther into the chamber. "The footmen and I would have races."

"Did you win?" he asked with a grin.

"I did—or else they let me win so they could keep their jobs."

"Let's pretend that you were the fastest girl in Cornwall." He eyed the length of the gallery. "Shall we put you to the test? See if you've still got your speed?"

She shook her head. "Gwen hates the sound of running on wooden floors."

The moment Tamsyn mentioned her aunt's name, Gwen and Jory appeared in their path. While Jory looked suspicious, his wife eyed Kit with interest, noting his military bearing and the quality of his clothing despite its rumpled state.

"Who's our guest, dearest niece?" Gwen trilled.

Tamsyn frowned at the never-before used sobriquet. "Kit, this is my aunt, Lady Shawe. Gwen, this is my husband, the Earl of Blakemere."

Her relatives' eyebrows shot up at the word *earl*. Belatedly, they bowed and curtsied. "You are most welcome to our home, my lord," Jory said with syrupy obsequiousness.

"Thank you, Lord Shawe," Kit answered coolly.

Gwen moved to press herself close to Tamsyn, wrapping one arm around her waist to hold her with uncharacteristic affection. "We were glad you were able to spare our Tamsyn so soon after your wedding. Can't do without her. The very light of our lives, she is."

Tamsyn plucked Gwen's fingers from her waist and nudged her aunt away. "Yes, that's precisely why you wouldn't buy me a new gown for two years."

Her aunt forced out a shrill laugh. "Oh, you're such an imp with your jests."

"Lord Blakemere will be staying with us for . . ." Tamsyn looked at Kit.

"For as long as it takes," he answered firmly.

Her pulse raced and her heart leapt at the resolve in his voice.

"If there's anything you need, my lord," Jory said deferentially, "you have only to ask."

"I'll be sure to let you know," Kit replied, his words icy.

Both her aunt and uncle hurried out of the chamber. Doubtless, after talking to the cook, Gwen would write many letters to let her friends and family know that she had a genuine *earl* and *hero* staying in her home. Jory would hide himself away in his study and bask in Kit's reflected glory.

Once her relatives had gone, Kit let out a low growl. "An obsequious pair," he muttered.

"It's not an average day at Chei Owr that sees an earl crossing the threshold," Tamsyn answered. "They're less . . . hospitable to blood relations." She grimaced.

His look darkened. "Damn them both."

"Better to be neglected than be the object of their scrutiny."

He didn't look cheered by her information. "I'd still like to flay them."

She patted his cheek. "I am most cheered by your bloodthirstiness." Which she was, in truth. She'd never had a champion before and the prospect elated her.

Tamsyn walked toward the door leading to the main hall, and the staircase that lay just beyond. "Shall I find you a room?"

She spun to face him when she realized that he had stopped walking.

"I thought the married couples in this house slept in one bedchamber," he said with a small frown. "Your parents, your aunt and uncle. And now—us."

What she wouldn't give to share a bed with him. To make love until they were as weak as fledglings. To feel his solid warmth beside her all night and wake in his arms.

Yet if he stayed with Tamsyn in her bedchamber, sneaking out before midnight to conduct the smuggling operation would be nigh impossible. "The bed in my room is far too narrow for two people."

"There's got to be other, wider beds." His voice was flat with enforced patience, yet there was a distinct sultriness and need in his gaze. "I'm so hungry for you, Tamsyn. I'll tear this house down to have you."

Heat curled through her, robbing her of thought.

Yet she glanced at the broken panes of glass in the windows. "You've seen the condition of this place. There's only one other chamber that could accommodate two people, and the wind cuts right through the gaps in the walls. The mattress is hosting a family of mice, too," she added.

"Then we stay at an inn." He took her hand, and the contact of skin to skin was drugging.

She shook her head. "I'm needed in the mornings to help in the village. The nearest inn is too far away."

He exhaled and looked down at their joined hands. His thumb stroked over her wrist, causing liquid heat to pool between her legs. She recalled with fevered clarity the night they had made love, the way he'd touched her, the pleasure they had created together. All of it came back in a flood of desire and a longing for closeness.

When he looked up at her, a sly, sensuous smile curved his lips. "There's something to be said for clandestine assignations outside of the bedroom."

"I know I can count on you to find the positive angle," she answered.

"I can show you many positive angles," he said with a leer. "There's so much we haven't tried. So much for us to discover. All the ways I can adore you." He narrowed the space between them and brushed his lips over hers. He smelled of wind and warm male flesh. "God, I missed you, wife. Your taste, your feel. The brilliance of your very soul."

She sank into him, into his kiss, and all that he offered. He pulled her close, his body radiating strength and purpose. Pressing her yielding body to his, feeling the sculpted muscle beneath his clothing, she felt both submerged in desire as well as powerfully alert and alive. Pleasure and joy suffusing her, she let her hand roam over his torso as she greedily drank in the sensations of his strength beneath her fingers.

They fit together as though hewn from the same rock. In him, she felt her perfect complement. Apart, they were strong, and together, they were unequaled.

Perhaps they had a chance. Perhaps this marriage had a possibility at survival.

Yet, tomorrow night loomed in her mind, keeping her from losing herself completely in his kiss and the hope of a better future. Heaven help her, but she had no choice.

She had to keep deceiving him.

Chapter 24

❧

$\mathcal{K}$it had seen abandoned homes in Portugal and Spain that looked better than this crumbling old brick house.

Years of neglect showed in the warped, water-damaged floorboards, in the vermin that freely traversed the corridors, and in the sunlight stabbing through holes in the roof. If ever the manor was the pride of the region—it *was* a baronial estate, after all—those days were long past.

Alone, he now ambled through a picture gallery. Dusty squares revealed where paintings had once hung, and he could only guess that the ancestors who'd built the house and worn the title were now gazing out on the parlors of newly rich merchants. He searched in vain for a portrait of Tamsyn or her parents. It seemed as though the painting of the late baron had been sold off.

Barring her possessing a miniature of her mother and father, Tamsyn likely had no images of her family. Nothing to hold on to besides memories.

Red fury hazed his vision as he strode from one empty space on the wall to the next. It was fortunate that neither Lord nor Lady Shawe crossed his path, because it would have been far too easy for Kit to chase them off the property with his pistol, no matter how they flattered him and plied him with blandishments.

Last night's dinner had been an exercise in discomfort. Lady Shawe had pressed him over and over again for London gossip, while Lord Shawe had boasted about his own youthful exploits as well as the influence he had as one of the area's few titled gentlemen.

Tamsyn had said very little at dinner, seemingly preoccupied. But when he pressed her later for some reason behind her quiet, she'd claimed exhaustion. He'd been uncertain about going to her bedchamber last night. So he'd lain awake in his uncomfortable bed, in his uncomfortable room, his mind full of her, his body urging him to action.

After leaving the gallery, he paced through the echoing corridors in search of her. All he encountered was the occasional apathetic servant. It was as though he'd become a ghost, haunting Tamsyn's home, forever trapped in the mire of her past.

He moved now, heading toward the stables so he could check on Empress, then stopped abruptly on the path leading to the outbuilding when he saw Tamsyn hurrying toward him. She wore a dark green dress that turned her hair as bright as a blaze and brought out the rosiness in her complexion.

Her gaze was downcast, her brow furrowed. She didn't seem to notice him until they nearly collided.

"Good morning," he said to her as she glanced up in surprise. "I trust you had a productive morning."

Her face went blank for a moment before she answered. "I was the picture of industry. Busy since the sun came up."

"We'll make a print of you and sell it at shops throughout the northern mill towns," he said soberly. "To inspire them."

"I can see it now," she agreed with a nod. "Armies of redheaded workers laboring away, turning England into a global giant. At least," she added, "where collecting eggs and sweeping stoops are concerned."

"Didn't know barons' daughters gathered eggs or did any sweeping," he noted.

"Samantha Markham and Lucy Temple are advancing in years. They don't move quite as nimbly as they used to." She lifted a shoulder. "Everyone else is so busy in the mornings it's hard to find someone to look in on Samantha and Lucy. So I do it."

He shook his head in admiration of her thoughtfulness. Many young women of her rank might deliver baskets of food to poor or elderly tenants, but wouldn't stoop to manual labor. Not his wife.

"They must have very clean hens," he observed, glancing down at her hands. "Not a speck of grime on you."

She tucked her hands into the pockets on the front of her apron. "I washed up before heading home." She gave him a smile that verged on being too bright, too forcefully cheerful. "Have you broken your fast?"

"I ate a moderate amount of toast and jam but my hosts force-fed me platters of compliments," he answered, which merited him a quick smile. "Tamsyn." Placing two fingertips beneath her chin, he stroked her soft flesh.

He peered closely at her. Shadows darkened beneath her eyes and brackets of strain surrounded her mouth. Something about being here clearly troubled her. Whatever it was, he couldn't wait to spirit her away from this manor.

Touching her was a sweet agony as awareness traveled through the length of his body. Last night had been tormenting, knowing that she was so close but being unable to go to her. Even if they hadn't made love, he simply wanted her beside him, near him.

At his touch, her pupils flared and her lips parted. He couldn't wait another moment—he had to kiss her.

She recognized his intent as he lowered his head, meeting him halfway. They kissed with a hot desperation, both of them too long denied the taste of the other. He cradled the back of her head, his other hand low on her back, urging her closer. She pressed tightly to him, and he felt all her sweet, yielding flesh beneath layers of clothing. He went fully hard within moments.

With her fingers threading through his hair, holding fast to him, he grew drunk on the flavor of her, on her very essence. He wanted to pull her down to the ground, to have them both lost to pleasure as he worshipped her, heedless of where they were or who could see.

God—he needed to get her away from this place, from her relatives, and whatever else seemed to trouble her.

Reluctantly, he pulled back enough to growl, "I need you back. With me. Doesn't have to be London—we can go anywhere. So long as we're together."

She squeezed her eyes shut. "I'm needed here, too."

"For how long?"

"Not forever." She opened her eyes, and her gaze verged on pleading. "Please, Kit. Let's not quarrel about it."

She looked so strained and stretched thin, it would be churlish to press her about it now. However, "We *will* discuss this. Soon."

He let her go when she eased from his arms, but the ache he felt at her loss was immediate.

"Care for a tour?" she asked after a moment.

Kit frowned at the sudden change in topic. "I've taken a thorough inspection of the house. Unless there's a secret dungeon I've missed."

Her laugh seemed a touch forced. "You've read too many of Mrs. Radcliffe's novels."

"I'm merely waiting for some *banditti* to carry me off and force me to wed their captain."

"We could take the tour farther afield," she offered. "I

could show you some of my favorite places. I promise this part of Cornwall isn't strictly devoted to toadying uncles and their derelict houses."

"I would like that," he answered. Here, at last, would be a chance to learn more about her—what she liked, what she loved. Each revelation was as precious as a pearl.

Somehow, he would make everything right between them.

THE ride into Newcombe was a short one. The way took them along the edge of the cliffs, then descended down into the tidy little village. Just beyond the village stood the bay, with fishing boats and other small vessels rising and lifting on the waves.

"That's Sam Franks's grocer shop," Tamsyn said, pointing to one storefront. A young, blond man wearing an apron stood on the front step and watched them pass with no attempt to disguise his curiosity.

"Jack and Ellie Edgar run the public house," she added, nodding toward the establishment. Men gathered in the window to stare, their interest in Kit as evident as the grocer's.

She seemed oblivious to the many inquisitive looks that trailed them, but Kit noticed. He saw more than a few men narrow their eyes with suspicion and caution. The women they passed on the street stopped and whispered to each other.

He'd had warmer welcomes from fallen Spanish towns. His body immediately responded, snapping into alert readiness. He could fight or flee at a moment's notice.

"This is Josiah Williams's all things shop," Tamsyn announced, bringing their horses to a stop. They dismounted. "We'll just pop in for a moment. I need to buy quills."

"Wait a moment," Kit said, holding up a hand. "Isn't that Nessa?"

The woman was walking down High Street with a basket hanging from her arm, looking preoccupied. She came to a stop as she noticed Kit and Tamsyn, her eyes wide with surprise.

"I hadn't seen her yesterday," he realized. "Why aren't you back at the house?" he asked Nessa.

"I . . ." The older woman seemed at a loss for words.

"She lives in the village," Tamsyn explained smoothly, "with her son, his wife, and her grandchild. She comes up every day to help me."

"So why is she here now?" he wondered.

"The baby's sick," Nessa said quickly. "And so is his mum. I'm looking after both of them."

"I can manage without her until they get well," Tamsyn added. "Come, let's leave Nessa to her errands so she can return home and nurse them." She tugged him toward the all things shop.

Nessa hurried away, and Kit frowned as he watched her disappear down a side street. But Tamsyn kept urging him into the shop, so he moved on.

The bell on the door chimed as Kit pushed it open, causing everyone within to freeze and stare at him. Kit nodded guardedly as Tamsyn strode in.

"Good morning, Josiah," she called out to a middle-aged man handing a customer a spool of thread.

"Miss Tamsyn," Josiah answered. His gaze flicked to Kit, then back to her, a question in his eyes.

"This is my husband, Lord Blakemere," she announced to the people in the shop. She made introductions, and though Kit didn't retain most of the customers' names, he felt their unease as though he'd fallen into a puddle of oily water in the middle of the road and hadn't cleaned his face.

"Pleasure meeting you," Josiah said after a brief, awkward silence followed the introductions. "Are you planning on staying long, my lord?"

"The duration of my visit hasn't been determined," Kit replied neutrally. "I only arrived yesterday."

"And you're staying at Chei Owr, are you?" asked a woman carrying a basket.

"He is," Tamsyn answered.

"It's fallen on hard times—no offense, Miss Tamsyn," she hastily added. "There are first-rate inns in Perranporth."

"If it's just the same," Kit said drily, "I'd prefer to be closer to my wife."

"Of course, of course." The woman nodded, but she shot a glance at Tamsyn. "We're, ah, fond of her, too, my lord."

"Oh, aye," the people in the shop chorused, and this, at least, was said with genuine feeling.

A faint blush stained Tamsyn's cheeks. "Some cut quills please, Josiah," she said to the shopkeeper.

He hurried to one drawer lining the walls and pulled out a long paper envelope, which he passed to Tamsyn. "Very fine prime quills. No seconds or pinions for you. Free of charge, Miss Tamsyn."

"You persist in saying," Tamsyn said wryly, "and I'll persist in refusing." She took a coin from her reticule, then gently pried open Josiah's hand before pressing the coin into it and curling his fingers around the money.

Though it made sense for a shop to extend credit to local gentry, it was odd that Josiah Williams wanted to refuse payment. As though he owed Tamsyn something.

"What are ye plans for the day?" an elderly man in farmer's clothing asked Kit. His accent was so thick it took Kit a moment to understand what he'd said.

"I plan on taking him on a tour," Tamsyn replied. "See the local sights, et cetera."

"Oh?" the older man asked with a pointed glance.

"The harbor and along the beach," she said. "*Some* of the coves. A few aren't precisely traversable, are they, Ben?"

"No, they aren't," the man agreed readily. "Best to stay away."

Everyone in the shop nodded vigorously.

"Because pirates use them for hiding their booty," Kit joked.

Tamsyn laughed rather loudly, and a few of the customers joined her.

"The day's getting ahead of us," she said brightly. "We'd best hurry along if we want to see everything. And there's so much to see."

"Planning on tiring me out?" he teased.

She pushed out another laugh. "It's very different from London. Early rising and early to bed."

When he lifted a brow at the word *bed*, a carnal pink tinged her cheeks.

He fought a growl, wanting to see that pinkness all over her body.

She interrupted his erotic thoughts as she announced, "Time to move on." She headed to the door and hurried outside as if sharks were intent on making her their supper.

"It was my pleasure to meet everyone." Kit bowed before he also took his exit.

"Small villages can be so guarded toward newcomers," Tamsyn said when he joined her in the lane. "I hope you won't judge them too harshly."

"They think highly of you." He stepped closer and smiled down at her. "For that, they cannot earn my enmity." Much as he wanted to kiss her, they were far from alone. He glanced at the all things shop window. Faces pressed against the glass disappeared.

As she led him toward the water, Kit sent one last look over his shoulder. The streets were suddenly deserted, and no faces appeared in the windows. He wanted to love the village because Tamsyn loved it. Yet coldness crept up his neck—as it often had in the moments before an ambush.

"THIS view from the harbor is the very definition of the word *charming*," Kit remarked as he and Tamsyn walked on the pier. Water lapped at the pilings, and the smartly kept boats rose and fell on the waves as though they breathed.

Fishermen mending their nets and tending to their vessels called out greetings to Tamsyn as she strolled on Kit's arm. Their gruff smiles faded as they greeted Kit with a wary, "Morning, my lord." He nodded in response, while all the muscles of his back tensed with the knowledge that he was being carefully watched.

Despite the cool reception from the locals, he'd spoken truly that Newcombe had a lovely harbor, especially when the sun broke through the morning haze and shone upon the water.

"I've always loved coming here," Tamsyn said as they stood at the end of the pier.

"Understandable," he answered. He glanced back at the fishermen, who made a pretense of working while covertly watching him. "It gives one a sense of possibility."

"And permanence," she added. "The village has existed for hundreds of years, maybe more. There have always been men here going out onto the water to get their sustenance from the sea, and their families have always waited on the shore for their return." She spoke with fondness, but also pain.

"It seems a precarious existence," he said softly, watching the way the breeze caught in her hair. At the water's edge, he could well imagine her the offspring of a handsome ginger fisherman and a seductive mermaid. Tamsyn was elemental, alluring—and elusive.

She caught him openly staring at her, but she didn't blush or look away. Instead, she held his gaze, her hazel eyes richly captivating. "All good things come at a cost."

"Sometimes the price is worth it," he murmured. Only through sheer force of will did he keep from skimming his fingertips down her cheek and lower, along her neck where her pulse gently throbbed.

She drew in a deep breath, turning her eyes toward the water. "This is my favorite scent—the wind carrying the smell of brine. If someone could distill and bottle it, I'd wear it like perfume."

"I can feel it chasing away any vestiges of London smoke lingering in my lungs," he noted. "Just the same, I like the way you smell now. Like flowers and salt." He enjoyed how she lowered her lids. "Mind, it's only the fact that we have an audience that's keeping me from rubbing myself all over you."

A tiny, sensuous smile curved her lips. Heat washed through him. He hadn't forgotten her taste, her feel. If anything, the time away from her had sharpened his need until it became a knife's edge, carving him from the inside out.

Damn her home's lack of a wide-enough bed. Beds weren't a precondition for lovemaking, but they surely were accommodating.

Seeking to shift the tide of his thoughts, he continued, "I can see why you were homesick in London. I'd miss a sight like this one, too."

"But you're a sophisticated city gentleman," she protested.

"Doesn't mean I cannot appreciate a lovely view. Why, I'd wager fifty pounds that if Londoners knew about this place, they'd flood Newcombe for a bit of scenic, restorative beauty."

She looked dubious. "There's no pavilion like at Brighton."

"Once I wagered with abandon," he said with a wry

smile. "Now that I must be more chary of my betting, I reserve it only for certainties. And without doubt, I'd stake money that this village would draw urban visitors by the hundreds."

"A lovely dream, but a dream nonetheless." She sighed and turned away from the view. "We'll just have to go on existing as we always have, balancing precariously at the water's edge."

Together, they strolled back down the pier. She guided him off to the left, toward a stretch of beach past a boardwalk, but asked, "Do you mind getting sand on your boots?"

He glanced down. He hadn't had room to pack an additional pair of boots, and the ones he wore were dusty from his journey to Cornwall. "These are already in a sad state. I may have to comfort my valet when it comes time to polish them." He didn't mention the time after Waterloo when he'd picked some dried mud off his boot, only to discover that his fingertips had come away red. The dirt had been saturated with blood. "What about your shoes? They look a trifle delicate for a trek across a beach."

"That's easily remedied." She bent down and quickly undid the ribbons of her shoes before stepping out of them. She wasn't wearing stockings. "Been doing this all my life."

The sight of her bare feet shot pure lust through Kit. He drew in a long breath, wrestling for calm. It might be considered a breach of decorum to make love with her on the pier, in full view of people who had known her since her birth.

Holding her shoes, she stepped from the boardwalk onto the beach, then grinned as she wriggled her toes in the sand. His breath caught at the sight of her unabashed joy.

"There's a series of coves we can walk to from here," she said.

He waved them forward. "Guide us there, intrepid leader."

They walked along the sand, from inlet to inlet, sheltered by the cliffs. The pale stone rose high, with the barest fringe of green grass peeking over the top, as if afraid to look down and see the vertiginous height.

For all the landscape's beauty, he was more transfixed by watching Tamsyn flirt with the water from the crashing waves. She held her skirts up, revealing her ankles. Like a sandpiper, she followed the line of sea foam as it reached up the damp beach and retreated again. At times, she would stay in place, allowing the water to cover her feet and soak into the hem of her dress.

He bent and tested the temperature of the water, expecting it to be warm. It wasn't.

"I've been thinking of you as part mermaid," he noted. "Now I know it must be true. How else to explain your ability to tolerate the icy water?"

"This is positively balmy from how cold it gets in the winter." She picked up a shell and handed it to him. "But from May to August, it's perfectly lovely for a brisk swim."

He turned the shell over in his hand. Such a fragile thing, so easily broken. But it weathered the sea and stood against storms.

Kit slipped it into his pocket, running his thumb over the grooves in the shell. He pictured the place on his mantel where he'd put it—no, better yet, he'd keep it in the table beside his bed, to take out and admire just before falling asleep.

"Who taught you to swim?" he asked.

She stopped walking and frowned. "I can't remember. It seems like I always knew."

That made him smile—thinking of her playing in the waves, the sun making new freckles on her skin, her hair damp and full of salt, like a creature of nature.

"Like I said, a born siren." He glanced up toward the

bluffs. "We're not far from your home," Kit noted. "If we kept heading north, we'd encounter the beach that's just at the foot of the cliff by the house. Is it part of the property?"

"It is," she said, and added quickly, "but no one goes there."

"Haunted?"

"Full of rocks. It doesn't make for a good walk. In fact," she went on, "we ought to turn back and go to the village to pick up our luncheon."

Kit remembered glancing down at the cove on her family property yesterday. From the bluffs, it hadn't looked rock strewn at all, only covered with more sand. There had been a rocky outcropping at the far end of the inlet—he wondered if that was what she meant.

The instinct that had kept him alive for years while fighting flared into alertness again. That sense of alert dimmed when he was with her, yet something in this place continued to needle him. Much as he wanted to, he couldn't ignore it or quiet the voices of doubt that whispered to him, telling him something wasn't right.

But he followed Tamsyn back down the beach, hoping against hope that for once, his instincts were false.

Chapter 25

Tamsyn was in one of her favorite places, yet unease kept its needles in her—poking into her neck and along her arms, keeping her in a constant state of apprehension.

Carrying their basket of food, she led Kit from where they had tethered their horses, down into the ancient forest's dell. Huge mature oaks shaded grassy banks sloping toward a creek, and the sunlight filtered through their leaves, turning everything cool and green. She tried to take comfort from the permanency of the place. No matter what happened in her life, the old trees would go on as they always had, the creek would continue to run, and all the living things that made this wood their home would persevere regardless of her tempestuous existence.

She cast a look over her shoulder to watch Kit as he ambled after her, a woolen blanket in his arms. His attention was fixed on the shadows between the trees, as though searching out hidden enemies. Yet he seemed to find the environment safe enough to glance upward at the leafy canopy and smile.

"This part of the world has more than its share of enchanted sites," he said, picking his way around a stand of ferns. "Hardly seems fair to the rest of the country."

"We take our enchantment seriously," she answered

with a solemn nod. "Woods like this are called *koswigow*. They're full of old magic." She stopped at a place where the ground was relatively level. "This will be a good spot."

"Are you certain?" He peered into the shadowy places beneath the ferns. "We might be trampling over the fairy folk's palace. I'll wind up with donkey ears or speaking only in gibberish."

"No need to worry," she assured him. "We're old friends, the *spyrysyon* and me. And you'd look charming with donkey ears." She pointed to the ground by her feet. "Let's put the blanket down here."

He did as she asked, laying down the coarse covering. "You haunt this spot as much as the fairies?"

"Nearly." She sank down onto the blanket, removed her bonnet, and began unpacking the basket. It would be a simple luncheon of pasties, ale, and strawberries—a meal she always enjoyed. "Some of the girls in the village were frightened of it here. Like you, they feared retribution from the *spyrysyon* for trespassing."

"I am not afraid," he said with a show of wounded pride. "I am extraordinarily cognizant of my surroundings." He laid his long body down on the blanket, propping himself up on an elbow and looking the picture of a gentleman taking his ease. "So you came here alone."

"Even when I was very small." She handed him one pasty. "My mother and father used to tease me and say they needed to tie a kite to my back so they could find me when I wandered away. I did that quite a lot," she admitted. She ran off more after her parents' deaths, seeking the comfort she couldn't get from Jory and Gwen.

"I wouldn't know anything about being born with wanderlust," he declared airily, then grinned. "When I asked for a commission, no one in my family was particularly surprised. It was said that two things were my main attractors—the scarlet uniform, and the chance to go abroad." He took a bite of pasty and made a sound of pleasure.

She also took a healthy bite. After chewing and swallowing, she said, "You must have looked very dashing in your uniform."

He gave a small shrug. "The most I could hope for was that I didn't dishonor it."

"Clearly," she pointed out, "your country thinks you didn't. Gave you an earldom to thank you for your service."

"That was Lord Somerby's doing," Kit demurred, running his hand back and forth over the blanket. He'd touched and held her tenderly with those hands, and she longed for the feel of them on her.

"Lord Somerby knew hundreds of officers," she noted, "and he didn't petition the Crown on anyone else's behalf. Just you." Gently, she asked, "Do you miss him?"

Kit was silent for a moment. "It's not as though I felt neglected by my father," he said contemplatively. "Third sons are usually afterthoughts, yet I wasn't overlooked or ignored. Even so . . ." His gaze turned inward. "Somerby was the first person who saw my potential." He took a sip of ale—with fascination, she watched the strong movement of his throat—and handed the flagon to her.

His touch lingered longer than necessary to hand her the flagon, sending quills of awareness spinning through her. "I believe you could do anything you set your mind to." She drank and set the ale down.

Kit looked at her for a very long time, his gaze unblinking. He came up onto his knees. "That's precisely what I think about you."

Warmth and agony twisted through her in a mystifying whirl. He gave her so much, and she repaid him with dishonesty.

"Tamsyn." His voice was low and searing.

A hot thrill shot along her body. She looked up and was ensnared in the naked desire in his eyes.

He moved with sleek fluidity, closing the distance between them. Her heart beat fiercely as he knelt beside her, cradling her head between his hands and tilting her face up. She let her eyes drift shut, holding herself in suspension, waiting. Wanting.

His lips found hers. With a soft purr, she arched up into the kiss. His tongue licked at hers, and she eagerly lost herself in the passion they stoked so quickly. Kit kissed her as though he'd been starving for her taste—despite their kiss that morning. She devoured him, too, feeling the liquid surge of need everywhere in her body, wanting the profound intimacy that two lovers shared.

They fell back onto the blanket, his body partially covering hers. As they continued to kiss, she stroked over his taut back, feeling the shift of his body beneath his clothing. When he raised up enough to pluck at the buttons of her spencer, she took advantage of his position and pushed his coat down his shoulders. Awkward with impatience, they worked to shed layers of garments—his coat and neckcloth, her spencer—until he was in his shirtsleeves and the front of her dress was spread open.

His hand slipped under her open bodice to cup her breast. She gasped as he found her tight nipple and stroked it. With each caress, sensation built, gathering between her legs. She shifted restlessly with growing desire. Against her thigh, she felt the thick ridge of his erection, and there was some comfort in knowing he wanted her as much as she wanted him.

At least her desire was honest. She could give him this. She could give *them* this.

He trailed his lips down her neck and found the bare flesh of her upper chest. But then he rose up, back onto his knees. She'd never seen him look so intent.

"Kit . . . ?"

"I want something, love." His hand stroked up her leg, slowly gathering up the fabric of her skirts. "I want to taste you."

She widened her eyes. At the Orchid Club, she'd seen people doing just that, but never had she thought she'd experience it for herself. "Here?" she whispered, excitement pulsing beneath that one syllable.

"It's only the trees and us," he answered. His lids lowered and his voice deepened. "I've dreamed of your taste for so long. And the look on your face when you come."

His candid, erotic words undid her. She went feverish everywhere.

In answer, she gave a small nod. He inhaled sharply, then leaned forward to capture her mouth for a long, deep kiss. When he finally pulled away, they both panted, their shared breaths hot and urgent.

As she lay back, resting on her elbows so she could watch him, Kit positioned himself between her legs. He removed her shoes, then reached up under her skirts and swiftly did away with her drawers, leaving her naked from the waist down. With both hands, he pushed up her skirts, baring her legs—calves, knees, thighs. Then higher.

He growled when he uncovered her sex. Fascination kept her gaze on him as he bent close and stroked his fingers through her red curls. He made another sound, low and dark, when he traced her folds and found them swollen and wet.

She couldn't stop her gasp as he caressed her, discovering where she was most responsive. He looked almost solemn as he circled her bud. Then he brought his mouth onto her.

Strength left her completely, and she had to lie back, her sightless gaze on the leafy canopy overhead while he licked and kissed and stroked her sex. His tongue delved into her, and she cried out in pleasure. He consumed her with unrelenting demand. Sensation filled each part of her, radiating out in golden rays, chasing away thought.

He lifted his head long enough to say huskily, "Touch yourself. Your breasts."

She could not resist his earthy command. Lifting her hands, she found the points of her nipples and lightly pinched them. She moaned in response.

"*Yes*," he rumbled, then put his mouth on her again.

As he lapped at her, he slowly thrust his finger in and out of her passage. Pleasure upon pleasure saturated her. She was spread out, shameless, the boundaries of herself melting away as Kit continued to devour her.

Her release came in a fiery wave. She flung herself into it with complete abandon, her cry high and long. Yet no sooner did the wave ebb, another grew, and when it crashed upon her, she couldn't stop herself from crying out again.

"Oh God." Her voice was no more than a mewl. "I want you inside me, Kit."

He reared back enough to unfasten his breeches and free his erection. Then he was stretched out atop her, bracing himself so that his weight didn't crush her. Their gazes locked. The witty, sophisticated gentleman was gone—now he was pure desire, and he wanted her.

He ran the length of his erection through her soaking flesh, coating himself in her wetness, before fitting the tip at her entrance. As he slid into her, he bared his teeth.

"Ah, love, you're perfect," he said hoarsely.

"Not perfect," she managed to gasp.

"To me, you are." He drew his hips back, then thrust forward. He stroked in and out with each word. "Every. Part. Of. You."

She reveled in the feel of him filling her, of her surrounding him, of them together and the pleasure they made. When she canted her hips to take him deeper, he groaned. And when he shifted his position so that with every thrust, he ground against her bud, she nearly wept with ecstasy.

Their pace increased as the frenzy took hold of them. He fucked her with single-minded purpose, making himself into a beautiful weapon of pleasure.

She came with a cry that left her throat raw. A few strokes later, Kit's body went rigid from his orgasm. After a long while, he sank down atop her, his breath rough and jagged.

Warmth and tenderness engulfed her. She petted the back of his head and pushed damp strands of hair from his brow. He nuzzled against her neck and pressed kisses to her throat.

Tamsyn didn't believe anything could be flawless. It simply didn't happen, not in nature, and not in the world of man. There was always something—a tiny defect, a slight fault—that prevented perfection.

This moment with Kit was nearly faultless. He had made her feel treasured, protected, adored, and given her such pleasure.

Yet nothing could take away from the fact that, by midnight tonight, she would have to lie to him. And if he ever found out about her dishonesty, there was every chance he would cut her from his life completely.

$\mathcal{B}$Y the time the sun set, Tamsyn's entire body felt tight as a spring. The lovemaking had been extraordinary, and she'd wanted to luxuriate in it for as long as she could. Instead, she had taken Kit to every landmark and vista, each view and prospect. Anywhere within a decent riding distance, she had brought him, with the excuse that she wanted him to see all the places that had significance to her.

He had to go to bed early tonight, and once he did, fall into a deep sleep without any chance of waking up in the middle of the night and searching her out.

They rode to the stables, and she cast a look of both worry and envy in his direction. He moved easily in the saddle, a man at peace with the world. She, on the other hand, was a mass of apprehension.

After they had dismounted and taken care of the horses, they made their way back toward the house. He laced their fingers together. Despite both the fact that they'd already made love today and her continuous disquiet about tonight, the press of his skin to hers brought forth a rosy bloom of need and an ache in her heart.

"I'm humbled that you showed me the places that hold meaning for you," he said warmly. "Seeing the beauty of this place and its power . . . I know you better now. Thank you."

Pleasure and dismay mingled within her. For all that she'd been trying to wear him out, she had also wanted to share her piece of Cornwall with him. He saw what it meant to her, and he valued that.

He stopped walking and kissed her quickly but tenderly. But the feel of his lips was too brief, because he pulled back enough to murmur, "Ah, there's something I meant to give you."

"Give me?" she said blankly. The astrolabe had been an extraordinary gift, and she'd tucked it away in the corner of her clothespress, hidden behind gowns and petticoats, in case a servant decided to claim it for themselves.

With a smile that verged on bashful, he released her hand and pulled something from his pocket. He held it up. "You left this behind in London. I hoped to see you wear it again."

The necklace he'd purchased for her. Its pearl and diamond pendant oscillated back and forth, almost hypnotic.

The urge to tell him everything hovered on her lips, to finally be done with all the lies and subterfuge and state baldly the truth of her situation.

She pressed her hand to her chest where her heart throbbed. "Oh, Kit."

"Shall I put it on you?" he asked as though hoping for a precious favor.

"If Gwen sees me wearing that," she said ruefully, "she'll turn chartreuse with envy."

"Let her turn any damn color she wants," Kit answered. "She doesn't matter." He motioned for Tamsyn to turn around.

There was nothing to do but hold herself still as he fastened the necklace's clasp. She glanced down at the pendant, her fingers unable to stop from caressing the creamy surface of the pearl, and her chest seized with agony and joy.

She turned back to face him. His gaze moved from the necklace to her face, his expression one of grateful pleasure. A hard lump formed in her throat.

"It's nearly time for supper," she managed to say. "I'll head inside and wash up."

"Washing up is a difficult and complex process," he said gravely. "I volunteer to lend a hand, just to make certain everything goes smoothly."

Her lips tugged into a smile. Her husband was an irredeemable rake. "We'd likely wind up missing supper."

"I fail to see the problem in that scenario."

"I'm hungry, and the cook refuses to serve food beyond set times." Though she craved the feel of him again, she knew that if she and Kit fell into bed together, extracting herself for tonight's work would be impossible.

"We'll forage in the woods like the *spyrysyon*."

But she shook her head. "I'd rather eat a hot meal than fumble around in the dark for sour berries. I promise—

another time I'll be more than happy to have you assist in my bathing."

He beamed. "Excellent. Now go." He gave her a soft nudge toward the house.

She headed up the path leading to the back door, but stopped short when she saw movement in the window. Was someone watching? It wouldn't be a surprise if either Gwen or Jory decided to spy on her and Kit. They had been completely disinterested in her when she'd been merely their niece, and even her elevation to being a countess hadn't drawn their attention. But with Kit in residence—a genuine *earl*—no doubt they'd seek some way to turn her marriage into their advantage.

In her room, she shut and leaned against the door. Her fingers stroked the necklace but it brought her no comfort. The world was a hard place, full of sharp edges and innumerable dangers. Even something, some*one*, that should have given her comfort only added to the peril.

Tears formed in the corners of her eyes and ran down her cheeks to pool in the hollow at the base of her throat. She pressed her hand to her thudding heart.

She loved Kit. Loved him, and that only made what she had to do all the more agonizing.

Chapter 26

It was useless for Kit to undress, get into bed, and pretend that he'd be able to sleep. Instead, fully clothed, he paced the length of his narrow room, sparking with restless energy and insistent thoughts.

The house moaned and creaked like an arthritic fisherman. He winced at the squeak of the floorboards beneath his boots. But he'd learned a trick when sneaking into a Portuguese *fortaleza* that had been commandeered by the French, and he used that skill now as he modified the heaviness of his gait and stuck closer to the walls, where the boards were less warped.

He ought to be splayed out in bed, sunk deep in slumber. Tamsyn had taken him from vista to castle ruin to abandoned mine, possibly determined to show him every sight within miles. Almost as though she was intentionally trying to exhaust him.

But that was ludicrous, wasn't it? She'd have no reason to deliberately exhaust him.

A mouse darted from one corner of the chamber to the other, pausing for a moment to stare at him with wary black eyes, uncertain of Kit's motivations.

It was a novel sensation to empathize with a rodent.

"I grant you safe passage," Kit murmured to the mouse.

Its whiskers twitched, and then it was gone, scurrying into one of the innumerable holes riddling the house.

Tamsyn's attachment to this neglected collection of bricks was understandable. It had been her home her whole life, and held the memories of past happiness. However, the presence of her aunt and uncle surely tainted those memories. He couldn't understand why she would voluntarily put herself under the same roof, not when there were much more pleasant, less painful options.

She'd barely eaten her supper and had hardly spoken. Lord and Lady Shawe didn't seem to notice or care. Kit did.

Impatience—and the demand to protect her—pushed at him, filling him with edgy force. He needed to get her away from this place. Surely he could hire some people to help the local women with their garden and chickens, thus freeing her from the callous disinterest of her relatives. He and Tamsyn could remain in Cornwall, if that was her desire. But they wouldn't stay in this house.

He'd tell her. Now. He couldn't wait another minute—he had to keep alive the fire that burned within her, before the weight of this house and her kin could extinguish it.

At once, he was out in the hallway, heading toward her bedchamber. He continued to stay close to the walls, careful to keep from waking the house with the creaking of his steps.

As he neared her room, he saw motion ahead and stopped—someone was quietly moving down the corridor. He pressed against the wall and peered around the corner. If one of her relatives was about, he didn't want to encounter them. Doubtless her uncle would try to talk to him and slather on more flattery.

But it wasn't Lord Shawe.

Kit's pulse pumped when he saw Tamsyn slipping through the shadows. She wore dark clothing and shielded the light from her candle, as if making certain no one would be aware of her presence. What the devil was she doing awake and dressed at this hour? Was she en route to his bedroom? His body leapt to attention at the thought.

But she didn't make the turn in the direction of his chamber. Instead, glancing around cautiously, she hurried toward the stairs leading to the lower level.

He crept quickly down the stairs, always keeping her in his line of sight. Yet she didn't go outside, choosing instead to go through a doorway that led to the basement. He'd discovered that door in his exploration of the house. Always curious, he'd gone into the basement but found it containing only the detritus and discards of a house. Nothing of note. He glided down the steps leading to the basement, then paused as she pulled a key from her pocket, fitting it into the lock on an old door. Kit had found that same door, but hadn't been able to open it. Thinking it led to more storage beneath the house, he'd dismissed it and moved on.

She opened it now and passed through into the darkness beyond, then shut and locked the door behind her.

Kit slid forward and took a penknife from his coat. He worked the knife in the lock until it gave a barely audible click. After waiting a moment to see if she came back to investigate, he followed, making certain to close the door.

He found himself plunged into a shadowy and twisting maze of corridors, bits of hay and stone dotting the rough floor. He wound his way from one passage to the next, always keeping Tamsyn in his sight. She moved purposefully, familiar with her route.

Nerves skittered along his skin. He squeezed his hands into fists, using the sensation of tightening muscle over bone to ground him.

She turned a corner and he paused so that she wouldn't

be aware of him. She stopped, too. The sounds of scraping stone reverberated in the passageway and a rasping, as if another door opened. Then her footsteps faded away.

He moved around the corner. But all he found was silent darkness.

Without the light of her candle, he couldn't see anything. Feeling around on the ground, he collected a few pieces of straw. Then, grateful that the War had trained him to keep knives and flints on his person, regardless of where he was, he took a flint from his pocket and set the straw to burning.

When it blazed to life, he started in surprise. The corridor came to a rubble-covered dead end, as though it had caved in long ago.

He turned in a slow circle. Where the hell had she gone? People didn't simply vanish.

Or maybe she was a changeling, after all . . . He shuddered.

Making himself still, he felt a slight, damp breeze coming from the wall to his right. He studied it. The wall looked to be made of plaster over wood, most likely with earth and stone behind it. Yet there was a small gap between the floor and the wall. A few stones were piled up nearby, as though they had been moved aside—revealing the gap. Putting his hand close to the space, the breeze pushed lightly against his palm.

He took a coin from his waistcoat pocket and nudged it through the gap. It clinked, as if falling down a step. The clinking continued until it faded away.

More stairs lay beyond this door. Stairs leading down to. . . . He calculated how far he and Tamsyn had traveled underneath the house, and inhaled the scent of the breeze. It carried the rich brine of the sea.

He frowned in surprise as he realized the stairs led down to the cove. Down to the very inlet that Tamsyn had avoided on her tour of the area, claiming it too rocky for anyone to traverse.

His spine tightened.

He straightened and felt along the wall to find a latch or lever that would open the door. Frustration sizzled when he could discover nothing. He had to get down to that beach.

There was only one other way to get there. Moving quickly, he sped back the way they had come, arriving back in the basement, and then ascending until he was in the house itself. He crushed the burning straw beneath his boot heel, and moved as noiselessly as possible through the manor.

In a moment, he was outside. There wasn't time to saddle a horse, so he ran at full speed toward the village.

Dark landscape swam around him as he passed fields and cottages. It was a waking nightmare—the shadowy landscapes rose up like those in the midst of dreams.

I'm awake, damn it. He clung to this thought as he ran.

He gave thanks for his good night vision, which had kept him alive on the Peninsula and now guided him to the village.

Everything in the small town was shuttered and quiet. Not a soul roamed the high street, all the citizens clearly in their beds. Out in the harbor, the boats moved with the motion of the water, but no one was about.

Kit hastened past the pier, making a sharp turn to get onto the beach. Running on sand made his legs burn, yet he kept going, speeding from one cove to the next. At last, he reached the edge of the inlet on her family's estate.

Crouching low, he scanned the scene.

His heart climbed into his throat at what he saw. The village had been empty because most of its inhabitants milled around in the sandy cove.

A woman walked among them, her movements sure

and purposeful. She lifted a lantern shaped like a watering can, and light from the spout fell across her face.

Kit bit back a curse.

The woman was Tamsyn.

His addled wits struggled to logically piece together what he saw. It truly was her. She must have emerged from the opening carved into the stone at the foot of the cliff. It appeared that large rocks had been concealing the opening, but they had been moved aside to permit entrance and exit.

A three-masted sailing ship was anchored several hundred feet from the beach.

It signaled to the shore with a light.

Kit scowled at the sight. He'd been in a considerable number of clandestine missions before—sneaking behind enemy lines in Spain to retrieve valuable information on troop movements—but this was England. This was peacetime. None of this was supposed to be happening.

Someone on land signaled back. It was Tamsyn, holding up her lantern. She covered and uncovered the spout with her hand. On the ship, the signal blinked in response.

At the far end of the cove, boulders on the sand formed a ridge that jutted toward the water. Men clambered over the rocks, then reappeared at the farthest end of the ridge. He couldn't tell what it was they dragged from behind the rocks. Angling for a better look, he sprinted forward and took cover behind a chunk of cliff that had long ago broken free and now rested on the sand.

One of the men turned and looked in Kit's direction, but he stayed hunkered down, holding his breath. Finally, the man went back to his work.

From his vantage, Kit saw that the men hauled what appeared to be a wooden walkway. No, it wasn't a walkway. It was a pier—the same used for mooring boats.

People waded into the water as they pulled the pier

around the stone ridge, pushing it out into the water before anchoring the end to the rocks.

A large rowboat disengaged itself from the ship and began heading in the direction of the pier. He watched with fascination as villagers formed a line leading from the pier to the opening in the cliff.

Finally, the rowboat reached the pier and men on the boat hefted something heavy into the waiting arms of the villagers.

Casks. The cargo they transported was casks. He didn't doubt they contained contraband French liquor.

Like a fire brigade, they passed their cargo from one to the other. Some staggered under the weight of the casks, but they were helped by brawnier, stronger men. The cargo moved toward the people at the entrance to the bluff, who brought the casks within.

All the while, Tamsyn strode up and down the line. Though she barely spoke, she directed the cargo's movement and paused now and then to consult with someone before stepping onto the slip and conversing with someone in the boat.

Kit sank down onto his haunches, the blood in his ears roaring louder than the surf as the truth finally revealed itself to him.

His wife was a smuggler.

His mind whirled as his body shook. It was impossible to make sense of anything with his thoughts and heart tumbling in confusion. What the hell should he do?

You've been in tight spots before, he reminded himself. *Take one step at a time.*

He seized on a thread of logic to help him move forward.

Years of warfare taught Kit that confronting her now could mean his death. Smuggling gangs carried bats and clubs in case they encountered customs officers. Doubtless the villagers would use the same weapons on him if he made his presence known. They'd beat him first, then ask questions later. They wouldn't much care that he was their leader's husband. He was an outsider and a threat.

The farmer had warned Kit about strange and dangerous doings in Newcombe, but never did Kit believe that *his wife* was at the center of it all. Ever since he'd arrived in the area, his military instinct had told him something was wrong—and here he had proof.

The only thing he could do now was get away without calling attention to himself. The rest he would have to figure out moment by moment. Now he had to work out the best retreat strategy.

He edged back, then retraced his steps along the beach. Despite his shock, he moved quickly, finding the darkest places as his mind spun.

No answers would come to him. Cold bewilderment receded, replaced by blazing anger.

She was a felon flouting the laws he and his men had fought to preserve. And all this time, Tamsyn had hidden this from him, knowing how he felt about crime. But as to the how of it, he could not begin to fathom. Questions pummeled him, questions that no one could answer. Except Tamsyn. She knew everything.

After reaching the village, he went back the way he'd come, walking quickly through the town. Though he kept himself aware of his surroundings, his thoughts were a morass that threatened to overwhelm him.

The way back to the estate offered no solace, only a choking sense of doom. It was all tied to this place— which was why she'd refused to leave.

The way the operation on the beach had moved with such practice and precision revealed that it had been going on for some time. She had been engaged in smuggling since before their marriage. They had wed with her holding this secret.

Why would she marry him? It made no sense. She only jeopardized the security of her smuggling endeavors by doing so.

Was nothing between them real? Was he merely her pawn?

"Fuck," he said aloud.

He'd lost his heart to her. Yet she'd played him false from the very beginning.

She worked in direct opposition to the Crown. For over a decade, he'd fought to protect his king and country, and all the while, she defied English law. And she had dragged him into her criminal world when she'd agreed to become his wife. Her callous disregard for the sacrifices of good men was anathema to everything he'd championed. But it hadn't mattered in the face of her criminality.

When he reached the house, stone encased him. His movements were heavy as he slipped inside, still careful to keep from being heard. Tired beyond reckoning, he climbed the stairs.

Part of him shouted that he should pack his belongings and ride away. Far from her.

Instead, he entered Tamsyn's bedchamber. He pulled a chair into the center of the room and sat.

Many times, he'd readied himself before ambushing the enemy. In that tense silence, he'd checked and rechecked his rifle, mentally reviewing how the ambush was supposed to transpire so that nothing could be left to chance. He had to be certain of his opponents' defeat to keep his own fear at bay.

This time, he wasn't armed with his Baker rifle. As he waited for his wife's return, he armed himself with her lies.

Chapter 27

Tamsyn's very marrow ached with weariness as she climbed the stairs and made her way toward her bedchamber. She'd never known such exhaustion, but that was the price of stretching herself thin for so long. For the first time in years, she had declined joining everyone at the Tipsy Flea for a postrun celebration.

She prayed for a deep, dreamless sleep, and was already beginning to unfasten the top buttons of her bodice when she opened the door to her room.

She barely had time to swallow her yelp of shock.

Fully dressed, Kit sat in a chair in the middle of the room.

His face was a mask as she shut the door behind her. He held his body rigidly, his hands tightly gripping the chair's arms.

Her weary mind leapt into action, searching for an excuse as to why she was awake, clothed, and roaming the hallways.

"Don't." His voice was low and flat. "Don't think of an explanation." He stood, and she instinctively backed up, until she pressed against the door. "I know."

Her stomach pitched and the room tilted. There was

no need to ask him *what* he knew. She understood. Somehow, he'd found out.

"Outside," she said quickly. "We can talk away from
the house. I don't want anyone to hear us."

He lifted a brow. "Your aunt and uncle aren't aware?"

"Please," she said, raising her palm. "We must go outside. I'll tell you everything."

That seemed to momentarily mollify him. They left
her chamber and she moved back down the stairs and out
the rear door of the house. As she wove through the weed-
choked garden, Kit's looming presence remained at her
back. He said nothing, yet she could feel his anger in unseen waves.

Like a prisoner walking to their execution, she exited
the garden through a gate, moving on until she reached
a fence at the edge of a barley field. Her sense of self-
preservation screamed for her to run and never come
back. Yet he would catch her if she tried, and it was pointless to flee.

She felt the slightest gleam of relief. The lies could
stop now. Everything would be out in the open, and her
deception—of Kit, at least—was at an end.

"How?" she asked, turning to face him. The night's
darkness wreathed him in shadow, but she sensed his furious expression. "How did you find out?"

"I followed you," he answered. "Down to the dead end
in the corridors beneath the house."

"I didn't hear you."

He gave a humorless laugh. "That's because I was a
damned good soldier." After a moment, he asked, "Did
you build them—the corridors, the false wall with the
door?"

"No," she answered. "My grandfather saw what happened to the aristocrats in France, and was terrified that

the thirst for noble blood would spread across the Channel. He hired Irish workers to construct an escape route from the house. It was only happenstance that there are also caverns beneath the manor. That's where . . ." She swallowed. "That's where we store the brandy and lace when they're brought ashore. There's another passageway that leads from the cavern to the stone shed you saw yesterday."

"The spiders' home," he said acidly.

A throb passed through her at the mention of her distraction. "A week after the goods are delivered, we bring them up to the shed, load them into our buyer's waiting wagon, and then he proceeds from there."

"I find it difficult to believe your uncle and his wife don't know any of this."

"They never go into the cellar," she answered. "Their servants are too lazy to investigate. For eight years, I've kept it hidden from them."

Kit cursed. "You've been smuggling for eight goddamned years." Briefly, he glanced away, as if unable to look at her. "I killed in the name of my king. I sent men to their deaths to protect my country. Yet all this time, you've flouted the law and made a mockery of the royal mandate. And by tying our names together, you've brought me into your reprehensible world, made me guilty by association." His voice throbbed with confusion and hurt. "Why?"

He'd survived the brutality of war, and she'd wounded him. Deeply. As he'd said, he had been a damned good soldier, and she'd flouted that. Shame was a brand upon her heart.

"The cost of a war is felt by many," she replied. "Newcombe was hit hard by taxes. There wasn't enough to pay for food. And the fishing had tightened up so that the catches were minuscule. Jory didn't take up my father's work of keeping the village afloat. When I'd go into Newcombe, I'd hear all the children and babies crying from hunger, and see the sunken eyes of the men and women." It pained her still to think of that time, as the village edged toward its demise.

"I grew up hearing stories of daring Cornish smugglers," she continued, looking up at the night sky. "They were heroes, not criminals. It came to me one afternoon after returning home from the village. Chei Owr had a secret way to the cove from the house and the passage to the stone outbuilding. Everything fell into place."

He said coldly, "A legal way to earn money didn't occur to you."

"Nothing would get the village back on its feet so fast," she answered, her voice tight, "or with such steady profits. I discussed it with everyone, and it was agreed we'd give it a try. There was nothing to lose."

"Except your lives," he bit out.

"Starvation makes people desperate. With children on the verge of death, would you make a different choice?"

He was silent.

"I went to a nearby town," she went on, "to a tavern known for being frequented by smugglers to get the operation set up. Nessa came with me."

"Eight years ago means that you were only sixteen."

"My parents had been dead for two years, and my father had always looked out for the village." Pride filled her now, as it had then, to see how he had asked after everyone at the conclusion of church, and how he'd never turned a villager away whenever they asked for assistance. "So it fell to me to take care of them. My childhood had come to an end when my mother and father died," she said without self-pity. "No one else had the means to do what had to be done. Just me." She lifted her chin as she spoke, "So I walked into that place with a hammering heart and a knife tucked into my garter."

Kit paced away, seemingly deep in thought. He whirled back to face her. "You married me and risked the whole operation," he accused.

"I had to," she said simply. "Chei Owr isn't entailed, and Jory is making plans to sell it." She lifted up her hands. "Without the house, we'd have no means to keep going."

"And your plan was to do what, precisely?" His question was brittle like frost.

Seeing no way to go but forward, she continued. "Word got to our buyer that our operation here was in trouble. He backed out." Bitterness clogged her voice. "Going to London seemed the answer to our problems. I could locate a new buyer in the biggest market in the country. There's always a need for brandy and lace, and we had a new shipment gathering dust here in Cornwall."

"That wasn't all you sought in London," he said cuttingly.

She ducked her head. "I couldn't find a buyer, and time was running out. I needed to find myself a husband, someone with money, who could purchase the house from Jory. Everything would be taken care of."

"You got a man who'd marry you," Kit noted. "Did you find your buyer?"

The day in the jewelry district was still vivid in her memory—and how close she'd come to being discovered by Kit. "I did. He agreed to take the goods off my hands when they came in from Cornwall."

Kit held up his index finger. "Hold a moment. You had smuggled goods in London? Where were they?"

"In"—she cleared her throat—"the cellar at the house on Bruton Street."

"And the staff never suspected."

"Mr. Stockton and two footmen had to be brought into confidence," she confessed. "I agreed to pay them a portion of the profits if they kept quiet."

His silence stretched on for an unbearable eternity.

Finally, he said through clenched teeth. "Nessa, the butler, the footmen. They were in on it. Everyone was—except me."

She tried to speak, but no words made it past her lips.

He planted his hands on his hips, and his scowl was so deep, she could see it in the darkness. "Why did you not ask me directly if you could buy the house?" he pressed.

"It would have been a huge expense. We had been wed such a short time, and then we learned the condition in Lord Somerby's will that gave me control of the money. I didn't know how you would have felt if I'd said I needed to spend the lion's share of our new fortune." She spread her hands. "I was afraid, so I said nothing. And adhered to my plans in secret."

"I was your dupe." The pain in his words cut her like a blade. "You used me."

"We used each other," she said. "To you, I was a means to get Lord Somerby's money. And what of your pleasure garden? You tried to make me care for you so I'd give you the funds to pay for it." She spread her hands. "Neither of us are guiltless."

His chest moved up and down as he drew in shallow, furious breaths. "That's your defense."

"It was for them," she said, waving toward the village. "I did it for them."

She took a step toward him, but he backed away. He moved slightly, and then put more distance between them. Finally, he turned and began walking.

"Kit? Where are you going?"

He whirled back and strode to her. "Not to worry," he said bitterly. "I won't go to the authorities. I won't have Lady Blakemere clapped in irons." He opened his mouth as if to speak more, but then shook his head and marched off into the night's shadows.

Her feet would not move to follow him. Everything within her was cold as granite, and just as heavy. She sagged against the fence behind her, using it to prop her up when she would have surely sunk down to her knees.

Fear gripped her throat tightly. Now that he'd learned the truth about her smuggling, he could destroy not only her, but Newcombe, as well. He was so bitter, so angry that she'd broken the law; there was every chance he'd change his mind and turn her in to the customs officers.

Pain engulfed her like a smothering blanket. Everything they'd built together had been destroyed.

What do I do?

Chapter 28

❧

*L*ike an avenging spirit, Kit roamed the surrounding countryside. Anger and sorrow and pain urged his legs into constant motion. Yet no matter what field he walked through, or bluff he stood atop, or crumbling castle keep he skirted, he never discovered the answers he sought— what to do about his wife and her smuggling.

He strode away from the coast and its beating surf, seeking silence. As if impelled by memory, he found himself at the edge of the forest where she'd taken him earlier. With grim determination, he moved deeper into the woods, bittersweet thoughts of their earlier lovemaking pulsing through him.

The hot wound of Tamsyn's deception continued to throb as he pushed his body to its limits. From the beginning, she had lied to him, even using their home as a place to store her contraband goods. He remembered how, the morning after they'd first made love, she had been absent from bed. When he'd found her, coming up from the house's lower floor, she'd said she had been handling a domestic emergency. Another fabrication.

She'd defied the law, as well. Wasn't that what he and his men fought to preserve? Had their injuries and deaths meant nothing to her?

He stopped at the clearing where they had lain. They had shared pleasure, but not the truth. Slowly, he crouched down and placed his hand on the dew-covered grass that was still flattened.

In the morass of his thoughts, one sang with a low and insistent note.

You weren't honest with her, either.

His fingers brushed over the grass, and predawn damp coated his skin. The coolness of the moisture jolted him, waking him from the cloud of his thoughts.

He stood and frowned at the leaves overhead, swaying in the darkness.

Perhaps their respective crimes canceled each other out. He was no stranger to morally ambiguous deeds. In Belgium, he'd shot a man in the back—but the enemy had been running to warn his comrades of the advancing English soldiers. He'd acted in a way that made his heart shrivel, yet it had been for the greater good.

She and the villagers defied the Crown and disregarded the law, but they had done so to survive. Adults could sometimes endure starvation, yet children could not. He'd seen the shriveled bodies of Spanish and Portuguese babies held in the arms of their wasted parents. That same fate could have befallen the children of Newcombe if Tamsyn hadn't intervened.

Whether or not that made his and Tamsyn's actions right, he didn't know.

The forest oppressed him now, choking him with its lush foliage. He hurried out of the woods, his strides taking him away from thoughts of what they'd created, and what they'd lost.

More landscape scrolled past him as he walked. The black night sky began to turn indigo with the coming of dawn, and shapes emerged from the darkness. Snug farmhouses and barns appeared. A handful of goats bleated at him as he passed their pasture.

The route he traveled sloped downward, and buildings grew more plentiful, until he discovered himself walking down the village high street.

Despite the earliness of the hour, people were already up and tending to their daily business. Women scrubbed at their washing or carried baskets. A sleepy child sat on the front step of a house, groggily playing with a doll. Out on the pier, men moved with familiarity on their docked boats, preparing their vessels before heading out for a day's fishing. Distantly, Kit wondered if their catch had improved over the years or if they still hauled up empty nets at the end of the day.

The people he passed continued to give him cautious looks. He couldn't blame them. He had no business being up at this hour and roving through the village like a specter.

They were smugglers, too. Their suspicion of him was well-founded. Yet no one knew that he was aware of their secret.

"Morning, my lord," one woman on her step murmured. She held a sleeping baby swaddled in a striped blanket, and gently jogged the infant up and down. Nessa came out of the house, watching Kit warily. The child and its mother looked perfectly healthy.

Nessa had lied to him, too.

He moved on without speaking.

No one in the village appeared gaunt or ill. There were no listless children dragging themselves along the street, followed by hollow-eyed mothers. Men weren't hunched with anger because their families' bellies were empty.

Kit had seen what famine did to people. So many villages on the Peninsula had been decimated by hunger.

One little boy in Portugal had followed Kit's unit for miles, begging for something to eat. Kit had given the boy his remaining bread and a hunk of cheese—though not before scraping off the mold.

The child's haunted dark eyes looked at Kit now, through the veil of time.

Starvation had come to this village, too. Eight years ago, it had withered flesh on bone and made stomachs angry caverns echoing with want.

Rescue had come in the form of one redheaded sixteen-year-old girl with an audacious plan. She had conceived and executed it, saving the lives of hundreds of people. Despite the losses she'd faced and the neglect she suffered at home, she did not abandon her need to help others. She persisted.

Kit walked to the seawall and sat down, looking out at the ink-dark ocean. At once, images of Tamsyn filled him—watching the water, inhaling its brine, walking along the edge of the foam on the beach. There had been so much life and joy in her, he couldn't help but share that happiness. Its reverberations continued even now, his heart lifting in time with the waves.

She had committed many crimes against his country, the one he'd been sworn to defend against enemies. Could he fly in the face of the law? Yet the government had taken from this village in the form of punishing taxation, endangering everyone. That wasn't right, either.

Uncertainty was a chasm, surrounding him on all sides.

Would he have done the same in her place? She'd taken a massive risk in order to help the villagers. She'd imperiled her own life. For them.

He studied the churning sea. He wasn't a waterman, but he understood enough to know that the ocean was never idle. It changed from day to day, from moment to moment. Yet it was eternal, too, despite—or because of—

its constantly shifting nature. One could try to predict its moods and movements, but there were times when there was no choice but to surrender to its changeability. It was either that or drown.

Making a choice was difficult and thorny. Yet he had to make one.

His thoughts wove through a labyrinth like Theseus searching for the minotaur. At the center of the maze, the beast awaited him. Did he kill it or learn how to live with the creature?

The answer came to him with sudden clarity.

He got to his feet, causing several heads to turn in his direction, but he paid them no heed. Instead, he traveled back up the high street, back on the road that led to Shawe's house—and Tamsyn.

TAMSYN paced moodily through the derelict garden her mother had labored over, as if trying to outrun her thoughts.

Soon after her mother's death, Tamsyn had tried to maintain the garden herself. She'd pulled weeds and pruned hedges to the best of her ability, but her knowledge about gardens was scarce, and she hadn't her mother's patience and skill in coaxing the plants to thrive. The books she'd studied had told her precisely what to do. Despite her following their instructions, the garden had withered.

It wasn't dead, but it didn't flourish. Whatever managed to remain alive did so out of sheer obstinacy.

We're much alike, she thought, stopping long enough to touch the jagged leaves of a shrub. She and the plant continued to exist because there was no other option other than surrender. It was said that the barony had been given to her ancestor because he'd fought against Cromwell at Worcester. Perhaps there was a little of the first Lord Shawe's blood left in her, keeping her on her feet when all she wanted to do was crumple to the ground.

Yet how was she to move forward? There was no enemy, no obstacle to overcome. Her fate, and the fate of the village, was in Kit's hands. She didn't know what he would do. Unsettled misery sat on her shoulders like a gargoyle, its claws digging into her flesh as it weighed her down.

Footfalls approached, the gravel crunching beneath the newcomer's feet. Tamsyn's body went still as her heart pounded. The footsteps were too heavy to be Gwen's, too quick to be Jory's. None of the male servants ever sought her out, since Gwen was the mistress of the house.

There was only one person who moved with such speed and purpose.

She forced herself to turn and face Kit, struggling to compose herself. Yet her heart sprang into her throat at seeing him approach, his gaze fixed on her.

He stopped a few feet from her and said nothing, studying her face for a long time. All the while, her breath came fast and the ground felt unsteady beneath her feet.

"I don't regret what I've done," she said evenly. "Not when it comes to the villagers. They were suffering and I had the means to alleviate that suffering. Perhaps another person, a better person, might have found another solution, but this was the one that seemed the best to me."

A muscle moved in his jaw, but he remained silent.

"In eight years," she said, her words low but insistent, "there have been seventeen weddings. Twenty-four children have been born. Fifteen burials took place. No one died because they didn't have enough to eat or because they couldn't pay a doctor. That was my doing, and I would gladly steal the diamonds from the Prince's waistcoat buttons if it meant Newcombe's survival."

Planting his hands on his hips, his gaze never strayed from her face. He looked like the soldier he was, sharply assessing the situation. Was she the enemy to him, or an ally? Perhaps she was something more complicated.

"If I have any regret," she went on, her eyes burning, "it's that I hurt you. I never desired that. I only wanted . . ." She blinked hard to stem the tears that wanted to run. "I had hoped that somehow, we could find a way to be together, to be happy, even as my deception drove a wedge between us." She quickly dashed her hand across her eyes. "Something occurred after you asked me to marry you. Something unexpected. I wasn't even sure if I wanted it to happen. But it did."

Summoning all her courage, she stepped closer to him. He didn't move when she placed her hand on his chest—but he didn't embrace her, either.

"I fell in love with you, Kit." Her smile was a fragile thing, easily broken. "The man who I'd wed as a means to an end was also the man I came to love. I love your clever mind, and the joy you find in the world, and the size of your heart. I love the way you cultivate friendships because you genuinely like people. I love that you never tried to make me into someone I wasn't."

His eyes were shining now, bright with emotion, and his chest heaved beneath her palm.

"Every lie I told you was like performing an amputation on myself," she whispered. "Cutting away perfectly healthy flesh while I fought to keep from screaming. But I had to choose—loving you, or the life of the village." She pressed her lips together. "So I made my choice. I made it, and I'm ready to face the consequences."

She dropped her hand and knotted it. Her fingers wrapped around her thumb and her fingernails dug into the flesh of her palm. "I can tell Mr. Flowers that I'm granting you complete, unrestricted access to our fortune. Bring a CrimCon suit against me. Say I was unfaithful. I won't contest it." Pain tore through her as she spoke, but she made herself go on. "All I ask is that you don't hurt the people of Newcombe."

A long moment passed. Tamsyn died and was reborn a hundred times as she gazed at Kit, her soul in her eyes and her fate in his hands. She searched his face for some sign, anything at all that revealed what he thought, he felt. Yet he remained steadfastly opaque.

Finally, his gaze fixed to hers, he cupped his hand around hers and slowly, carefully, uncurled her fingers.

"You'll break your thumb if you throw a punch with it tucked under your fingers," he said lowly. He arranged her hand so that it formed a strong fist. "Better. More force and less chance of injuring yourself."

She frowned. "Are you asking me to strike you?"

"I want you to be able to defend yourself," he answered. "Firearms are good for only one shot, and they aren't very reliable. Plus there's a chance you could kill someone, which is a crime punishable by death. If there isn't anything around to use as a weapon, effective use of this"—he lifted up her fist—"can be devastating. Don't be afraid to use it on a customs officer if he's coming after you. Aim for his nose or throat. Hitting the solar plexus," he continued, resting her hand on the center of his chest, "can knock the wind out of someone and give you an opportunity to run like hell."

She stared at him as her pulse raced. A tutorial in self-defense was not what she had expected from him.

"There's always a knee to the groin," she said lowly.

He grimaced. "Brutal and devastating."

"Generally," she said, failing to keep her words level, "when the lawbreaker is advised on better ways to defeat the law, it's seen as an endorsement of their illegal activities." She licked her dry lips. "Is that what you're saying, Kit?"

He wrapped both his hands around her upraised fist. "As you said, neither of us is guiltless. We've both done things . . . things that aren't necessarily right, but they aren't wrong, either." He exhaled. "It's a complex world. We try to control it with laws and Thou Shalt Nots and etiquette manuals. We try . . . but when it comes down to it . . . we can only do the best we can. Hope we hurt as few people as possible. Sometimes it can't be avoided." His lips formed a small, wry smile. "Sometimes it's necessary. Like what you've done here, for the village."

Her chest began loosening, the knot in her belly unraveling, but she was afraid to look too closely at what she felt, and what he meant.

"I was responsible for hundreds of lives, too," he went on softly. "Each time one of my men died, they took a piece of me with them—because I hadn't been able to protect all of them. But had it been in my power, I would have done anything to make sure they returned to their families. I fought and planned and killed, for my country, yes, but for my men, as well."

"Kit." She imbued his name with all her aching hope.

"My love," he answered. His gaze was warm, and he lowered her fist before cupping the side of her face. His palm was warm against her chilled flesh. "I'm here. I understand. And I know what has to be done."

She had been the one responsible for everything for so long. The burden eased from her shoulders, yet her heart refused to fly free until it knew for certain what Kit intended.

He pressed his lips against her forehead before tilting her head back so their gazes met. "On my way back here, I realized what we have to do. We'll stick with your plan to buy this house from your uncle." He smiled down at her. "The smuggling must continue. And, if you'll have me, I'll serve as your second-in-command."

She gazed at him with wide eyes. "You speak truly?"

"I jest about many things," he murmured, "but not this. Not you. My sweet, brave, scofflaw bride." He permitted himself a scoundrel's smile. "They'll sing ballads about us and sell prints of our daring, infamous exploits in the shops on Paternoster Row."

"No need for infamy," she said gently. Her lips trembled as she spoke. "We only want to keep the village alive and thriving."

He ducked his head in acknowledgment. "Perhaps I got a little swept up. However," he added more soberly, "in this field, you have more experience. I cede to your expert knowledge."

"I need to hear it again." Her breath came quickly. "You aren't going to report me to the customs officers? The smuggling doesn't have to stop?"

"Precisely right." He wrapped his arms around her. "I'm here to help, however I can. Because it's the right thing to do. And because I love you."

He brought his lips to hers, and, throwing her arms about him, she kissed him back with all the desire and joy and love that filled her like an ocean. Gratitude poured through her, leaving her giddy on thankfulness and Kit's kisses.

When they finally broke the kiss, she said in a hurried whisper, "We'll have to act quickly. Jory keeps avoiding me, but he'll talk to you. Tell him you want to speak with him about a business matter, then offer to buy Chei Owr. He'll quote you an exorbitant price, but if you offer him a lump sum in cash, he'll have to accept your offer."

Kit chuckled. "It's a shame we didn't have you on the Peninsula. With your clearheaded tactical expertise, the War would have been over in a fortnight."

"I had other battles to fight," she said.

"And you'll go on fighting them," he added. "But not alone."

Energy surged through her, making her feel as though she could lift the heaviest boulder or climb the steepest peak.

Someone stood beside her. Someone loved her. Things she had yearned for, while believing that her wishes were hopeless, had finally come to pass.

Chapter 29

$\mathcal{M}$uch as Kit wanted to spirit Tamsyn off to the much-touted inns in Perranporth and share a bed—along with a night of athletic, imaginative lovemaking—he had to make an offer on the house as soon as possible.

The first order of business after that would be getting Tamsyn's aunt and uncle out. Once the loathsome Lord and Lady Shawe were gone, he and Tamsyn could concentrate on moving the latest shipment of contraband. There was also the matter of finally making repairs to the crumbling manor.

When he'd been fighting overseas, he'd made certain that he had clearly defined objectives arranged in the most logical and achievable order. It saved him and his men from poorly executed, disastrous missions. He applied that same principle now. The stakes were just as high.

He and Tamsyn had hoped to talk with Lord Shawe as soon as possible, but he was absent all day. And when Kit and Tamsyn went down to supper that night, Lord Shawe didn't join them at the dining table.

"Where's Jory?" Tamsyn asked her aunt.

Lady Shawe took a delicate sip of soup, dabbed her lips with a napkin, and then set the square of fabric down very deliberately before answering in a lofty voice, "He's in Newquay. He'll be back tomorrow."

Clearly, there was nothing to be done until the man himself was back from the neighboring town. So they endured another tedious dinner.

When Lady Shawe excused herself to retire for the night, Kit rose and bowed with minimal politeness. Once the baroness had quit the room, he turned to Tamsyn. "How do you manage it?"

"Manage what?"

He glanced around, then spoke in a low voice. "Sharing a roof with these people when you're hiding a secret from them. It makes my gut churn."

"My greatest challenge was keeping them from finding out," she answered in a whisper. "For months, it gnawed at me. I barely ate and couldn't sleep."

His heart contracted, imagining her so alone and so troubled, with little solace.

"But I overcame that fear," she continued lowly. "Because I had to." Darkness crept into her eyes. "It's not nearly as easy keeping a secret from someone you care about. It cuts you over and over again as though you're plunging a knife into your own chest."

He strode to her and raised her chin for a kiss. "We're done with hiding from each other. We're a united front now."

"We are," she answered.

When Kit walked Tamsyn to her bedchamber, he lingered at the door.

"Not sharing a bed with you is a bitter pill to swallow," he muttered.

"We could try evicting Gwen from her room," Tamsyn suggested. "But even if we could get her to leave, I don't want to sleep on a mattress *they* shared." She shuddered.

"A fair point," he conceded. "But I have a solution. It isn't perfect, but I'm used to conditions that aren't ideal." With that, he strode to his bedroom, gathered up armfuls of bedding, and marched back to Tamsyn's room.

"What are you doing?" she asked as he arranged the blankets and a pillow on the floor next to her bed.

"Making up a pallet, of course."

"But the floor is bare wood," she protested. "That can't be comfortable."

He shot her a look. "Compared to some of the places I slept on the Continent, this is luxurious."

"Kit," she said, her hands on her hips, "you cannot sleep on my floor when a somewhat-decent bed is just down the hall."

He curved his hands over her shoulders. "Now you're just offending my soldier's pride. Besides," he added after pressing a quick kiss to her mouth, "from now on, I never want us to sleep apart."

"I want the same," she said ardently. Then she gave a massive yawn.

He chuckled. "Weary is the woman who fights many battles."

"There are so many." She stretched out her arms and he avidly watched the lithe movements of her body. "I'm wrung out, but my mind is spinning like a pinwheel."

"The night before a battle was never easy," he said with a nod. As he spoke, he undid the fastenings of her clothes, stripping her down bit by bit. "I knew that if I didn't get enough rest, I'd be in even more danger. Weariness makes a man clumsy and unable to react quickly." He peeled off her gown, and then worked on her underthings. "So when I'd lie down in my tent, I'd imagine I was in the safest place I could picture. In my case, that was a little dell near my family's country estate. I'd go there to climb trees and watch clouds."

He slipped her loosened stays off her body and set them aside. Soon, she only wore her shift. All the while, she kept her gaze trained on him. He continued, "I'd picture myself there, lying on my back, the warm breeze on my face and the scent of green growing things all around me. Nothing and no one could harm me there. I was safe."

She went to the bed, pulled back the covers, then patted the mattress.

"You don't have to sleep on the floor," she murmured. "We'll be snug in bed together."

He didn't need to be asked twice.

Her eyes were shining as she watched him quickly disrobe. Though he normally slept in the nude, it seemed a wiser course of action to leave on his smallclothes, just in case something happened during the night. Still, it made him grin to see Tamsyn's gaze linger on his torso, and then drift lower.

He growled when she licked her lips. "Insatiable," he accused.

"Give me a taste of something delicious," she replied, "and I'll want it again and again."

She stretched out on the bed and he climbed in beside her. The bed complained loudly at the extra weight, but he didn't care. He doused the candle, then gathered her close in his arms. She was silken and sleek, and his body roared its demands. "It won't be long," he vowed. "Then we'll have an enormous bed of our own, and not leave it for at least a fortnight."

"*Two* fortnights," she murmured. "Three." Within seconds, her breath deepened and came slowly. She was asleep.

Smiling ruefully, Kit closed his eyes. There would be other nights for them to create pleasure together. For now, he'd content himself with the simple, glorious pleasure of holding her.

Moments later, he slept.

*B*REAKFAST came and went and still no sign of Jory. Tamsyn felt ready to scream and tear logs apart with her bare hands. Instead, she made herself sit peaceably in the drawing room and attempt to read a book.

"I've read the same paragraph half a dozen times," she complained to Kit. "My concentration isn't helped by your pacing, I might add."

"It's either this or whittle something," he answered as he made another circuit of the chamber. He took a slim knife from his pocket and eyed the leg of a table. "Don't suppose anyone will miss this."

She held up a hand. "Keep pacing, if you must. Better that than you turning the house into kindling."

Kit slid the knife back into his pocket and resumed pacing. Ceding defeat, Tamsyn set her book aside and stared moodily out the window. It was a breezy day and the oaks and elms outside shook with the force of the wind. Normally, she loved windy days—they filled everything with life, even mundane little clumps of weeds—but today her nerves jangled and jarred with each gust.

She straightened and Kit stopped pacing when someone came through the front door. Judging by the footsteps, it was more than one person. Male voices conferred lowly, then two people walked deeper into the house. More footsteps grew louder as someone came nearer and nearer to the drawing room.

The door opened and Jory strode in. Tamsyn immediately got to her feet. She didn't like the smirk her uncle wore—particularly because he aimed that same smirk at Kit, rather than Jory's usual obsequiousness and toadying in Kit's presence.

"Home from a first-rate trip," he announced smugly, shutting the door behind him. He tucked his thumbs into his waistcoat pockets. "Dined with excellent company and we had much to talk about."

Kit came straight to it. "I understand that you plan on selling the house. We want to purchase it."

Jory's grin widened. "Oh, do you now? I find that right fascinating, so I do. I'll warn you now, Blakemere, my terms are steep."

"Doubtful you'll get more money than we'll offer," Tamsyn said, crossing her arms over her chest.

Her uncle ambled with deliberate slowness to the fire-place, ran a finger down the mantel, then wiped the dust off on his trouser leg. "Here's how it's going to work," he said, turning back to face them. "You're going to give me twenty thousand pounds—"

"What?" she yelped. The house couldn't be worth more than ten thousand.

"And then," Jory went on, "the next year, you'll give me twenty thousand more. And so forth."

Tamsyn's stomach dropped.

"You're fit for Bedlam," Kit growled.

"Maybe so," Jory agreed pleasantly. "But then, I'm not the one running a smuggling gang, am I?"

She barely resisted the urge to slam her fist into Jory's face. The need to fight tightened her muscles, and her neck protested when she turned her head to look at Kit. The cold fury in his face was terrifying as he stood poised to fight, balancing on the balls of his feet and his hands forming fists at his sides.

"A wild accusation," Tamsyn said, her voice seething with fear and fury.

Jory threw her a contemptuous look. "You'd been act-ing strange ever since his lordship arrived. Something was afoot. I followed you out to the garden yesterday. Heard a few things. Heard what you've been doing beneath my own roof."

Tamsyn's stomach pitched. In the garden, she'd been too consumed with her thoughts, and hadn't heard Jory at all.

Her uncle vied for a sorrowful expression. "Fair broke my heart," he said mournfully. "The gel I'd fed and clothed and kept out of the rain wasn't nothing but a viper. An ungrateful viper at my bosom."

Anger was a living thing that raged within her, demanding release. He had ignored her for years, and now he saw her only as something to be exploited.

"Must say," he went on, "eight years is a damned long time. Me and Gwen didn't have a crumb of knowledge about it." He crossed his arms over his chest, and his look of woeful reproach faded. "That time's over. Now you pay me." His voice hardened with his threat.

"The hell we will," Kit spat.

"Ah," Jory sighed, "I thought you'd give me trouble. So I took myself to Newquay yesterday and brought back with me two customs officers."

Shock reverberated through her as if someone had detonated a bomb. Jory didn't give a damn that they were of the same blood. Her uncle couldn't wait to betray her.

"As we speak," he continued blithely, "they're having a spot of tea in the parlor with Lady Shawe."

"Blackmail," Kit snarled.

Jory shook his head. "No need for ugly words."

"But that's what it is," Tamsyn insisted hotly. "We don't agree to your demands, you sic the customs officers on us."

"I invited them to Chei Owr," Jory acknowledged. "For tea. Just being polite to the local law. And if it happens that you don't agree to my terms, then"—he shrugged as if the matter was out of his hands—"I tell them everything."

Tamsyn's rage grew as her mind desperately searched for a way out. But none came.

Jory threw up his arms as a shield when Kit took a threatening step toward him.

"What's to stop me from beating you senseless?" Kit said tightly.

"Lady Shawe also knows about your smuggling," Jory muttered. "Told her yesterday. If anything happens to me, she'll spill everything to the customs officers." He lowered his arms and breathed with relief when Kit backed off.

"You're a son of a bitch," Tamsyn spat.

Her uncle clicked his tongue. "Here I thought going to London would make a lady out of you."

"Go bugger yourself," she snarled.

Jory strode to the door and opened it. "Two minutes. That's all the time you get to make your decision. I hope it's the right choice."

Her uncle walked away.

Kit slammed the door behind him. He looked around the chamber, his eyes burning. "Anything here you don't value?"

"The vase," she answered bitingly after a moment. "It's Gwen's."

Without a word, Kit strode to the painted china vase, then threw it against the wall. It shattered loudly, filling the room with noise and pieces of ceramic.

"That should be his fucking head," Kit growled.

Panic and anger and desperation clashed within her. "If we pay him, he'll just keep coming back for more and more."

"If we say no," Kit concluded grimly, "he'll turn us over to the authorities. Because of my title, we might not be hanged, but we could be transported. Damn it." He dragged his hands through his hair. "All he did was overhear us. He might not have proof."

"Maybe he found some." She rubbed at her face. "Or he's hoping that his threat is enough to make us bow to his demands. Even if we wanted to, we couldn't meet his terms."

Kit said through clenched teeth, "Wish I had a goddamn bayonet to ram into his chest."

She straightened her shoulders, drawing on the courage that had kept her going all these years. "I think I know what we have to do."

"Tell Shawe to go hang?" Kit suggested with a vicious snarl.

"Exactly." She prayed she was making the right decision.

Her husband gave one clipped nod.

A moment later, the door to the drawing room opened. Jory entered, followed by two men wearing riding officers' uniforms.

Tamsyn's heart seized at the sight of them. She had fled men like this on more than one occasion, but here they were, in her home.

"Lord and Lady Blakemere," Jory said snidely. "This is Chief Inspector Edwards and District Officer Wright."

The customs men bowed. She stiffly nodded in response.

Her uncle looked back and forth between Kit and Tamsyn with a gleeful, expectant look. "Well?"

Kit gave her another slight nod. She took a deep breath. "No," she answered.

"As you like," Jory said brightly. He turned to the customs officers. "Arrest these two in the name of His Majesty. The charge is smuggling."

Tamsyn's heart pounded as her uncle pronounced her fate. Yet she held her ground.

Edwards and Wright murmured in surprise, and Kit swore softly under his breath. The air in the room became charged.

After a moment, Edwards said slowly, "These are serious charges to be brought against a nobleman and his wife."

"Their title didn't stop 'em from smuggling contraband," Jory answered.

Wright asked, "Have you any proof?"

A calculating look crept into Jory's face, and hope within Tamsyn died.

"I do," he answered. "Come with me, and I'll show you everything."

Chapter 30

"Follow me, all of you," Jory said. He left the drawing room and headed toward the front door. Wright trailed after him.

Tamsyn's feet were bolted to the floor. She couldn't move.

Kit was at her side in an instant, wrapping one arm around her waist, supporting her. "Love—"

"My lord, my lady," Edwards said, gesturing toward the door. He wore a stern expression, one that would brook no argument.

She and Kit couldn't flee and they couldn't thrash her uncle. There was nothing to be done but move forward— and pray that she could find an explanation for whatever evidence Jory provided.

Tamsyn had always kept an alibi ready if ever she was caught. She had planned to admit to the charge, but say that she'd been coerced by a ruthless criminal overlord to commit the crime.

Her old alibi wouldn't work, though, not with Kit included in the accusation.

"My lady," Edwards said more insistently.

Tamsyn exhaled, then moved out of Kit's protective hold.

"After you," the senior officer said, glancing at the door meaningfully.

There was no running now. No hiding. She had to face her uncle's threat—but Kit would be beside her. It was and wasn't a comfort. There was no denying that she had brought him into this disaster, and if there was punishment to be meted out, he'd get a substantial share of it.

She, Kit, and Edwards moved through the house. The sun shone too brightly in her eyes when she emerged outside, and she squinted to make out the forms of Jory, Gwen, and Wright waiting in the drive. Her aunt's expectant smile kindled more fury within Tamsyn.

Like hell will I let her see me squirm.

But what was Jory's evidence? If she knew, maybe she could come up with a reasonable excuse.

He hadn't led them to the basement. He'd said nothing about the locked door, either, or the secret corridors beneath the house.

She seized hold of this hope. Perhaps he didn't know about any of it. If he'd been aware of them, he would have said something—wouldn't he?

Don't look at Kit. Not with all these eyes on us.

"All here?" Jory asked, looking around.

"Every one of us, my dearest," Gwen answered.

Jory clapped his hands together. "Right, then. Hope you don't mind a little walk, gentlemen," he said to the officers.

"Just get on with it, my lord," Edwards answered brusquely.

Her uncle deflated a little, robbed of milking the moment. Scowling, he strode in the direction of the village.

Feeling like a condemned prisoner, she walked after Jory while her mind whirled. Last night, she and the villagers had been careful as always to conceal signs of their movements, smoothing over their footprints in the sand and returning the pier to its place of concealment.

Had they forgotten something? Or had Jory found a villager willing to confess to the crime in exchange for compensation or leniency?

The procession of Jory, Gwen, the customs officers, Kit, and Tamsyn moved down the hill, taking the road directly into Newcombe's high street. As they entered the village, she fought the urge to twist her hands together anxiously.

Kit walked with the upright bearing and steely expression of a soldier heading into battle. Gone was the insouciant charm, the insolent winks. Regret stabbed her—he'd wanted to leave the world of soldiering behind, and she'd brought him right back into it.

People in the street stopped and stared at the sight of Tamsyn with customs officers. Children clung to their mothers' skirts, and men gathered at the door to the Tipsy Flea. Nessa came out of her house, with her family trailing behind. Their eyes gleamed with alarm and their postures were wary.

Tamsyn discreetly gestured for calm, struggling to allay so many fears. When Denny Oates reached for a thick board, clearly intending to use it as a cudgel, she gave a minute shake of her head. She wouldn't condone violence against the riding officers—and it wouldn't solve the problem.

Jory led them quickly through the village, then down to the boardwalk, and the beach beyond it.

God help us, we're going to our cove.

Walking on sand was never easy, but each step made her breath come in ragged gasps. From one inlet to another, they continued relentlessly on. Her mouth went dry when they finally arrived at the cove.

There had to be something she could do. Some way to stop this from happening. But it unfolded relentlessly.

Fear threatened to strangle her as Jory marched up the

sand. He neared the opening in the cliff through which the smuggled goods were brought into the caverns. The opening was disguised with large rocks, but perhaps Jory knew what they concealed. As they got closer to the secret entrance, she managed to stop herself from looking at Kit with alarm.

Her uncle kept walking. His continuing steps kicked sand on the rocks blocking the opening but he didn't spare it a single glance as he trudged onward.

She nearly sank to the sand in relief. Surely, he would have pointed out the opening to the customs men if he knew about it.

Her relief perished quickly as Jory made straight for the rocky outcropping at the farthest end of the beach. He stopped beside it and pointed.

"There," he said exultantly. "All the proof you need."

Kit went to Tamsyn, taking her hand and giving it a squeeze. Perhaps it was an attempt to reassure her, or maybe it served as a signal to get ready to fight, then flee.

She prepared for both eventualities, making herself light on her feet and recalling Kit's instructions on how to punch someone.

"Forgive me, my lord," Edwards ventured. "I see only a collection of rocks."

"It's what's on the other side of them," Jory shot back. Moving with the stiffness of middle age, he scrambled over the rocks. When he reached the top, he called back, "Up here."

Tamsyn's breath sawed through her as she watched both riding officers scale the rocks. Hands on their hips, they stared down at the other side. Wright removed a pad of paper from his pack and sketched what he saw.

"You see?" Jory crowed. "It's a pier. I found it yesterday after I heard her in the garden talking of her crime. They use it for their smuggling. Haul it out into the water, and then the boats can land and unload their damned cargo." He sneered at Tamsyn. "Drag them away. There's the evidence."

Edwards climbed down from the rocks and walked purposefully toward her and Kit. "Can you explain this?"

"What's to explain?" Jory cried, awkwardly lowering himself from the rocks. "I've already told you—"

"I'd like to hear from Lord and Lady Blakemere," the senior officer said, his voice measured.

"It's . . ." Tamsyn's ability to dissemble deserted her. "The purpose of that pier is . . ."

"It's the private dock, naturally," Kit said in a matter-of-fact tone. "For the rowboats bringing the sea bathers from town."

Tamsyn suppressed her urge to look at Kit with the bewilderment she felt.

"My lord?" The senior officer frowned in confusion.

Kit gestured as he spoke animatedly. "For visitors who want to bathe in the sea but want a sheltered place to do it, we will ferry them from the pier in the village to this spot. It will spare guests of more delicate constitution from struggling to walk over sand. Everyone will wear bathing costumes, of course," he added with a nod, "since women and men will have access to the water. We'll have bathing machines and people to act as dippers."

"What the bloody hell are you talking about?" Jory snapped, stalking toward them.

"A dipper is someone who holds a person in their arms and dips them into the water," Kit explained. He turned to the customs officers. "They're at all the best seaside resorts. Excellent especially for ladies who might not have the ability to swim."

"Not *that*," Jory said tartly. "The whole sodding bit about bathing machines and dippers—you're babbling nonsense."

"Nonsense?" Kit raised a brow. "Shall I tell them, Lady Blakemere?" he asked, glancing at her with a fond smile.

"By all means," she answered, utterly mystified.

Kit wrapped his arm around her waist and pulled her closer. He beamed at the customs men. "My wife and I have decided to turn Newcombe into England's most sought-after seaside holiday destination."

As the riding officers murmured their interest, Tamsyn pasted a smile on her face—even though her insides were a riot of shock, amusement, and disbelief. Newcombe— the next Brighton?

"There's no such scheme," Jory spat.

Kit glanced at him coldly. "Lord Shawe, your opinion on the matter is not being solicited."

"But—" Jory protested.

"A seaside resort," Edwards said skeptically.

Without pause, Kit began speaking with excitement. "We built the pier first to test if it was possible to ferry people from town to the cove, and it was a rousing success. But the introduction of the ferries is just one of the many features and improvements we will be undertaking." After gently releasing his hold on Tamsyn, he strode back toward the village. "Please, sirs, follow me."

In contrast from their grim plod before, their procession now worked in reverse as Tamsyn and the others hurried after Kit, who walked with wide, eager strides. "We'll have tents and chairs to hire," he called over his shoulder, waving toward the beach. "And refreshment kiosks selling lemonade and ices."

They reached the boardwalk, where dozens of villagers who had been standing and watching now scattered in different directions and busied themselves with menial tasks. Even Nessa pretended to vigorously sweep her front steps.

"For those who want an oceangoing adventure," Kit

went on, pointing to several moored vessels, "they'll hire a boat to take them out on the water. Luncheons will be provided, of course."

"Of course," the junior officer seconded.

"Quickly, please," Kit directed, moving from the pier to the high street. Here again, more villagers gathered in curious groups, then hastened in various directions, like fish startled by the approach of a shark.

"We'll have a tea parlor," Kit continued as he walked, gesturing toward the shops that fronted the high street. "There will also be a shop selling toys, one offering local handicrafts for sale. The women make excellent baskets and corn dollies that anyone with taste will demand for their home. You see the public house," he went on, pointing toward the Tipsy Flea, "but there will also be a dining room that will be open to both sexes. Traditional fare such as stargazy pie and pasties will be served, as well as Continental dishes for our more sophisticated visitors."

Kit stopped their procession in front of the all things shop, and he beamed at the customs officers.

Tamsyn held her breath. Would they believe him?

Slowly, the men nodded.

Tamsyn risked a look at Gwen and Jory, who gaped at Kit. Suddenly, they turned their furious attention to her.

Her back stiff and her mouth tight, Gwen stalked to Tamsyn. Red spots of anger stained her cheeks.

"Nonsense, all of it!" she snarled. "There's no scheme. This is nothing but glib obfuscation."

Tamsyn drew herself up. "I assure you, aunt, this plan is real. We haven't even gotten to the part about the musical pavilion."

Gwen sputtered. "Musical . . . ?"

"Indeed," Kit added smoothly. "Plans are already being drawn up in London by one of England's top architects. The pavilion will go there." He pointed to a rise at the end of the high street, now home to a chicken coop and a pair of goats. "The animals will be relocated, naturally."

"It will house a stage with an orchestra pit," Tamsyn went on, shaping the imaginary space with her hands. "There will be music of all varieties performed, and during the peak season, theatrical works will be staged. Classics and modern pieces, including premieres of the Viscountess Marwood's work. She and her husband are close friends," Tamsyn added, hoping the viscountess would forgive her for shamelessly name-dropping.

"Where will all the visitors sleep?" the senior officer wondered.

"Two hotels in the French style are currently being designed," Kit answered. "One on the high street, there." He indicated a series of sheds housing boats that needed repair. "The other will be a short walk from the center of the village, for visitors who want a bit more seclusion. Should demand outpace supply, we'll build more."

His face purple, Jory barreled toward the customs men. "They're making this up! There are no plans to turn this waterlogged blight into a seaside resort. It's all twaddle to hide their real purpose." He glowered at Tamsyn. "Smuggling."

She met her uncle's anger with her own, squaring her jaw in defiance.

"Wrong, Shawe," Kit replied frostily.

Edwards looked pensively around at the high street. Villagers crept out in groups of two and three, anxiously watching the riding officers.

"You," the chief inspector said, pointing toward Sam Franks, who stood on the step of his shop. "Come here."

Slowly, cautiously, Sam approached, casting worried looks over his shoulder at the other villagers watching the unfolding events.

"Sir?" Sam asked warily.

"Tell me about the scheme to transform this place into a holiday destination," the officer commanded.

"Mr. Franks isn't part of the planning committee," Tamsyn said quickly.

Edwards lifted a brow. "Surely he knows *something* about it."

Wide-eyed, Sam looked at Tamsyn. She gave one tiny nod, praying her gesture wouldn't be seen by the customs men.

"It's, uh, a substantial alteration," Sam improvised. "Many changes. There's talk of . . . a . . . music festival during June and July. Yes," he said, warming to his subject, "and a singing competition."

"The winner gets ten pounds," Kit threw in, "and a silver cup with their name engraved on it."

Though it wasn't possible to read Edwards's expression, he said to Sam, "You can return to your place of business."

"Yes, sir." Sam bowed. "Thank you, sir." He hurried inside, but stood right in the window and stared at the assembly on the street.

"Lord Shawe," the chief inspector said, turning to Jory. "Have you any additional evidence against Lord and Lady Blakemere?"

"I . . ." Jory's mouth opened and closed. He looked frantically at Gwen, who could only offer a helpless shrug.

"I think that means 'no,' sir," the junior officer said.

Edwards put his hands on his hips, a movement which was echoed by Wright. The silence that followed was the longest of Tamsyn's life.

Finally, Edwards spoke. "Without any further proof of your allegations, and in light of Lord and Lady Blakemere's thorough explanation, I see no reason why this inquiry should proceed any further. We have found no evidence of smuggling here."

Tamsyn pressed her lips together tightly to hold in her cry of triumph.

His eyes shining with exhilaration, Kit sent her the briefest of smiles before smoothing out his expression.

"Lord Shawe," Edwards said sternly, "in the future, you would be advised to have actual proof of a crime before making such a serious accusation against a titled gentleman, particularly one as distinguished as Lord Blakemere."

As Jory stammered, the chief inspector turned to Kit and Tamsyn. "The plans for this village sound delightful. Please do let me know when construction is complete. I think my missus would enjoy it very much."

"We'll be sure to reserve a room with an ocean view." Kit stuck out his hand, and the officer shook it.

Both officers bowed at Tamsyn, then walked back in the direction of Chei Owr. As they ambled up the road, more and more villagers came out of their hiding places to talk animatedly amongst themselves.

Gwen lurched toward the step of Sam's shop and sat down heavily, her gaze vacant. Like a flag in high winds, Jory shook with apoplectic rage. His chest puffing out and his arms stiff at his sides, Jory stormed up to Kit. Her uncle started to speak, but Kit cut him off.

"Now *I'll* tell *you* how it's going to work," Kit said, his voice low but firm. "You are going to sell me the house for the sum of one pound, and then I'm giving the house to my wife so it will belong to her even in the event of my death."

Tamsyn stared at him, victory ricocheting through her body like a bullet.

Gwen roused enough to yelp, "One pound!"

"Then," Kit continued as if Gwen hadn't spoken, "you

and Lady Shawe are going to clear out of Cornwall and never return. London will be off-limits to you. Find some other corner of the world that can tolerate your stench."

"Here, now!" Jory exclaimed. "I ain't going to do any of that. And you can't make me."

Kit's smile was vicious. "The Crown has made me an *earl*. I have the ear of very powerful men—including the Duke of Greyland. I see by the chalkiness of your face that you've heard of His Grace. All I have to do is whisper one word to him, *one word*, and you and your lady wife won't be welcome anywhere. Not in England. Not in Scotland or Ireland. And certainly nowhere on the Continent. A well-connected man, is the duke."

Feeling herself blaze with justice, Tamsyn crossed her arms over her chest. "From the day you arrived to bury my parents and take possession of Chei Owr, you overlooked me. All you cared about was your own gratification. Ponder that in your ostracism," she said, her voice charged with feeling. "The girl who only wanted your love is sending you into exile."

Her uncle had the waxy appearance of a cadaver. "H-how are we supposed to live?" he stammered.

"No one's taking away the income from the barony," she said icily. "That's still yours. Chei Owr, however, will belong to me."

"But . . . but . . ." Jory stuttered.

"Ingrate," Gwen spat, struggling to rise. "After all we did—"

"You did nothing." She took Kit's hand and held it tightly. He looked down at her with a warm, encouraging expression, and her heart felt full. She pointed up the hill, toward Chei Owr. "Go and pack," she commanded. "Take only what you came with ten years ago. The rest is mine."

For several moments, neither her aunt nor her uncle moved as they sputtered like fish.

"March!" Kit ordered, sounding every inch the commanding officer.

Jory hurried off with a speed that belied his years. Gwen followed, casting baleful looks over her shoulder. Finally, they crested the hill and disappeared.

A hot wash of relief poured through Tamsyn, nearly blinding her.

Gone. They were gone. And Chei Owr was hers.

Kit raised her hand to his mouth and kissed it. "Love," he said, beaming, "you were magnificent."

For many moments, she couldn't speak, too overwhelmed by emotion. "The credit goes to you," she said at last. "Making up that tale about turning Newcombe into a seaside resort." She shook her head in awe. "No one could tell it was a fabrication."

His gaze fixed to hers. "It doesn't have to be a fabrication."

She raised her eyebrows. "Actually have the bathing machines and the tearoom and build the musical pavilion?"

He brightened. "Yes, actually," he answered, energy growing in him as he looked around at the village. "A frivolous pleasure garden will generate income for a score of people. Instead," he went on animatedly, "we put that money into the village. Transform it into a choice destination for wealthy Londoners. Everyone in Newcombe will have honest employment. No more dependency on sporadic fishing catches—"

"And no more smuggling," she concluded. Her mind whirled with the idea. "Beyond belief, preposterous." Her breath came quickly. "Wonderful."

"It is, rather," he said as if astounded by his own cleverness.

"Do you think we could do it?"

He stroked his palm down her cheek. "I've said it before, love," he said gravely. "There is *nothing* you cannot do."

She wasn't concerned that many villagers hovered nearby. She didn't give a damn if the Archbishop of Canterbury looked on. Her husband needed kissing, and by God, she was going to kiss him.

Cupping the back of Kit's head, she brought his mouth to hers. He was warm and firm and deliciously masculine. She kissed him with all the passion that pulsed through her.

Someone whistled. She didn't care.

Finally, she and Kit broke apart. "We'll have to ask the people of Newcombe if they'll agree to the plan," she murmured.

He eyed the numerous faces surrounding them. "I'm confident that they'll approve of whatever you propose. After all, they *did* sign on when a sixteen-year-old girl suggested that they take up smuggling." He shook his head. "Fearless woman."

She couldn't stop the smile that wreathed her face. Everything within her brimmed with gratitude and joy—especially for him.

The past couldn't be changed. The pain they'd both experienced couldn't be erased. Hurts and wounds, however, faded.

There might be scars, but scars meant survival.

She and Kit had been alone in their battles before. Yet now, they fought and endured. Together.

And they would thrive.

Epilogue

Two months later

"*B*righton, Margate, Portsmouth," Langdon declared, spreading his arms wide as he looked out at the sparkling water. "They'll be deserted once word gets out about Newcombe."

"Alas for Prinny and his Pavilion," Kit added with an unrepentant grin.

Greyland waved his hand dismissively. "He'll find some other way to bolster his flagging ego. Perhaps he'll declare war on Andorra."

"With any luck," Tamsyn said hopefully, "it will be a very *brief* war. One that lasts a half an hour."

"From what I've heard," Lady Greyland added in a conspiratorial tone, "the Prince Regent can't last more than two minutes."

"After sobbing over his insufficient manhood, Prinny will realize the key to his health will be an extended stay in Newcombe," Kit affirmed, smiling at his wife and friends. A small folding table had been set up on the boardwalk, surrounded by five chairs currently occupied by Kit, Tamsyn, Langdon, and the Greylands. A teapot and cups had been brought out, as well, for refreshment.

There was far too much bustle and activity on the high

street for anyone to sit and take a leisurely tea. Even from where Kit and the others sat, the sounds of construction rose above the crashing waves and gulls' cries. Hammers, saws, and men's shouts punctuated the air.

Military training, Kit had discovered, provided the exact resources needed for the metamorphosis of a sleepy fishing village into a fashionable seaside resort. Since the expulsion of Lord and Lady Shawe and the purchase of the manor house, not a day went by that didn't witness Kit and Tamsyn reviewing plans and overseeing countless projects.

Fortunately, Kit's experience taught him the benefit of delegation. Weeks earlier, he and Tamsyn had journeyed to London to interview people to manage and supervise the massive project. They had met with dozens of architects, urban planners, and engineers before finally settling on Monsieur Anselme Durand, the son of a Quebecois architect and his Algonquin wife. Monsieur Durand's supervision ensured that Newcombe's progress didn't stumble.

Their work didn't end at the village, either. The manor house was undergoing a transformation, as well. Scaffolding surrounded the aged structure as workmen labored. Kit couldn't begrudge the noises of renovation, even if it meant he and Tamsyn were unable to spend long, leisurely hours abed in the morning.

Only today, he'd been awakened at first light by Tamsyn's lips sliding down his abdomen, heading lower—and then the hammering outside had started. Still, a small amount of temporary sexual frustration was worth the price if it meant the resurrection of his wife's familial estate.

He never tired of seeing her smile as she watched everything progress. She grumbled a little about the constant presence of workmen at the house, but her complaints were halfhearted.

Their guests from London didn't object to the noise, either. They had journeyed from the capital to see Newcombe for themselves after Kit had written them full of praise. Upon their arrival, Lady Greyland had taken one look at the harbor and said, "If we don't back this project, Alex, we're a pair of damned fools."

"You are no one's fool, Cass," her husband had replied solemnly.

They now sat down for tea on the boardwalk, having spent the morning touring all the construction sites.

"Monsieur Durand told me the hotels are already taking reservations," Tamsyn said, then laughed in disbelief. "The foundations have just been laid, and we're reaching capacity."

"We're ready to meet the demand," Kit answered confidently. Energy and resolve surged through him. Thinking of the discussion he'd had the previous day with Monsieur Durand, he felt both satisfaction and humility.

The architect had presented him with a preliminary drawing for Newcombe's future home for veterans. It would house two dozen severely injured men on a full-time basis, with twelve more beds for temporary guests taking the sea air. War had made him a hero and earned him a title, but at last he could give back and honor the men who'd fought and died.

He saw Tamsyn laughing at something Langdon said, and was struck breathless with gratitude. She'd given him so much—her determination, her drive, and the sheer pleasure with which she met each new challenge. Their marriage had been based on convenience. Hurried vows had concealed secrets that had shadowed the tentative bond between them. Then it had changed. Evolved, becoming stronger, deeper. And so had he.

Fighting had shaped him into a soldier. Being Tamsyn's husband had made him a worthier man.

A man who could make love to his wife for hours, days, weeks, and never tire. He wanted more and more and more. Not just of her body, but her entire self.

She caught him looking at her with ardent carnality and blew him a kiss.

Was it possible for a man to perish from happiness and adoration? He might be the first.

Langdon's drawl cut into his adoring thoughts. "I may need a sea cure myself after watching you two worship and fawn over each other."

"I'm certain you can find a crab or lobster to seduce," Kit answered. "A crustacean might be willing to overlook your shortcomings."

Before Langdon could snap a retort, a boy ran across the boardwalk, heading toward them. He carried a folded piece of paper and fought to keep hold of it in the wind.

"Yes, Charlie?" Tamsyn asked when the child ran to her side.

"Got a letter," the boy gasped, breathless from his run. "For Lord Langdon."

"That's me." Langdon took the letter. He fished a coin out of his waistcoat pocket and handed it to Charlie. The boy grinned and clutched the coin tightly as he ran off.

"What is it?" Lady Greyland asked as Langdon unfolded the letter and perused its contents with a frown.

"I'm being summoned back to London by my father." With a sigh, he tucked the missive into his coat. "He sent the letter with a carriage, which is waiting at the house."

"Nothing dire, I hope?" Tamsyn asked.

"He likes to tug on my strings now and then, just to make certain I'll dance to his tune. The price of being the heir." He rose. "Unfortunately, I'll have to return immediately." After bowing over Tamsyn's and Lady Greyland's hands, and slapping Kit and Greyland on the shoulder, he straightened his coat. "Keep me apprised of the village's progress. It's a damned sight more interesting than anything happening in London."

He strode away, and Kit wondered how long before his friend found his way back to the pleasures of the city. Despite Langdon's words to the contrary, there was one thing in London that he couldn't resist—the Orchid Club, and its beautiful manager.

"I think I'll take my wife for a walk along the beach," Kit announced. Tamsyn immediately got to her feet.

"By all means," Greyland said, rising. "I'd like some privacy so I may seduce my own wife."

"You don't need to seduce me, Alex," Lady Greyland chided affectionately. "I'm yours already."

"It never hurts to practice," the duke replied gravely.

"Avert your gaze," Tamsyn directed Greyland. When he did, she bent and removed her shoes.

"Give them to me," Lady Greyland said with a wink. "You might want both your hands free."

Tamsyn handed the duchess her shoes, then reached for Kit's hand.

Leaving the Greylands, they walked out onto the sand together. Kit soaked in the sensation of the sun on his shoulders, the fresh sea air washing over him, and the feel of her skin against his.

The breeze carried with it the sounds of construction from the village, each fall of the hammer sounding, briefly, like gunfire. Edginess rose up within him.

Tamsyn tugged on his hand, and his tension seeped away.

He would always be a veteran. The war was part of him, marking his body and his mind. Yet he could live with the shadows when there was so much light in his life.

"When you said no," he murmured, "you saved me."

"I said yes to your marriage proposal," she objected.

"You denied me the pleasure garden," he reminded her. "I would have poured myself into an illusion of peace."

"You don't wish for what might have been?" she asked.

He shook his head. "What I have now far outpaces any dream or fancy I might have once had." He glanced at her, and the clean line of her profile. In his pocket, he still carried the seashell she'd given him months earlier, unwilling to consign it to a lonely life in his bedside table. "I'm just grateful that you were desperate enough to marry me."

She smiled warmly at him. "They'll have to change the old saying—for us, at any rate."

"And what saying is that, love?"

She stopped walking and wrapped her arms around him. He brought her close and smiled when she touched her lips to his and whispered, "'Marry in haste, *rejoice* at leisure.'"

Thomas Powell, the future Duke of
Northfield, has longed for the sensual and
mysterious manager of the Orchid Club
since the moment he saw her . . . but will
she dare to give in to temptation?

Find out in the next
London Underground novel . . .

Dare to Love a Duke

Coming Fall 2018!

UNFORGETTABLE ROMANCES FROM
NEW YORK TIMES BESTSELLING AUTHOR

Lynsay Sands

An English Bride in Scotland

978-0-06-196311-7

Annabel was about to become a nun, when her mother
arrived at the abbey to take her home . . . to marry the
Scottish laird who is betrothed to her runaway sister!
From the moment Ross MacKay sets eyes on Annabel,
he is taken with his shy, sweet bride. And when an
enemy endangers her life, he'll move the Highlands
themselves to save her.

To Marry a Scottish Laird

978-0-06-227357-4

Joan promised her mother that she would deliver
a scroll to the clan MacKay. But traveling alone is
dangerous, even disguised as a boy. When Scottish
warrior Campbell Sinclair lends his aid, she is more
than relieved . . . until he surprises her with lingering
kisses that prove her disguise hasn't fooled him.

Sweet Revenge

978-0-06-201981-3

Highlander Galen MacDonald is on a mission of
revenge: kidnap his enemy's bride and make her his.
When he realizes Kyla is delirious with fever, he
wastes no time in wedding her. While Kyla is grateful
to the Scottish laird for saving her from marrying a
loathsome man, she is just as furious that Galen has
claimed her for his bride.

LYS7 1017

At Avon Books, we know your passion for romance—once you finish one of our novels, you find yourself wanting more.

May we tempt you with . . .

- **Excerpts** from our upcoming releases.

- Entertaining **extras**, including authors' personal photo albums and book lists.

- Behind-the-scenes **scoop** on your favorite characters and series.

- **Sweepstakes** for the chance to win free books, romantic getaways, and other fun prizes.

- Writing **tips** from our authors and editors.

- **Blog** with our authors and find out why they love to write romance.

- **Exclusive content** that's not contained within the pages of our novels.

Join us at
www.avonbooks.com

AVON
An Imprint of HarperCollins*Publishers*
www.avonromance.com